Praise for *Prison Shadows*

"Dr. Den Houter has created a sympathetic protagonist, a rarity in today's literary world. Travel with Clifford on his riveting journey for psychological and physical survival.

"Suspenseful, well written, and superbly researched, *Prison Shadows* is a must read for anyone who appreciates crime novels."

—Katharine Crawford Robey, author of *Cardinal Coat and Other Stories* and *Tor and Raven Are Friends*

"Clifford Ratz turns to drugs for comfort, self-styled altruism, and profit to compensate for a failed marriage and strained family relationships. An astute cop and a traffic infraction speed up Clifford's downward spiral into incarceration and its grim picture of violence, corruption, and despair.

"Clifford is a magnetic character whose successful return to society is applause-worthy. But his return is as dismaying as it is cheerful, due to a dear family member's continued manipulations putting Clifford at risk.

"*Prison Shadows* is a realistic and compelling psychological suspense novel that fans of crime fiction will want to read."

—J.C. Konitz, author of *Becoming Kate, a Novel of Second Chances*, and *Herald, the Christmas Dachshund*

PRISON
SHADOWS

KATHRYN DEN HOUTER

Kathryn Den Houter

MISSION POINT PRESS

Readers are encouraged to go to www.MissionPointPress.
com to contact the author or to find information on how to
buy this book in bulk at a discounted rate.

Published by Mission Point Press
2554 Chandler Rd.
Traverse City, MI 49696
(231) 421-9513
www.MissionPointPress.com

ISBN: 978-1-954786-95-0
Library of Congress Control Number: 2022906890

Printed in the United States of America

This book is dedicated to my late husband, Leonard Den Houter (1948-2006).

He graced this world for only a short time but left an enduring legacy.

His steadfast love for family, his passion for justice, and his self-sacrifice are remembered with deep gratitude.

His compassion for the less fortunate sings in the hearts of his four children:

Jonathan, Jenna, Jessica, and Benjamin.

Contents

1   Powell, Michigan   1

2   Ingham County, Michigan   3

3   Herman and Celia Ratz   16

4   Jail   20

5   Marquette   42

6   Michigamme State Prison   53

7   Prison Antics   68

8   Outliers   79

9   Sharmbee   90

10   Delores   109

11   Vince and Sue Attwood   115

12   Clifford's Interview   133

13   Officer Blak   140

14   Stuck   159

15   Maggie Sweetwater   171

16 The Waiting Begins ... 177

17 A Mountain of Red Tape 183

18 Showdown 186

19 Echoes of Freedom 193

20 The Attwood Farm 212

21 Last Confessions 221

22 Baby News 243

23 Baby Blues 271

24 Out of the Shadows 280

25 Family Tear 288

26 Courage to Change ... 301

27 The Pit 321

28 Trail Cam 329

29 "I Have a Warrant..." 332

30 Cry of Contrition 348

31 Knitting Together 357

Acknowledgments 368

About the Author 370

PRISON
SHADOWS

1 Powell, Michigan

June 1987

Inching along like a snake on its belly, a car with headlights off pulled alongside the road and parked with just the faintest crunch of tires on gravel. Two men opened the doors and closed them carefully so as not to awaken the inhabitants inside the lone trailer sitting next to the towpath. The pitchy night encircled both men like a shroud. It had rained hard just before nightfall and the damp chilly air sculpted a vaporous mist, blurring the lines between grass and trees. The overcast sky blotted out any star or moonlight. Darkness crawled into every dimension, suffocating any hint of light.

The men walked side by side, hunched and intense. A distant sound of crackling footsteps and rustling underbrush disrupted the hush surrounding the fir trees. Grabbing their flashlights, the sharp beams pierced the darkness. Glowing eyes stared at them—frozen in fear. With a sudden dash, a deer bounded through the pines into the distant open fields. Its hooves kicked up the pine needles, triggering a sharp sweet smell.

They resumed walking, looking back, checking to see if anyone in the trailer had started investigating. The lights were still out. In front of them, just a trace of the towpath was visible, and a flashlight beam lit the way. A "No Trespassing" sign in neon letters appeared out of the mist, but they pressed on, inching their way toward the shadowy woods. The men trudged through ferns high from summer growth and underbrush wet from the evening's rain. Their shoes, pants, and legs were damp, and their weary bodies cold.

Beyond the woods, a field of even rows emerged as they quickened their pace in excitement. Their flashlights beamed up and down, twirling around the field, certifying their discovery. They snatched off some of the vegetation, noting a leaf with spiky points, smelled the earthy, unmistakable scent, and tucked samples in their pockets.

2 Ingham County, Michigan

October 1984

The back window of his black Toyota flashed red, an undulating terror. Fight or flight instincts jammed into Clifford's head. His shoulders sagged as a wave of resignation washed over him; his gut ached as he pulled over.

In the next telltale moments, the cop checked his license plate and pulled up information. He placed his hand on the trunk of Clifford's car confirming he had been there and moved briskly to the driver's side window.

"Officer Kent here. You were swerving. What's your name?"

"Clifford Ratz."

The cop's astute brown eyes scanned the front and back seats, one hand hovered over his holster as his free hand gestured.

"Your driver's license and registration."

Fumbling through the glove compartment, Clifford found the registration tucked inside the maintenance manual and retrieved his license from his wallet. Reluctantly, he presented both items to the officer as if offering up his own execution. The officer strutted back to his flashing vehicle and retrieved more information. Clifford knew what was coming and just wanted it over. It seemed to take an eternity.

Another police car screeched to a stop, its red light flashing. *Backup*. Clifford shuddered. An odd sensation pulsed from the top of his head to his feet.

"Get out of the car. There's a warrant out for your arrest," the officer said, with one hand firmly on his holster.

Clifford hesitated, hoping it was all a miserable nightmare. He'd ridden this rodeo before and was suspicious of the justice system.

"Get out of the car!" the cop said.

Clifford opened the door and placed his feet on the ground. The cop pulled him upright, yanked him away from the driver's side door, and slammed it. He swiveled Clifford around and jammed his face on the hood. "Hands on top of the car!"

Knowing he was guilty, Clifford swallowed hard and complied. Officer Kent frisked him and felt something in his right pants pocket. Fearing a weapon, the officer reached in and withdrew a packet of cocaine. He seized it as evidence.

"Okay, let Oakley do his thing," he commanded the newly arrived canine officer. Oakley jumped out of the car, sniffed the ground, darted around the vehicle, checked the tires, and staked out the trunk. He put his front paws on the back bumper and barked, which prompted the officer to open the trunk. There he found about forty one-pound bags of marijuana—almost twenty kilos.

"Okay, I'm taking you into custody," Officer Kent said brusquely. He handcuffed Clifford. "You have the right to remain silent. Anything you say can and will be used against you in a court of law. You have the right to speak to an attorney before speaking to the police, and to have an attorney present during questions now or in the future. If you can't afford an attorney, one will be provided for you at the government's expense. Any questions?"

Clifford's shoulders slumped as he shook his head. Officer Kent grabbed him by the arm and shoved him into the back seat of his squad car.

Clifford knew the cops wouldn't believe him if he told them this was the first time he bought crack cocaine, so he remained silent. *They wouldn't understand I'm upset about my mother. Listening is not one of their strengths— actually, most of them don't seem to give a shit. Would they treat me better if they knew my mom didn't want to live anymore? Hell no.* Clifford had left her moaning in her bed, because his father wanted him out of his sight.

"You better leave, son," his father said. "She always puts on a show for you." Knowing he would only make matters worse, Clifford left his parents' home—his heart in turmoil. He wanted to blast that sadness out of his mind—maybe some crack could do it. He loved his mother; she was kind, smart, and warm-hearted. Many of his growing-up years revolved around their mother-and-son team, ganging up on his father and sister. Herman was a mild-mannered man with a quiet demeanor, seemingly a kind and gentle person, but he had a heart that was filled with guile. He was competitive, stubborn, and judgmental. Nobody, except his daughter, thrived under his care.

The arguments with his father were *never* productive. Clifford lost every argument. If Clifford raised his voice just an iota, the father would explode, "If you raise your voice at me, this discussion is over." Herman would then posture like a charging gorilla. Clifford tried to stifle his anger and explain his position, but his father never listened, so out of frustration, he'd raise his voice. As predictable as the sun rising, his father would walk away in a huff. This happened over and over again. It was a big fat no-win situation for Clifford.

Herman put his wife, Celia, in no-win situations too. She was stuck, repressed into nothingness. Once Clifford left home, Herman dominated his wife and squeezed out every ounce of independence. His identity consumed hers. She was null and void. It was like he gaslighted her. With no one there to take her side, she was defenseless against his brand of evil.

Saddened and troubled by the possible demise of his mother, Clifford smoked pot, and it worked for a while—it eased his anxiety. His friends were in the pot-smoking culture and he fit right in. Most of his clients were either his age or older; many were flower children. Several of them struggled with late-stage HIV, and an older gentleman was battling cancer. He sold to a couple of much older women—grandmothers with severe joint problems. *I'm an angel of mercy. I have the answer for their crippling diseases.* He convinced himself that he was rushing into the shadow world to capture the best stuff for his friends.

Maxwell, one of his drug connections, laughed at the irony of marijuana when he said, "Just you watch, one of these days they'll make marijuana legal and you'll be able to buy it in the grocery store like beer and wine. Growers' stock will go through the roof." Unfortunately, Clifford had a poor sense of timing. Luck eluded him most of the time and eventually, pot became his nemesis.

"Your dad is coming upstairs. Get to your room pronto!" His mother shouted. "You smell like you've been smoking again, and you know how he feels about that." She tried to protect her son by salvaging the situation. Clifford heard his father's footsteps on the stairs. He sprinted to his room, shutting the door behind him.

"Dammit! I smell pot! Is Clifford home?" Herman charged. "That kid drives me up a wall. Why can't he stop doing that? Time for another talk."

Trying to understand her son, Celia probed for the reason. "It seems like he smokes late in the afternoon after school's out. Maybe that's how he takes out his frustration. He still gets good grades. He's at the top of his class."

"He might get good grades, but dammit, he doesn't have a lick of common sense—none!" Herman grumbled. "Clifford! Come downstairs and eat supper."

There's no way in hell I'm eating a meal with that jerk. He'll scowl at me from across the table and by the end of the meal, my stomach will be in knots. I'd rather be hung from the rafters by my thumbs. I'm not going to stop smoking pot. He's too dumb to understand. Besides, I found a good source of pot in Lansing. I'll be the kingpin for the group before long. They need me.

Herman knocked forcefully on Clifford's bedroom door, which was no surprise. "We've got to talk, son."

"Alright," Clifford said preparing himself for a blast. Herman walked in and sat on the bed, sucking in air to relax. He tried the buddy-buddy approach. Even though his voice was as calm as it could be, it was like fingernails on a chalkboard to Clifford.

"I've got to tell you something. I've put you and Maribelle in a trust and you'll both be sitting pretty after I'm gone. You need to know if you become a pothead, I'm changing my will and giving all the money to your sister. You better clean up your act, son. Think about it." Herman stood up and stomped out.

OMG, I think he means it this time. I don't want her to get my money. She'll hold it over my head forever. Dad has played with me, teased me about writing me out of the will. All of his threats push us farther and farther apart, and he wonders why I get stoned. I explode inside when I hear his voice. His threats make me want to smoke even more … Shit, if it's the smell that gets to him, I'll figure out a way to freshen up. Or, I could say screw it and go underground and live in my own hermit world.

HERE I AM, RIDING *in the back seat of the squad car. And, they have an outstanding warrant for my arrest.* He regretted the night when he'd bought weed from an undercover cop. Oblivious to the true intention of the transaction, he started counting out his money. Alarmed by the shiny metal handcuffs he spotted in the cop's jacket, he ran, stuffing the money back into his pocket. *Phew*! *Mission aborted*. He shoved his way into a vast crowd with the cop in hot pursuit. Pivoting around into an alley next to Restaurant Row, he searched for a place to hide. He jumped into an open dumpster and closed the lid. Something caterwauled—he turned to his right and was frightened by two glowing eyes. *Raccoon? Cat? Possum? Whatever it was, it had to go.* He grabbed the critter by the nape of its neck, opened the lid, and threw it out. It was a cat. Clifford stayed inside the dumpster until the coast was clear.

His instincts told him they would find him later at some point. *But, why on the night I purchased crack cocaine for the first time?* His luck was never good, and this was worse than a nightmare about Wanda, his ex.

OFFICER KENT TURNED RIGHT onto Cedar Street. The sign read, "Ingham County Jail." He hauled Clifford out of the back seat and brought him to the bullpen for booking and evaluation. They placed him in the custody of a corrections officer while they checked his identity, reason for arrest, and his general demeanor. The next step was fingerprinting and pictures. They snapped a mug shot, took pictures of any scars, and checked for tattoos.

"Any birthmarks?" the intake officer said. Her attitude screamed, "I abhor my job and I hate anyone who makes it difficult for me."

"One on my right ear."

Clifford recalled how his mother tried to erase his birthmark by using lemon juice three times a day. It worked for a while but would come right back. She tried melaleuca, calendula, and steroids prescribed by a doctor. Nothing worked, but her concern convinced Clifford she loved him. He carried her love with him wherever he went.

"Turn around; let me get a shot of that." She grabbed his shoulder.

Clifford flinched and pulled away. "Don't touch my ear!" he snapped. It was his holy ear, an appendage Mama nursed and obsessed over.

"Turn around. Pull your ear lobe forward."

Shrinking, Clifford obeyed.

She clicked the keys on her keyboard and described the birthmark for his file.

A male corrections officer took over. He took off the handcuffs and ordered Clifford to strip down. He checked for anything lodged in his body cavities, had him cough, and sent him to shower. A guard exchanged his clothes for an orange jumpsuit and fastened a blue band on his wrist. The jumpsuit stood out like a neon sign shouting, "I am a prisoner!" The officer gave him a matching pair of orange Crocs to wear. *Fashion statement?* No shoestrings were allowed, an attempt to prevent suicide; and shoestrings could be weaponized. The officer followed the intake procedures to the letter. They took his clothes and put them under lock and key. If released, they would give them back, but if he went to prison, a family member or friend had to collect them.

His pockets were empty. *No goods delivered; no money received.*

The intake worker gave his file to the guard through a slot in the door. "Do you want to see your mug shot?"

"Sure."

Clifford stared at his picture before handing it back.

"The next step is getting you to the infirmary for medical screening. Follow me."

Once in the infirmary, Clifford sat hunched forward on the waiting room bench, elbows on his knees. The officer was in guard pose behind him. *I hate my mug shot. I look broken, like scum. What's happened to me? When I graduated from high school, I was going places. I was going to be a doctor. I was salutatorian of my class. Everyone, including Mom, wanted me to go into medicine.*

"Clifford was such a cutie pie," she would say.

Mom always favored me—when she cut my hair, she saved my curls and pasted each blonde wisp of hair on my picture around my head. I looked like one of those little angel things. Maybe an angel-imp describes me better. My sister was jealous of me. When I talked, Maribelle drowned me out by yelling so loudly nobody heard what I said. When Mom gave me a treat, my dang sister would grab it out of my hand and run away. I never beat her up, but I wanted to. She has such a big honkin' nose. But go figure, Dad loved her best.

There was still a hint of an angel in Clifford's face. His eyes were a cerulean blue, playful and tempestuous, driven by a high-powered brain. Clifford was engaging, charming in his own way. Each smile sparked a glint in his eyes, and his eyebrows were linear but expressive. His nose was Grecian, firm and strong. He had firm jowls outlined by a well-shaped beard and the stubble of a five o'clock shadow. His most impressive feature, however, was his sensual lips. They were sealed, lock-box tight, guarding deep hurts inside. He opened them only when he had something to say. The blonde curls left long ago and were replaced by dark brown hair with sorrel highlights. After his doping and drugging excess, his hair became unkempt and grimy. He stood six feet tall and sported a stout, full-bellied frame. His strong body came from his father and it served both of them well.

As Clifford waited for the doctor, he observed the sights and sounds of the jail. He felt trapped in déjà vu, bringing him back to his high school gym class and the concrete walls. Clifford hated gym and dreaded the naked bodies prancing around the shower stalls. The smells of the jail were similar and sickening. The disinfectant liberally dispensed by the janitor's mop in the infirmary failed to overpower the odor of human sweat. He felt his stomach churn.

The environment was clinical and cold. Orange jumpsuits walked from one place to another, creating gray shadows on long slabs of white concrete. The strips of fluorescent lights glared on the sheen of the finger-marked chrome railings. Somehow, all this whiteness didn't fit the inhabitants—the rejects of society. Some evil hearts stalked the hallways, but others were like Clifford, down on their luck. The chrome strips around the doorways and walls signified an indestructible permanence to the place. For the inmates, the hallways were their ticket out of their cells to the day rooms, the commissary, phones, the infirmary, and the cafeteria. Although closely watched and guarded, they felt free for a short while.

Sitting on the bench, Clifford witnessed a shift change—no fanfare, just quick movements, like musical chairs. The guards seemed to drop into place. Doors would open and close in a flash. The day's intake workers, mostly women, brought in a box of doughnuts and coffee. The guards waited and watched the women, hoping to snatch a doughnut before leaving their shift. There were brief conversations as the guards found their place. The smell of coffee agitated the inmates, made them hungry for breakfast.

"Why did you send him to the infirmary?" the doctor asked.

"He has a history of substance abuse."

"Are you on any medication?" The doctor asked Clifford.

"No."

"Well, he looks fine to me. Take him back to the holding pen."

The officer walked him down the hall and opened a heavy steel door to the holding tank. The smell of alcohol, a noxious blend of beer, wine, and hard liquor, almost floored him. The officer handed him a rolled-up mat. Clifford took it in hand and looked for a place to sit. He yearned for sleep. There were six faces watching him, all at different levels of intoxication. It was a six-man cell with benches and a toilet, but no sink.

"You've got one phone call. The morning shift will

take care of you." He walked out, latching the door. The resounding clunk of steel and the finality of the metal click of the lock left an indelible memory. It was something he would *never* forget.

"Ratz?" an officer said. "You can make your call."

Clifford was ushered out of the holding cell and into a room of phones. He dialed home. When his mom picked up, a mechanical voice instructed her to accept reverse charges.

"Mom? Are you there?"

Finally, her voice came through.

"Hi, son. Where are you?"

"Ingham County Jail."

"Oh no," she exclaimed. "Why are you there?"

After a lengthy pause, he said, "They arrested me last night for having pot in my trunk."

"Your dad and I know you smoke—a lot, but are you dealing drugs?"

"Yeah, some," he paused. His voice changed. "Please bail me out!"

"Your dad isn't here now. I'll talk to him when he gets home. Have they set bail?"

"As far as I know, they're doing that right now. If you call the jail this afternoon, they should have the details."

"When can I talk to you again?" Mom asked.

"I don't know. Ask them."

"Bye, son." Her voice trailed to a whisper, disheartened.

Waiting was hard for Clifford. He didn't trust people to come through for him. His friends let him down so many times, he'd lost count. After a while, relying on others made him cynical. He was a loner who depended on no one.

Clifford was relieved Mom had answered. Dad would have seethed with anger inside but kept a cool exterior. Clifford saw his pattern for thirty-five years, over and over again. He'd shut down. Clifford wished he'd just yell and get over it. Mom would have to deal with his ornery sulk. He'd remain sullen for days and she'd pester him to get it off his chest. His inertia frustrated her and now that he was retired, it meant even more sulking and more dissatisfaction. *Will Dad lift a finger to help me out of this jam? Probably not. Damn him.*

3 Herman and Celia Ratz

Breaking this news to Herman about Clifford was like having all her teeth pulled, painful and not productive. Celia's phone rang.

"Need anything from the store?" Herman asked.

"Nope. Don't need anything. When are you coming home?"

"Gotta get some gas on the way, so in about a half an hour. Why?"

"We'll need to talk when you get home."

She called the jail to find out about Clifford's bail. "Hello, this is Celia Ratz. My son, Clifford, was arrested last night. I'm wondering how much money we need to bail him out."

"I'll check. Stay on the line."

Celia was on hold for over ten minutes. Her anxiety escalated.

"Mrs. Ratz? The judge is finishing the paperwork. Do you want to stay on hold? It will be a couple of minutes."

"I'll wait." She paced—*what a miserable way to start the morning*. Celia needed the information to form a doable plan before Herman got home.

"Mrs. Ratz? I'm looking at the report and the judge is requesting thirty-five thousand dollars bail. He's been dealing drugs. There was also a warrant out for his arrest stemming from an incident a month ago. He eluded the police. The judge wrote in the report that he's a flight risk."

"Did you say thirty-five thousand dollars?"

"Yes."

"Holy crap!"

Celia hung up without saying goodbye. Her stomach churned. She grabbed her Valium and washed it down with a swig of water. She needed relief—big time. Herman drove up the driveway.

"Hi, sweetie. What's up?"

Slumped in a living room chair, Celia barely looked at him.

"I got a call from Clifford," she said. "Sit down. I have something to tell you." Herman braced for whatever was coming. Stoic, unlike his wife. "Clifford is in the Ingham County Jail." Herman scowled—then, a long, stony silence.

"Was it drugs?"

"Yes."

"He's been smokin' a long time. I'm not surprised he got caught."

"It gets worse," Celia said. "He's been dealing."

"Ah, is he *that* stupid?" Herman put his head in his hands and shook it back and forth. "He's goin' to be the death of me. Does he expect me to bail him out?"

"I don't know. He's pretty down. I called the jail to find out how much bail would be. Are you ready for this? Thirty-five thousand."

"What?!" Herman jumped out of his chair, threw up his hands, and paced back and forth. "That's a huge amount! We can't afford that. Why is it so much?"

"He had a warrant out for his arrest. He eluded the police a month ago. The judge thinks he might jump bail."

"How can such a smart kid be so *stupid*?" Herman said. Celia sat motionless and didn't answer. "I will *not* risk any more money on that kid. He'll have to sit it out in jail. Maybe he'll learn his lesson."

Celia shook her head. "I thought you would say that, but I feel so sorry for him. Ever since he got the divorce from Wanda, that wacky woman, he hasn't seen much of his kids. He loved those kids. After that happened, he hasn't been himself. I'll check with a bail bondsman to find out how much their services would cost. I have four thousand left from my inheritance."

"That's foolhardy! We can't waste any more money on him."

Celia leafed through the Lansing phone book, looking for ads for bail bondsmen. She picked the one with the largest ad and called. Herman headed for the bathroom.

"Hello, this is Celia Ratz. My son's in jail. How much would it cost to bail him out?"

"How much is his bail?"

"Thirty-five thousand."

"That's high."

"I know. They said it was because he eluded the police a while back when they tried to take him into custody."

"We charge ten percent up front. That's our fee. We tell the court that we'll pay the full bond if the defendant fails to appear for his court date. So, if your son doesn't show up, we'll lose a lot of money. It's too risky for us to enter into an agreement with you."

"Do you know of a company that would take the risk?"

"There's a small company in Mason that might do it for twenty-five percent down."

Celia did a quick calculation in her head and realized it was more than double the money she had. "Thank you for the information," she said, hanging up. It was a hopeless situation. "This is too big for me to handle," she mumbled.

4 Jail

The jail was a warp zone inside. The two in for DUIs were stone silent, heads hanging down as if overripe apples on a tree. Simon, in for murder, intimidated Clifford with his weird, laser-focused, but distant stare. He was a puzzle and looked like the Jesus picture Clifford saw hanging in his hometown Baptist church. While his face resembled Jesus's, Clifford didn't think Jesus was nearly as wide or muscular. Simon's hair was a dark brown, his features even, and his pale lips seemed frozen in a faint delicate smile. *It probably masks an inner rage … or maybe not. Is it rage?* Clifford wasn't sure, so he stared back, hoping to crack who or what the man was. Simon's face turned white, fists pumped red, and his smile became a sneer. Clifford backed off.

Norm, in for nonpayment of child support, was a jolly sort of fellow. Short and talkative, he chattered through the thick air between Clifford and Simon.

"What you in for?" he asked. "Is this your first time?"

"Drugs, and yes, it is my first time."

"Smokin' or dealin'?"

"Both."

"Yeah, I used to smoke, but once the kids came, my

f**king ex confiscated it. All she left me with was booze, and that has its own problems. You got kids?"

"A boy and a girl."

"How old are they?"

Clifford wanted to swat him—like offing a mosquito. He wouldn't shut up. "I've got to get some sleep," Clifford said, determined to stop the yammering.

Saturday morning came and the two DUIs bailed out, leaving Clifford and three others in the holding cell. Clifford hoped his parents would bail him out too. That didn't happen on Saturday. He didn't know it then, but it wouldn't happen on Sunday either. In the meantime, he spent time talking to Steve, the one sitting next to him on the bench.

"What're you in for?" Clifford asked.

"Destruction of federal property," Steve said. "My sister tried to yank my tether loose with a pair of pliers."

"Did she do it?"

"No, she just bent 'em real good."

"Someone bailing you out?"

"There ain't no damn way. I don't know nobody who gots the money to bail me out."

"I haven't heard anything from my mom and dad either," Clifford said.

When Clifford heard the groan of the steel door, he hoped the officer would have a message for him.

"Jackson?"

Jackson was fast asleep but poked his head up when he heard his name. "What?"

"You're bailed out."

Jackson shook the sleep out of his eyes, brushed his hair back, said a quick goodbye, and walked out. The hard thud of that door sealed the holding cell, leaving Clifford, Steven, and Simon behind. It stayed that way throughout Sunday. *Maybe Monday, things will change.* Once again, the door clunked open.

"Ratz? Your attorney is here." The guard said, nodding to the man standing next to him.

"I'm Neil Pastoor. Your parents hired me to defend you. Follow me to the room off the hallway."

Clifford followed him, noting his peculiar gait. It was somewhere between a hobble and a limp involving both feet. The two sat down and Clifford sized him up. Neil's dress was conservative—tweed jacket, bowtie, and button-down shirt. His dark curly hair framed an expansive face. Piercing brown eyes lurked behind round, dark-rimmed glasses. His straightforward demeanor elicited trust, but his sardonic laugh bugged Clifford.

"You have a spotty record here," Neil said. "There's domestic battery from May of '72." He continued reading Clifford's rap sheet. "There's auto theft on your juvenile record—looks like you took your dad's car without permission. And there's a drug sale where you eluded the police." Neil looked up. "Was it a sting operation?"

"Yeah, it was a setup. I connected with someone I thought was a university student, but when I realized he was a narc, I jammed the money in my pocket and ran my ass off."

"There's no indication they made an arrest, but they made the last one from two nights ago stick. You had quite a load to deliver … almost twenty-five pounds. That's big time. Where was it going?"

"I deliver to people who have medical issues … a few for recreational use. Sometimes, they have so much pain they can't see straight, and pot helps them manage it."

"Well, drug trafficking is a felony. You could get three to five years of confinement if not longer for that … depends on the judge's mood. I'll convince the judge that it should only be three years, because it's your first major brush with the law. How do you want to plead: guilty or not guilty?"

"It's clear I'm guilty. I guess that's what I'll plead."

"I'll meet you in court in a few hours." Neil shook his hand, shuffled out, and left, spouting his irritating laugh.

The officer ushered Clifford back into the holding cell. An hour later, he returned, handcuffed him, and took him to a vehicle waiting outside. Surrounded by heavy plastic shields to keep him locked into place, he rode in the van for two miles, through small business districts and residential streets. It stopped by a stately brick building graced by a brass eagle atop a clock tower. *Why do these old courthouses look like decorated wedding cakes? What the hell is that all about? Why not something more somber like a tomb, painted black or steel gray? Wouldn't that give it the gravitas it deserved?*

Clifford shuffled into the courthouse, escorted by the officer. They detained him in another holding cell to await his arraignment.

"Clifford James Ratz," called the bailiff. He unlocked the door, grabbed Clifford's arm, and walked him to a long rectangular table, where he sat to Neil's right.

"I read over the documents again," Neil whispered. "My best advice is for you to plead no contest rather than guilty. It will give me a little more room to negotiate."

Clifford nodded. He scanned the courtroom, noticing the prosecuting attorney to his left and the galley behind him filled with people. With a sudden jerk of his head he smiled when he saw his mom. Dad sat next to her, scowling. He stared straight ahead, looking at the back of Clifford's head. Clifford smiled but gritted his teeth as he turned back.

"All rise!" said the bailiff. Clifford joined the throng of those standing.

"You may be seated," the judge said. She was an attractive middle-aged woman with long dark hair. Clifford tried to meet her eyes, but they were hidden behind a wedge of black bangs and horn-rimmed glasses. She was unreadable.

I wonder if she'll be fair. Will she believe I was just trying to help sick people and chill out a little? I'll soon find out.

"Clifford James Ratz. Please stand. You have been charged with a felony. You are accused of intentionally trafficking a controlled substance, a drug of dependence. How do you plead?"

"No contest, your Honor," he said, looking squarely at her.

"Your Honor," Neil interposed. "This is Mr. Ratz's first drug trafficking offense. Until now, he has been a law-abiding citizen."

"That might be, Mr. Pastoor, but this is a major crime

and he possessed an excessive amount. What was he going to do with all of that marijuana?"

"From my discussion with him, he did not involve minors and he sold only to adults who used it for pain management."

"This is a drug of dependency, and that's the problem," the judge responded. "Mr. Ratz, for your crime you could be sentenced from three to five years in prison." Turning toward the prosecuting attorney, she said, "Do you have anything to say about setting his bail?"

"Your Honor, Mr. Ratz eluded the police during a previous incident," asserted the prosecutor. "He's a flight risk and has drug charges pending. He will likely make every attempt to complete those transactions, and such as it is, he's a menace to society."

"Understood. Bail remains the same."

Three to five years without freedom was a terrifying thought. His eyes, smeared by disgrace, dropped to the floor. The judge's words, "confinement for five years," screamed in his head like an echo in a dark chamber. He had so many questions. *Why is my bail so high? Why five years? I don't have any other convictions. Where in the hell is my attorney?* He dragged his feet all the way out the door. The expression on his mother's face begged for eye contact. He didn't look up. Clifford climbed into the van and turned his face away from everybody. The purring of the engine, usually a comfort for him, didn't soothe his anxieties. He knew where he was headed.

CLIFFORD HEARD THE GROANS of two steel doors before he reached Dorm D, where he would wait until sentencing. It was a large cement block room with six narrow bunks—one man per bunk. Each man sat on his cot. An older television with a cable box was fastened to one wall, and at the far end was a toilet, shower, and sink. It was a make or break place. Blank eyes stared back at him. The officer removed Clifford's handcuffs and he walked into the cell.

"Go make up a bunk," the officer said. He handed Clifford a towel, two sheets, and a goody bag of soap, a small tube of toothpaste, and a toothbrush.

Clifford made his bed, noticing the only window was to the left of his bunk. He glanced outside at a courtyard with a rusty generator and weeds growing between the spread of gravel. It was a grim place made bleaker by the steel gray overcast of the Michigan sky, common in early winter. Clifford had five cellmates. Derrick and Leroy, in for murder, were from Detroit.

"Ain't no room for us in Detroit," Derrick said, "so, Ingham County gots us—they gets paid by the state of Michigan for keeping the bunks filled—the mo' prisoners, the mo' they gets paid. Geez, why rehab us? They'd lose money."

Sid, in for selling drugs, wore a green wristband. "My wristband is blue," Clifford said. "Why is yours green?"

"It means I've been sentenced and serving time," Sid mumbled.

Stew, also wearing a green wristband, was charged with growing marijuana on his dad's farm. Randy had been convicted of stealing from a vending machine and evading the police in a high-speed chase on the county's back roads. He wore a yellow wristband, which meant he'd broken his parole and was serving his mandatory forty days.

The corrections officer rolled a cart of individual trays into Dorm D at 6:30 a.m., 11:30 a.m., and 4:30 p.m.— like clockwork. Meals were a big event. He slipped the trays through a metal flap just below a tiny glass window in the door.

"Chow … chow time!" Stew shouted to wake the others. They dimmed the lights for six hours, from midnight to 6:00 a.m., even though they didn't sleep at night. Nighttime was when they talked. They slept through the day, waking up only for each meal. Snoring and showering were the main topics of conversation. For privacy, one of them donated a sheet to drape across the shower stall. Each took turns. Shower time reminded him of the mass showers after gym class. He sat on the edge of his bunk, staring at the floor. There was no way Clifford wanted to strip nude in front of them. They poked at him and badgered him until he gave in.

Derrick was the champion snorer. He tortured all five of them. They threw pillows at him and tried the water treatment, but nothing worked. They got back at him by teasing him relentlessly.

"What sound does a T-Rex make when it's sleeping?" Randy asked. The other five shook their heads. "A dino-snore," he quipped, laughing at his own joke.

"Randy, that's some dumbass shit," Derrick jabbed.

"I've got a good one," Leroy announced. "A Detroit cab driver and a preacher arrived at the pearly gates—

Saint Peter takes the cab driver first and brings him to the best part of Heaven, but he brings the preacher to the second-best part of Heaven. The preacher asks Saint Peter 'Why?' After all, he served God for many years. Saint Peter said he based it on merit from how many people they brought closer to God.

'On merit?' the preacher said. 'I headed a congregation of seventy people for years. I preached my heart out. What did he do?'

'True,' Saint Peter said. 'But while you were preachin,' people were snorin,' but while the cab driver was drivin'… the passengers prayed their butts off!'"

"Amen to that," Derrick said with a chuckle.

"Hey, I've got a better one," Stew said. "Three guys were at a deer camp, bunked two to a room. No one wanted to share a room with Steve because he snored like a bitch. The first night, John sleeps in his room and comes to breakfast the next morning all f**ked up, bloodshot eyes and everything. They asked him what happened. He says, 'Steve snored so loud I was awake the entire night.' The next night it was Gary's turn. In the morning, Gary says, 'Steve shook the roof. I couldn't sleep a wink.' The third night was Herb's turn. Herb is a big hunk of a guy who loves to fish and hunt, a real manly man. The next morning Herb comes to breakfast all bright-eyed and bushy-tailed. The other guys ask him what happened. Herb said, 'After we got ready for bed, I tucked Steve into bed and kissed him good night, so he sat up all night watching *me!*'"

Laughter bounced off the cement walls.

DERRICK LEFT, AND RUMOR had it that he went back to Detroit to stand trial. Clifford still hadn't heard anything from his parents—not even a phone call. Later that day, he was summoned by a corrections officer, handcuffed, and brought to a small room near the cell. A gentleman introduced himself as a social worker. His purpose was to ask some questions. "It's a mental status exam," he said. The questions were simple, and Clifford was sure he passed.

The next day, Neil shared some good news. "I wanted to tell you in person. I've talked with the prosecuting attorney, and both of us agreed on a reduced sentence. Instead of five years in prison, the prosecutor will ask the judge to give you a sentence of three years followed by parole, the time to be determined later."

"That sounds much better, but it still sucks. Thanks, I guess."

"The date for sentencing is next week, Friday, and the judge should be on board with the three years."

"So, I'll be facing that same judge again?"

"Yes." Neil stood. "Make sure you thank your parents for hiring an attorney for you. You got much better treatment that way."

"I will. Have you spoken to them?"

"Yes, just this morning. They should be calling you this afternoon."

"Thanks." Clifford shook Neil's hand. Clifford was relieved to know that someone on the outside had his back.

IT SEEMED STRANGE NOT to have Derrick in Dorm D. They were becoming a team—kind of like pulling for each other. Rumor had it Derrick might be acquitted, although juries were unpredictable. Sid was a hoot. He made Clifford laugh, making the time go faster.

The door scraped open to a specter so unwelcome, it sent shivers up his spine. Simon Dean, from Clifford's bullpen days, entered with a sneer. Simon snatched the goody bag and sheets out of the officer's hands and steered his massive body to the bunk next to Clifford's.

"Shit," Simon mumbled. He stared at the floor. Clifford watched him out of the corner of his eye. Simon seemed calm, but he reminded Clifford of the silos on his uncle's farm, cool on the outside, but dusty and combustible on the inside. If by accident or on purpose one ignited, a huge explosion would blow the place apart. A hot light bulb, a cigarette, a lightning strike, almost anything could ignite a fire storm.

Clifford's cellmates sensed Simon's hair-trigger mien and withdrew into a tense silence. They did *not* want to aggravate him. He was a tinderbox, a disaster waiting to happen.

Aroused by the grind of the door, Simon lifted his head.

"Ratz. You have a phone call," the officer said. Clifford stood, setting off a chain reaction.

"What the hell!? I've seen yo' ass before," Simon yelled. Clifford kept walking. The door shut behind him.

"Clifford? This is your mom. Are you alright, sweetie?"

"I'm not doing okay. There are some horrible people here."

"Y'all know when you wallow with pigs, expect to get dirty." Sometimes Clifford laughed at her clichés, but not today.

"When are you and Dad going to bail me out?"

After a lengthy pause, she said, "That's too much money for us, so we got you a good attorney instead."

"Shit," Clifford mumbled. "I guess that's better than nothing…. Thanks, Mom. I think he's fighting for me, and I appreciate that, but Mom, there's a very dangerous guy in the cell with me."

"I told you, never corner someone you know is meaner than you. Stay away."

"I don't plan on *cornering* him, Mom. He's as big as a f**king house."

"Clifford! Watch your language!"

"Sorry… but Mom, he's out to get me. This is serious."

"Meanness doesn't jes' happen overnight."

"That makes no sense to me. What are you saying?"

"Something happened to him that made him mean. Maybe you could just listen and be kind."

"Aw, Ma, that will never work."

"By the way, Sharm's been asking about you. She wants to come visit you."

"Really? I'd like to see her … but I'm ashamed for her to see me in this place."

"Don't worry about that. Sharm loves you no matter what."

"Tell her to call me Sunday afternoon. I'll wait for her call. What's she been up to?"

"She's doing pretty good in school, but she's got a tattoo on her neck—it's a rose inside a pig's mouth. She thinks it's beautiful, but it's really ugly. She did get rid of that goth boyfriend and tried out for the spring play."

"That girl is always changing. I'd like to talk to her, but I need more money in my account before I get a phone call from her. I have to pay five dollars for fifteen minutes. Would you put some money in my account?"

"Okay, I'll put more in." A beep signaled. "Our time is up. I'll call again soon. Love you."

UNSURE WHAT TO EXPECT when he returned to his cell, Clifford dragged his feet.

"Move your ass," the officer said. "I've got shit to do."

When Clifford walked in, he found Simon sitting on his bunk. *Do I ask him to move? Remember what your mother said about cornering someone meaner than you. He's itching for a fight. I should call a guard. Simon's out of line.* Clifford went to the window and waited for a guard to come by with the meal cart.

"Officer, someone took my bunk," he yelled.

Simon smirked.

The door opened. "What's going on here?"

"I came back from a phone call and found him sitting on my bunk."

"Come on, Dean," said the officer. "Get your ass off his bed. You know you can't do that."

Simon shuffled back to his bunk, waited for the officer to leave, and gave Clifford a contemptuous look.

"You f**king snitch." He lowered his eyes, balled his fists. "I should poke both your eyes out." Simon stood, grabbed the front of Clifford's shirt, and locked an arm around his neck. Clifford grunted and clawed at Simon's huge bicep. Sid, Stew, Randy, and Leroy charged, but Simon shook them off and threw Clifford down on the concrete. The four men worked as a team, slamming into Simon and pushing him backward until his head bounced off the block wall. With a flurry of swear words, they wrestled him to the floor.

"Cut it out—Get your damn teeth off me!—Shut your f**king mouth!—Settle the hell down!—What's your damn problem?—What in the hell did Clifford ever do to you?"

Stew and Randy gripped his legs, while Sid and Leroy each held an arm, which were impossible to control. They kept at it until Simon's arms twitched and then relaxed.

Clifford slipped out of the knot of human bodies and found his way to his bunk, breathing heavily and shaking. He was grateful for his cellmates' protection. Simon simmered down and lay limp against the back wall, tired from his adrenalin rush.

"Keep one eye open when you sleep, you SOB. It always happens at night," Simon mumbled.

That bastard…. Threats must be in his DNA.

There were many things Clifford wanted to say, but was convinced Simon would take them the wrong way. He didn't want his words to incite another fight. Clifford knew Simon must have a hell of a backstory. *It doesn't take a lot of common sense to know that hate breeds hate.* Knowing his cellmates talked during the night and slept through the day, Simon's threats didn't bother him. *Simon is crushed—at least for now.*

The door opened. "Ratz," the officer called. "Your attorney is here."

"Have a seat," Neil said as Clifford entered the room. "They scheduled your sentencing for tomorrow. Like I said before, the prosecutor and I have agreed on three years because you don't have a previous record. However, he did ask me about the domestic abuse incident. Tell me about that."

"My ex-wife, Wanda, and I married young, at nineteen. We had two kids before we were twenty-five. I was working hard at the Pontiac plant to bring home the bacon and keep a roof over our heads. Wanda threatened to divorce me, and the worst of it was she pitted the kids against me. I came home from work one night—she'd been drinking. The kids were sick and there was nothing to eat in the house. I lost it, but I never hit her. I took several swings at the kitchen wall, punched holes in the drywall. Wanda got scared and called the cops, but she didn't press charges." Clifford paused. "When I was fourteen, I took my dad's car for a joy ride. I drove it out of the garage before he left for work. I was just being a teenager. I got pulled over for speeding. They had an APB out on me. I told the cop I did it because I hated my dad. The cop got red in the face and yelled, 'We don't tolerate daddy-haters.' I've never forgotten what he said."

"That's pretty close to what I'm reading on your sheet," Neil said. "One more question: Did your parents call?"

"Yeah, my mom called."

"All the calls coming in and out of the jail or in the prisons are recorded. Please remind your family and friends not to say anything incriminating. Is that clear?"

"Are the conversations between you and me recorded?"

"No. That's illegal because of attorney/client confidentiality."

"Good.... being in jail makes me distrust everyone."

"In this system, that's the best way to be."

CLIFFORD DAWDLED BACK TO his cell, dreading another conflict with Simon. *Thank God that creep is asleep. I'm going to flop on my bed and relax.* His mind wandered to his past life as a family man—his most painful time. He slogged out a living to keep his wife and children fed and sheltered. He wanted them happy, but was stretched so thin he became ornery. All his hard work and good intentions seemed to count for nothing. He juggled too many balls. At one point, all the balls dropped and scattered everywhere, leaving him heartsick and stuck with the financial strain of alimony and child support. The only redeeming part of that life was his daughter, Sharm.

Pretty as a picture, and tiny as a peanut, Sharm was Daddy's girl. When Clifford worked on his car, she would bring him the tools he needed. Yard work meant the two of them would dig and pull weeds side by side. She was his little shadow. They lit up when they saw each other, like old souls meeting after a long journey. She was funny and bright like her daddy. They shared the same sense of humor. He spent an afternoon with her before he got busted. They ate Coney dogs and laughed a lot. It was a breezy relationship with no judgment or pressure. "Fun times only" was their motto. In the spring, they relished going to Potter Park Zoo. They laughed when the apes scratched their butts and when the giraffes snatched food with their black curling tongues. The groan of the door jarred him out of his reverie.

"Ratz? You have a phone call." Half expecting his daughter, he hustled from his bed and followed the guard.

The phone system at the jail was bogged down by interruptions and wait times before the caller got clearance to talk.

"Daddy? I can't hear you. Are you there?"

"Yes, I'm here."

"What happened, Daddy? Why are you in jail?"

"I don't want to talk about it," Clifford said. "Grandma will fill you in."

"Did you do something stupid?"

"I guess you could say that."

"I have a birthday next month. I'll be sixteen. I want you to be there. Will you be out by that time?"

"I don't know."

"Can I come to visit you?"

"Yes, you can come during visiting hours after school. The best time is between three and four. Why don't you plan on calling me Sunday afternoons? Would that work for you?"

"Sure, that'll work. I broke up with Andy."

"Smart girl. He wasn't good enough for you."

"I know. He was a control freak, always trying to tell me what to do. He'd turn green with jealousy. I was afraid of him when he got angry."

"Will you do a favor for me? Do well in school, you hear?"

"Okay, Daddy. Did Grandma tell you I got a part in the play?"

"No. She told me you tried out. So, you got a part. That's great."

"It's a small part, but they told me I'm an ingénue. Grandma said I got it because I'm pretty."

"That you are. You remind me of a yellow tulip, sunny and happy. You are the sunshine of spring. I love you, honey—just the way you are!"

"I love you too, Daddy. Grandpa and Grandma just drove up. I need to go."

"We'll talk next week. Good to hear from you." *How she came out of Wanda, I'll never know. Sharm does not take after her mother, not one smidgen. Sharm and I think alike about most things. I don't care what everyone says; I look forward to seeing her tattoo. Knowing Sharm, it's got to be creative and clever. I miss my daughter so much. If she got herself in a jam, I'd die for her. Her life is more important than mine.*

He hung up the phone and nestled his head in his arms on the metal counter. A wave of sorrow washed over him—life seemed so cruel.

"Get up," the guard ordered. "It's time to go back." Clifford pushed the chair out, stood up, and dragged his feet all the way to his cell.

Only four cellmates were there—Simon was missing.

"Where's Simon?"

"We don't know," Leroy said, speaking for the rest. "A guard came and took him away … hopefully back to hell."

Clifford's spirits lifted knowing he could have a better night's sleep without Simon around. He wanted to be rested for sentencing in the morning.

"ALL RISE!" THE BAILIFF announced. "The Ingham County 30th District Circuit Court is now in session with the Honorable Judge Mavis Cartright presiding."

The judge entered from an anteroom and stood behind the bench. "You may be seated. Those here for the Clifford Ratz case, please come forward." Neil and Clifford filed to the front and sat at the table to the judge's left.

"Mr. Skewes, do you have a recommendation for sentencing?"

"I do, your Honor. Mr. Pastoor and I have come to an agreement that Mr. Ratz should be sentenced to three years in the state prison system." The judge remained silent, but her eyebrows rose above her eyeglasses, questioning their decision.

"Mr. Skewes and Mr. Pastoor, please approach the bench," she ordered. Her voice lowered to a whisper. "I'm confused by this. He committed a felony—he had a huge load of contraband. He needs longer than three years to reform."

"Your Honor," Neil said, "Mr. Ratz is sorry for what he has done and recognizes it hurt his community. But

I must say, he is a very bright man. He was salutatorian of his high school class. He began making bad choices trying to support his family after a difficult divorce. He knows he needs to pay for his crime."

"Very well. Where did he go to school? He's about the same age as my daughter."

"I think it was Mason, but I'm not positive."

"Mr. Ratz." Her eyes drilled Clifford. "You will serve three years in a state prison for your crime. Please use this time to think about what you've done and how you might better contribute to society. Do you have any questions?"

"No, your Honor."

Clifford followed Neil out of the courtroom. "You got a pretty good deal, and you might be released sooner for good behavior."

"Do you know what prison will be taking me?"

"It might be a couple of days before we know. It depends on where they have vacancies."

The handcuffs made it impossible to shake Neil's hand, so they nodded to each other as he was escorted to a transport van. Clifford became anxious about what was next. Michigan had prisons in the thumb area and in the UP, but those were too far away. Sharm wouldn't be able to visit him. Jackson Prison was only a thirty-minute drive, and he hoped they had an opening there. He had no choice in the matter—he was at the mercy of the prison system and the Department of Corrections, the DOC.

Clifford, stuck in the fog of anxiety, didn't notice that Simon was still missing. Finally, he looked about and saw Simon's junk scattered on his bunk like shells on the seashore. "No word on Simon?"

"One of the inmates said he's in Detroit awaiting the outcome of his murder trial," Stew said. "He's been there for the better part of a week. How did your hearing go?"

"Not too bad, I guess. I got three years and my lawyer said I might get out sooner for good behavior. I'm worried about where they're going to send me. I don't want to go too far away. I won't be able to see my family."

EARLY IN THE MORNING, just after they finished eating breakfast, the familiar clanking-rattling sound filled the cell.

"Ratz, leave everything behind and come with me."

Like a lamb to the slaughter, he followed him out. The officer put belly chains on him. A chain went around his waist, and the handcuffs were attached to the chain. Another long chain went down his legs, and his ankles were shackled. Clifford slid his right foot forward, and then his left until he got to the van, where he froze. Simon was handcuffed to the seat—bawling like a baby. Clifford turned stubborn. The guard had to lift him into the van; he was stiff as a board. He hauled him to a bench attached to the side wall and locked him in. Simon and Clifford sat across from each other, a gruesome reminder of how they first met.

This is worse than my darkest nightmare.

"Where are we going?" Clifford shouted.

"Marquette," the driver replied.

"No! I can't go to Marquette!"

"Too bad. So sad. There are worse places—you could be going to hell," the officer said, with a devilish laugh.

Simon stopped crying to curl his lip at Clifford, but soon became sullen, stared at the floor, and fell asleep. Clifford checked to make sure Simon was securely shackled. *If he gets loose, he'll kick my ass again for sure. It's going to be a hell of a long ride.*

Clifford had made the trek to Marquette as a boy scout. It was a camping trip to see Pictured Rocks and various waterfalls cascading off the granite cliffs in the Upper Peninsula. The trails were rugged, but the nature was awe inspiring. From that experience, he knew it was a four-hundred-mile trip to Marquette and would take about six hours.

I wish I was a teenager again, hanging out with boys my own age and looking forward to new adventures like joking around, eating ice cream, and camping. The night sky filled with stars ... and sparks from the fire ... and fireflies were all good times. Oh well. What's done is done. Three years is a long time to be locked away in cells full of Simons. I've got to outsmart them. Hell, I've got to keep breathing.

5 Marquette

"The UP [Upper Peninsula] today is still among the least populated regions of the lower forty-eight states. It's a rough-and-tumble land of woods and swamps and your corner towns, where logging remains the only industry to thrive (iron mining was once the mainstay, but 598 of the peninsula's six hundred mines have closed, victims of the ailing domestic steel industry), and the largest city, Marquette, has a population of less than twenty-five thousand." —*The Living Great Lakes* by Jerry Dennis

The highway slid through Lansing without offering a view of the famed Capitol building. Clifford saw only Lansing city limits on his left. On the right, they cruised by the famed university town of East Lansing, home to Michigan State University. Clifford's failed attempt as a college student flashed before him. He was a young buck when he had met Wanda at Harper's Bar on Albert Street.

What the hell did I see in her? She was short and cute, a barfly, sitting alone at the end of the bar. Our eyes met, locked, and hers beckoned. I smiled and against my better judgment said, 'Why not?' And like some mysteri-

ous gravitational pull, we became lovers. After a night of hypnotic sex, I wanted more. I couldn't get enough. Sex with Wanda was addictive.

Both of us were students at Michigan State, but not sure who we were or where we were going. Our sex life was present tense and erased all apprehensions. It defined us and our lives. Kevin arrived nine months later, and we loved our baby boy. He was a delightful baby, slept through the night and reached each developmental milestone right on time. Wanda wanted to study child development and own a day care center. In a way, real life was her training. We dropped out of college, moved into an apartment in Lansing, and I went to work on the night shift assembly line at Fisher Body. Wanda stayed home with Kevin and was a good mother to him.

Sharm was born two years later, and that's when things got rough. Sharm was colicky and our marriage teetered on the edge of collapse. I was frustrated because I had to sleep during the day to be ready for the night shift, so that meant Wanda had to keep the kids quiet. When I went to work, she was all alone at night with a screaming baby. It was a chaotic mess and ultimately, it didn't work out.

Suddenly, Simon moved. Clifford snapped to, fixed his eyes on his nemesis, and double-checked the security of Simon's shackles. Simon opened his eyes, but they rolled back in his head. He started shaking, small tremors at first, then more intense. He frothed at the mouth.

"Officer!" Clifford shouted. "Simon's sick! He needs help."

The officer realized Simon was in trouble and told the

driver to pull the van to the side of the road. The guard grabbed a sweatshirt from the front seat and climbed inside the back door. He checked the time, cushioned Simon's head with the sweatshirt, and waited. Between each violent contortion, Simon's body stiffened, his teeth clamped down with a powerful force, and his iron jaw clenched shut. His legs shook so wildly the van rocked. Instead of fear, Clifford felt compassion for him. Simon, the murderer, was helpless in the grip of this horrible malady. The officer checked his wristwatch again and directed the driver to head to the Clinton County jail in St. Johns.

"I'll have Doc Spenser check him over," he said. "He's calming down some, but it's been over five minutes."

By the time they reached the jail, the seizure had subsided. Simon was sweating profusely. The officer helped him sit up, but he was limp with exhaustion.

"He needs some water," Clifford said. Simon, foggy-eyed, nodded and smiled. *He's thanking me. Maybe we'll watch each other's back in prison.* The officer gave him a drink from a small water bottle, and he seemed to come around.

Doctor Spenser climbed into the back to examine him. He had Simon track his finger with his eyes, felt his forehead for fever, and checked for any possible injuries. "He's fine. Does he have medication for his seizures?"

"Nothing was mentioned in his file," the officer said.

"I've got some Tegretol in my office. I'll send it with you. Follow the directions on the bottle," the doctor said, hopping out of the van to get the medicine.

"Give this to Doctor Murray at Michigamme. He'll make sure he gets the proper dose."

The van pulled away from the curb and headed toward Marquette with Simon and Clifford in the back looking at each other. Simon fell into a restorative sleep and stayed that way for several hours. Out of the corner of his eye, Clifford spotted signage for the Au Sable River, which released a flood of memories. Once again, he recalled the boy scout memories with his friend, "Matt the Rat." They'd developed a reputation as the cutups of the group. They laughed at anything and everything and goofed around from morning until their heads hit their sleeping bags at night. The Au Sable River was considered one of the more challenging rivers to canoe. Maybe a river flowing at three miles per hour didn't seem like much for an experienced canoeist, but it was Clifford and Matt's first time. After a brief demonstration from their leader about how to navigate the water, Matt and Clifford pulled the canoe offshore, climbed in, and started paddling. They were an accident waiting to happen. Clifford was in the front, paddling with all of his might. He propelled the canoe swiftly and forcefully through the water. Matt was in the back, charged with steering the boat. It worked for a while because the river was wide, and they raced ahead of the other scouts, singing and laughing together. Around a bend, halfway through the trip, they encountered a long peninsula dotted with evergreens, which created a passageway so narrow it would have challenged an expert canoeist. With Clifford still paddling full speed ahead, Matt steered too far to the right. The canoe slammed into a pine tree, dumping Matt and Clifford overboard. Gasping for air, they surfaced, frantically searching for the canoe, which had bounced downriver. They pulled themselves out of the water onto the peninsula and waited for the rest of the group.

Right away, the leader saw what happened and instructed one of the boats to retrieve their canoe. "You boys look like drowned rats!" he said, coining the name "Matt the Rat." The scouts rescued the canoe, but their paddles were missing. "You two boys will have to portage the canoe the rest of the way."

Clifford and Matt resigned themselves to lugging the canoe up the bank to a trail overgrown with bramble. They followed the river back to camp.

Gazing out the window, Clifford knew the Au Sable River would be frozen over and the trees bare and gray. It was mid-December after all, but his memories were as green and alive as if it were yesterday.

THE VAN CLIMBED NORTH along Highway 75. Snowmobiles roared next to the main highway, packing the snow until it glistened like glass. The vehicles lurched and slowed depending on the hills and dips on the trails. To his right, he spotted a sign which read, "Arbutus Beach." This conjured up his first encounter with the arbutus flower—a masterful work of God. The scent was like nothing he had smelled before. It was a strong spicy fragrance unparalleled by the most expensive perfume. He'd found small bunches on the shady glens during his early spring walks with Sharm. She'd caressed the little pink trumpet-shaped flowers and rubbed the blossoms under her nose so she could fully inhale the delicious scent. *Sweet days, sweeter memories.*

Beyond the roads and ditches, endless rows of evergreens flashed past Clifford's window. The white and jack pines ignited his memories from fourth grade and of his French-Canadian teacher, Mrs. Bouchard. She came from the Upper Peninsula and was proud of it. Her father and brother were lumberjacks and patriarchs of the dwindling lumber industry. She shared her lumberjack stories with her students and described the pines as icons of Michigan's northern woods.

During the pioneer days, cutting timber was the state's main industry. Acres upon acres were harvested to build factories and homes in the Northeast. Lumber from the west side of Michigan bordered by the Lake Michigan shoreline was sent to Chicago to frame massive architectural structures and family homes. Hardworking lumberjacks spent entire winters in the camps sawing down pine trees, hauling them to sawmills, and rolling them downriver in the spring.

Teams of horses hooked to timber wagons transported lumber to buyers. In the winter, when the snow made the trails impassable, they iced the paths so the logs could be hauled by sleigh. Clifford smiled when he recalled Mrs. Bouchard describing pocket pasties.

The cooks at the camps sent pasties with the lumberjacks for a warm, nourishing noon meal in the woods. The delicious pasties were sized and shaped to fit inside their pockets to keep both the pasties and the men warm. Inside each was a chunky mixture of rutabaga, venison, other meats, potatoes, and turnips, all baked to perfection.

Lumberjack tales were a staple in the north woods. Clifford, prompted by Mrs. Bouchard, remembered reading *Legends of Paul Bunyan, Lumberjack* in fourth grade. Folk legends crowed about Paul Bunyan's great strength and skill as a logger. It was said that every time he stomped through the forests with his seven-foot stride and eight-foot frame, he created a lake. His footprints were everywhere in northern Michigan. Clifford relished reading the crazy stories of the imaginative critters concocted by the lumberjacks as they worked in the woods. There was the Fillyloo, a mythical crane that flew upside down. The Teakettler, a small stubby-legged dog with ears like a cat that made a whistling sound like boiling water in a teakettle. Then, there was the Hidebehind, the Goofus, and the Hangdown, all figments of their imaginations.

Mrs. Bouchard described evening scenes in the bunkhouses of the logging camps where lumberjacks drank whisky, ate hearty meals, and told stories of mythical creatures. Late at night, one could hear rounds of raucous belly laughs. The night ended by extinguishing the fire in the fireplace, turning off the kerosene lanterns, and the grand finale—slumber and loud snoring.

Thoughts and other memories flooded Clifford's semiconscious mind. He tilted his head back and daydreamed. *I remember seeing a show on TV about a van full of convicts hit by a train. Two of them escaped into the woods, running for their lives. They were chained together, so working as a team determined their survival. What if a situation forced Simon and me to escape together? Would we survive?*

A sudden jerk jarred Clifford out of his daydream. The wheels skidded on a patch of black ice and the driver slammed on the brakes. This created an out-of-control spin. *Idiot!* Fortunately, there was no traffic on the road, so the driver controlled the skid. Simon woke up and looked around with fear in his eyes.

"What happened?" he asked.

"The driver slid on some ice and spun the van around," Clifford said. "It's okay now."

Simon rolled his eyes in disgust and hung his head between his shoulders, trying to find more sleep. His head bounced like a bobber in the water. *Is he a friend or foe? I've seen him helpless with a seizure and piss in his pants. That's blackmail material. Would it be enough for us to call a truce or would he want me dead, silenced forever?* Clifford thought about it for a long time. *I'll be nice but watch him close—so close my body will feel his wind, and the movement of his soul.*

Clifford waited for Simon's head to bob up before he spoke to him. "We're close to Mackinaw City. Have you been here before?"

"No," he said. "What's the big f**king deal?"

"You can see the Mackinac Bridge from here. There it is," Clifford exclaimed, as he pointed to the massive steel girders buttressing the sky. For him, the view of the bridge and the Straits of Mackinac never got old; it was always as if he was seeing it for the first time. His excitement never waned.

Clifford had smoked his most memorable joint on the Mackinac Bridge on Labor Day twenty years ago. Daylight was dawning when he and his friend Ralph shared one before the other bridge walkers arrived. Leaning on the steel railing and looking out, they could see the land masses of the Upper and Lower Peninsulas. Lake Michigan and Lake Huron flowed together under the bridge—a magnificent sight.

Simon remained silent, but his permanent sneer disappeared and his eyes opened. It was as if a little bit of his child had come out to play. Clifford had never seen a glint in his eye before, but he was certain it was there, if only for a short time.

"Who built it?" Simon asked.

"The state of Michigan. The architect was a man named Steinman, I think. It's the fifth-longest suspension bridge in the world and considered one of the safest," Clifford continued. "Over there is the Grand Hotel on Mackinac Island."

"I've heard of Mackinac Island before," Simon said.

Immediately after crossing, the van turned left to go west on Highway 2. Lake Michigan's ever-changing shoreline, cold, yet captivating, lapped along the highway. The constant thrum of the waves moving from form to formlessness and back again hypnotized Clifford. December was a dicey month in the UP—one never knew whether the waves would be frozen solid or freely moving as they laced the shore. The winter was a bit warmer in the north country this year, but that could change in an instant.

Clifford was edgy. The specter of Michigamme Prison

loomed larger in his mind as the van headed toward his future. Jail inmates warned him about the cruel treatment there. They'd had a long history of escapes and bloody riots. After he heard the vegetable masher story, he'd been terrified. A simple kitchen utensil killed one and injured three other inmates. Violence scared Clifford. His face yellowed and his guts quivered. He had an urge to run away. If only he could.

Leroy had told Clifford there were two kinds of prisoners, the J-cats and the cell soldiers. J-cats had that name because they were in what the guards called the "J" category—completely insane. They screamed and shouted during the day and screeched and bellowed at night. The fierce loneliness of living in a cell reduced them to animals. They stunk because they stopped grooming and taking showers. They'd lie in their own urine and feces. Their stench was worse than a dead animal carcass. Sometimes they'd grab their shit and throw it at guards or other inmates. He told Clifford not to get too close to them. Clifford recoiled in disgust. *Who'd want to be close?*

Cell soldiers threatened any and everybody in the dorm, but they *never* left their cell. They terrorized with words and hurled threats, promising to bash out brains and stab people to death. They were the bullies; all talk but no action. Clifford would have to learn to tune them out or he'd turn into a J-cat himself.

Clifford's chest quaked. The saddest part was his family was too far away to visit him regularly. Phone calls would have to suffice, and they'd have to agree to pay the charges for collect calls. That was especially frustrating for Clifford because he took pride in being financially independent. He expelled a weary sigh, hoping he would survive the scourge that lay before him.

The trip was not over quite yet. He saw road signs for Rapid River and Gladstone, the last leg of their journey. They turned north onto Highway 41.

"I have to take a leak!" Simon shouted.

"We're about twenty minutes out," the guard said. "Hold it!"

"F**k that. I don't know if I can."

"There're no bathrooms out here," the officer responded. "All I see along the road are bait and tackle shops. You have to wait." The driver sped up, trying to appease Simon. Although Clifford didn't complain, he was ravenously hungry after the long six-hour journey. "We'll be there in less than twenty minutes."

The highway made a wide smooth turn alongside the deep blue of Lake Superior, the northernmost of all the Great Lakes. The deep waters of this inland sea cast an icy cerulean hue. Clifford considered this lake bewitching, mighty, and massive. The next turn was a sharp left bound for something far less inviting—a circular drive into Michigamme State Prison. Clifford's eyes widened at the structure—a medieval castle with its protruding rotunda, elongated windows, and turrets with pointed roofs. His imagination turned to Bram Stoker's horror story, *Dracula*. The castle was just like what he saw before him. Clifford had assumed that prison would look just like Ingham County Jail. But that jail was built in 1958, and Michigamme in 1885. There was no resemblance; they were architectural opposites. He looked at it more closely and a sick feeling hit the pit of his stomach.

6 Michigamme State Prison

The van circled to the back of the building and parked. The guard unlocked Simon from his metal bench and ushered him through the door labeled "Admitting." The driver and Clifford remained in the van waiting for the officer to return. Forty-five minutes later, he unlocked Clifford's chain from the bench and escorted him through the door. The guard handed over his paperwork and unlocked the belly chain, leaving only his wrists handcuffed. Clifford was brought into a small room adjacent to the main office. An armed officer dominated the room. In his right hand, he held a flashlight, which he aimed at Clifford's face.

"I'm Officer Blak," he said gruffly. "You need to respond to each and every command I give you, and do it promptly. Is that clear?"

"Open your mouth … wag your tongue up and down," Officer Blak commanded with rapid-fire speed. "Run your hand through your hair … brush your ears back and forth." Satisfied, he took Clifford's handcuffs off. "Take your clothes off." Clifford begrudgingly complied. "Lift your penis and scrotum … turn around … lift your foot up … lift your foot up! Now, bend over

… spread your butt cheeks … open them up … cough three times," he demanded as he directed the flashlight beam up his crack…. Damn it! Stand still," he barked.

The officer took his time as he inspected each orifice and every article of Clifford's clothing. Standing there buck naked was mortifying. Officer Blak ripped away his dignity. No shred of his humanity was left. *Why are you doing this? I want to scream and claw your eyes out.* He stood stock still. Officer Blak handcuffed him and before he ushered him out of the room, he grabbed and squeezed his buttocks. With a fiendish sneer he said, "Remember, you're fresh meat! This is a little foreplay to get used to the idea."

Clifford gave him a cold stare and remained silent.

Officer Blak yanked him around and escorted him to Dorm O for Level 1 inmates. They passed through a narrow, well-lit hallway to cell 173. The hall guard unlocked it and gave him bed sheets and a paper-thin blanket. Clifford went numb as he walked inside. The bars slammed shut and locked him in. Inside the cell was a toilet without a cover, a sink in the corner, and a second bunk on top of his, empty. *I wonder if I'll have a cellmate. That could be a good thing—or, very bad. Nothing to do but wait and see.* A kitchen worker pushing a meal cart stopped by his cell and handed him a brown bag of food.

"Thank you," Clifford said.

The worker grunted a reply and headed back the way he came.

Home, sweet home—too bad it didn't come with an

instruction manual. I'll have to figure it out the hard way. Maybe there's nothing to understand, I only need endurance.

He looked out his window and saw four feet of snow, a row of bare-naked trees, and a gun tower high above the grounds. Armed guards in the watch tower monitored every movement at the prison. A sudden ruckus of voices exploded as the dormitory door opened. The clanking of doors created a clumsy rhythm of opening and shutting. Inmates, herded by guards, filed past Clifford's cell. Hoping to avoid eye contact, he curled into a fetal position and hid in the shadows of the bottom bunk. He snapped to when he heard the sounds of supper.

"Chow! Chow! Dorm O, line up!" The guard yelled. Cell doors opened and a line formed. They marched en masse to the mess hall. Clifford brought up the rear. The inmates went through the food line, took a plate of food from the servers, found seats, and the mealtime bedlam began.

"Yuck, f**kin' salmon loaf with spuds tonight."

"Who's the new punk?"

"Where's Delores?"

"There she is. Hey, Delores! We've had salmon loaf two weeks in a row. Please, please, cook something different."

"Lay off her, Porky. She's doin' a good job." The clamor of the voices grew louder and louder.

When Delores came into the room, the chaos died down. They seemed to listen to her much of the time.

"Gentlemen, Christmas will be here in a couple of weeks and I need someone to help me in the kitchen. Let me know if you're interested."

Dinner was over in fifteen. The men lined up, headed back to their cells, and were locked in for the night.

Bringing up the rear suited Clifford. He didn't have to watch his back.

I worked in the kitchen at MSU during the first semester in college. It was fun. I wonder if they pay a prisoner for kitchen work. I should stop by and talk to Delores.

He asked the officer in charge if he could talk to her about helping in the kitchen during Christmas. The officer nodded.

"I'll come back to get you in five," he said.

Clifford peeled off the line and headed toward the kitchen. Delores, manhandling a massive stainless-steel industrial dishwashing machine, stood with her back to the door. Pressured steam shot up each time she rinsed a rack of dishes. A hairnet held her bun tight and her apron was tied with a crisp bow in back. Delores reminded him of his grandmother, a strong, no-nonsense woman. Delores had a large frame held up by stocky legs with mammoth shoulders for a woman. *She's built like a linebacker.* Her shoes were misshapen from bulging bunions. *Just like Grandma's.* They were black with standard two-inch heels, fastened with laces. Sensing someone behind her, she limped around on her right foot. Delores's eyes were steady and attentive.

"You need something?"

"I'd like to help over Christmas."

"Put your name, cell number, and when you were admitted on the clipboard over there."

"Do you get paid?"

"Twenty-five dollars a week."

Clifford raised his eyebrows in approval.

"When would you like me to start?"

"I have to check on a few things. I'll get back to you."

"I worked in the Union at Michigan State when I was a student there. I liked the work."

Delores felt familiar somehow, like a member of the family. He wanted to work with her.

As promised, the guard returned to take him back to his cell. Clifford found someone sitting on the top bunk, smiling. His heart sank because he was hoping to have the cell all to himself. He retreated to the lower bunk, but soon an upside-down head dropped into view.

"I'm Pete. Who are you?"

"Clifford."

"What brought you to this godforsaken place?"

"I don't want to talk about it."

"Man, you sure are a tight ass," he chuckled. "My story is a real shit fest," he said. "Want to hear it?"

"Sure."

"My ex is a bitch. She's been keeping the kids away from me. I got pissed off, so I followed her up north when she and her scumbag boyfriend took the kids camping near Sleeping Bear Dunes. I found their campsite, took my binoculars along, and watched them like a hawk."

"Why?" Clifford asked.

Their conversation ended suddenly by an explosion and a flash.

"Fire!" someone yelled. "There's a fire in the first cell by the door."

Waves of smoke tumbled down the narrow hall, setting off the fire alarms. The warning marshaled the fire brigade as all the cell doors in Dormitory O clanked open.

"Line up and march outside," the officer commanded.

The instigator of the fire dashed outside with lightning speed, making a run for the fence. He effortlessly scaled the wall but as he reached the concertina wire, the guard in the watch tower fired, shooting him in the leg. With a bloodcurdling scream, the escapee dropped to the ground, writhing in pain, with blood squirting from his wound. An officer applied a tourniquet, which slowed down the blood flow. They lifted him on a stretcher and took him to the infirmary.

"Let that be a lesson to you boys. Do *not* try to escape," the officer said. "It's *stupid*! We always get you back, and we make your life even more miserable."

The inmates from Dormitory O were silent as they headed back to their cells. The fire was out but the acrid-smelling smoke permeated the hallway, and the air was blue. The inmates coughed and complained, which prompted the guards to set up fans at the end of the hallway to get rid of the fumes. By the time the fracas was over, it was midafternoon. Clifford and Pete flopped on their bunks and took a nap.

The officer's warning about the dangers of escape didn't help Clifford's nerves; it made him more anxious. He wanted to smoke a joint so bad his brain went into overdrive. He curled into a fetal position to self-soothe.

He even thought about sucking his thumb like he did when he was a kid. *What if they found out? They'd have a field day.* Restless, he sat up and put his hands over his face and hyperventilated.

"You okay?" Pete asked.

"Watching that kid trying to escape and the blood streaming from his leg really got to me."

"It got to me too."

"I worry that I'll get dragged into a bad situation in this prison."

"Aw, I wouldn't worry about that. Most of the stuff people worry about ain't never gonna happen anyway."

"That's true," Clifford responded. "But I'm afraid I'll get bullied, blamed, or blackmailed for doing something I didn't do."

"An old farmer once told me your fences need to be horse high, pig tight, and bull strong," Pete said chuckling at his own words. "Put a good fence around you."

"Line up for chow!" the guard commanded.

All the cell doors opened as the inmates lined up for dinner. Clifford brought up the rear. Pete was in front of him, and Clifford realized how huge he was. Close to six feet six inches, he weighed well over two-hundred pounds. He towered over Clifford. Their conversation seemed to make his anxiety go away—at least for a while.

Delores was just inside the door of the mess hall. She whispered something to the officer in charge before she left to go back to the kitchen.

"Hot damn, we got lasagna tonight!"

"Are there breadsticks with it?"

"Hell, I don't care about that. What's for dessert?"

"An apple," he frowned.

"Marquette's my kind of place: three hots and a cot," a new inmate said.

"Home, sweet home."

Prisoners snickered.

The inmates took their plates from a server and found a place to sit. Pete and Clifford sat together. An officer whispered something to Clifford as he walked by. Delores wanted him to stop by after dinner. She'd given him the nod to start work the next day.

CLIFFORD SHOWED UP FOR work in the kitchen at four in the morning, just as Delores said. She pointed to the apron on the hook and the hats on the shelf, and he put them on.

"Now, you look official. Do you know how to scramble eggs?" she asked.

"Yes'm."

She handed him a large wire basket filled with brown eggs. Clifford spotted dung on a few of them—he gave her a questioning look.

"When you wash the eggs with water you destroy the protective coating," she said. "We get them fresh from the farm, where the trustees work."

After rubbing the crap off with a rag, Clifford got busy cracking the eggs in three industrial-sized frying pans. He was making breakfast for over one hundred men. He whipped and stirred the liquid until it firmed. His arms grew tired. When he finished, he ate his own breakfast of eggs, buttered toast, and bacon, sitting at the counter.

"Plan on staying here when the rest go back to their cells," Delores said. "I've got a project for you."

Clifford waited patiently for Delores to take a break and give him work orders. She was a working machine.

"I have white cardboard sheets in the back cupboard," Delores said. "Bring them over here to the table. I'd like you to push out the twenty angels along the dotted lines, sprinkle them with glitter, and hang them from the ceiling. Any questions?"

He shook his head and soon became engrossed in the project. Content to stay busy and away from the other inmates, he eyed them with suspicion. *I don't know where I fit in and who I could trust.* It would take more time to figure that out. Meanwhile, the kitchen felt safe. He finished the angels and hung them from the ceiling. *They make a hell of a difference!* They shimmered in the light and transformed the bleak dining room into a place with some holiday sparkle. He stood back and admired his work. After cleaning up, Clifford looked for the hall guard to take him back to his cell.

The next morning, he headed to the kitchen with a bounce in his step. He smiled at the angels dangling delicately from the ceiling as he walked through the dining room. Delores put him to work making pancakes for breakfast. She also got him going making stuffing for the turkeys, and pies for Christmas dinner.

CHRISTMAS IN PRISON WAS like dreaming about the star of hope without being able to see stars in the sky. The customs inside were different from those on the outside.

Nothing was given for giving's sake—there were *always* strings attached. If a piece of candy was left on the bunk of a newbie, they wanted something in return—perhaps a sexual favor. The prison staff gave the inmates large bags of candy for Christmas. Inside were Reese's Peanut Butter Cups, Hershey candy bars, Honey Buns, and Grandma's Cookies, to name just a few. This candy became currency to exchange for something better like hooch, drugs, or cigarettes. On Christmas Day, the cells would open up with a babble of voices and the dormitory turned into the craziness of the New York Stock Exchange, bustling with trade deals, selling this and buying that.

"You like Honey Buns? You got hooch?"

"Yeah, I've got a pint of real good shit."

"I'll trade a bun for it."

"Two buns and a Hershey for a half a pint!" Silence.

"Take it or take a hike."

"You're a damn crook … but yeah, okay."

One inmate liked Reese's Peanut Butter Cups so much he sold one spliff for two cups. By the time the dealing was done he had a full bag of Reeses. The spliffs had more tobacco than marijuana in them, so the guards didn't pick up the smell. This tempted Clifford, but he resisted, reminding himself to stay clean. His goal was to get out on good behavior as soon as possible, so trading candy for a spliff was too risky.

On Christmas Day, a few of the lucky inmates received visitors. In the visiting room, a.k.a. the dance floor, was a decorated Christmas tree with wrapped presents underneath. One prisoner offered to take pictures of the families with their inmate relatives, which they could keep as a memento. Clifford was not one of the lucky ones. His family did not show up. The trip to Marquette was seven hours of winter driving and the weather was dicey. There was a snowstorm in Gaylord, and the Upper Peninsula was covered with a sheet of ice. A phone call would have to be enough. The wall phone was shuffled around from one inmate to another. Finally, Clifford got his turn.

"Merry Christmas, Mom," Clifford said halfheartedly. "What are you guys up to?"

"Oh dear, it's my sweet boy," Celia exclaimed. "How are you doing, sweetheart? I've been so worried about you. I miss you."

"Mom, calm down! I'm doing okay. I miss you, too."

"Santa came and brought you a couple of gifts. Have they been treating you well?"

"I'm still alive. I've worked in the kitchen all week getting ready for Christmas dinner. I made apple and cherry pies and stuffed the turkeys. I have to go to work in an hour, so I wanted to give you a call first."

"Is the food good there?"

"It's not the greatest. I miss your Christmas treats—the gingersnaps, the pfeffernüsse cookies, and the stollen."

"I'll send some your way, or are packages seized by the officers?"

"Could be—there are some fat-assed guards around here." Clifford chuckled.

"Sharm is here and she's beggin' to talk to you. Son, watch your mouth!"

"Hi, Daddy. Are you okay?"

"I'm alright, but I sure do miss you, my little bee."

"It's not Christmas without you. If the weather wasn't so nasty, I would have convinced Grandpa to take me up there."

"Maybe all of you can come to see me when the weather warms up."

"We will. You can be sure of that. I love you so much."

"Your dad is here," Clifford's mother interjected. "Would you like to talk to him?"

"Sure."

"Merry Christmas, son. Are you okay?"

"So-so. I get three hots and a cot."

"Follow all the rules so you can get out early. We miss you."

"Time's up. Got to go. Goodbye, Dad."

A mechanical click followed by a white noise cut off the conversation. Clifford handed the phone to the next inmate in line.

When Clifford got to the kitchen, he put on his apron and hat. Delores was wrestling the turkeys out of the ovens; heat poured out.

"Here, let me help you," Clifford said, rushing to her aid. He grabbed hot pads and took the heavy pans off the oven racks. They must have weighed thirty pounds each. He lined up all five turkeys on the long metal table, an impressive sight.

"Why didn't you get the precooked slices for dinner and make it easy on yourself?" Clifford asked.

"Don't tell anybody, but I think this is my last Christmas here. I wanted to make this meal real special for the boys."

"Where are you going?"

"I'm retiring before I lose my mind. Shhh! Keep it a secret."

"I'll miss you." Clifford's shoulders slumped.

The rest of the crew bounded into the kitchen, grabbed their aprons, and settled into their workstations.

"Damn, Delores, you made a hell of a spread. The roasted turkeys smell delicious."

"What kind of pies did you make?"

"I made cherry and apple," Clifford said. "Delores made pecan."

"Wow, this looks better than the shit my mama makes," Jerome said.

Delores's face lit up with a pleasant smile. "Gotta make it a Merry Christmas for you guys."

ALL THE CHRISTMAS FESTIVITIES and kitchen duties exacerbated Clifford's usual midwinter cold. He coughed and wheezed so much he decided to go to the infirmary. He hailed a guard to take him to Brooks, the new medical center at the prison. Clifford's watery eyes, red nose, and incessant sniffling were convincing enough.

Brooks Medical Center was the cleanest and brightest place in the prison. Two panels of fluorescent lights ran parallel to each other and were the full length of the waiting room. To his surprise, Simon was sitting on the bench across from him, just like when they rode up together in the van. Simon nodded an acknowledgment. Clifford responded in kind. He waited for Simon to speak first.

"Keepin' your ass out of trouble?" Simon asked.

"So far, I've been working in the kitchen and keeping my head down."

This precipitated an unexplainable silence.

Fearfully, Simon looked directly into Clifford's eyes. "Watch your back in the kitchen."

Simon turned his body to scan which guards were in the room. He waited for one of them to leave before he spoke again. "We can get any drugs we want in Level Five—coke, smack, weed, and a new one called crystal something. The buzz in my block is that the dealers are working through the kitchens, so you—" The guard came back.

"Do you want to meet at church in a couple of weeks?" Clifford asked.

"Sure, why the hell not."

Clifford looked at Simon and nodded, grateful for the information and the possibility of meeting him in the future.

There wasn't much privacy when seeing a doctor; the guards peered through the windows of the treatment rooms at all times. After a doctor examined Clifford, he said, "An antibiotic would help you lick that cold." He gave him a bottle of pills. "Take one a day with food." With that, Clifford was escorted back to his cell.

Simon's comments bothered him. He never saw any drug deals going on in the kitchen, although the corrections officers met in the dining room next door. They came in for coffee at five in the morning before their shifts started at six. Clifford went to work at four in the morning, so he kept his eyes and ears open to find out what the guards were doing.

A group of six uniformed officers met way in the back of the large dining hall. Occasionally, they would tell jokes and laugh, but when the conversations took on a serious tone, they huddled together. There was no way he could hear the conversation. Just before dispersing, Denton, one of the officers, reached into his pocket and handed something to Officer Blak. Clifford craned his neck around the kitchen door to get a better look. Officer Blak gave him an icy stare. Clifford quickly looked away and grabbed a spatula from a nearby table. He certainly didn't want them to accuse him of eavesdropping. *Watch out ... trouble's brewing.*

7 Prison Antics

Pete, Clifford's cellmate, attended a church service every Sunday. He prayed for the well-being of his children and for the comeuppance of his ex-wife. Somehow, he hoped God would even the score. Pete told Clifford the rest of his story about his eventful trip to Sleeping Bear Dunes, which led to his arrest and ultimate conviction of parental kidnapping. Pete had followed his ex and her boyfriend to a camping spot near the dunes. He set up his tent two campsites away, kept a low profile, and waited for the opportunity. The two lovers left the children, ages nine and eleven, sleeping in the tent and went off for a moonlight swim in Lake Michigan. Pete tiptoed into their tent and woke them up.

"Shhh! It's Daddy," he said. "I got a call from Grandpa saying that Grandma is very ill. He's hoping we'd be able to come to Wisconsin to visit her—it might be the last time."

"What's wrong with her?" his son Jeremy asked.

"She had a stroke."

"What's a stroke?"

"We don't have time to talk about it. We have to get on the car ferry to cross Lake Michigan. Put on your shoes and grab your clothes." Hayley, the nine-year-old, started to sob uncontrollably. Pete picked her up, carried her to the car, and they headed off to Ludington to catch the Badger. Feeling comfortable being with their daddy, the children fell asleep in the back seat.

When his ex and her boyfriend returned from the swim, she got hysterical and called the police. She knew it was Pete and promptly gave the police his license plate number and a thorough description of his car. They put out a "be on the lookout" alert, and within three hours they apprehended him, before they could embark on the Badger. The police took the children to the police station in Ludington and returned them to their mother.

Pete sighed and hung his head after telling the story. He wasn't ashamed of what he'd done; he was sorry they caught him.

"My mother used to scold me in her Dutch accent when I lied as a child. She would say, 'Da lies have so short a legs dat truth catches up, and den truth takes dem over.' Mother's words were very wise," Pete said ruefully.

The next Sunday, Pete invited Clifford to the church service after breakfast. A guard escorted them outside the prison walls to the chapel. In contrast to the elaborate architecture of Marquette Prison, the John W. Rice Prison Chapel was a plain building with an unusually steep roof, the best design to prevent the accumulation of snow. Inside the interdenominational chapel were two wooden sculptures, one of the Virgin Mary and the other of Christ on the cross.

"Breathtaking," Clifford said.

"After the service, I'll tell you how those came to be," Pete whispered.

A priest from the city of Marquette led the service. He provided a humble homily of Christ's sacrifice and the need for repentance.

"The story of the statues is pretty cool," Pete said on the walk back to their cell. "Roney, an inmate, was a gifted sculptor who worked mainly in wood. The warden commissioned him to sculpt the two statues you saw. He finished the statue of the Virgin Mary in record time and began sculpting Jesus on the cross. As the face of Jesus emerged out of the wood, he stopped short and went into a period of contemplation. The figure was coming alive for him. Some months later, after the Easter celebration, he was motivated to complete that sculpture in time for the dedication in June of 1964. I think he embraced Jesus Christ and had a true conversion. I find it amazing that in the darkest of places, light breaks through. How cool is that?"

Clifford nodded.

TIME SPENT IN THE kitchen got edgy. The group of six officers, the coffee clubbers at the far end of the dining room, were a rowdy, tacky bunch. Topics ranged from hot women, to wiener dogs, to fishing, to hunting, and shooting at the firing range. Jokes about women brought out a cascade of laughter. Clifford glanced their way as he peeled potatoes, sliced vegetables, and stirred the eggs. He didn't dare make eye contact. Officers Blak and

Denton huddled together after the rest had left. They watched for onlookers as Blak slipped something from his pocket into Denton's. *What are those assholes up to? I wonder if Delores knows about this. It has to be drugs. It's got to be big money for them to take that kind of risk.* On his way back to Cell Block B, Officer Blak strutted past Clifford, glared at him, and hurled a threat.

"Have you heard what we do around here to daddy-haters?" Blak said with a smirk. "In Block B we stuff your head in the john, flush and repeat, and flush and repeat again. Sometimes they drown, sometimes they don't, but they always get a free shit-shampoo. We don't take kindly to daddy-haters."

Clifford remained stone-faced; his eyes fixed on his chores. He looked up only when Blak left for Cellblock B. *That son of a bitch knows about me. He's trouble ...*

PEG-LEG WAS A LIKEABLE old guy with a wooden leg, kind of the mascot of Dormitory O. He'd been the head hallboy for many years. His usual routine was to take two mops, one saturated with soap and water, and the other one dry. He'd mop an area, return the mop to the bucket, then shove the bucket backward as he dried the floor with the other mop. As Clifford watched him from his cell, Peg-leg backed down the corridor drying the floor. The bucket had failed to travel its normal distance. The mop handle was aimed straight at Peg-leg's butt, and it landed right there.

"Get away from me, you degenerate creep," the old man growled. When he turned around to see who goosed him, he discovered the mop handle. Embarrassed, he looked both ways to see if anyone had seen the romp. Clifford muffled a laugh and didn't make eye contact.

"You didn't see nothin'!" Peg-leg said urgently. "And you keep it to yourself!"

"Your secret is safe with me."

THE NEXT MORNING, CLIFFORD woke up later than usual. He rushed to his workstation in the kitchen. Delores stood in the kitchen doorway, apron on, and arms akimbo. "You're late!"

"Sorry," Clifford said as he scampered to get the eggs. He cracked and stirred the eggs, and cracked and stirred some more. "Could I ask you something?"

"Sure."

"Why are you retiring?"

"The politics of this place is getting to me," Delores said. "It has gotten to the point that it's downright corrupt."

"What do you mean?"

"Some of the guards lead a double life." As she spoke those words, a pandemonium of noise exploded in the hallway by the kitchen. A guard came running down the steps from the auditorium upstairs. He stomped past the kitchen doorway.

"Ed's been stabbed—multiple times," he shouted. "Call an ambulance."

Two officers carried him down the stairs, blood

pooled on each step. They placed him on a stretcher at the base of the steps and waited by the front door.

"Ed just had a cup of coffee in the dining room with the other officers," Delores said. "Dear Lord, something bad's coming, and I don't mean just poor Ed. I feel it in my bones."

Other officers followed the blood trail to the auditorium, checking for anyone lurking there. Finding none, they locked it up tight to make certain no one disturbed the crime scene. An ambulance screamed up the circular driveway with flashers on. They raced Ed to St. Luke's Hospital in Marquette.

Meanwhile, Captain Brewster and his crew upended every trash can in the yard, assuming that was the most logical place to discard a knife. Officer Blak located the bloody coveralls with a single bloodstained glove in the pocket in the yard shack. They didn't find the knife, so they felt certain it was somewhere in the auditorium. The crew tore the auditorium apart. It was a desperate search since they didn't want another inmate finding it. They searched every nook and cranny. They finally found it, along with the mate to the bloodstained glove, deep inside the piano. With the knife safely in hand, they sounded the alarm for lockdown. Everyone, including Clifford, returned to their cells.

A tower guard saw an inmate enter the yard in coveralls and go into the shack. They detained the inmate when he came outside.

"Where are your coveralls?" an officer asked.

"I wasn't wearing any," the inmate said. The officer

had conflicting information, so he strip-searched him and put him in quarantine.

When a murder was committed in the prison, it was rare that someone snitched. Inmates got even with the snitches. But when they pronounced Ed Debouch dead, one witness came forward and was willing to make a report, providing he was protected.

Burly said, "Harvey and I were standing on the back-kitchen dock when Officer Debouch walked by. That's when Harvey said, 'How would you like to get one of them pigs?' I said, 'Hell no, I ain't doing no such thing,' and I went back to my cell. Harvey is sick! I want him to stay the f**k away from me."

The murder investigator discovered another assailant in the auditorium, but at the last minute, Frank changed his mind and ran. Willard and Burly became the main witnesses at the trial. For safekeeping, they were transferred out of Marquette Prison until the trial date. Harvey was found guilty and given another life sentence and sent to a different prison.

Clifford returned to his workstation when the lockdown was over.

"Senseless murder," Delores said, "What a shame."

CLIFFORD RECEIVED SEVERAL CARDS around the Christmas holidays, but Sharm waited to send him a card until Valentine's Day. It was a couple of pages long, and luckily passed the scrutiny of the guards.

Dear Daddy,

I think about you every day. I'm super busy, and some things have happened in my life that I want to share with you. I turned sixteen in January.

Thank you for the Twix candy bar—you know it's my favorite.

I'm dating David, a senior at Mason High. He's cool, but he's sick and tired of school, although he's determined to finish his senior year. I respect him for that. But me—I'm not so sure I want to stick it out. David and I have talked about running away together. I told him that if we do, you would be the first stop before we take off for places unknown. I miss you so much.

I met a friend of yours yesterday at the park. It was just after school let out. She was waiting for a friend. Her name is Lorca Lemham. She's a sweet lady, but all crippled up from arthritis. She looks like an old grandma. I like her very much. She asked about you. When I told her where you were, she was sad. She asked for your address, so I gave it to her. You'll probably hear from her soon.

I'll write you again in a few weeks. In the meantime, take care of yourself and stay out of trouble. I'll call you Sunday afternoon.

I love you very much.

Sharm

Clifford couldn't remember anybody by the name of Lorca Lemham. Was it someone from his childhood? He considered Lorca to be a weird name for a woman, and even for a man. The person looked like an old grandma—so he decided it must be a woman. A flash of insight came to him. He and Sharm had played word puzzles when she was younger. They developed their own code by scrambling letters into different patterns. They used this method to keep messages a secret from Wanda, because she was always reading Sharm's diary to find a way to control her. He scratched his head and tried to recall the pattern, and what he figured was putting the last three letters starting from the back to front at the beginning. He tried that and discovered the name really was: C-a-r-o-l for the first name, and H-a-m-m-e-l for the last name. *I know her—she bought pot from me. Now I know why she used a code! Sharm's a smart cookie. But, why did she give Carol my address? That's stupid. The guards will screen it, and she might be arrested. I need to tell Sharm to let Carol know I don't want to get letters from her. She might get into trouble. I'll say it would make me upset to hear from Lorca.*

Early in the evening, the phones got the most use. Clifford had to wait in line.

"Sharm?" The collect call message interrupted. "Sharm? Thanks for accepting charges. I'll pay you back," Clifford said. "I got your letter and wanted you to tell Lorca right away that I don't want any letters from her. It would upset me too much to hear from her."

"Okay, Daddy. I'll let her know. Is everything okay?"

"Yes, sugar. I was disappointed that you might quit school, but I'll write a letter to you very soon." Clifford exhaled his tension; the bases were covered.

CLIFFORD SHIVERED IN HIS cell. It was the month of February in the arctic north, and minus twenty-five below zero. He wore every stitch of clothing he had in prison, plus the thin blanket he received the first day. He wrapped himself up like a burrito to conserve his body heat and waited for the sun to shine through his window.

In spite of the cold temperature outside, Johnny from Dormitory O tried to escape. His cell was just two down from Clifford's. According to the buzz, Johnny buried his white bed sheets in the snowdrifts along the wall of the outdoor bullpen, which was the outdoor exercise yard. The yard was surrounded by a twenty-foot-high concrete wall. He found a small gap in the wall by post five. When he walked outside to exercise, he tied the sheets together with a knot at the throwing end. The knot caught in the post five gap, and Johnny pulled himself up and over the wall. There was a security fence on the other side, which he had to get over. Wiry and strong, he found a way, but his jacket snagged on the concertina wire. He left it behind and escaped into the woods. The alarm sounded a lockdown and a strip search was ordered for each member in Dormitory O. Inmates groaned. They were disgusted by the lockdown and strip searches.

Three days later, Johnny returned to his cell—frostbitten, with his head wrapped in bandages—to recuperate. "What in the hell happened to you?" his cellmate asked.

"Jim Johnson, the son of a bitch, nailed me," he said. "I was walking by a lumber camp when a guy with a shovel over his shoulder came toward me. He nodded and said, 'Howdy,' and walked right past me, but then he blasted the back of my head with the shovel and took me into custody. Come to find out, he was the f**king sheriff of Marquette County and boss of the lumber camp. That asshole was on the lookout for me."

Clifford had an eerie feeling that Officer Blak was on the lookout for him. His menacing presence seemed to be everywhere, lurking around in the dark hallways.

8 Outliers

Clifford sat in the fourth row, gazing at the Virgin Mary, waiting for Simon. Running late, Simon galumphed through the chapel door and scanned the cluster of ten inmates scattered around the room, looking for Clifford. He turned his head and locked eyes with Simon. Muscular and surly, and yet self-conscious, Simon was uncomfortable, like a fish out of water. He sat on a chair next to Clifford. Each nodded.

"What happened to your face?" Clifford asked, noticing a scabbed-over scratch from his left eyeball to his chin.

"Belcher raked me in the yard," he said. "The bastard never cuts his nails. That pussy uses them as weapons."

"Did you go to a doctor?"

"Hell, no."

"What's happening in Cellblock B these days?" Clifford asked, talking low.

"Nothing good. There's a lot of jerks and weirdos in there now," Simon whispered. "You know that guy Ed who got murdered?" Simon looked around to see if anyone was watching. "The scuttlebutt was he was about to snitch on some guards selling drugs. Harvey was just the patsy. He didn't have nothin' to lose—in for life anyway." Clifford just nodded his head and remained silent. "Have you ever thought about escaping?" Simon asked. "This would be a good place to do it. There are only two guards and twelve inmates in here. I might give it some thought. Meet you here next Sunday?" Clifford nodded. Simon stood and left.

Clifford sat there, sorting out what Simon said. *I don't want to try to run—if I follow the rules and keep my nose clean, I should be out in maybe two years. I'm not surprised about Ed—it explains why it happened. Delores was right when she said it was a senseless murder.*

The priest never did show. The snowplows were still clearing the roads.

The guards ushered the inmates back to their cells. While sitting on his bunk, Clifford felt the warm sun coming through his tiny window and his mind drifted to some unfinished business with Sharm. *I wonder if she contacted Carol.* Most of all, he was concerned about her running away and becoming a school dropout. Other thoughts drifted through his mind. He remembered Sunday afternoons when he was growing up.

As long as he could remember, Sunday afternoons were boring times as a child. He grew up in a conservative home—his parents followed the fourth commandment, which says Sunday is a holy day of rest. They didn't allow entertainment like going to see a movie, or even swimming with friends. His family belonged to a United Brethren Church and they took their religion and rules of the sabbath seriously.

Clifford rebelled. The code was constricting—like a prison. During his teenage years, he chose a different path and became part of the local drug culture. This was his religion of choice. The high from smoking pot settled nicely in his bones, helped him chill, and smooth out his anxieties. Not only did he learn how to relax, he also found a way to relate to others. His pot-smoking friends became a brotherhood of like-mindedness. They traveled through the world of trips—good and bad ones—and helped each other. Once he settled into that path, the next step was figuring out how to keep getting the good stuff. When he got his driver's license, he found dealers in the university town of East Lansing. He listened carefully to others to determine the reliable dealers. Soon, Clifford became known as the go-to person for the best pot in the city of Mason.

When he reflected on his life in high school, he considered it a laughable double-life. He was smart and diligent, and the teachers loved him. He obeyed the rules, understood the value of fair play, and didn't need to grandstand during class. He was confident in his abilities and helped others. His achievement of class salutatorian was no surprise. He was a model student who turned out As with ease, but if the teachers had known his dark side, they would have been flabbergasted and in disbelief. Clifford spent much of his energy hiding his secret life by compartmentalizing his conflicting values and crafting a persona of pleasing others.

Sharm, now a sophomore at the same high school, chose not to have Clifford's double life. She was enticed by the hippie life. The freedom from hypocrisy felt right and her desire for sexual experimentation intrigued her. Clifford understood her nonconformist streak because he was driven by the same desires. However, he would always be the dutiful parent and encourage her to finish high school.

Dear Sharm,

I hope this letter finds you well. Each day I spend in this miserable prison, I am comforted knowing that I am one day closer to coming home. I miss you. Please think carefully before dropping out of school. The trajectory of your life will change forever and not in a good way. It will be harder to find decent employment without a diploma and you won't be able to go to college without finishing high school first. You are a bright young lady and dropping out would be a missed opportunity. High school can help you discover your strengths. Sharm, at least promise me one thing ... that you'll talk to a counselor before you make the final decision. Mason High has good counselors on staff who will give you wise advice.

I love you,

Daddy

SIMON AND CLIFFORD MET in the chapel the next Sunday. This was not the time or place to consider escaping. It was the first week of March and a ferocious snowstorm with gale-force winds rolled off Lake Superior. The prisoners shivered as they felt the full force of the wind coming from the lake a block away. The snow fell in torrents so thick only a dim light from the sun penetrated the wall of white. It was like an icy fog. The chapel provided only temporary relief from the cold concrete prison walls. To ensure the local priests would bestow their weekly blessing, the officials had to turn up the heat in the chapel. This morning the priest from St. Albans, made it through the snowstorm. He never looked at his audience. Instead, his eyes cast to the heavens as if begging for inspiration from on high. He shared a homily from Isaiah 5:16: "I have put my words in your mouth and covered you with the shadow of my hand." He talked about two kinds of shadows. One shadow was sinister—it came from dark places. The other was a protective shadow that came from the light—one being ominous and harmful while the other was nurturing. Simon was spellbound.

"My dad was a black shadow, a dark one from hell," Simon said. Clifford looked at him wide-eyed, listening.

"When you were a boy?" Clifford asked.

"Yes, when I was a small boy. The asshole would come home from the night shift at the factory—drunker than a skunk," Simon whispered. "The f**ker would open my bedroom door after I went to bed and his dark shadow would cover me. It scared the shit out of me. I couldn't move a muscle."

"Did he beat you?" Simon was silent, shifting his eyes to the floor.

"Yeah, but only if the bitch said something to him about what I had done or not done that day. I never knew if I was goin' to get the shit beat out of me, or if he'd just walk away. I was so f**king scared."

"Was the bitch your mom?"

"Yeah, the she-bitch. If I had a seizure, my old lady would get so pissed off because she said I had an evil spirit hanging out inside of me making me go crazy. I knew I'd get beat. She'd have Dad beat the devil out of me."

"That really sucks! I'm sorry, friend."

"You saw one of my seizures. Do you think I've got evil spirits inside of me?"

"Absolutely not!" Clifford said in a loud whisper. One of the guards walked toward them. "Lots of people have seizures," Clifford said softly. "Your brain is short-circuiting—you have *no* control over that! It's a medical problem. That's what the medication is for…. Has it been helping?"

"I think so. I haven't had another one since I've been in here. I used to have them once a month."

"Good! Keep taking the medicine!"

"HAVE I TOLD YOU about Simon?" Clifford asked Pete.

"No."

"He's unforgettable!" Clifford said. "I met him in the Ingham County Jail. He's a murderer from Detroit. I almost shit my pants, I was so scared of him. He'd walk around with a dark cloud swirling above his head, ready to snap and twist into a violent tornado. My first brush with death was with him. I found him sitting on my bed just to taunt me, but I didn't want to confront him, so I called a guard and ratted on him. Man, was he pissed off!"

"What'd he do?"

"He slammed me up against the concrete wall and tried to choke me." Clifford stood up, pacing back and forth. "If it hadn't been for the other cellmates, I wouldn't be here today. He's Goliath-strong!"

"This time around you got a better cellmate," Pete said smiling. "Probably, you'll never see him again."

"Not so. He's here in Cellblock B. We rode up to Marquette together chained to opposite sides of the prison van. Halfway through our trip, he started to drool, his eyes rolled back in his head, and he had a full-blown seizure. Yesterday in the chapel, he told me about his childhood. His mother said he was demon-possessed and thought a good thrashing was the only way to get rid of the seizures. His dad beat the crap out of him after every seizure. Of course, that just made him meaner." Clifford paused, hung his head. "I feel sorry for the guy."

"His parents were simpletons. Even I know it's a medical condition … not caused by demons!" Pete said.

"I can't stop thinking about him."

The alarm sounded for lockdown, and both Pete and Clifford rolled their eyes and wondered what was coming down. The bedlam was coming from outside the prison by the admitting station. They heard chains rattling as they slammed against metal surfaces. Horns were blaring and the tower guards fired shots. Clifford jumped up and peered out his window. It was midafternoon and typically the calmer part of the day. Escapes were more likely at twilight or in the early morning.

"There are two vans out there and a ruckus like I've never seen before," Clifford said. "That's all I can see."

Pete joined him at the window and scratched his head.

"Sometimes the safest place to be is locked in a prison cell," Pete said. "Probably, Simon feels safer; at least his dad can't get to him."

"Those kinds of demons follow you wherever you go," Clifford said.

Outside of his window and across the bullpen, Clifford could see the final phase of the construction of a new building. The buzz was that MIPC (Michigan Intensive Program Center) also known as MIPSY, had offices for counselors, classrooms, a visiting area, and an exercise facility. Behavior modification programming was all the rage in the prison reform community, but the inmates launched rumors of being subjected to brain control, lobotomies, and electroshock therapy. Paranoia set in, spreading from ripples radiating through the water like a skipping stone. There was no stopping them. The prisoners panicked. One particularly pernicious rumor was that the central core of the star-shaped building moved in a clockwise direction while the four outward wings moved in a counterclockwise direction. The prisoners were convinced that the opposing directions would keep them so dizzy they would lose control and eventually, lose their minds.

The alarm blared across the prison grounds. Level One inmates were allowed to have dinner in the dining hall, but all the rest had to go into shakedown. This meant they had to stay in their cell while each prisoner and his cell would be searched. The dining hall was abuzz with rumors of a prison transport that went awry.

The prisoners went berserk, tearing up seat covers, setting fires, and breaking windows. They totally destroyed the interior of the van, and brutally assaulted one of their own. Even though the prisoners were chained together, the despised member of the group was thrown out the window, left to dangle in the wind. They did not want to go to MIPSY. Because the thirty-six prisoners were left out of the communication loop, they had no way of sorting truth from fiction, and their paranoia festered.

Two weeks after the van incident, a guard was escorting an inmate to MIPSY and without forewarning, the inmate shoved the officer down and escaped into a wing of the building. Fourteen angry prisoners seized control of two wings of the center, destroying furniture and making weapons from shards of glass and broken wood. Using a bullhorn, Captain Brewster sounded a warning and gave an ultimatum.

"Give it up or be gassed."

His order was met with a barrage of bottles, sticks, and eating utensils. He responded by pitching tear gas canisters into the section seized by the prisoners. They gave up, and the behavior modification program was suspended for further review.

Even though MIPSY was a separate building on the prison grounds, Level Five inmates had to succumb to a shakedown. Simon did not fare well. His Tegretol was seized. The officer searching his cell wasn't smart enough to know the difference between a contraband substance and prescribed medication. Later that night, he had a violent seizure. He slammed his head against the cement, causing it to swell into a welt the size of an egg. He blacked out, and woke up choking on his own vomit and shivering from the cold.

DELORES HAD A LOT to say the morning after the riots in MIPSY. "What happened in that building was wrong, but mostly stupid," she opined. "How do you expect prisoners to stay calm and rational when they don't understand what's happening to them? Most of them are in prison because they don't trust anyone. Behavior modification has to be clearly explained. The inmates in Level Five are on the verge of rioting too. During the shakedown they found all kinds of weapons … meat hooks, baseball bats, boning knives, clubs, lengths of metal pipe, shivs, screwdrivers, a sledgehammer, and all kinds of drugs. Doesn't make me feel safe."

"Me either," Clifford said stirring the scrambled eggs.

THE SHAKEDOWN WAS OVER, and Clifford hoped he would see his friend Simon in the chapel. It was a bright, cloudless Sunday morning in the Upper Peninsula. Early May was a teaser—one never knew if it would be warm or cold. That day it was warm, and Clifford enjoyed his walk to the chapel. As usual, he sat in the fourth row and directly in front of the Virgin Mary. The priest from St. Albans was presiding over the service again. Clifford recalled the last time he heard his talk and marveled at his choice of scripture. It spoke to Simon's heart and was an epiphany for Clifford. Since then, their relationship had taken on a new dimension. Clifford glanced back over his shoulder after hearing a sound. He gasped when he saw him. Simon, nearly lifeless, shuffled toward him, so different from their last meeting.

"Sit," Clifford said motioning to a chair. Simon plopped down next to him, exhausted.

"They took the medicine away from me." Simon's eyes deadened.

"When?"

"During shakedown … they thought it was illegal drugs," Simon shuddered. "I had a seizure last night, hit my head hard, and I don't remember much else other than waking up choking on my own vomit."

Clifford stood and signaled to the guard by the door to escort them to Brooks. The chapel service was no longer important. "I'm tired of this crap. Get up, we're going to the damn clinic."

9 Sharmbee

Clifford was elated when a thick letter arrived. He opened the torn flap, which meant an officer had read it and tossed it into the "Passed Inspection" tray. Prison officials made no attempt to hide their tampering with the mail. He was sure it was a birthday greeting, but the rounded bulge of the envelope indicated there was more.

Dear Daddy,

Happy birthday! This birthday makes you thirty-six, I believe. I miss you so much.

I am planning a trip to Marquette at the end of this month. If my boyfriend won't take me, I will hitchhike. I'll do whatever it takes to see you.

Clifford laid the letter on the bed and reminisced. *Little Sharm. She buzzed around like a little bumblebee. Her bounce filled the room with life. She had boundless energy. All the while she sported an impish smile.* His eyes shifted out of reverie and he continued reading.

David and I want to go to prom, but Mom is being mean. She won't buy me a prom dress. She keeps saying, "Your ne'er-do-well father is in prison, so he's not sending me any money. Take it up with your worthless dad. See if he can afford a prom dress."

"What a bitch!" Clifford snapped.

How does she expect me to send money to her from f**king prison? She just keeps the money for herself and that asshole Kevin anyway. Sharm never gets any of it. Kevin's a mama's boy. What about the two-hundred dollars I sent her from my job in the kitchen? I worked hard for that. Wanda the bitch-witch will never be happy. She's never satisfied. Sharm is just a little girl. Why can't Wanda at least pretend she cares for her daughter? He punched his pillow and resumed reading.

I thought I could ask Grandpa if he had some money, but that didn't turn out very well.

He said, "Buying a prom dress is a waste of money. I put money into a fund for your college education every month. That's what I think is important."

But, Daddy, don't you think I should have a little fun once in a while? Other girls buy dresses, and their boyfriends sometimes get a shirt to match. Their pictures are so cool.

Clifford's anger escalated to rage. "Wanda and my dad put me in no-win situations. Those assholes are treating my daughter like she's a piece of shit," he said.

"What's up with you?" Pete asked, roused from his afternoon nap.

"My ex and my dad frustrate the hell out of me," Clifford grumbled, throwing the letter on the floor. "They're so much alike I can never win with them. They only care about themselves and their stupid ideas." Grimacing, he added, "I'd choke the shit out of my ex if I could. That bitch won't buy Sharm a prom dress and let her feel pretty for her special night."

"You're getting upset about a *prom dress?*" Pete questioned. "That's ridiculous."

"You don't understand," Clifford bristled. "This is just the tip of the f**king iceberg."

"Do you have any money saved from working in the kitchen?" Pete asked.

"I was saving money for some land or a house when I get out," Clifford said, still smoldering.

"Maybe you could give her some of the money and she could find a way to get the rest," Pete said.

Clifford looked at Pete, scratched his head, and pulled the mini-safe out from under his bunk. He fumbled with the lock, his hands shaking with utter exasperation. He grabbed a tattered envelope, opened it, and took out a roll of five ten-dollar bills. It was only fifty dollars. He didn't know how much prom dresses would cost, so he wasn't sure it would be enough. He didn't have a checking account, so he'd have to send the money in the mail. Sending money to Wanda's address would *not* be the best idea. *She'd steal it, spend it, and keep it away from Sharm. I'll send it to Mom with a note. She'll help Sharm get a prom dress. For once, my pretty little Sharmbee will get one over on her mother. I love it. It's well worth the money.* After making the decision, he retrieved the letter and continued reading.

I saw Lorca. Three more friends came along: Yliem, Norsha, and Nortame. They have become my friends, and I want to help them. Life is hard for them. Daddy, I want you to know that when I read your last letter about finishing school, I talked to a counselor at Mason High. You're right—they know what they're doing. I decided to finish school and David is doing the same. I hope this news pleases you, Daddy.

I'm hoping you can talk some sense into Mom. It's hard living with her.

I love you always,

Sharm

Clifford could feel his blood boiling. It was no use talking sense into Wanda. She was like a concrete wall with no way to break through. The only way he could manage his anger was to outsmart her.

The last part of the letter surprised him. How did she ever meet so many women he'd sold pot to? Carol, Sharon, Emily, and Tameron were flower children from the sixties. They were aging poorly. They smoked pot daily just to cope. Three of the four friends were on disability and not able to work. Carol was a parapro, a paraprofessional. She helped certified teachers with their students. When Carol was done working at school, the four of them got high together, and sometimes their group expanded into a larger circle of friends. They wanted the good stuff, the expensive stuff, guaranteed to get the job done. A little went a long way and was cheaper in the long run.

Sharm had a cute way about her—she was approachable. With her bright pixie face, coquettish blue eyes, and engaging smile, she pulled people to her like a magnet. She was petite, just under five feet, and one would think she was easily intimidated, but she wasn't. Her voice was loud and brusque, the voice of authority. Her courageous self-confidence made her listeners think she knew what was best for them. She had an uncanny intuition like a soothsayer, or maybe even a prophet. People gravitated toward her like a moth to fire.

Clifford hoped that at least one of her schoolteachers would help his little bee discover her gifts instead of saying, "Are you really Kevin's sister?"

"Yes," she would say, bowing her head in shame. She knew they were mocking her flighty ways and wondering why she couldn't be a stellar student like her brother Kevin.

Clifford knew Sharmbee had a load of crap to overcome. Her mother favored her brother. Now, her daddy was in prison for selling pot, and she had a personality that did not take kindly to the expectations of school. She was told to shut up, sit down, and stop talking.

Clifford hoped some good luck would come her way. *I wonder if she will ever find her place?*

CLIFFORD WAITED FOREVER FOR Sharm to get back to him. Time moved slowly. Clifford waffled about whether his actions were the right ones. Should he have involved his mother, Sharm's grandmother? *Was going to prom really that important? Maybe Pete was right—getting irate about a prom dress was stupid.* Clifford had been wrong so often in the past. In the future, he wanted to do things right.

His wait was eased when Peg-leg, the old man with the wooden leg, cruised by his cell with his mop bucket. He sang a catchy tune sounding like an old sea shanty with a driving rhythm. It reminded Clifford of Gordon Lightfoot's song about the Edmund Fitzgerald.

Pray tell who knows the love of dear God
if the waves swallow us whole.
The hear sayers looked at rough Whitefish Bay,
but nary a word did they say.

"Hey, Peg-leg," Clifford asked. "Is that song about the Edmund Fitzgerald?"

"You got it," Peg-leg grinned. "It's Lightfoot's tune, but I made up my own lyrics. I was sitting here in prison when it happened."

"That was in the 1970s, wasn't it?"

"Yup, November 10, 1975, to be exact. It sank in Lake Superior about two-and-a-half hours east of here, and northwest of Sault Saint Marie."

"Was the weather bad here, too?" Clifford asked.

"For sure. Hurricane-force winds with waves up to thirty-five feet—a killer storm."

"Was it an old ship?"

"Sorta. I think they built it in 1958, but it was a beauty!" Peg-leg exclaimed. "I saw it coming through the Soo Locks when I was a kid. At that time, it was the largest ship on the Great Lakes. For seventeen years it shipped iron ore from Duluth, Minnesota, to the steel mills in Detroit, Michigan."

"That must have been a sight to behold."

"If I remember the numbers right, it was about 730 feet long and weighed almost fourteen thousand tons."

"It must have been a nasty storm to sink a ship that size."

"Wicked nasty. I feel bad for the families," Peg-leg said. "But Gordon Lightfoot made the Edmund Fitzgerald a legend." He pushed the handle of his mop forward down the hallway and kept singing.

Inside, the doomed men hollered their end
as the massive waves made them shudder.
The brave, kind men with their tears full spent
said goodbye to the fathers and mothers.
Superior rolls and swirls to make their graves
down under …

When Peg-leg made another pass with his mop on the way to a different cellblock, Clifford struck up another conversation.

"Hey, Peg-leg. What you in for?"

"Murder."

"Who'd ya kill?"

"My Aunt Jean."

"Why'd you do it?"

"She was a rich old biddy," Peg-leg said matter-of-factly. "A car accident left me with miserable pain. I asked her for more money to buy drugs to ease my pain—my nerves were shot. She helped me before, but that time she said no."

"Do you feel bad about it?"

"Nope." He continued on his way, singing.

So twenty-nine men in heaven chant a dirge of a ship lost down under.
Superior's beauty is never lost despite dreams rent asunder.
A legend lives on for daughters and sons in the winds of a dark November.

A LETTER CAME FROM Sharm. Clifford was thrilled.

Dear Daddy,

I am so excited. Grandma and I went shopping for a prom dress yesterday.

It is a beautiful dress—or, maybe I should say it's cute. When I think about a dress being beautiful, I think about something long and elegant. This dress is short, knee-length, and it flares out. It is yellow with white polka dots. It has a halter top with a princess-cut bodice. I think it's adorable and one of a kind. I'm sure I'll be the only one wearing this dress at the prom. And, by the way, I found some black patent-leather shoes, too. They have a black-and-white polka dot bow on top. I hope David likes my dress.

Clifford flipped to the second page of the letter and something fell on his lap—a picture of Sharm wearing her new dress. Adorable! *My little Sharmbee! With her black short-cropped hair, I swear she looks like a cute little bumblebee.*

> Prom is this coming Saturday. It will be fun. I'll give you a call after the prom to let you know how it went.
>
> I love you, Daddy.
>
> Sharm

Clifford took her picture to work to show Delores.

"You sure have a cute daughter," she said with a smile.

"You haven't heard her voice. She's got a husky voice like Tallulah Bankhead," Clifford laughed. "But for me, she's a keeper."

Clifford waited for her phone call, or maybe a letter. Two Saturdays came and went, then, three and four, but he heard nothing. *I hope she's okay. Her mother might have grounded her from using the phone. Wanda is probably retaliating because I maneuvered around her to get a prom dress for Sharm. She's like that; she always gets even.*

Finally, after a long four weeks, a letter came. He was hopeful she had a fun prom night and that her mother was fair to her.

> Dear Daddy,
>
> I have horrible news. I have never felt so sad in my whole life. I am not sure I should share it with you. It's something I would never tell Mom. I have to tell someone, so I will tell you, but you must never, never tell anyone else.
>
> Please promise me. I trust you, Daddy, and I know you

won't hurt me, but I am so ashamed. I'd just die if my friends find out, and I don't want Lorca and her friends to know. Make sure you never tell Grandma. It would hurt her too much.

Clifford read on as he braced himself for some horrific news. *Maybe she and David had a brush with the law. Did she get caught smoking pot? Is she pregnant? Was she kicked out of school?* Clifford continued reading the letter.

Mom would never help me out. I know you would, but you can't. David and I had a big decision to make.

Clifford knew it was something major. Sharm was usually transparent about her life, especially with him. The letters and spaces were black and white on the pages, but Clifford knew she was sobbing, and her eyes were filled with tears. Little water spots were scattered on the pages of the letter, probably tears.

Daddy, it was the hardest thing I've ever done. My period was late, and I had more than the usual cramping. I got so sleepy and nauseated. I just wasn't myself. I didn't know who to talk to, so I turned to David. He's only seventeen and I'm sixteen—we're too young to be parents. We didn't know what to do.

David's friend Riff had this happen to him, and he shared information about an abortion clinic in East Lansing that helps minors. So, David called them up and made an appointment for the next day.

What a sad turn of events. One minute, I thought she

had the world by the tail, and the next moment she's in the depths of despair. Clifford was not one to sanction abortions. He had thought about the possibility with Wanda, but they were fleeting thoughts. At this stage in life, it was a relief not to have that on his conscience. He had high school friends that did the "trip," as they called it, to an abortion clinic. Deep in his heart, he knew this action didn't mean she would become unpregnant; it was more grievous than that. The truth was they were parents of a dead child. He was pretty sure thoughts about the abortion would bedevil them in their adult years. This gave him chills. For Clifford, taking a life was one of the worst things a person could do.

It was so scary, Daddy. David dropped me off, so I was all alone. The first thing I had to do was watch a movie about choices. But, do you understand? I was caught in a trap—I was trying to claw my way out of it. I knew I wasn't old enough to be a parent—how could I support a baby? I didn't want to tell Mom. She wouldn't help me anyway. I didn't want her to see me pregnant. They gave me a test called an ultra-something. I saw something moving inside my belly. I started to cry, and I couldn't stop. I covered my eyes until I got through it. They asked me what I wanted to do, and I told them I didn't want to be pregnant anymore. They brought me into another room, gave me something for pain, and took a long instrument and just sucked it out of me. I feel much better now. I don't cry as much. David tells me I did the right thing. He paid for it. They scheduled him for an STD test. What is that, Daddy? David was pretty angry about that. I still plan on visiting you before the end of the month. It will have to be on a weekend because I still have high school classes. I wish I had happier news, but now, I have fewer worries and life will just go on.

I love you, Daddy.

Sharm

He laid back on his bunk and let the letter drop on his chest. He fell into an anguished sleep. There was nothing he could do—it was a done deal. Upon waking, the deep shadows of night charged through his tiny window. He felt the coldness of the cement walls, and was overcome by a strong, driving urge to smoke a joint. He didn't want to wake Pete, so he stuck his arm through the bars and quietly gestured to the guard at the end of the hall. The guard approached.

"Hey, man, do you know how I could get some pot?" Clifford whispered. "I just got some bad news and pot would sure calm my nerves."

"I know a guard in Cellblock B that sells the stuff," he said. "I'll see what I can do."

Just the possibility of getting some stuff eased his mind. Clifford slept through supper, and woke up famished. Thankfully, he remembered the peanut butter crackers and two cans of pop he purchased from the canteen. He scrambled to find the stash under the bed and scarfed down the snacks. He lay back down on his bunk, wishing himself to sleep, but a good night's sleep eluded him. He woke up every hour on the hour, between two and four in the morning. He washed up and put on clean clothes. He signaled to the guard to open the cell, and the officer escorted him to work.

When the shift changed, the night guard whispered to Clifford. "I called my friend, and he said he could get the stuff, but it's going to cost you," the guard said. "You got money?"

"Some," Clifford responded. "How much?"

"Sixty dollars an ounce."

"What!? That's double the amount I used to pay."

"It's illegal and risky to sell in prison."

"I have twenty-five dollars," Clifford said. "I'll have to wait until I save more. Does he sell pretty good stuff?"

"It's the best there is."

"What's his name?"

"You don't need to know."

"Do you get a cut?" Clifford asked.

"Why do you want to know? I could lose my job if I'm not careful," the guard said. "It's dangerous business."

"I'll keep that in mind." Clifford said as he headed to the kitchen, where he stirred eggs for breakfast and chopped the ingredients for lunch salads. *Sixty dollars is a lot of money. It will take me two more weeks of work to be able to afford it. Before, I could always get the money I needed. I'm sick of being in this place.*

Delores was in rare form that morning. She chatted on and on about a new boat she bought to go fishing in after she retired. "I can't believe that I'll be free of this place in two weeks," Delores exclaimed. "I've got so many things planned for when I retire."

"I'm sure going to miss you," Clifford lamented. "Have they named your replacement?"

"There are two in the running. Shirley will be here next week, and then, Travis is coming the following week. I'm doing an on-the-job interview for each of them. I'm sure one of them will work out."

"When are you going to make the announcement?"

"The beginning of next week."

"Before you leave, give me your address and I'll write you once in a while."

"I don't want anyone to know where I live, so I'll give you the number of my post office box. Make sure you don't tell anyone about my retirement. Okay?"

"Your secret is safe with me."

After breakfast was served, Clifford went back to his cell. He passed Pete heading out to the exercise yard.

"You sure were noisy last night. Trouble sleeping?" Pete asked.

"Yeah, I did. I got an awful letter from my daughter. I'll tell you about it sometime."

A couple of days later, Clifford sat on the edge of his bunk, grabbed his writing tablet and pen, and began writing a letter to Sharm. He had given it enough thinking time and had to get it off his chest. He was certain Wanda would read her mail, so he would have to be guarded about what he wrote.

Dear Sharm,

I am so sorry you are feeling sad and that you feel so alone. David is not a good boyfriend. He's not treating you with the respect you deserve. He took the easy way out. Promise me if you feel sick, you'll see a doctor. Being sixteen in this world is tough. I wish I could have helped you. I am pleased that you felt safe enough with me to share your inner thoughts. You are a wonderful daughter. Don't ever forget that! Keep working on your studies because education will give you a better future. You make me proud!

Love always,

Daddy

THE NEXT DAY, A guard summoned Clifford to the visitors' center. "Ratz, a young lady is here to see you."

He tucked the letter in his chest pocket and walked to the visitors' center. He sat on a cold chair, placed his elbows on the metal counter, and waited. He knew his visitor was being thoroughly searched for contraband and weapons. The administration had just hired a female corrections officer to search female visitors. Clifford was not looking forward to the routine strip search given to prisoners after the visit.

Sharm was twitchy, not her usual self, but Clifford beamed, delighted to see her. "What a surprise! How did you get here?"

"I hitchhiked."

"Oh, no! You said you were going to, but I didn't believe you. I thought you were kidding. That's not safe," Clifford scolded. "Did you run into any trouble?"

"One truck driver was a little scary," she said as she plopped into a chair. She eyed the plexiglass screen between them. "But my masculine voice unnerved him," she smiled and looked coyly at Clifford.

"Did you play those tricks?" Clifford snickered.

"Yup, it works every time"

"Fess up. What did you do?"

"He started to hit on me, so I rolled my eyes to the back of my head, messed up my hair, and bellowed out a guttural shriek. His eyes widened, he recoiled—thought I was a witch for sure."

"What did he do then?"

"He dropped me off at the next gas station and said, 'Goodbye, Sybil.'

"I rolled my eyes to the back of my head one more time and slid my butt out of his truck."

"You are too much," he laughed. "Did they search you when you got here?"

"Yeah, that was miserable," Sharm retorted. "I didn't have to take my clothes off, but she checked out every nook and cranny."

"Just remember, they're recording our conversation."

"Is that what the flashing red light above us is all about?"

"Yeah, I think so," Clifford said. "I got your letter last week and wrote back." He reached into his pocket and slid the letter under the shield. "It's cryptic—wanted to keep it a secret from Wanda. I was pretty sure she'd open and read it. I'll mail it this afternoon. I don't want them is confiscate it."

"I came all this way because I desperately needed to talk to you," Sharm said.

"What I left out in the letter was that David did not take good care of my sweetie. He took the easy way out by just dropping you off."

Sharm became silent, listening intently. Tears welled in her eyes as she recounted her first real trauma. Frustrated by not being able to hug her father, Sharm made a heavy clunk with her head on the plexiglass separating them. The rattling sound alerted the guard. They made eye contact and Sharm straightened up. Clifford lifted his hand as if to soothe her, but the partition made it an empty gesture.

"You are a brave girl by facing this ... issue all by yourself. I wish I could have helped you through it."

"But Daddy, David was there."

"Not really. He just wanted to get out of a jam," Clifford continued. "You asked me about what STD means. It means sexually transmitted disease. If David gave you anything, you must get to a doctor for some medicine. Most of these diseases are curable, but you must get help right away."

"I feel okay. I don't think he gave me anything."

"Stay alert to any changes, okay?"

"I will."

"How are you going to get back?"

"The same way I came, but I have enough money for a one-night stay at a hotel in Marquette before I head back. I bought my prom dress on sale, so I saved some of that money for this trip. Thank you for sending the money to Grandma. The two of us had a great time shopping."

"I got the picture. You looked adorable in that dress," Clifford smiled, and then his face became sullen. "Our time is about up. Make sure you keep up at school—it's your ticket to success. I'll be worried about you, Sharm. Please, please give me a call when you get back. I'll be waiting on Sunday evening."

"I will, Dad. I promise."

They blew each other a kiss. Clifford watched his little girl exit out the big steel door as he waited to be strip searched and escorted back to his cell.

A SIZZLING WARMTH FILTERED through Clifford's window. Sitting on his bunk with his bare back to the window, he shivered with delight. *Damn, that feels good.* Even though May in the Upper Peninsula could be icy cold, today it was warm, and the sun drenched the matted earth with huge swathes of light. Clifford hoped this signaled spring and better times ahead. His thoughts turned to Simon. He hadn't heard from him in a long time. The same guard who was willing to get pot for him was stationed at the end of the hall. Clifford waved to get his attention.

"Whatcha need?" he asked.

"Could you ask your friend in Cell G about Simon Dean?" Clifford asked. "I haven't seen him around."

"Dean has been in the hole for the last ten days."

"Really? What for?"

"He beat Belcher within an inch of his life. He's still in the hospital."

"How's Simon?"

"It was a fierce fight—a lot of blood," the officer said. "He got some deep scratches and bruises, but he's okay. He should be out of the hole soon."

"If you see your friend in G, mention to him that I would like to see Simon in church one of these Sundays."

"And the people in hell want iced tea." The guard

turned and walked away. "I'm not your damn messenger service."

Clifford grinned. *He'll tell him when he sees him. So, Belcher finally got under Simon's skin. If you get on his bad side, he'll kill you. It's like he has a switch that goes from light and easy to pitch-dark insane. When two hurting machines collide, they suck into the other's darkness and swirl up together like a tornado. Simon's wrestling with a ton of demons, so one little poke and he explodes.*

Sunday afternoon crept into twilight. After dinner, Clifford sat in the visitors' center waiting for Sharm's call.

"Ratz, you have a phone call," the officer said. With a sigh of relief, Clifford waited for the prompter to permit the call, and then heard Sharm's voice.

"I made it home okay, Daddy. Thank you for your support and advice. You are my very best friend. I wish Mom wasn't such a meanie. She's so tight with her money."

"Don't let Wanda get to you, sweetie," Clifford said. "She gets under everyone's skin. I might have a little money to give you. I'll send it to Grandma's house, so Wanda won't get it."

"You're the best, Daddy."

"You are my best friend too, sweetie," he said. "Make sure you keep up with your studies and find better friends at school, okay?"

"I will, Daddy. I love you." The call was over, short and sweet. Knowing she was safe put his mind at ease. Clifford hummed as the guard walked him to his cell.

10 Delores

"**G**entlemen, I have an announcement," Delores shouted above the din of the lunchroom. She waited for their attention. "I'm retiring. Friday is my last day. I will no longer be your cook. Travis will be replacing me."

An epic uproar filled the room.

"Dammit, Delores, why you leavin' us? Don't they pay you enough? We'll miss the hell out of you *and* your pies!" Their comments bounced back and forth off the walls. The cacophony turned into a loud chant. "Don't leave! Don't leave! Don't leave!" Utensils, plates, and cups thumped on the tables—it was pure pandemonium.

Fearing the worst, the guards rushed to the dining hall, clubs in hand. What happened next surprised everyone. When the prisoners saw the guards, they stopped their antics and became silent. The inmate closest to Delores started to laugh and the rest of the prisoners followed his lead. The guards were astonished, so Delores informed them that the inmates were protesting her retirement.

"Oh, I didn't know," one of the officers said. "The warden didn't tell us. When are you leaving?"

"Friday will be my last day."

"You'll be missed. I guess these cons let you know how much they care about you."

"They certainly did. They're good men—every one of them. I'll miss them, too."

The prisoners chatted as they exited the dining room, smiling and nodding at Delores as they passed by.

STAN, THE COOK FROM Cellblock B, approached Clifford.

"I want to do something special for Delores on her last day. Everyone likes her. She's a great lady. Would you be willing to help with the decorations and food prep?"

"Sure," Clifford said. "Just let me know what you want me to do."

"I'll talk with the warden this afternoon and get back to you tomorrow."

"Do you want to meet somewhere after breakfast?"

"I want it to be a surprise, so make up a reason to come over to my kitchen. Tell the guard you need to borrow a bag of sugar or something."

"Okay, I'll see you at ten," Clifford said. "Will that work?"

"Sure."

Clifford was brightened by the prospect of a retirement party for Delores. After all, she was like a mother to him during his miserable imprisonment. He worried about what his life would be like without her greeting him each morning. They had worked side by side, shared intimacies about their lives, and hung together after Ed's murder. Their friendship ran deep.

At ten the next morning, Clifford met Stan in the kitchen.

"I talked to the warden, and he gave the go ahead on the party. The warden will request that she make a bag lunch for the prisoners on Friday. Then, at two in the afternoon, we'll have a nice dessert spread for everyone."

"Do you want me to do the decorations on Friday?" Clifford asked.

"No, you can do them tomorrow. We won't be able to keep the decorations a secret from her, but that's okay. Delores is a fan of the Spartans and Michigan State, so we'll do everything in green and white. Streamers from the ceiling would be fine."

"Where are the streamers?"

"I'll buy some after work tonight," Stan said. "I'll frost and decorate a retirement cake and bring the refreshments for everyone. I would like you to make an ambrosia salad for the event because some of the guys don't like cake. Delores always has bananas in her kitchen, so grab twenty of them and bring a large can of peaches. Last time I checked, the peaches were in the basement pantry. I'll get the coconut and the maraschino cherries, but you'll need to get the whipped cream out of the freezer in Delores's kitchen. Bring the peaches as soon as you can, and bring the bananas and whipped cream on Friday morning. They need to be fresh."

"That's a lot to remember," Clifford said.

"If you forget something, call me."

"Okay."

Clifford planned to decorate the dining hall that night after Delores went home. After breakfast, a guard escorted him to Stan's kitchen so he could get the crepe paper streamers. Stan was mixing the cake for the party and had one large bowl filled with yellow batter and the other with chocolate.

"Looks like you're making a marble cake," Clifford said.

"No, some of the men don't like chocolate. So, half of the cake will be yellow and the other half chocolate. I'm going to use white frosting and decorate it with green and white roses. Should look pretty nice," Stan smiled.

"I'm here for the streamers."

"Oh, that's right. They're in the bag on the counter."

When Delores went home for the day, he went back to the dining hall to decorate with crepe paper in hand. He tore lengths of crepe as evenly as he could and hung them up with scotch tape. He alternated the green and white strips. When finished, he gazed up at his work and grinned. It looked festive.

The next morning, Clifford started his kitchen work as usual. He greeted Delores and was pleased with her surprise reaction to the streamers.

"Someone knows I'm a Michigan State fan."

Clifford smiled as he scrambled the eggs and chopped vegetables for the salad. When the eggs were just the right consistency, he set the pan on the warmer and slipped downstairs to fetch the peaches from the pantry. Confused by the number of doors in the basement, he finally found the pantry halfway down the hall. There was a sudden loud scuffling sound on the floor above, followed by a violent banging and random thuds. Alarmed, Clifford sprinted down the hallway and dashed up the stairs. The kitchen was eerily quiet.

Where's Delores?

"Delores?" Clifford shouted. "Where are you?" Panicked by no answer, Clifford scrambled through the kitchen. He searched her workstation, the dining hall, the bathroom, and finally, the utility room—where he found her sprawled face down on the concrete in a pool of blood. He knelt down beside her and felt for a pulse.

It was faint. Clamoring to his feet, he slipped on the blood pooling around her chest. Righting his impending fall, he called out.

"Help! We need an ambulance!" He ran toward the hallway. "Delores has been stabbed!"

The officers from the morning coffee group charged past him into the kitchen. Officer Blak rechecked her pulse and declared her dead.

"Where were you when this happened?" Officer Blak demanded, giving Clifford a hard look.

"I was in the basement getting a can of peaches for her party. I heard a scuffle and climbed the stairs as fast as I could."

"So, you were the last one to see her alive."

"Her *murderer* was the last one to see her alive," Clifford answered.

"Well, we don't know who killed her," Officer Blak stated. "So, you're a suspect—the number one suspect."

Clifford's eyes widened. *Why would I kill her? It would be disastrous if they tried to pin it on me. Is someone setting me up?*

"Strip search him," Blak ordered. "Then, lock him in his cell, and get Captain Brewster. We need to get to the bottom of this."

A guard left the room to find the captain. The horror of Delores's murder would stay with Clifford, the ghastly image seared in his brain. Once full of life, and eager for retirement, Delores's body lay motionless with a river of blood oozing out of her sides. Her hairnet lay on the floor and strands of hair were pulled out of her tight bun. One foot was bare, her shoe sideways beside her, a reminder of her ferocious fight for survival. Clifford's eyes fixed on the bow of her apron. She had tied that bow with precision behind her back every day for thirty years. It was starched, perfect, and untouched by the scuffle. That was the last image he saw before a guard hauled him back to his cell.

Pete was reading on his bunk. Surprised Clifford returned early from his kitchen duties, he lifted his head.

"What's up?"

"Someone murdered Delores."

"What! What did you say? Someone murdered her? When did this happen?"

"Early this morning," he mumbled. "I don't want to talk about it."

Clifford just wanted to lie on his bunk and sleep. The smell of her blood, the stillness of her body haunted him. The murder scene was etched on his eyelids forever. Every time he blinked, he saw it. He couldn't find his tears because his insides were frozen. *I need to rest; maybe I'll discover it was just a bad dream.*

11 Vince and Sue Attwood

Sitting in his office with a view of the Michigan State Capitol, Vince Attwood, a state employee, answered his phone. "Attwood."

"Vince, this is Margaret. There's an emergency in the Upper Peninsula; the cook was murdered. Michigamme State Prison is in lockdown. I need you to interview each suspect. This usually helps shake out the truth—and you're good at it."

"How soon do I need to get up there?" he asked. Vince had promised his wife a vacation at the beginning of summer break.

"You need to be there by Monday of this coming week," she said. "You'll get mileage and a place to stay for the week."

"You know you can count on me, but I promised my wife I'd take a vacation with the family next week."

"Take them with you. It's beautiful in the UP this time of year," she coaxed. "See if you can find a hotel suitable for your family, and I'll run the numbers."

"Okay, I'll get back to you later today."

Vince was Margaret's right-hand man, which he considered a high compliment. She was a respected attorney, the head of the Department of Corrections, and his boss. Margaret called on him to investigate all the major prison crimes. His police training came in handy. He had spent five years on the Lansing police force and worked his way up to detective. When he did an honest evaluation of his career choice, he realized he didn't like being a cop; a cop's thinking was too black and white, and rule bound. His friend Mel suggested he look into becoming a lawyer, so he applied to Cooley Law School in Lansing. Being recently married with a wife to support, he couldn't quit his current job, so he took classes at night. The coursework and the time commitment had been a challenge, but he never regretted taking the plunge. His legal training allowed him to look at issues in a different way, helping him understand the complexities. Vince had acquired the skill needed to look at both sides, and the many dimensions of criminal behavior.

He had a mountain of paperwork to complete before he could leave for a week. He didn't have time to make phone calls to hotels in Marquette. He called his wife, Sue, and asked her to find a family-friendly hotel near Michigamme State Prison. After mentioning the possibility of taking the family on a trip up north to the UP, he detected excitement in her voice.

"There's been a murder up there and Margaret wants me to investigate the crime," Vince explained. Taking the family along on a business trip was new for him. Rarely did he talk about his job, since much of it was confidential. Combining business with family time would take getting used to.

"I've never been to the UP," Sue said. I've always wanted to see what it's like."

"Great. Let me know before four this afternoon because I have to run it by Margaret."

"I'll get right on it."

SUE CALLED JUDY, A teacher friend of hers from the UP, to get the scoop on hotels in Marquette.

"So, you're going to the UP," Judy said. "Lucky you. I miss that place."

"Vince is filling in for Davis Spar," Sue said. "He's the administrative law judge at the prison. There was a murder there last week and the prisoners are on lock-down."

"Not good. Those prisoners are aggressive and nasty. It can be a real powder keg. My grandpa was a guard at that prison for twenty years," Judy continued. "It has a terrible reputation and is considered the most violent prison in Michigan."

"Do I need to worry about Vince's safety?"

"I don't think so. The guards are well trained."

"Thank goodness." Sue breathed easier, but was not entirely convinced.

"The architecture of that place is fascinating," Judy offered. "It's Romanesque, if I remember correctly from my art history class. The façade of the buildings is sand-stone, quarried from local pits. The windows and doors are highlighted by a vibrant red sandstone. When you're there, take a look at the administration building; it's impressive. It's a three-story octagonal rotunda topped with a cupola. The archways, spires with high pointed roofs and arched windows, are reminiscent of medieval castles."

"It's hard to believe a prison is an architectural marvel," Sue said. "But I'll keep an open mind."

"Oh, by the way, something happened in 1950 you should know about. My grandpa's scrapbook has a copy of the newspaper article from the *Mining Journal* about the incident. I'll send you a copy. As far as hotels are concerned, I recommend Tiroler Hof. Check it out and see if you like it as much as I do."

Sue researched the hotel and found it was an Austrian-themed resort on the shores of Lake Superior. It claimed to be an accommodating place for children, and the pictures showed ample acreage around the hotel for their family to explore. Judy's suggestion was a good one. She knew Sue well enough to know she needed a safe place for her children to run and play. A two-room suite cost a reasonable seventy-five dollars a night. Margaret gave her stamp of approval. Taking a vacation paid for by the state would be a first for their family.

A few days later, she received the article from Judy. The headline from the *Mining Journal* was dated July 7, 1950: "Three Prisoners Attack Governor."

The story that follows detailed an unbelievable kidnapping attempt on Michigan's Governor G. Mennen Williams.

"Three Prisoners Attack Governor"
Around supper time at the Marquette State Prison, three inmates came out of the kitchen with knives.

They lunged toward the governor, slashing at anyone standing between them and the governor. Their intent was to seize and hold him hostage, and demand they be set free. Three prison guards were wounded, and one inmate was shot.

State Police Sergeant George Kerr, the governor's bodyguard, shot and killed John Halstead, a long-term prisoner. Kerr suffered multiple knife wounds in his back and hand during the melee.

Albert J. Haukness, 131 Arch Street, a prison guard who suffered fractured forearms while attempting to assist the governor, is convalescing at home.

At the bottom of the article, Judy had written a comment: "Albert Haukness was my grandpa."

Amazed at this article, Sue phoned Judy.

"Judy, I just got the article. I've never been to the UP, but what a fascinating place! It's full of stories. Your grandpa was a hero. Thanks for sending it. Is there anything else I should see while I'm up there?"

"Stories are everywhere in the UP. It does have some quirky things about it," Judy laughed. "The one must-see is Pictured Rocks in Munising. It rivals the Grand Canyon, and the ferry ride is worth the time. I recommend it. Fill me in when you get back."

"I'll give you a call, and thanks for the information."

AND SO, THE PACKING project commenced. They filled large Tupperware bins with clothes for warm and cold days. They needed plenty of diapers for Sarah, the baby. Each child had their own bin, and when they were stacked, they nearly filled the back of the station wagon. Knowing Vince would need the car, Sue carefully planned the meals and packed food they could prepare and eat at the hotel. They put their suitcases in the back of the station wagon, along with the largest bin, which was crammed full of building blocks, jump ropes, balls, coloring books and crayons. On top of the bins sat a lunch for the trip, which consisted of peanut butter and jelly sandwiches, carrot sticks, fruit, and lemonade.

The journey seemed to take forever. They drove up Highway 75 north, crossed the Mackinac Bridge to Highway 2, and merged onto Highway 28 to Marquette. A straight shot would have been about seven hours, but with three small children, pit stops, and a picnic lunch, it took ten long hours.

TIROLER HOF HOTEL, A quaint chalet overlooking Lake Superior, was even better than expected. A rosy sunset bedazzled them with a light dance on the deep blue waters. All eyes were fixed on the magical play between the water and sun. Even the bouncy toddler pressed her face against the car window and stared. Behind the hotel was a large stretch of woods with spring flowers and walking trails. The three children squealed with delight. Tiroler Hof promised to be a fun place to run, play tag, and discover nature's treasures. When Sue surveyed the grounds, she spotted a picnic table in the side yard, perfect as a command station for meals, toys, and a med station for the inevitable cuts and bruises.

Looming in the distance, just south of the hotel, was Michigamme State Prison. Long sunset shadows hovered over what looked like Count Dracula's castle. Sue felt uneasy having their precious children near such a menacing place. For Vince, it was a perfunctory matter, business as usual. As an attorney for the Michigan Department of Corrections, he had been in almost all the prisons, and knew all there was to know about the penal system. His nonchalance reassured her.

THE NEXT MORNING, AFTER a few kid issues during the night, Vince kissed Sue on the cheek and headed to work. Her day started with the usual childhood routines: diaper changing, face washing, teeth brushing, dressing for the weather, and eating breakfast on the pocket-sized table in the hotel suite. As they headed to the command center, Sue stressed the importance of staying quiet so they wouldn't wake the other hotel guests.

All three children scurried from the hotel, running in three different directions. The day was chilly but sunny. John happily sprinted across the expansive lawn and looked out over Lake Superior. Samantha, nicknamed Sam, helped Sue organize the crafts before she skipped off to play with her brother. Sarah toddled bow-legged in circles until she dropped to the ground, giggling. The fresh air, nature, and spirited play were a welcomed change from the hectic pace of getting ready for preschool every day. So far, their vacation proved to be first rate.

Vince's experience was anything but first rate. He

returned to the hotel disgruntled. His shoulders were hunched forward, his tie loose around his neck, and his shirt stained. The children ran to hug him but froze when they sensed a dark mood.

"I have to get in the shower right away, When I walked through Cellblock B, the inmates threw piss and crap at me before I left."

"They did what?" Sue exclaimed. Vince headed for the shower, dropping his clothes on the floor.

"Throw my clothes away."

Picking them up gingerly, touching them as little as possible, Sue put them in a plastic bag and set them outside the door of the suite. Vince's mood changed after showering. He smiled, relaxed in his fresh clothes, and joined everyone for a simple supper of chicken tenders and fries. Sarah fell fast asleep in Sue's arms. The children were exhausted from playing hard in the chilly air, so she put them all to bed. She and Vince needed to talk.

"What's going on at the prison?" Sue asked.

"It's a long story," he sighed. "The inmates, especially in Cellblock O, are agitated because of the murder. Delores was a much-loved cook in that unit. She announced her retirement the day before they found her body in the utility room. She had been stabbed multiple times with a kitchen knife, which they found next to her body. Strangely enough, there were pellets spread around the murder scene. It seems a box of rat poison tipped over during the scuffle. They sent those pellets to the lab to make sure it was rat poison and not something else. Nobody has confessed. The guards and some prisoners are convinced it was one of Delores's kitchen workers by the name of Clifford Ratz. He's worked with her since he arrived from Ingham County last year. He was convicted on a nonviolent drug charge—a Level One inmate."

"Level One?"

"They follow the rules. I interviewed him today; he's pretty tame," Vince replied. "No assaults on his record, and he is easy to get along with. Usually, they're on the road to the reintegration units."

"It seems like murder isn't something he'd do."

"That's what I think, but nobody named any other suspects. It's frustrating."

"It's got to be tough conducting those interviews."

"It is," Vince said. "The rest of the inmates are upset because they're all on lockdown."

"You mean they're confined to their cells until you resolve the situation?"

"They're in lockdown until I complete all the interviews," Vince continued. "I think Clifford is being set up. I interviewed him today and he was so despondent he could hardly talk. He sobbed and said Delores was like a mother to him. He repeated over and over again that he didn't do it. I believe him."

"Is there any evidence proving he *is* the murderer?" Sue asked.

"At this point, the only evidence they have is circumstantial. He was the last person seen with her. The group investigating the murder found fingerprints on the knife and on the box of rat poison, so they sent those to the lab today. We should know tomorrow."

"Who do you think is setting him up?"

"I'm not sure, but tomorrow I'll interview two more inmates," he continued. "Evidently, last month the prison guards discovered some drug-related infractions, and the hearing officer before me found himself in the middle of a hornet's nest. He recused himself from the case since he couldn't remain impartial. I think this is all tied together somehow."

THE NEXT DAY STARTED with the usual rustling noises upon waking. The children whispered to each other, excited about playing outside. Random morning trips to the bathroom signaled the beginning of the day. Sue changed Sarah's diaper and dressed her warmly for playtime. The other two dressed themselves, ate cereal, and brushed their teeth after breakfast. She heard Vince shuffle to the bathroom, his footsteps dragging. It was like he knew it was going to be a tough day.

John and Sam dragged the box of toys outside and began constructing a building similar to Tiroler Hof. Sarah expressed her newfound freedom by running pell-mell on the lawn. Neatly dressed in a suit, Vince gave Sue a kiss, said goodbye to the children, and drove off. *Dear Lord, please keep him safe so he will return home to his family in one piece. Amen.*

For the children, it was a day filled with fresh air, popsicles, hot dogs, and ice cream. The Lincoln logs, coloring books, and puzzles made the day fly by. Suppertime came and went, and the sun settled in the west. It was the children's bedtime, so Sue read their favorite stories and tucked them in. A sobering darkness surrounded them. Sue washed the dishes, organized the toys, and set out the clothes for the next day. Still no Vince. She tried to make herself believe everything was okay, but was sick with worry waiting for him to return.

Clearly exhausted, Vince finally lumbered into the hotel. After a curt greeting, he made his way to the bathroom, showered, and changed clothes. Sue hauled two folding chairs out of the closet, grabbed a couple of beers out of the mini-fridge, and found a place to roost on the small patio outside their suite. They had privacy, but could hear the children if they needed them. Sue waited for Vince to join. All cleaned up and ready to relax, he sat next to her. He sighed, silently gazing at the stars as he sipped his beer.

"How did it go today?" she asked.

"It went," he replied. "It was a very long day. The results came back from the lab. Clifford's fingerprints are on both the knife and the box of rat poison. And yes, it was rat poison." Vince shook his head, drained and disappointed by the results. "I feel certain he's innocent."

"You mentioned you were going to interview the man involved in the drug smuggling operation. How'd that turn out?"

"A man named James Denny was one of them—he's a scary guy," Vince opined. "He's in close custody, which is the most restrictive supervision. He's been known to be crazy violent and prone to escape. The guards keep a close eye on him."

"Does he have any connection with Clifford or Delores?" she asked.

"Allen Henry, one of the best officers at the prison, is

helping me with the case. We haven't found any connection. We verified that at the time of the murder, Denny was sitting in his cell. It's a puzzle. Tomorrow, I interview Murray Saul, one of Denny's accomplices over the years. He's a big guy—looks mean, but he's pretty passive, only a Level Two."

"So, he's compliant most of the time," she stated.

"Yeah, he needs more supervision than Level One, and he's not ready for a reintegration unit. Saul was accused of delivering the drugs. Every once in a while, he's violent. I'm pretty sure he's Denny's fall guy. Should be an interesting interview tomorrow." After a few more sips of their beers, Vince and Sue went inside. The night air was too cold for comfort.

THE FOURTH DAY OF their summer vacation was troublesome. Vince left for the prison, hoping for some kind of resolution. The sky was overcast, and it was cold—just above forty degrees. Sue bundled up the children, but could still see their breaths as they played. They looked like the little engines that could, puffing smoke and chugging up the mountainside. There were more injuries than usual, so they ate lunch early. The phone rang.

"Something bad happened," Vince said.

"Are you okay?" Sue asked.

"I'm okay, but Clifford attempted suicide."

"Really? How awful!"

"He apparently couldn't handle being accused of Delores's murder. Slit his own throat."

"Do you think he'll make it?"

"I don't know. He's in the ICU now. I planned to interview him about the lab results today, but that's going to have to wait."

"Where did he find a knife to do it?" Sue asked.

"That's a story in itself. I'll tell you about it when I get back."

After lunch, the children played tag outside. When their hands were freezing and their noses like icicles, they went inside to warm up. They huddled around the television, so Sue put *Dumbo* on the VCR for the afternoon's entertainment. They had an early supper of cheesy macaroni and hot dogs and a warm bath before going to bed.

Vince arrived after they were asleep, his overcoat only half on, too exhausted to cover his shoulders. His mood was dark from the events of the day. He flopped in a chair. The burden he was carrying was getting heavier by the minute.

"Did you have supper?" Sue asked.

"Yes, I grabbed a hamburger on the way home."

"Anything new?"

"No. Henry and I are puzzled by the lab results. Everything points to Clifford, but I'm sure he was set up … but by whom? Nobody's talking."

"Where did he get the knife to cut himself? I thought they strip-searched him before he went into lockdown."

"They made a big mistake! Travis Hillman, the new cook, started working the day after Delores was murdered. He didn't know where to find the food or the cooking supplies, so he asked a guard to release Clifford from the lockdown to help him in the kitchen."

"Oh no! I bet he hid a kitchen knife in his jumpsuit before he was taken back to his cell."

"That's exactly what happened. He slit his throat after his cellmate left for the exercise yard. When he returned, Pete found blood everywhere, and Clifford was unconscious. It's a miracle they got him to the hospital on time."

"How long before you'll be able to interview him?"

"I really want this job assignment to be done, so I plan to interview both Saul and Clifford tomorrow. Then we need at least one day to do some sightseeing. I hope we can take the family on the ferry to see the Pictured Rocks. I hear it's beautiful."

THE FAMILY COMMAND CENTER was busy the next morning. The children charged out of the door, ready to play and release their pent-up energy. Building toys were strewn about like a straggle of scattered treasures. They tried to create a farm by fashioning a barn, a farmhouse, and a corn crib. Soon the crayons, especially the red, yellow, and green ones, were worn down because of their drawings of the sun, the spring flowers, and the green grass. In the late morning, they had root beer floats as a special treat. Sue noticed storm clouds forming in the west around noontime and was certain an afternoon rain would force them back inside. They stayed out as long as they could, but soon, the black clouds tumbled their way. They made a mad dash inside just before the storm broke and the clouds dumped a torrent of rain.

The children plastered their faces against the windowpanes, looking longingly at their play yard. They were hoping they could play outside once the storm had passed.

"Mommy, Mommy, look!" John said. "There's a rainbow." Sam clapped her hands and Sarah followed with her version of excitement, jumping and stomping. The sun was peeking through the clouds and a brilliant rainbow stretched over Lake Superior, casting out rain showers.

"Yes, you're right. The sun is out, but let's give the grass a little time to dry," Sue said as she put *Cinderella* in the VCR. Patience was not one of their best qualities, but they begrudgingly sat in front of the television, staring at the screen and glancing out the window. "Okay, let's go outside and play." They hauled the toys to the command station; Sue dried the table and placed the boxes on it. Sam and Sarah decided to play ball, and John headed for the walking trail.

"Stay on the trail!" Sue shouted, a little uneasy and not sure where the trail might lead. She had to remind herself he wasn't a baby anymore and would soon turn eight. Michigamme Prison was in that same direction, just over the hill.

A loud noise made her turn around. Sarah was wailing. Sam had thrown the ball hard, smacking Sarah in the face; a bloody nose ensued. Preoccupied with comforting Sarah and managing the nosebleed, Sue forgot about John. It wasn't until afternoon snack time that his absence sparked her maternal instinct. *Where's John? Why isn't he back yet?* She put Sam in charge of Sarah and headed for the trail. "John? John? Where are you?"

she yelled in her best mega voice. Silence. No answer. She ran toward the hill away from the trail. "John! Where are you?"

"Up here on the top of the hill," he yelled back. "I found something cool."

"I was so worried about you. Thank heavens you're okay." Sue pressed on up the hill and through the trees, spotting a golden dome gleaming in the sunshine. "What on earth did you find?" She approached what looked like a miniature building.

"It's a tiny church—like the girls' playhouse."

What a marvel! It had a white stucco façade with gold trim and a round stained-glass window above the arched doorway. Around the outside were several small windows with curved tops, and the turret to the left of the main entrance was a hexagon encircled by narrow rectangular windows painted blue. On the very top was a golden onion dome.

"Mom, there's a clock by the tower in the back," John said. "Come, look."

Sue followed him to the back of the chapel and caught sight of Michigamme State Prison through the mangle of trees. It was a top view, replete with heating units, chimney flues, and concertina wire. The prison was frighteningly close.

"I need to check on Sam and Sarah and bring my camera back here to take some pictures," Sue said. "Follow me back, John. We'll bring the girls up here to see your discovery."

They all climbed the hill to look at John's treasure. The girls wanted to go inside, but all the doors were locked tight. Sue lifted them up to peek inside the windows, but it was too dark to see anything. To the left of the entrance was a small plaque:

> WE BUILT A CHAPEL ON THE HILL.
> WE REARED IT AND LEFT IT THERE
>
> FOR SOMEONE WHO IS AS MUCH IN NEED
> AS WE WERE.
>
> SEPP & ANNEMARIE HOEDLMOSER
>
> BUILT 1967-1970

Sue took the children's picture in front of the chapel as the late afternoon sun shimmered through the spring leaves. The picture would take a prominent place in the photo journal of their vacation.

Vince came home for supper around six, carrying two large boxes of pizza. The children were ecstatic. Friday was take-out pizza night, just like at home. Vince's forehead was tight and creased, a sure sign he had a headache. Sue could tell he needed to vent, but there was too much commotion. They would talk once the children were in bed.

"How'd the interview go with Saul?"

"Very interesting," Vince replied. "I hit a nerve because he got extremely agitated after I asked him about Delores. He stood up, slammed his fist on my desk, and lunged at me. I pushed the emergency buzzer before he could grab me. He let out a roar, lifted up the front of my desk, and shoved it at me. Two guards restrained him and took him to his cell. He didn't go willingly—he snarled and spit at me."

"That's horrible. Vince, you could have been seriously hurt!" Sue grabbed his hand and held it to her chest, over her heart.

"I'm okay. Don't worry about me," Vince continued. "Saul exploded when I asked him about Delores's retirement announcement."

"That's odd. I wonder why?"

12   Clifford's Interview

Like so many murder-suicide cover-ups, Delores's demise had enough complications to mystify even the most astute detective. Several questions bewildered Vince. *How can such a tightly contained unit such as a prison not know what's going on? I wonder if someone was afraid of what Delores would do once she was out of reach and beyond the prison walls. Was she being blackmailed? Or, was she the blackmailer? Could it be that once she was in retirement, they would lose control? How do I prove it?*

Vince decided to interview Pete, Clifford's cellmate, to find out about Clifford's relationship with Delores. Pete was chatty and the interview was a monologue: "At Christmas, Delores baked damn good hams with all the trimmings. She decorated the kitchen and the dining hall with girlie stuff: angels, red bells, and blue stars. Clifford worked his butt off helping her decorate. On New Year's Day, they had turkey, so it was like Thanksgiving all over again. Clifford stuffed the turkeys with dressing and added sugar and orange zest to the cranberries. The kitchen smelled damn good—baked turkey and oranges. Delores and Clifford treated the inmates like family."

After Pete's interview, Vince was more convinced

than ever of Clifford's innocence. *Why would he kill her? He doesn't have a motive.*

THE PRISONERS ON LOCKDOWN were growing more restless by the day. Vince had one more interview—Clifford. Lockdown would be lifted once his interview was completed. Vince scheduled it for Saturday, hoping Clifford would be well enough to speak. Vince would hand the paperwork to the hearing officer who recused himself, so he could pick up the ball where he left off. Not solving the murder frustrated Vince, but he was relieved that the end of his job assignment was close. The truth lurked somewhere in the shadows of malicious lies and half-truths, and it would haunt him until justice was served. Clifford deserved vindication.

ON SATURDAY MORNING, VINCE slipped quietly out of the hotel room so as not to awaken his family. He drove to St. Luke's Hospital for the interview with Clifford. A volunteer at the front desk checked his identification and pointed him brusquely toward the elevators that would take him to the second floor. Once off the elevator, he saw two prison guards stationed at the end of the hall outside Clifford's room, standard protocol. The purpose was to protect the community from Clifford.

This is laughable. I've seen this so many times. Don't they understand he's a nonviolent criminal? He turns anger in on himself and becomes depressed. His MO is not violence! What he needs is a therapist, not armed guards.

Before he entered Clifford's room, Vince flagged the doctor standing by the nurses' station.

"Are you Dr. Benet?" Vince asked.

"Yes," he said as he begrudgingly set aside his chart and lifted his eyes over his spectacles.

"I'm Vince Attwood, the hearing officer for Michigamme Prison. I need to interview Clifford Ratz. Is he able to answer a few questions?"

"He severed his vocal cords with a knife. I've done surgery on them, but it will take months to heal. It's possible he'll never speak again. Writing the answers out is the only way he can respond to your questions. He gets a couple of calls each day from his family who live in the Lansing area. Please use caution and be patient with him—he seems like a nice enough guy."

"He is. Writing a response will work."

"Committing suicide by slitting your throat is very rare and is one of the most painful recovery periods," Dr. Benet said. "He's heavily sedated for the pain."

Vince opened the door to Clifford's room. Suffocating odors assaulted Vince, which suggested his room might be the least desirable room in the hospital, not uncommon for prisoners. The mixture of bleach, urine, and pureed food—a putrid combination of smells—nearly floored him. He stepped back into the hallway, took a deep breath, and tried again. He entered quietly and approached the raised bed. In front of him was a wan, weak-looking man in his thirties. His neck was bandaged and stabilized by a neck brace. Vince waited for Clifford's eyes to open.

"Good morning. I'm Vince, the hearing officer in charge of investigating the murder of Delores Kin. I have some questions I hope you can answer." Clifford's beseeching eyes changed to a stony stare; he turned away.

"I think you're innocent. You don't appear to have a motive, but I need your help if we're going to get to the bottom of this."

Clifford's expression changed. "Write your answers on the tablet," Vince said. "Let's get started. I sent the knife used in the murder to the lab for fingerprinting. Your prints were all over it. Where and when did you use the knife?"

Clifford scrawled his answer. His neck brace prevented him from seeing his own writing.

I use knife in kitchen often

"Did you use the knife the day of the murder?"

Yes

"What did you use it for?"

Cut vegetables for salads

"Did you do that before Delores came in that day?"

Yes

"The guard that found the body said he saw you in the kitchen with her that morning. Do you remember seeing the guard?"

Yes, He gets coffee before his shift

"What happened after that?"

I go to basement for peaches—I hear loud noise upstairs—like a fight. I ran upstairs.

"Let me get this straight. You were chopping vege-tables in the kitchen when Delores came in to start her shift. So, she was alive when you left to go to the base-ment to get peaches. Is that correct?

Yes—three officers in kitchen: Officer Blak, Rodney, and Trent. They grabbed me and locked me in my cell.

"If you can, please describe the murder scene."

Blak taped off room—Delores face down in blood—hairnet on floor—one shoe off next to her—apron still tied.

"Did you see the box of rat poison tipped over and on the floor?"

No

"Do you use rat poison?"

Yes, every week—put poison on vents for rats

"Where did you get the knife to cut your throat?"

Travis asked for help in kitchen—I got knife there

"That's enough for now. Thank you, Clifford. I'll give my write-up to Davis Spar, the hearing officer who works at the prison. He'll get in touch with you soon." It had been a two-hour interview. The sedatives for pain were wearing off, and Clifford was getting agitated. Vince was tired too. He would leave a directive for Davis to inves-tigate Officer Blak's role in this ordeal.

It was pushing noon, and Vince had promised his family they would drive to Munising to catch the ferry to see Pictured Rocks. It would take an hour to get there, so they'd have to rush.

Vince returned to the hotel, and he and Sue stacked the Tupperware containers in the back of the station wagon and drove east to Munising. Both had received glowing accounts about Pictured Rocks from different friends. Highway 28 trailed along the scenic coast of Lake Superior. The children's eyes were fixed on the lake all the way from Marquette to Munising. It was refreshingly quiet in the car—no poking or teasing. Vince drove, but was not really present. Sue knew her husband well enough to know his thoughts had drifted to Clifford. *That murder will haunt him until all the pieces fit and Clifford is cleared. If Vince believes Clifford was set up, then I'm certain he was.*

"Mommy," John exclaimed. "There's the ferry." The ferry swayed back and forth next to the dock, getting ready to receive passengers. John and Sam were excited as they boarded, but Sarah cowered and whimpered. The movement of the gangplank and the vastness of the water scared her. Vince calmed her by lifting and carrying her on board.

AFTER THEIR FERRY RIDE, Vince and his family made the six-hour drive back to their home in Powell. With brute determination, he hauled the Tupperware containers out of the station wagon and dumped them in the middle of the living room while Sue supervised each child's bath, read them a bedtime story, and heard their prayers at tuck-in time. When all was finished, Vince and Sue plopped on the sofa, sighed, and finished sorting out the week ahead.

Continuing to mull over the events earlier in the day, Vince walked upstairs to his home office. A menacing red light blinked on his answering machine. He pressed rewind, endured the screeching bleep, and listened.

"This is Davis Spar. I'm in a jam. Somehow, Officer Blak got wind of his impending interview, and he's threatening to have the warden kick me off the investigation. Call me back and let me know who has read your report. This case is getting nasty."

Vince immediately dialed Davis.

"Got your message," Vince said. "What's up?"

"Officer Blak jumped all over me after you left on Friday. He acts like he's in charge of this investigation. What's with that guy?"

"I suspect him of involvement somehow—he's over-reacting. He was the first officer on the scene of the murder—like he was waiting in the wings to take control."

"Well, I'll tell you one thing. I don't like being threatened. Who else has seen the report besides the warden?"

"Nobody. I showed it to the warden so he could lift the lockdown. I'm going back to work on Monday. I'll give Margaret a copy, then."

"Humph. There's too many ears in the cornfield," Davis opined.

"If you want help with the investigation, talk to Margaret. She might be willing to send me to Marquette to help. Just let me know," Vince offered.

"I'll think it over. Thanks for getting back to me right away."

13   Officer Blak

Officer Blak swaggered into the private room off the warden's office, lips curled and eyes cold. Despite his hostile demeanor, he was handsome enough with his erect posture, dark hair, and sepia-toned skin. His blue eyes were vacant—as if something was missing. Perhaps he had no conscience, or maybe, a mind that couldn't handle complexities. He was an enigma.

Davis had successfully lobbied Margaret to include Vince in the investigation. The Blak interview was next, and Davis needed moral support. They had worked together before and were an effective team. They began hatching plans in the interview room.

"We need a strategy," Vince said. "He's as cunning as a fox and knows the ropes regarding prison investigations."

"I know. First, we need to determine if there are other men involved. Second, since there is no DNA evidence on him, we need to catch him in a lie. Third, the big question is whether Clifford is being set up."

"I'll be the bad cop and you be the good cop," Vince suggested. "That should move things along quickly. Are you okay with that?"

"Sure. I'll call him in." Davis used the intercom. "Officer Blak, please come in."

Officer Blak entered. Seeing Vince, his face tightened.

"I didn't know there would be two guys interviewing me."

Davis motioned for him to have a seat. "Thanks for coming in today. I understand it's your day off," Davis said. "Do you mind if we call you Gene?"

"That's fine."

"Would you like some coffee or water?"

"No, I'm good," Blak said. "So, Davis, you're the 'good cop,' right?"

"I'll jump right in," Vince said. "You were the first guard on the murder scene. Is that correct?"

"Yeah."

"You were unusually prompt. Where did you come from?"

"The hallway at the end of the dining room."

"Why were you there? Don't you work in Cell B?" Vince questioned.

"I do, but I have coffee in the morning with some guys before the shift starts. We were heading to our workstations."

"You and who else?" Vince asked.

"Rodney Stine and Trent Deter."

"Is that all?"

"Yep."

"A witness said you called for Captain Brewster to begin an investigation," Vince continued. "You had already taped off the murder scene. Is that correct?"

"Yes."

"Wouldn't Captain Brewster bring crime scene tape when he came? Where did you get it? Did you have it in your pocket?"

"Yes, I carry it with me in case of an emergency."

"Is that the usual protocol?" Vince questioned.

Blak shrugged. "It's what the hell I do!"

"Describe the murder scene to me."

"Delores was sprawled, face down on the floor," Officer Blak said dispassionately. "She had been stabbed several times in the chest—according to the coroner, five times. There was crap on her body from a box of rat poison. The box was on the other side of the room."

"Anything else you remember?"

"Nope."

"Seems your version has missing information," Vince said. "You never mentioned Clifford being at the scene, which surprises me."

"That piece of shit's the one who committed the damn murder," Blak said. "When he called for help to cover his ass, I ran to the kitchen."

"Clifford said he could feel a pulse, but you pronounced her dead as soon as you came into the kitchen. Is that correct?"

"I've dealt with death many times. Clifford doesn't know shit about anything."

Davis interjected. "Do you know of anyone who would have wanted Delores dead?"

"She ratted on an inmate by the name of Saul about some drug infraction a couple months back. I'd check him out," Blak said. "He's the only one I can think of."

"By the way, Clifford was the first one on the scene

and said the box of rat poison was on the shelf, *not* on Delores's body." Vince fixed on Blak's eyes. "I wonder how that happened."

Blak stiffened and glared at Vince. The blood drained out of his face and he pumped his arms, trying to leash his anger.

"Well, thank you for coming in on your day off," Davis said. "We'll contact you if we need anything more."

A few minutes after Blak's interview ended, there was one loud pound on the door; Wayne Korhonen, the warden, entered.

"Just heard," he announced. "Clifford's doctor will discharge him from the hospital later this afternoon. We'll put him in Cellblock B."

"Why in Cellblock B?" Vince gasped. "He'll be with lifers and hardened criminals."

"He's the prime suspect in Delores's murder," Wayne said. "That's where he has to be until trial."

"For God's sake," Vince protested, "They'll torture him!"

Wayne grinned. "The guards won't let that happen."

"Right," Vince said, shaking his head. "I have a few more questions for Clifford, so I'll need to talk to him tomorrow."

"We'll see if he's up for it," Wayne said. He abhorred small talk, so he forcefully shut the door as he exited.

Vince thought the warden was an odd duck. He talked weird and had mood swings. His nervous twitch and his answers to questions were monosyllabic. *Maybe it's because he's Finnish.* Being terse was a characteristic of the Finns, and Wayne seemed to be more clipped than most. According to prison gossip, he came from the Finnish community in Duluth, Minnesota, but quickly adapted to life in the Upper Peninsula. He made the prison hum like a well-oiled machine, with a hyper-focus on details and procedures. He was rumored to be hooked on methamphetamine, but no one knew for sure whether a doctor prescribed it for an attention disorder or if Wayne used it recreationally as an aphrodisiac. The staff learned to brace themselves for his mood swings, manifested in outbursts of anger and unpredictable behavior. But for the most part, his decisions about the prison were on point, so his job was never in question.

Vince left the interview room unsure about the next day. Did Davis want to team up with him for more interviews? The news about Clifford was unsettling, and he felt compelled to do something about it. Margaret had scheduled him for three days at the prison, and then he was back in Lansing. He considered it his moral responsibility to see Clifford before he left the area. The Lansing office preached the ethics of avoiding personal feelings with inmates—but, Clifford was different. Vince considered him a target of cruel and unusual punishment, which in his mind was not acceptable.

Vince checked into the Tiroler Hof Hotel and asked for a secluded room with a view of the lake. He was exhausted from the drive and the emotional drain of Officer Blak's interview. He needed to relax and get a good night's sleep. Room 165 was at the very end of the hall and away from the traffic in the lobby. It felt right. He found Belgian chocolates in a petite box on his pillow and specialty soaps and shampoos with citrus smells. He pulled back the curtains and opened the window wide to soak up the fresh breeze from Lake Superior.

"Ahhh!" Vince exhaled his toxic emotions, collapsed on the bed, and napped for a while.

He woke up thinking about the next day. He would be tied up in interviews with Officers Trent Deter and Rodney Stine. They were the first ones at the murder scene. Vince suspected a drug conspiracy, but Delores's part in it was still unclear. The most probable reason for her murder was information she knew and kept secret. Maybe Clifford knew something, so he *had* to talk with him tomorrow.

Before retiring for the night, he called Sue to check on the kids and to say good night.

"How's it going, babe?"

"I just put the kids to bed. They miss their daddy-hugs," Sue said. "How's everything up there?"

"Just routine stuff. I'll be tied up most of the day tomorrow doing interviews. The warden said Clifford was discharged from the hospital today. Here's the kicker; they placed him in Cellblock B."

"With the lifers?"

"Yeah, I don't know what they're thinking."

"Are you going to see him?"

"I'm making a point of seeing him tomorrow. I feel for the guy."

"By the way, I have a surprise for you, but I won't share it with you until you come home," Sue said.

"I don't know if I can wait."

"Believe me. You can," Sue chuckled. "It's a good surprise. Sweet dreams, honey."

Vince scratched his head, trying to interpret what she said. He gave up, showered, and fell into bed. Tomorrow was going to be a full day.

The first interview was with Rodney Stine. He gave consistent and accurate answers, which parroted what Officer Blak had said. Stine had been walking through the corridor by the kitchen when he heard Clifford's shout for help. Officer Blak motioned to him to come along to respond to the alarm. He pulled the tape out of his pocket and asked Rodney to mark off the murder scene.

"Do officers usually carry tape in their pockets?" Vince asked.

"No. I was surprised when he took it out of his pocket, but I did what I was told."

When asked about the murder scene, he described it like Blak did—except for one thing. The box of rat poison was by her right arm, not away from her body like Blak described.

"Did you notice if Officer Blak moved anything?"

"No, but I was busy stringing the tape around the counters and tables. I wasn't looking in his direction."

"Well, that's all for right now," Davis said. "We'll contact you if we need more information."

Wayne opened the door and popped his head in. "Attwood, if you want to see Ratz, now is the time. He's awake and able to talk. You'll have to go to his cell. We can't cart him down here."

"Okay." Vince turned to Davis. "Go ahead and start the interview with Trent. I'll be back soon."

A guard opened the steel door to Cellblock B. Madness and pandemonium were everywhere. Shivs, eating utensils, and metal cups clanged and clattered on the bars from every direction. "Just because we've got Delores's murderer here doesn't mean you have to be lunatics," Officer Blak shouted. The noise was deafening. Blak's voice was like a squeak of a mouse—nothing could break through the tsunami of voices.

"Hang him! Hang him! Hang him!" the inmates chanted. "He's a motherf**king bastard," another prisoner shouted above the mayhem. Vince walked purposefully to Clifford's cell and waited for the guard to unlock the door. Some inmates, curious about Clifford's visitor, dulled the roar. They wanted to know what was going on. Clifford was able to sit up, but his voice was a low rasp.

"Hello," he hissed.

"I have a couple more questions. I'll be quick and quiet," Vince said. "Why do you think someone killed Delores?"

"She planned to expose the guards involved in a drug scheme after she retired," Clifford whispered.

"Why do you say that?"

"After Ed Debouch was killed, she said, 'The politics of this place is getting to me—it's corrupt.' Now, I know why she said that."

"Is there anything else you need to tell me?"

"That's all I know for sure."

Knowing Clifford's time in Cellblock B would be agony, Vince left with a sick feeling in his stomach. He needed to check on the Trent Deter interview but by the time he arrived, the interview was over. Davis hadn't found anything suspicious and had ended the interview early. Denton Stokes was the last interview, which would happen the following day.

Vince drove to the hotel in a stupor of fatigue. The day's events drained him, and he needed a nap. He enjoyed the burst of fresh air as he opened the window. He took a deep breath and exhaled completely. The lake breeze was as refreshing as ever. Housekeeping had tidied the room and he devoured the chocolates he found in the tiny box on his pillow. He plopped down on the bed and fell into a deep sleep.

He woke up to a pitchy, moonless night. The view out the window was a thick wall of dark and the lake was a black hole. No traffic, no people noises, no glare from the city. But, he felt a diabolical presence.

"Vinceeee. Vinceeee, boy," a ghostly voice whispered. "You're in over your head, asshole. Walk away … while you still can."

Vince jumped off the bed and dashed to the window. "Who's there?"

An evil laugh punctured the air. "The boogeyman."

"What do you want with me?" Vince asked, convinced it was not his imagination.

"We … want you to drop the f**king investigation of the guards."

"And let Clifford take the fall? That's not happening," Vince snarled.

"Then, you're screwed … Now!" the man screamed. The hotel door thundered and shuddered as a man shouldered it open. The lock chain pulled taut but held. After a brief pause, Vince cringed to the screeching whir of a saw. In less than a second, the chain parted, and a masked man barged inside.

Vince fell back on his police training and lunged at the intruder. Putting him in a headlock, Vince slammed his head into the floor, rattling the windows. Winded and cursing, the man struggled to his feet on the rebound. Vince charged him, fist drawn back to swing, but someone charged through the rear window and grabbed him from behind. Restrained and outnumbered, Vince conceded the battle and lowered his head. He was at their mercy.

The men, both masked, tied his hands behind his back and pushed him into a chair, tying his feet to its legs. The thug who came through the window used duct tape to bind him tightly to the chair. Vince couldn't move. Before taping his mouth, the first man asked, "Will you drop the investigation?"

"I don't have the power to drop it. It's a directive from Lansing."

"Stop it now! If you don't … your sexy wife and useless brats will pay for your mistake."

"Killing me or hurting them would be the stupidest thing you could do. They'd know for sure the guards were responsible and Lansing would send someone to take my place." On the outside Vince appeared unflappable but inside his pulse was racing, and his guts were rolling. The thought of someone hurting his family sent shivers creeping up to his scalp. *My sexy wife? Dear God.*

Police sirens wailed in the distance. The men's eyes widened, filling with fear. The first man said, "Did you disconnect the alarm like I told you?"

"Hell yeah, I disconnected it. I'm sure I did!"

They dropped the roll of tape and the rope and clambered out the window. Vince listened as they ran up the hill to the woods. He couldn't move, but they left without taping his mouth.

"Help! I'm in room 165. They tied me to a chair!"

The police knew exactly where he was. They kicked open the door and bounded into the room, guns drawn. After clearing the room, an officer checked the bathroom and broken window while his partner turned to Vince.

"They climbed out that window and ran up the hill and into the woods," Vince said, as the officer cut through the tape.

"Justin, call Investigation," the officer in charge said. "We've got a crime scene here." He exited out the back door and beamed the woods with his flashlight, checking for movement.

"What's your name?" Officer Justin said after making the call.

"I'm Vince Attwood, an administrative law judge and former detective. I'm conducting interviews into the Delores Kin murder. The prison guards are being interviewed, and the criminals who attacked me threatened to harm my family if I didn't stop. Those thugs were either guards or hired by prison guards."

"Do you know who they are?" Officer Justin asked.

"No, they both wore masks … How did you get here so fast?"

"They have a good security system here. When your assailant disconnected the alarm by the back door, the warning light came on at the front desk and video cameras were turned on. The employees know to call the police when that happens. This hotel is only a block away from the prison, so they added that feature to provide security for hotel guests."

"You got here so fast I thought someone must have tipped you off."

"They have a video of the guy who came through the back door. He put his mask on just before he entered the building, so we have a head shot of him without a mask."

"I'd like to see his face. I might recognize him."

"The manager is in the office next to the check-in desk. I'll let him know you're coming. I have to stay here to meet the detectives. They might want to interview you. I'll let you know when they come."

Vince approached the manager. "I'm the guest in 165. I'd like to see the video."

"How are you doing? That was an awful experience," the manager asked.

"I'm still processing it. Good thing you have a state-of-the-art security system."

The manager nodded and smiled. "Justin said you were coming. Have a seat."

The video captured a white male, average height, partially bald and about forty years old. His facial features were clear. He slipped the mask on *after* he disconnected the alarm. *Stupid!* He seemed vaguely familiar, but Vince couldn't place him. He shook his head, thanked the manager, and inquired about another room.

"My room's a crime scene. I'll need other accommodations to sleep."

"Sure. We have a room on the second floor, ready and open. Room 240," the manager said, handing him a pass card.

"That'll work."

The following day at the prison, Vince checked the message in his notebook. It read, "Final interview—Denton Stokes." Vince met Davis in the rotunda, grabbed a cup of coffee, and headed to the interview room.

"Last one and then I head back to Lansing. I had a hell of a night last night," Vince said. "Two creeps broke into my room and attacked me. They tied me to a chair and demanded we stop interviewing the guards. They didn't have guns, so they weren't planning to kill me, but they threatened to hurt my family if we didn't stop."

Davis's jaw dropped. "What the hell is going on?"

"Extortion," Vince surmised. "They're guilty as hell. We're onto something."

"What did you tell them?"

"I told them no way, not happening."

"Did they leave when you stood your ground?"

"No, they bolted when they heard the police sirens. They scrambled through the window and headed for the woods behind the hotel." Vince smirked. "They've got to be pretty dumb. The police detectives are investigating the incident right now. I saw one of the men on a security video, but I didn't recognize him."

"Are you still up for interviewing this last guy?" Davis asked.

"Absolutely. There's no way I'd stop now, not after they threatened my family."

Davis clicked on the intercom. "Wayne, send Denton Stokes in for the interview."

"He's not here yet," the warden said.

"Let us know when he arrives."

While they waited, Vince detailed the events of the night before. They chuckled about their major miscalculations. They obviously didn't research the hotel's security system, which was far more sophisticated than just a door alarm.

"Denton's here."

"Bring him in," Vince said.

In walked a forty-year-old, partially bald, white male of average height. Denton's face flushed.

Vince, sitting in the interviewer's chair, smiled and nodded. *He's the man on the video. I'm sure!* A war between cop Vince and lawyer Vince ensued. His palms were sweating, and shivers rushed from his tailbone to his skull.

The son of a bitch. I'll make an arrest right here and now and have Davis call the cops. Shit! I don't have handcuffs. Hold on, you're a judge … Make sure he gets his due process. Does due process come before law and order? Technically yes, but what's right is right and what's wrong is wrong. I'm so f**king tired of that reasonable doubt bullshit. Calm down … It's possible someone coerced him into committing the crime. Dammit all to hell!

Vince appeared unflappable, but his posture was rigid and alert. He sat glued to his chair, glaring at the suspect until finally, the inner war became too much. He stood.

"I need more coffee. I'll be right back." Vince stepped

out of the interview room into the warden's office. "We've got the suspect. Call the police."

The warden looked at him with a curious expression. "Denton Stokes, a suspect? You're out of your mind," the warden exclaimed. "I'm *not* calling the cops."

"Then, I'll call them," Vince snapped. He grabbed the receiver and dialed. The warden slammed his hand on the cradle.

"Let me handle this," the warden pleaded. "Bring him into my office."

"Either I call the police with your phone or I drive to the police station."

"You're *not* using my phone and that's that."

Vince left in a mad dash and drove to the Marquette police station. He asked for Justin, one of the first policemen at the crime scene.

"What's up?" Justin asked.

"Davis and I were interviewing Denton Stokes and I recognized him. I'm sure he's the man I saw on the security video last night. You need to bring him in for questioning."

"Where is he?"

"As far as I know he's still with Davis in the interview room at the prison," Vince said. "I'll head back there and continue the interview."

"I'll get Jim and drive out, ASAP."

Vince was sure Davis wondered what had happened to him; he had been gone far too long for just a coffee refill. The warden had obstructed justice and his behavior baffled Vince. *What part is he playing in all of this? This investigation might go all the way to the top.*

Davis's interview with Denton was winding down when Vince walked in. "Sorry I'm late, I was side-tracked," Vince said matter-of-factly, hoping to keep Denton under his watchful eye until the police came. "I have a few questions that need answering. Denton, why would anyone want to kill Delores Kin?"

"I don't know," Denton answered confidently. "She was a nice lady. The only incident that comes to mind is the report she filed against Saul. You might want to check him out." Vince asked him a few questions about where he was at the time of the murder, and wanted his description of the murder scene.

Vince stalled long enough until out of the corner of his eye he saw a police cruiser approach the prison grounds.

"Where were you last night about nine o'clock?" Vince asked.

"I was home with my family," Denton answered. "You can ask my wife."

The door flew open and the detectives barged in, showing their badges.

"Are you Denton Stokes?"

"I—I am," he stammered. "What's going on?"

"We'll be taking you to the police station for questioning. Put your hands behind your back." They read him his Miranda rights as they handcuffed him. Jim took his arm and ushered him into the back seat of the police cruiser. Davis was mystified by all the commotion.

"What in the hell did you do?" Davis said, shaking his head. "That's some cup of coffee."

VINCE DROVE SOUTH OVER the Mackinac Bridge to the peninsula below. The investigation was far from over, but it cast a dark shadow over the very men who were hired to enforce the law. He was convinced the guards were operating a drug ring. They made a killing with that underhanded racket. The prisoners wouldn't squeal because the guards were their main suppliers. The innocent guards wouldn't blow the whistle because the crooks would make it hell for them, maybe even kill them like they did Ed Debouch. Delores Kin was their only wild card. She had refused to play their game. Vince suspected she overheard their conversations during morning coffee and threatened to expose them. If they were busted, the consequences would be dire; they would lose their jobs, pensions, and probably do time. Their lives would be ruined. So, they entrapped Clifford, an innocent victim. Just thinking about it made Vince's blood boil.

Crossing the bridge was a mental Rubicon, bringing him out of his raging hell. His thoughts turned to home, family, and wife. She'd mentioned a surprise. *I wonder what that's all about. Did she receive an inheritance from her aunt who recently died? Or is she planning to have my parents over to celebrate the fourth of July? Maybe she's pregnant. Will John, Sam, and Sarah have another sibling? Stay cool, buddy. You'll find out soon enough.*

It was a long six-hour trip. Vince pulled in the driveway at nine that evening. Sue had the kids in bed, but they squealed when they heard the garage door open. John and Sam flew down the stairs.

"Daddy! Daddy's home!" Sam said, reaching out

with open arms. Vince picked her up and did the Daddy-daughter twirl. John was next with a big-hearted hug and a fist bump. Daddy and Mommy were both home and safe; the children would rest easy.

"Time for bed," Vince said. "We can play tomorrow."

As the children disappeared, Vince kissed Sue as his shoulders slumped into an embrace. He felt safe for the first time in three days.

"A lot has happened since our phone call two days ago." He pulled her over to the couch and described in minute detail the assault, the threats, the demands, and the wail of the police sirens. Sue listened without comment. When finished, he put his head on her shoulder and she tenderly kissed his forehead.

She chuckled and mumbled, "Sexy wife, eh?"

"I'm afraid I have to agree with that accusation," he said, drifting off.

"Do you want to know the secret now or later?" Sue asked, rousing him.

He grinned. "Now. I think I know but go ahead."

"What do you think it is?"

"We're going to have another baby?"

"You're right, but how did you know?"

"You announced your other three pregnancies the same way."

"So, you're saying it never was a secret?" Sue teased him with a poke in the side.

"Never was," Vince beamed. "But I have a secret wish."

"What's that?"

"I want another boy. Then, we'll have two of each— that would be super! Can you make that happen, please?"

Sue smiled. "We've got a fifty-fifty chance. We'll have the ultrasound in a couple of weeks, so we'll know by then. Can you wait that long?"

"Guess I don't have a choice."

Vince stood up, pulled her to her feet, and held her hand as the lovers ambled to their bedroom.

UP AT SIX O'CLOCK, Vince drove forty minutes from Powell to Lansing. He was very proud of his family; they were a bright, loving bunch. As much as he disliked the monotonous drive, and a job that involved tons of paperwork, he knew it would give his family a higher trajectory if he persisted with his state job. The day-to-day grind of his employment was a selfless contribution to his family's well-being. Sue and Vince were expecting their fourth child, so he renewed his commitment to the state of Michigan.

14   Stuck

Voiceless and battered, Clifford gave thanks for his brain, which was all he had left. He could read and think and form ideas. He had his book friends stacked up on both sides of his cot. At a moment's notice he could open one and slip into another reality. He ravenously consumed books about justice, crime, and the prison systems. One book, *All the King's Men* by Robert Penn Warren, grabbed Clifford's attention.

> *(The law) is like a single-bed blanket on a double bed, and three folks in the bed and a cold night. There ain't ever enough blanket to cover the case, no matter how much pulling or hauling … Hell, the law is like the pants you bought last year for a growing boy, but it is always this year and the seams are popped and the shankbone's to the breeze. The law is always too short and too tight for growing humankind.*

THE WEATHER WAS GOOD, so Clifford ventured out to the exercise yard. Simon sneaked up behind him and bumped him forward. Clifford turned around, not knowing whether to smile or glower at him. Ever since he was in Cellblock B, Simon joined in with the name-calling and nasty chants: "woman killer," "daddy hater," and "kitchen garbage."

"How're you doin', man?" Simon asked. Clifford scowled and ignored him. "Don't be mad at me," Simon continued. "I'm just doin' what I gots to do to survive this place. After solitary, I got so buggy, the psych-doc put me on brake fluid. I slept twenty-four-seven for a week."

"Sorry."

"And, I'm sorry you got the shaft. They's some f**king dirty guards 'round here."

"Line up! File out!" the guard on duty shouted. "Keep your mouths shut and your hands to yourself. Do you understand?"

"Yep," Simon and Clifford said in unison. They lined up and walked through the doorway into the bullpen. Two guards stared them down, driving them to opposite sides of the yard; their conversation ended abruptly.

I'll bet Simon has some dirt on the guards. Will he snitch or dummy up? I need to find out.

Yard time ended and the inmates filed inside. Clifford whispered, "Simon, meet me in the chapel this Sunday."

"I'll try."

"No talking, assholes!" The guards separated them.

The fear of losing his mind haunted Clifford. Reading and thinking forced him to keep a grip on reality. Just reaching for and touching a book reassured him; they were concrete proof there was life beyond the four walls of his cell. They could cage his body, deprive him of love, and trample on his self-esteem, but they could *not* control his mind. He would make sure of that. The horrors of Cellblock B were unimaginable. The chanting was the worst. Officer Blak led the chants, his favorite one being "daddy-hater." It was the same one he whispered brushing past him in the kitchen. Officer Blak had free rein to mortify him any time he was on duty. His voice ranged from an inaudible whisper to a loud rant. The jeers crucified Clifford—emotional torture. The loud crescendo of shouts bounced off the walls, so Clifford muffled the noise by covering his ears with a pillow.

"Coward. Ratz is a pussy," they mocked. Their laughter was an evil contagion.

The relationship between the keeper and the kept mystified Clifford. *Why do the inmates act like guards? Wouldn't it make more sense for us to support each other and band together?* He remembered reading the account of the Patty Hearst case in the newspapers. She identified with her abductors, took on their behaviors, followed their commands, and refused to testify against them. *I believe the reports called it the Stockholm Syndrome. I'll research it when I get to the library tomorrow. Have to keep my brain going.*

ON SUNDAY MORNING, A guard escorted Clifford to the chapel. He sat in the fourth row in front of the wooden statue of the Virgin Mary. This was the first time he had been to worship since his attempted suicide. He did not see Simon. The service began with the priest from St. Albans presiding. He read the passage in Philippians 4:8:

"Finally, brothers and sisters, whatever is true, whatever is noble, whatever is right, whatever is pure, whatever is lovely, whatever is admirable, if anything is excellent or praiseworthy, think about such things." Clifford liked the passage, but the homily was insipid, his message not helpful. The final hymn, however, was inspiring.

ALL THINGS BRIGHT AND BEAUTIFUL

All things bright and beautiful,
All creatures great and small,
All things wise and wonderful,
The Lord God made them all.
He gave us eyes to see them.
And lips that we might tell,
How great is God Almighty,
Who has made all things well.

Suddenly, harmony filled the room. Someone sang tenor, and a beautiful baritone joined in behind Clifford. He turned around to find Simon singing his heart out. Clifford was dumbfounded, surprised he could sing so well. Simon was sitting four rows behind him. On the way out, as Clifford filed by, Simon slipped a wad of something into his chest pocket. The guards watched them like hawks. Clifford trembled with fear, keeping his eyes focused straight ahead. He desperately hoped the guards wouldn't search him. Once back in his cell, he lay down and pretended to be asleep. He fished the wad out of his pocket, smoothed the wrinkles from the Kleenex, and read the note.

"Officer Black, Rodney Stine, and Trent Deter are jackpotting you. Denton Stokes is the mule. Sorry. Be careful."

Clifford read and reread the names. He knew what a mule was, but the word jackpotting confused him, so he decided to ask one of the legal beagles who pored over law books in the library.

"Can I ask you a question?" Clifford whispered to an inmate.

He looked up, squinted through thick coke-bottle glasses. "You just did."

"What does jackpotting mean?"

"It means an inmate is in prison because of trumped-up charges."

"Yeah, that describes me," Clifford said. "I'm being blamed for a murder I didn't commit."

"The Delores Kin murder?"

Clifford nodded.

"The murderer jackpotted you; you're the fall guy. You need to get yourself a good attorney."

"Who would you recommend?"

"Maggie Sweetwater is the best. The bitch is expensive and *anything but sweet*," he said.

"By the way, what's your name?

"Stew."

"What're you in for?" Clifford asked.

"Embezzlement."

"How do I get a hold of this Sweetwater?"

"I'd use the phone." Stew scribbled a number and handed it to Clifford.

"Thanks."

"If you need anything else, let me know." He smiled. "I hate crooked cops … just saying. Good luck."

Clifford walked to the guard standing by the library door and was escorted back to his cell. He slumped on his cot. *Where can I get money for a good lawyer? No damn options. Dad? I'm not sure he'll be willing. Dude, grow a pair. Go find out.*

DAVID AND SHARM RAN away together, finding solace in each other's arms. She couldn't tolerate the thought of losing her father. He was her only champion. Without him life would be unbearable. *Why would he commit suicide and leave her alone?* At least David was someone she could lean on, someone who could take care of her.

"I want to see Daddy," Sharm fluttered her eyelashes. "Will you drive me to Marquette, please?"

"I thought you wanted to go to Las Vegas to get married?"

"I want to see Daddy first."

"That's six hours up and back," David said.

"He tried to kill himself. I might never see him again."

"Oh, alright," he sighed and pulled over to the side of the road. Checking for traffic, he made a U-turn and changed direction.

THE REUNION HAPPENED IN the visitor's center.

"Sharmbee!" Clifford exclaimed in an ecstatic whisper. "I was worried I would never see you again."

"I was worried I would never see *you* again," Sharm repeated. "Why did you hurt yourself, Daddy? Life can't be that bad." Dark tears ran down her face from her mascara oozing off her eyelashes. Clifford caught a glint from her nose ring. *What the hell is that hideous thing? My Sharmbee looks like a whore. Is she rebelling? I can't look at it.* Clifford gazed at the floor.

"Yes, it was," he said. "They accused me of murdering someone I cared about and they trumped up evidence to prove it. I don't want to spend my life in prison, but it looks like I probably will."

"Maybe they'll find the person who really did it."

"Let's pray they do," Clifford said, looking down. "What's going on in your life?"

"Are you sure you want to know?" Sharm asked, trying not to make eye contact. "Like they say, sometimes ignorance is bliss."

Maybe I don't. Clifford paused.

"I'm not happy not knowing, so I might as well know."

"Oh, Daddy you're too much!" Sharm smiled. "I love you, and that will never change."

"I love you too, sweetie."

"David and I are running away."

"Where are you going?"

"Las Vegas to get married."

"What?" Clifford was livid. "You're *not* old enough!"

Her rebel sparked. "You only have to be sixteen to marry in Nevada."

"Are you sure?"

"Yes, I've checked," she said.

Clifford's throat tightened. He couldn't say another word. Frustration and disappointment choked him. Still, his love for her was steadfast and all consuming. *She's not my little girl anymore.* He exploded into sobs.

Sharm had never seen her father like that. In shock, her eyes widened and filled with tears. She swallowed hard and cleared her voice, getting ready to speak.

"Maybe I better go, Daddy, I'm making you miserable." She paused, stood up and pressed a kiss through the plexiglass.

Sharm's life is teetering on a razor's edge. Her future is grim. I had hoped she would learn from my mistakes, but that's not happening. It's like she's my shadow, living out my dark side. I still love her, and I know I would die for her if it came to that.

Clifford's eyes stayed glued to the floor as he walked back to his cell, an attempt to hide his tear-stained cheeks. Turning away from the bars and gawking prisoners, he tried to rest. He skipped two meals to sleep it off and woke up in the late evening, famished. After checking his stockpile of food under his cot, Clifford tried to satisfy his hunger with the usual peanut butter crackers and pop at room temperature, but he was still hungry.

I just have to forget about eating until breakfast ... I

feel like I'm in a deep pit and I can't find my way out. Is there anybody who can help me?

Clifford summoned the courage to call his father the next afternoon.

"Dad, this is Clifford."

After a long silence, Herman said, "What do you want, son?"

"I need help."

Another long silence.

"What goin' on?"

"I'm being blamed for a murder I didn't commit."

Clifford wanted to spill the names of the guards that Simon listed, but he knew his conversations were recorded. "I need an attorney. Neil, my last attorney, is just too far away. I have the name of a lawyer from Marquette who's supposed to be good."

"Sounds like you *do* need an attorney." Herman agreed. "Why are you calling me? Need my permission?"

"I need money to hire one," Clifford said point-blank. There was silence on the other end of the line.

"You've been expensive these last couple of years. I feel like I'm throwing money down a rat hole," Herman continued. "I'm still paying the bills from your last attorney."

"I'll pay you back, I promise."

"I don't know, son," Herman grumbled. "I don't have a lot of cash right now. I'm retired and Social Security doesn't pay much. I've got money for you in a trust when I die. Maybe I can reconfigure that, so you can get the money early."

"I need the money now, so do what you have to do."

"Alright, I'll get on it."

"MAGGIE SWEETWATER LAW OFFICES," a perky mechanical voice answered. "How can I help you?"

"This is Clifford Ratz. I need to talk to Maggie Sweetwater."

"I'm sorry, she's not in right now. Would you like to speak with one of her associates?"

"No, I want to talk with her. Can I leave a message?"

"Yes, hold on, I'll get you to her voicemail."

Her message spooked Clifford. It sounded just like Sharm. She had a husky voice, kind of sexy. "If you have a legal need or an itch to stitch, I have the remedy. Leave your name and number, and I'll get back to you."

Clifford felt optimistic. Maybe she would help him stop his slide into the snake pit.

For three days, Clifford sat in the phone room waiting for Maggie Sweetwater to call. Blak had to clear the call before he could talk with her.

"Ratz, Maggie Sweetwater is on the phone. That bitch has never helped anyone get out of prison yet. You're wasting your money." He rolled his eyes and handed over the phone. "Remember, only fifteen."

"Yes, this is Clifford Ratz."

"How can I help you?"

"I need a good lawyer."

"Well, I'm a lawyer but only as good as my last case. What's going on?"

"I've been wrongfully accused of a murder," he answered, looking around for Blak.

Clifford could hear Blak snigger from the other side of the room.

"Is it the Delores Kin murder?"

"Yeah."

"I was wondering when I'd get the call. That's a messy situation," Maggie opined. "We better find a time when we can talk privately at the prison."

"I like that idea, but first I need to know how much you charge."

"I need a five-thousand retainer up front and once that's used up, it's two-hundred-fifty an hour. If you're still interested, let me know the day and time for a visit."

"I'll get back to you sometime today or tomorrow."

Clifford thought the fee was reasonable. His next call was to his dad to check on the money.

"Dad, how are you coming with getting me money from the trust?"

"That's one tangled mess to try to undo. The bank trustees are hard to work with." Herman continued. "I had to hire a lawyer to convince them that you needed the money right now and that you have no other sources available."

"I appreciate your effort," Clifford said. "I talked with the attorney about an hour ago. She said her fee is five-thousand up front and two-hundred-fifty per hour after that. She has a reputation for being one tough attorney."

"Damn, son, that's a lot of money … Ah, to hell with it. I guess we don't have a choice."

Knowing he had money backing him eased Clifford's anxiety. Once again, he had to leave a message on Sweetwater's machine.

"One o'clock tomorrow works. I'm in Cellblock B."

15 Maggie Sweetwater

Never fear shadow. It simply means there's light shining somewhere nearby. —Ruth E. Renkel

"**R**atz? That Sweetwater woman is here to see you," Officer Blak said with an assessing stare. He mumbled, "Watch out. She's a real bitch," as they walked down the corridor.

Clifford's first impression of Maggie Sweetwater was her personification of passion. She was a country song waiting to be written. But that was only the first layer of who she really was. Taller than most men, she was close to six feet two inches tall, barefoot. As a descendant of the Ottawa band of Indians in the Upper Peninsula, she sported a full round face and wide-set eyes. The Ottawas were known as shrewd traders and the best barterers of the north country. Her fiery eyes were quick and discerning. Clifford sensed she knew good as well as she knew evil; nothing escaped her. Most importantly, she seemed to have a warm spot in her heart for victims. Clifford suspected she had represented many people like him over the years and was ready to pounce on any evildoer.

He liked her and was confident she'd get the job done. Long bangs hid most of her brown eyes. Her lips were ready to snap into a mean sneer at any moment. Each finger flaunted a flashy silver ring with turquoise stones. Underneath a dark blue suit jacket, she wore a peasant blouse with colorful beadwork. Her gathered blue skirt hit her leg mid-calf, and in three-inch stilettos, she towered over Clifford.

"Hello, I'm Maggie Sweetwater."

Being in her presence was more than sharing a room; he felt an empathetic understanding of his pain, almost like an embrace. There was a magnetic field drawing him to her. His feelings were similar to what he had felt for Delores, which was a deep respect for her strength and compassion.

"I'm Clifford Ratz," he said, reaching out for a firm handshake.

"How can I help you?"

Clifford began a long litany of his miserable time spent in Michigamme. He shared the incriminating events that led up to his incarceration. She got the entire story from his first brush with the law at fourteen, up to and including Delores's murder. It was like confessing to a trusted priest. She listened attentively.

"I've received inside information from Simon, another inmate," Clifford said. Reaching into his pocket, he gave her the wad of Kleenex with the names Simon scribbled. Maggie examined them and her brows lifted.

"Officers Blak, Deter, Stokes, and Stine," she read. "Those guys are trouble. I'll check this out. Well, Clifford, I think you have a solid case. I can help you," she said with a broad smile.

"I have money for your fee. My father is sending you the five-thousand retainer."

"I'll get the ball rolling. The first part is the discovery phase. Let's plan on meeting at the same time and place in a week. If you have any questions, call my office."

"Will do." Clifford nodded, and they shook hands.

Maggie strutted out the door, flinging her black braids over her shoulder.

That's one hell of a woman! She's like a tornado, hurricane, and volcano all rolled into one. It seems like she likes me well enough. I hope she's not put off by my scar. He rubbed his neck. Clifford smiled as he motioned Officer Blak to escort him back to his cell. *We've got the goods on you … You son of a bitch.*

THE FOLLOWING WEEK, AS Maggie entered the room, Clifford couldn't help but ogle her. He admired the way she looked, how she walked, her voice, and her elegant hand gestures. He yearned to be her lap dog, stroked and cuddled. Maggie, however, was all business. Placing her papers on the table, she got straight to the issues at hand.

"The prosecuting attorney shared compelling information. Denton Stokes is in custody," Maggie announced.

"No shit!"

"He broke into Vince Attwood's hotel room and threatened to harm his family if he didn't drop the investigation of the guards."

"Man, that dude's f**ked in the head!"

"This might wrap up quickly. They'll be checking the names on Simon's note today sometime."

"The guards are cannibals, and Officer Blak is the worst. He's known for stirring up mayhem in Cellblock B."

"My first husband was a full-blooded Indian and proud of it. He died in prison. He was a good man who cut deals with the wrong people," Maggie shared. "I'm pretty sure the guards egged them on." She looked down to suppress tears.

Clifford sensed she'd had a hard life; her compassion came from somewhere. Clifford grasped her hand and gently held it. Maggie looked up with tender eyes, slipped her hand out from under his, and placed it on her lap.

"I was determined to fight injustice, so I went to law school. I had two little boys and no money, but I had enough drive to conquer Mt. Everest." Clifford nodded with respect. Maggie sighed and walked out of the room, her heels clicking staccato on the concrete. Clifford cradled his head on his arms at the table and watched her leave. She took the warmth from the room with her, leaving him cold and empty.

MAGGIE WENT BACK TO her office and sorted through her previous cases. She was sure she had a case involving Officer Gene Blak. Her fingers flicked through her folders until she found it under the Ms—*Tyler Morse v. Offi-*

cer Gene Blak. Three years ago, she represented Tyler Morse, who witnessed a drug transaction and a money exchange between the warden and Blak. Tyler disclosed this information in a letter to his son, and he reported it to the Department of Corrections. Officer Blak and the warden denied the allegations, and the investigation was terminated. As a result, Officer Blak targeted Tyler and hammered him with an onslaught of emotional abuse. Tyler's son hired Maggie to defend his father. She wrote a strong letter reminding them of Tyler's right to sue if he was subjected to cruel and unusual punishment. Her letter successfully stopped the harassment, and Tyler was able to finish out his sentence without incident.

I thought the name sounded familiar. His reputation as a drug trafficker is probably warranted. I'll call the prosecuting attorney tomorrow to find out the status of the case against him.

"Dale, this is Maggie Sweetwater. Anything new happening with the Denton Stokes situation?"

"It's popping like popcorn," he quipped. "The investigators spent four hours questioning him. To pressure him into telling all for a reduced sentence, they reminded him of the mandatory prison time for burglary, battery, unlawful restraint, and extortion. He recognized himself on the security video and turned white as a ghost. He knows he's in deep shit."

"It isn't like you to push for a plea bargain."

"This time it's different," Dale said. "Those guys at Michigamme have been livin' on the edge of the law far too long. I wanna get the whole bunch of 'em."

"I know what you mean," Maggie added. "I previously defended an inmate who Blak harassed after he squealed on him about a drug deal he witnessed."

"If we play our cards right, we'll finish those guys."

"I'm the attorney for Clifford Ratz. They set him up for a fall. He's charged with the murder of Delores Kin."

"Well, sit tight. I'll have some news in a couple of days."

16   The Waiting Begins ...

Although Clifford trusted Maggie, his anxieties never left him. He paced back and forth in his cell day and night. One of the inmates taunted him. "Are youse a Ratz in a maze?" he said. Clifford thought about it and laughed, lifting his spirits a bit.

"No, I just know something big is coming down," he answered. "I feel like I'm stuck at the top of a Ferris wheel and someone took their hand off the go button. I want to get down and push it myself." He kept pacing.

What is Maggie up to? I don't want to hound her, but why doesn't she give me a call? She holds the key to my freedom ... and my heart. I write her letters every day but I'm too afraid to send them. I'm ashamed of the ugly scar on my neck. I hope that's not a turnoff for her.

He walked around the edge of the cell and touched each corner he passed. Walking in a trance, he was like a caged animal with nowhere to go and nothing to do.

"Ratz, you have a phone call," a guard announced.

"This is Maggie," she said. "I've got good news and not so good news."

"Give me the not so good news first."

"Denton Stokes is the only one so far who's been charged, however, they're working on a plea deal. If he implicates the others in the drug ring, he'll get a reduced sentence. Sit tight, and let the judicial process run its course."

"Maggie," Clifford said. "I—I would like to—see you—sometime."

"I know … But there are lots of other women out there who would love you. You're a really nice guy, Clifford, but I'm your attorney. Our attorney-client relationship needs to be protected and maintained … as is."

"I've never asked before, but are you married?"

"Yes."

"Okay, Maggie. I understand," Clifford said sadly.

"I'll give you a call in a couple of days. Goodbye."

Back in his cell, Clifford lay on his bunk, broken-hearted. *Maggie is out of reach. Maybe someday I'll find someone like her, but first I need her to get me out of this place.*

"CLIFFORD!" MAGGIE EXCLAIMED TWO days later on a phone call. "I have some great news. Denton Stokes signed a plea deal. He's become a CI, what they call a confidential informant, and because he doesn't have a previous criminal record, his information has credibility. The detectives will grill him for names, criminal activities he witnessed, and administer a lie-detector test. The next couple of days will be very interesting. I should have more information soon."

"Please, call as soon as you know something," Clifford pleaded.

"I will, possibly by the end of the week."

As the days merged together, he paced his cell, trying hard to keep the fog out of his brain. Prison life had aged him. He walked by the little mirror over his sink and gasped when he saw his hair thinning and turning gray. His voice was getting stronger—a little louder than a whisper, but the raised scar on his neck stayed an ugly purple-gray. No matter how hard he tried to pull himself straighter, his posture slumped forward. He drew a calendar on his cell wall to cross off the ticking hours of each day, urgently trying to take control of his life. Two days seemed so far off. He paced faster and faster until he literally jogged around his cell.

"Stop, Clifford. Stop!" the other prisoners shouted. "Asshole, stop, dammit!"

Clifford collapsed on his cot, curled into a fetal position, and slept. He woke up feeling entombed in a stygian darkness. *Am I losing my mind? I need to get a grip and fight for my sanity.* Strangely comforted by a low snore in the next cell, he remembered where he was, and that Maggie was fighting for him. He sat up to wait for the dawn, reassured by her promise that she would call him by the end of the week.

"CLIFFORD, THIS IS MAGGIE. Denton Stokes has implicated Gene Blak, Trent Deter, and Rodney Stine. He made it very clear they are the guards who murdered Delores Kin."

"So, that means I'm off the hook?" Clifford dropped to his knees, crying tears of gratitude.

"Slow down. They probably will dismiss this charge,

but it's going to take some time for the wheels of justice to turn. So, you *have* to be patient with the process," Maggie implored. "Furthermore, Stokes named you in his statement saying that you had nothing to do with Delores's murder." Maggie continued. "He characterized the murder as being a drug-related incident. The best statement from the CI is that you had *nothing* to do with the murder of Delores Kin."

"Maggie, I *have* to get *out* of this place!" Clifford cried. "Dear God, I want to get out of this place! What are my next steps?"

"I'll talk to the prosecuting attorney on Monday and ask to have your charges dropped. It depends on what he wants to do. If he wants to investigate further, that could take two years or more. Also, you have some time remaining on your previous conviction. I'll inform you of his plans."

"Two years! Two years!" Clifford shouted over the phone in his raspy voice. "I can't spend two more years in this hellhole. I'll go f**king nuts if I have to wait two days!"

"Clifford!" Maggie said. "You must be patient! Justice takes time … Now, enjoy your weekend. Goodbye."

The guard escorted Clifford back to his cell. *Enjoy my weekend? All I know are dull, boring hours that coalesce into a gray blob they call a day, which is indistinguishable from the day before. I feel like I'm sinking … sinking … sinking … Maggie, pull me up! Jesus, pull me up!*

Clifford prayed through the night and the next day. He fasted, sweated, and cried. His prison neighbors were strangely quiet as they watched his heart turn inside out.

Clifford opened his eyes and Simon grasped his cell bars, face distorted as he wedged between the bars, pushing to get as close to Clifford as he could. Simon's eyes were closed in supplication, tears streaming down his face.

"Simon, my friend," Clifford said. "Are you praying for me?"

"Yeah," Simon blubbered. "You's been treated real bad." Clifford nodded in agreement. Simon continued, "Them guards are gonna cook in hell!"

"Amen. They killed my friend, Delores. And then, the f**king bastards tried to hang me for it. Hell's too good a place for them."

"PHONE CALL FOR RATZ," a guard announced. Clifford stood up and was escorted to the community room. "She said her name was Sharm."

"Daddy, how are you?"

"Better than I was yesterday," he said. "What's goin' on with you?"

"David and I are married," Sharm offered. After a long pause, she added, "And, we're going to have a baby. We want to do it right this time."

"I hope it works out for you," Clifford spoke softly. "When's the baby due?"

"Sometime in the spring."

Clifford wanted to share what was going on with his case but didn't want to give her false hope. "I would like to meet the newborn."

"I'll try to bring the baby to see you, but I always

worry about the spring weather in Marquette. It's full of surprises."

"I look forward to holding the baby," Clifford smiled. "How's your grandpa and grandma doing?"

"Grandpa is grumpier, and Grandma is looking forward to being a great grandma."

"Life moves on. There's no stopping it," Clifford opined.

The transmissions cut off, replaced by white noise. Monday morning and afternoon came and went with no word from Maggie. In the evening, after her normal working hours, she called.

"I have wonderful news for you. The prosecutor's office worked all day on your case. They reviewed your file, consulted with Wayne Korhonen, and Davis Spar at the prison. They also contacted Vince Attwood from the Lansing office."

"So, what's the great news?"

"All of them, not just some of them, agree you should have the charges dismissed. But don't get your hopes up too high. I still have to contact Margaret Dunn, the top attorney at the Michigan Department of Corrections—she's a tough cookie. She'll be in her office tomorrow."

"So, I have to wait some more? Right?"

"We should have her answer by tomorrow," Maggie said. "The next step is setting a court date for the judge so he can review your case. It's important we get a date before the holidays because the courts shut down around that time. I'll call you tomorrow before the end of the business day."

"I'll be in the phone room, waiting."

17 A Mountain of Red Tape

"**M**s. Dunn, this is Maggie Sweetwater. I'm the attorney for Clifford Ratz. He's the prisoner accused of the murder of Delores Kin."

"Yes, I know the case. Vince Attwood filled me in on the details. Let me set up a conference call. I'll put you on speaker and have Vince join us." Maggie heard a few bleeps and a brief conversation before Vince chimed in.

"Hello, Maggie," Vince said. "I worked with you about six years ago on the Nate Ryder case."

"I vaguely remember him. It was an assault and battery between two inmates, if my memory serves me."

"Yes, it's a miracle Nate survived the assault," Vince said.

"I'm calling about another matter," Maggie said. "I'm representing Clifford Ratz, the accused in Delores Kin's murder."

"I've been following the case closely. I have a stake in that game. Officer Blak and Denton Stokes hog-tied me in my hotel room and threatened bodily harm to my family if I didn't stop investigating the prison guards. I want those bastards arrested."

"I'm aware of the incident. I'm calling because the prosecuting attorney wants to drop the charges against Mr. Ratz. I need approval from Ms. Dunn before we can set a date to have the case reviewed."

"I have complete confidence in Mr. Attwood," Margaret asserted. "He's been the investigator on this murder case from the beginning, and he strongly believes that Mr. Ratz was set up to take the fall for the guards. The evidence points to the guards as the guilty parties. You have *my* approval," Margaret said.

"Thank you," Maggie said. "I'll let you know if there are any changes."

"I'll call the prosecuting attorney and make sure the case goes smoothly from this end," Vince said. "The charges against Clifford should be dismissed."

Maggie hung up and smiled. *Looks like it's unanimous; everyone thinks the charges are bogus. But, the opinion of the judge is the only one that matters.*

Getting a hearing with the judge before the holidays was no simple matter. She called the prosecuting attorney to pressure him for a court date, but his secretary answered. "Dale won't be in until Monday. Do you want to leave him a message?"

"No, I'll leave the message with you," Maggie said, frustrated by the red tape. "When he calls you at the end of the day, let him know I need a court date for my client, Clifford Ratz—he's been in a bad place far too long."

The prosecuting attorney called first thing the next morning. "Maggie, this is Dale. I took another case off the docket after it settled, so I'll slip you into that slot. It's the twenty-fifth of October. Does that work for you?"

"Yes, that works," she replied.

"I'll firm up that date and get back to you."

"Thanks, Dale."

With the approaching court date for the hearing, Clifford recognized the wisdom of Maggie's words: "The wheels of justice move slowly." A month away seemed like an eternity. Clifford had much too much time to reflect on the horrors of prison life. *These lost souls haunt the hallways and evil predators at the top of the food chain cannibalize the weak. Victimization is as common as breathing. It's time to leave and never, ever come back.*

18   Showdown

"All rise," the bailiff announced. "The Ninety-Sixth District Court of Marquette County is in session with the Honorable Judge Roger Magnus presiding."

"You may be seated," Judge Magnus said. Following the shuffle of feet and squeaks of the benches, the judge called out, "Clifford Ratz, please stand."

Maggie and Clifford stood. They looked squarely at the judge.

Maggie navigated the courtroom like a pro. Her self-assured presence evoked confidence. Clifford was certain she could be mistaken for an attorney trained at Harvard or Yale. She had that presence about her—no second guessing, keenly competent, and seasoned. He watched her interact with the judge like the professional she was, her eyes even and fixed on him.

"Mr. Ratz," Judge Magnus said, "Over the last month, I have pored over your file, and had several conversations with Wayne Korhonen about your behavior at Michigamme State Prison. I especially took time to review the charges against you."

The courtroom doors burst open and then slammed

with a loud bang against the walls, echoing in the room. Gene Blak barged in.

"This is a miscarriage of justice!" he shouted. "Ratz is guilty! Three witnesses saw him at the scene. I know he's the killer, " he yelled, shaking his fist at Clifford.

Fearing mortal danger, Maggie and Clifford dropped to their knees and ducked behind their chairs and under the table. The spectators, expecting gunfire, fell to the floor and covered their ears. In a flash, the bailiff subdued Blak and handcuffed him. A fellow officer patted him down but didn't find a weapon. Blak's eyes were fierce like daggers. He squirmed and spit at the bailiff.

"Get that man out of here!" Judge Magnus demanded. "Take him to the county jail and book him on contempt … as a starter." The spectators crawled to their knees and slowly stood up, some shaking. They hung on to the benches in front of them. Maggie and Clifford didn't stand until they were sure Blak was out of the courthouse.

"We'll have a fifteen-minute recess," the judge ordered, briskly pounding his gavel.

Clifford was shaking so hard, he could barely stand. They chose to remain seated in the courtroom until the recess was over.

"Officer Blak is a raving lunatic," Clifford whispered.

"He knows his number's up," Maggie said.

"But can't he see this makes him look guilty as sin?"

"He's a sociopath and a hothead. He chooses to believe his own lies," Maggie said.

"I just want to get as far away from him as I can."

"I don't blame you," Maggie said. "The ones I hate the most are those who lie to hurt others. They don't deserve to walk the earth."

"All rise!" the bailiff announced. "The Ninety-Sixth District Court of Marquette County is in session with the Honorable Judge Roger Magnus presiding."

"You may be seated," the judge said. "Mr. Clifford Ratz, please stand. I have reviewed your file, and it is clear you should not have been charged with this crime. The charges are dismissed."

"Thank you, your Honor," Clifford exhaled his tension, and tears formed.

"Furthermore, I will remand this case to the parole board for review. They will make any further determinations. It is clear from my discussions with the warden you have not imbibed or illegally trafficked drugs while in prison. You have a clean record."

"Your Honor, permission to speak," Maggie requested.

"Proceed."

"Mr. Ratz has served five months in Cellblock B in a maximum-security unit, and Officer Gene Blak has tortured him." Maggie handed the judge a document specifying the incidents of abuse. "Mr. Ratz was originally placed in Cellblock O, a minimum-security unit," Maggie continued. "Please consider paroling Mr. Ratz with time served. At the very least, please order that Mr. Ratz be returned to Cellblock O until this matter is resolved."

"Ms. Sweetwater, I will take that under advisement and get back to you."

"Thank you, your Honor."

Clifford squeezed Maggie's hand, hugged her, and whispered, "Life is sweet." She smiled and they walked out of the courtroom together.

"I'll give the judge a couple of days to think about my recommendations, and then I'll give him a call," Maggie said. "This might turn out very well for you."

"Maggie, thank you for all you've done," Clifford smiled. An officer approached and took him back to his cell.

Here I am in Cellblock B, but at least Officer Blak won't be there to harass me. His ass is sitting in the county jail. Clifford walked past Simon on the way to his cell. *This might be the last time I see Simon. We've been through a lot. I'd like to help him. I wonder if Maggie could find a way to get him out of here. First, I must get out of here myself, get a job, and then I can pay for his defense.*

"Chapel on Sunday?"

"You got it," Simon replied.

IT WAS ALMOST NOVEMBER, and snow buried the north country. Glare ice coated the sidewalks and the chapel was freezing cold. Nobody was there except Clifford and his guard. *Am I early? Where's Simon?* He took his usual seat in front of the wooden statute of the Virgin Mary and waited, closing his eyes. *Dear Jesus, you've heard my prayer—I am eternally grateful. Help me be patient and find the resolve to take the next steps in my life. Trusting you is how I survived, and my only hope for a better future. Amen.*

Someone turned on the heat, and warmth emanated from the four corners of the chapel. The priest welcomed Simon and Clifford, the only two present, and read the scriptures from Romans 15:13: "May the God of hope fill you with all joy and peace in believing, so that by the power of the Holy Spirit, you may abound in hope."

"Gentlemen, I would like to end my homily with a poem written in 1918 by Theodore Shackelford. He speaks to us even today."

O Hope! into my darkened life
Thou hast so oft' descended;
My helpless head from failure's blows,
Thou hast defended;
When circumstances hard, and mean,
Which I could not control,
Did make me bow my head with shame,
Thou comforted my soul.

When stumbling blocks lay all around,
And when my steps did falter,
Then did thy sacred fires burn
Upon my soul's high altar.
Oft' was my very blackest night
Scarce darker than my day,
But thou dispelled those clouds of doubt,
And cheered my lonely way.

E'en when I saw my friends forsake,
And leave me for another,
Then thou, O Hope, didst cling to me
Still closer than a brother;

Thus, with thee near I groped my way
Through that long, gloomy night
Till now; yes, as I speak, behold,
I see the light! the light!

Simon and Clifford sat motionless, captivated by the words.

"Clifford," Simon said haltingly. "Youse bring out the best in me. I hope you get out of this place and have a good life."

"I think it will happen. Simon, you're a good friend," Clifford said, turning to look at his buddy. "Promise me you'll never lose hope?"

Humbled by Clifford's kindness, Simon answered. "I promise."

"RATZ," THE GUARD SAID. "Pack up your things and come with me."

"What? Where?" Clifford said waking up from a nap. His eyes were half shut, and his brain foggy.

"I have orders to take you to Cellblock O."

"Oh, the order came through. Wonderful!" Clifford shouted. The prisoners in Cellblock B clanged cups and silverware on their bars, and started shouting. Some clapped and cheered, while others yelled threats.

"Dirty dog Clifford got a break! Not fair. Sleep with one eye open, pussy boy," someone shouted.

Clifford scrambled to collect his clothes, the snacks under his cot, bathroom paraphernalia, and the mountain of books he was planning to read.

"You've got a lot of shit," the guard remarked. "I'll get a pushcart." Clifford stacked it full, pushed it down the hall, and gave Simon a fist bump. Their eyes met for a brief moment, and without words, they said what they needed to say.

Clifford turned and walked out of Cellblock B. *I'm finally out of this hell hole. Maybe, just maybe, freedom is around the corner.*

"RATZ," THE OFFICER ANNOUNCED. "Phone call."

In the middle of reading a book, he sat up and stepped around his clutter. "Who's calling me?" Clifford asked the officer.

"Ms. Sweetwater."

"Hi, Maggie," Clifford said. "I hope you have good news. I'm sick and tired of waiting."

"I don't know. Judge Magnus has set another court date for the end of the week.

"Why?"

"I don't have an answer for that."

19   Echoes of Freedom

Sue, hugely pregnant with their fourth child, answered the house phone.

"Vince here. I just heard they released Clifford from prison."

"Great news!" Sue exclaimed. "This is one of those times the justice system worked."

"Well, sorta," Vince opined. "It worked further down the pipeline, but I believe prison is not the place for nonviolent drug criminals. It hardens them. You create bigger problems for society. I called to ask your opinion on something."

"I'm all ears."

"Your friend Jane Bartman runs a transitional house for prisoners south of town. Right?"

"Yes, I've known Jane for years."

"Does she have a good reputation?" Vince asked.

"The best. She's always been good with people, organized and professional."

"I've heard that too. I'm going to call her to see if she has room for Clifford. He needs a break."

"I'D LIKE TO SPEAK with Jane Bartman."

"I'm Jane, how can I help?"

"This is Vince, Sue Attwood's husband."

"How is Sue doing?"

"She's pregnant with our fourth child. The due date is at the end of the month."

"Fourth!" Jane exclaimed. "You have three going on four children, now? I lost track after two. Congratulations."

"Thanks."

"Do you know if it's a girl or a boy?"

"Sue knows, but she's keeping it a secret."

"Say hello to Sue for me. You work for the DOC, right?"

"Yes, I do. I'm hoping you can help me. I have an inmate from Michigamme State Prison being released on time served in a few days. The parole board is suggesting a transitional home for him. You come highly recommended. Sue can't say enough good things about you. My question is: do you have any openings?"

"As of noon tomorrow, I have an opening. One of the residents found an apartment and is moving out."

"Could you put a hold on that opening? Clifford Ratz is the name of the inmate, and I believe he'd do well under your care. He's nonviolent, and just a nice guy."

"I'll reserve the spot, but get his records to me ASAP. I need to run it past the board."

"I'll call the warden as soon as we hang up and get back to you with that information"

"PLEASE PUT THE WARDEN on the phone." Vince's voice was edgy—still miffed by his last encounter with the warden. He remembered Wayne disconnecting his call to the police. He still wondered what part he played in the drug trafficking problem in his prison.

"What's this about?" the receptionist asked.

"Clifford Ratz."

"Hold on," she said.

"Wayne here. What do you want?"

"I found a suitable placement for Clifford. They're holding a spot for him in a transitional housing unit."

"In Lansing?"

"No, Grand Rapids."

"Is that the one run by Jane Bartman?"

"Yes."

"She has a good reputation," Wayne said. "I've set aside one hundred dollars for his gate money. It should be enough for a bus ticket to Grand Rapids. I'll give my stamp of approval for that placement."

"I have another favor to ask."

"What's that?"

"Jane needs his records ASAP to run it by her board and make sure the placement is right."

"I'll get on that this afternoon."

"Thank you." Vince was certain hyper-conscientious Wayne would get it done.

"CLIFFORD, THE WARDEN WANTS to see you," the officer announced.

"Do I need to take my things?"

"Yes."

Clifford packed his belongings in a cardboard banker's box his mother sent along with his favorite snacks and a package of civilian clothes. He had all the clothes he needed for his release date—a Carhartt jacket, gloves, sweatshirt, boots, slacks, and new underwear. Clifford was looking forward to seeing his family on Thanksgiving Day.

"Could we stop by the prison library on the way?" Clifford asked. "I have a couple of books to return."

"Sure."

Clifford had a spring in his step—he sensed the finality of this chapter in his life. He turned around and gave one sweeping glance at what was behind him. He was stung by the oppressive misery on the faces of the other inmates, the scratched steel bars, and the dirty white chipped walls. Sad—so sad. The only people from the prison he would miss would be Simon and Delores. *Simon's story is not over. I'll see him again. I'll never see Delores again in this life.* Clifford looked at the bindings of his half-read books before he handed them to the librarian. He'd have to wait to finish reading them until he was a free man.

"Well, Clifford your time here at Michigamme has been eventful to say the least," the warden said. "The judge is releasing you on time served. You're a very lucky man."

"If you say so," Clifford said, his face deadpan.

"I have one hundred dollars gate money for you. According to the parole board, you have to wear an electronic monitor on your ankle. I'll have a guard secure the device before you leave. Once you arrive in Grand Rapids, your next step is living in a transitional housing unit. You have been placed at a facility with a good reputation. A guard will drive you to the bus station in Marquette and make sure you get on the bus and head in the right direction. The bus leaves at twelve thirty in the morning and you'll arrive in Grand Rapids about two thirty in the afternoon the next day. That's fourteen hours of riding, but you'll be able to sleep. I'll have Travis pack a couple of bags of food for your trip," the warden continued. "There'll be a police officer waiting for you at the bus station in Grand Rapids and he'll drive you to the housing unit. Once there, ask for Jane Bartman. She'll make sure you follow the terms of your parole." The warden paused. "Questions?"

"I can't think of any."

"All the best. Remember, a life of crime only brings misery."

Clifford was in complete agreement. Wayne Korhonen—the man, not the warden—reached out to shake Clifford's hand. It was firm.

He was escorted to a holding cell near the intake office, and he waited for the van to take him to the bus station.

Finally, Clifford climbed into the prison van and turned around for one last look. *It's darker and more ominous than Count Dracula's castle.* Determined to focus on what was ahead, he fastened his seat belt.

No chains, no handcuffs, no strip searches, no condemnations, and no more verbal abuse. Clifford smiled as he cruised by the dimly lit streets of the city of Marquette. Michigamme Prison chronicled a year of his life, but it felt like an eternity. The prison had wounded his soul and created scars that would never go away. The newfound freedom was only a faint echo of what he had been before all this began. He would never regain the innocence of that first freedom before prison changed everything. Now, it all seemed more complicated and more sinister. *I doubt that will ever change.*

THE BUS RIDE WAS refreshingly lonely. Pitch dark outside, the inside of the bus was lit only by the red EXIT sign. The smooth hum of the tires and the faint gasoline smell lulled him to sleep. Clifford and two other men on the bus slept through much of the journey. Nothing was visible for miles except for an occasional yard light beaming from a farmstead. Clifford woke to a foghorn sounding in the distance. He looked out to see hovering lights outlining the Soo Locks in Sault Ste. Marie. He slept again until he felt the sun through the window anointing his head with warmth. It was daybreak, and the sunrise glowed across the horizon illuminating the Mackinac Bridge. This majestic bridge inspired Clifford time and time again. He watched Lake Michigan and Lake Huron flow together, and he recollected the time spent with Simon traveling to Marquette. It seemed like ages ago.

At the next stop, several passengers boarded. Three women and two men moved through the narrow aisle. They clung together like family. Two women sat across from Clifford and the men claimed the seat behind them, but the third woman chose to sit next to Clifford. She was an older woman who wore a dark coat that made her look like a woolly mammoth. Clifford could barely see her face, which was hidden by a paisley kerchief. Clifford sighed, leaned his head against the window, and tried to nap.

To his surprise, his electronic ankle monitor began signaling. It sounded like a low rumbling fart with intermittent pauses. Clifford panicked. *Shit! How do I get this thing to stop?* He bent forward, lifted his pant leg, and looked for some kind of button. There was nothing but a plain strap locked on his ankle. *I wonder why the GPS is sounding off. Wayne didn't tell me what to do if this happened. Should I explain what's happening to the woman next to me?* She ignored the first few sounds, but soon she raised her head and gave him a puzzled look.

"I'm sorry, ma'am," Clifford said. "I am wearing a monitor around my ankle and I'm not sure why it's making this sound."

"What's a monitor?" she asked with a thick accent.

"I was released from the prison in Marquette. The monitor is part of the condition for early release."

"You prisoner?"

"Not anymore." At that confession, she stood, and in a huff, found another seat. Clifford's insides churned. *What if this is how I'll be treated in the free world? I feel like a social outcast.* He hung his head, closed his eyes, and forced himself to ignore it. Thankfully, the monitor stopped signaling in five minutes.

The sights along the highway drew Clifford's attention away from his humiliation. He refused to feel sorry for himself. *She doesn't know what I've been through. I know I can find something worth living for. I'll be a grandfather soon. Mom and Sharm are waiting for me. I'm even looking forward to seeing Dad.*

The bus stopped in Charlevoix to gas up. Clifford had leftover change in his pocket from the gate money, so he hopped off the bus and went inside to buy a candy bar. He bought a copy of the *Detroit Free Press* to see what was happening. The newspapers in prison were always a week or two old. Reading current news was a luxury. The front-page headlines were the Iran-Contra affair; the DC-9 Continental Airlines crash in Denver, killing twenty-eight; and the Korean Air 707 explosion. London was suffering from the fire at the King's Cross tube station, with thirty-one dead. *The world hasn't changed a bit, but it's better than the crap I endured in prison. I can run away from it.*

Clifford climbed back on the bus, brushed by the group of five, took his banker's box out of the overhead, and moved to the back. He enjoyed the breathtaking views of Lake Michigan and the east and west bays of Traverse City.

The rolling panoramic views on Highway 131 heading south toward Grand Rapids were magnificent. The traffic increased an hour before the bus approached the city. Church spires and modern glass-plated office buildings were part of Grand Rapids's skyline. The bus driver slipped around the northern section of downtown on Highway 131 and exited to the Indian Trails Bus Depot. Clifford stood, grabbed his banker's box, and waited patiently for those ahead of him to disembark. He ducked to look out the windows and scanned the depot for a police officer. He'd have to wait to go inside to get a better view. The officer was just where the warden said he would be. He recognized Clifford and the two made eye contact. The officer approached and shook Clifford's hand.

"Enjoying your freedom?" he asked.

"Yeah," Clifford smiled.

"We'll head south to Jane Bartman's place. You're a lucky man to get a placement there; she treats ex-cons like family. She'll greet you at the door and give you a tour." The officer drove south to the facility and pulled up by the curb to a green, two-story house in a residential area. "This is it."

The officer escorted Clifford to the door. "Jane, I'd like you to meet Clifford." She greeted him, just shy of hugging.

She was an animated, squat woman with loads of energy. She was so welcoming he couldn't stop smiling. *She looks and acts just like Delores.*

"Welcome, Clifford," Jane said, extending a hand. "Set your box in the corner over there and I'll give you a tour. Your bedroom is on the first floor, and Matt is your roommate. You'll have one of the twin beds." Jane continued, "We rotate chores for everyone who lives here. You're on mopping duty this week. Here's the closet with the mops. Mop the kitchen floor after dinner every night, and the bathroom two times a week. Any questions?"

"Do we eat dinner together?" Clifford said in his raspy whisper.

"Yes," Jane answered, puzzled by his voice.

"Do you live here?"

"No, I live next door, but I spend most of my waking hours here. Richard is in charge when I'm not here," Jane continued. "A requirement for living here is attending AA meetings every day, seven days a week—it meets at the VFW hall just down the street."

"I'm not an alcoholic," Clifford said abruptly.

"Maybe not, but something you did got you in trouble with the law. The twelve-step program is the best there is, and it keeps you on the right track. Also, we have a group meeting about the goings-on in the house every Wednesday at noon. That's when we have a pizza lunch. There are eight of us here."

"Where is everybody?" Clifford didn't see a single soul.

"At their jobs. Everyone here works in the community. With Thanksgiving and Christmas around the corner, there's always a need for workers. I'm waiting for a call from a local baker. He packages Christmas goodies. I think you'd like that job. Oh, before I forget to mention it, a van from Grace Church comes here at nine on Sunday mornings to pick up whoever wants to go to church. I go there myself; they have a well-attended contemporary service."

Sensing the tour was over, he went back to the foyer to get his box and brought it to his bedroom. "I like to read. Is there a library nearby?" he asked as he met her in the hallway.

"It's five blocks east of here. But the terms of your parole don't allow you to go to the library. Your tether will be programmed for this house, church, AA meetings, and your job. We'll go over those instructions once you've settled in your room. In the meantime, if you want books from the library, I can pick them up for you."

"Thank you. I would appreciate that," Clifford rasped. He understood why Jane had a good reputation. She cared.

The privacy of being alone in his room was wonderful. Clifford took the clothes out of his box and put them in the drawers and hung up his jacket and shirts in the empty closet. He stashed the treats his mother sent in the nightstand next to his bed. Stretching out on the bed, he felt like a young boy visiting a friend's house. The bed was more comfortable than the prison cot, and it was quiet. Not having the chaos and mayhem around him was a great blessing. After a brief power nap, he woke to sounds in the kitchen. In his mind's eye he saw the refrigerator opening and closing, heard feet shuffling and pans clanking. *I wonder what the kitchen crew is making for dinner. Mmm, onions frying, and hamburger browning. Maybe we're having sloppy joes or spaghetti with meat sauce.* He heard the clanking and sliding of the dishes and flatware being carried from the kitchen to the dining table. Certain the food was close to being served, Clifford walked out of his bedroom.

"Hey, the new guy's here. Add another plate," the kitchen boss shouted. "Hope you like spaghetti."

Clifford nodded. He gave a thumbs up—his voice was odd, so gestures worked better sometimes.

"I'm Matt, and chief cook this week."

"I'm Clifford."

"Have a seat; the food is on the table."

Clifford found a chair closest to his bedroom door and looked mostly at his plate. He was comforted by the easy laughter and good-natured kidding. Seven men, including Clifford, sat around a large round table. Table manners varied. Elbows and spills were ignored. There was an air of tolerance; all were accepted.

"Have you met Jane?" asked an ex-con.

"Yes."

"She really makes this place hum. My name is Josh. What's yours?

"Clifford."

"Are you from around these parts?" Josh asked.

"I'm from Mason, near Lansing."

"I know the town. I have an uncle who lives there. How did you get here?"

"The warden from the prison in the UP sent me here."

"Usually, they send you to a unit in your hometown. Anyhow, welcome. This place is the best."

CLIFFORD WASN'T SURE IF Jane's place was the best. Maybe it was, or maybe it seemed best because prison was the worst. Anything, even a chicken coop, would have been better than prison. He was skittish about AA; it was like the first taste of sour medicine, but it proved to be helpful. Clifford realized his addiction was marijuana, and once he accepted that he needed help, he made steady progress. Taking a moral inventory of himself was a kicker, but he persevered through the difficult self-assessment. It took Clifford ninety days to work through the twelve steps, which was the required length of time at transitional housing. *Maybe they understand that it takes ninety days to make it work. It must be part of the plan.*

Three months quickly disappeared. He got along well with his roommate, Matt. Only one incident shook him to the core. Clifford was able to save money from his work at the bakery. One Friday, he cashed his check at the bank and planned to start repaying his dad back for the lawyer he hired. His mom and dad came for a visit on Sunday afternoon, so he hid the money in an envelope under his bed. Sunday morning, when he got home from church, the money was gone. Someone had stolen it. Clifford was baffled and angry. Who did it? How did they know where it was? He brought it up at the Wednesday group meeting, but no one talked. He talked to Jane about it, and she suggested that he buy a mini-safe.

"Those safes aren't very secure. Someone could probably open it with a screwdriver," Clifford said.

"You're probably right. It would just slow 'em down, but they wouldn't want anyone seeing them carrying it out of your room," she answered.

"Does this happen often?"

"Yes, these guys are ex-cons and when they get the whiff of money lying around, they can't stop themselves."

"I'll just keep it on my person or in the bank," Clifford said.

"That's the best way to go."

CLIFFORD WORKED EXTRA HARD improving the relationships with his family. He knew he was a changed person,
but his parents saw him the way he used to be, a miserable failure. His parents were ashamed of his criminal behavior, so he accepted any affection they gave
him with gratitude. He had gained insight and wisdom
throughout his harrowing ordeals. Herman appreciated
the efforts Clifford made to pay back the loan. Clifford
knew he was on the right track when his father gave him
an especially warm hug at the end of the visit.

Sharm and David were another story. They came to
visit him one Sunday afternoon. Sharm was miserable.
She was seven months pregnant and ready to pick a fight
with anyone who looked at her wrong. David needed a
cigarette, so Clifford set three chairs around the patio
table on the deck. He wanted to follow the rules of the
house.

"When's the baby due?" Clifford asked.

"I've told you a million times," Sharm snapped. "April
fourth."

"I'd like to buy something for the baby," Clifford
appeased. "What do you need?"

"Everything."

"Okay, what do you need most?"

"A crib," David chimed in. "We have a small apartment, so we'd have to put the crib in the living room
close to our bedroom door."

"If we don't get a crib, we'd have to pull out a dresser
drawer and put the baby there," Sharm grumbled.

"I'll get you a crib, but I don't have a car. I'll order one from Sears in Lansing and have them deliver it to your apartment."

"That would be nice of you," David said. Clifford stood up.

"I'm on the supper crew, so I have to get dinner started. I'll call you when I get the delivery date and time from Sears. Take care, and good seeing you." *I don't think those two are going to make it. Sometimes there's never enough wisdom, love, or money to make it right. They didn't even ask about my freedom and how my life has changed. That's okay. I'll help anyway I can. I hope they're not beyond it.*

Clifford was grateful for much of his new circumstances. His work at the bakery was a low-pressure position. He liked working with food since his time with Delores in the prison kitchen gave him a good skill set. He packaged holiday cookies through Christmas and New Year. They asked him to stay on through Valentine's Day. Clifford liked his boss; Raymond was a short wiry guy with an easy laugh. Every break, Raymond stepped outside the back door to smoke a couple of cigarettes. Clifford joined him to chat and they talked about the weather and politics. Clifford's raspy voice didn't seem to bother him. He just listened more intently to make out the words through his throaty crackle. Working through Valentine's Day would just about complete his three-month stay in transitional housing.

"CLIFFORD, YOUR THREE MONTHS here are almost over.

You and I need to set up a plan for your next steps," Jane said. "What time do you usually get home from work?"

"I'm usually home by three. I take a short nap before supper."

"Let's set up a meeting around four. Would that work?"

"Tomorrow or Wednesday would work best for me."

"Okay, tomorrow at four it is," Jane said.

Clifford was hoping she could find a way to get the tether off his ankle. He was self-conscious when the low rumble sounded without warning. He found out the weird noise came from the GPS checking on his where-abouts.

"YOU'VE DONE A BANG-UP job here," Jane smiled. "You and Matt were a great team. Raymond thinks the world of you and is sad to see you go. You've followed the terms of your parole and have done your chores around here without complaining."

"Speaking of compliance, when can I get this tether off?"

"I'm not sure. Let me check."

Jane leafed through his file. "It says here that you have to wear it for a minimum of six months, but longer if you break the terms of parole."

"I guess I have to be patient," Clifford sighed.

"There is something important we need to talk about," Jane continued. "Raymond praised your work ethic and your skill set, but he shared the frustration he had with your voice. He couldn't recommend you working with the public."

"What do you mean? Did he say my voice was offensive or too soft?" Clifford asked.

"Perhaps he means that you would put people off. Communicating with the public is tricky, and a whispery voice would get in the way of getting the message across."

"Oh."

"Sometimes I have to strain to hear you," Jane said. "The reason I brought this up is because it's part of our job to point you in the direction of suitable employment. Working with the public is not a good option for you. I've made an appointment for you with a career counselor this Thursday at two in the afternoon. I've talked to Raymond about dismissing you early from work on that day."

Clifford was silent and dejected. "I guess Thursday would be fine."

"Good. I'll arrange transportation."

Walking back to his bedroom, his shoulders slumped. *Is my old depression coming back for an unwelcomed visit? I regret attempting suicide—I cut myself off at the knees. I feel like I'm doing the dog paddle in ten-foot waves. How can I find a job and support myself? Sharm isn't doing well, and I need money and a car to be able to help her.*

Thursday came, and Jane drove Clifford to the counseling office. He walked into a testing center and was given a battery of tests. It took three hours to finish all the assessments and he never even met the counselor. The receptionist scheduled an appointment for Clifford to come back in a week.

That evening, Matt and Clifford settled down for bed.

"My daughter Sharm is pregnant and really bitchy," Clifford said.

"Hormones can really mess with one's head, going up and down," Matt said as he mimicked riding the waves. "Being pregnant is a temporary condition, so 'this too shall pass' puts things into perspective."

"Seems like God could have figured a better way to keep our species going."

"I couldn't agree with you more," Matt laughed. "Lights out!"

CLIFFORD WAS EAGER FOR the appointment with the career counselor. The receptionist walked him down the hall and introduced Mr. Freeman.

"Have a seat," Mr. Freeman continued. "I've had a chance to review your tests, and the results are quite interesting." Clifford listened intently. "Your overall IQ is 129 and in the superior range, which means you are in the top five percent. The *Big Five Personality Assessment* presented a lot of information about who you are. You scored high on introversion, low on openness, high on agreeableness, very high on conscientiousness, and high on neuroticism. Putting that in plain English, you are disciplined, careful, and helpful. Also, you tend to be practical, prefer routines, and generally are thoughtful and reserved. Unfortunately, you are anxious and pessimistic, which can undercut any confidence you may have, which compromises your self-esteem as well."

Clifford was amazed by the results. *I should have had this done before. It would have helped me find a better path.* "What's next? What do I do with this information?"

"Good question, Mr. Ratz," Mr. Freeman answered. "First of all, you are bright and have a lot to offer."

"Raymond, the boss I have now, says because of my vocal injury, I can't work with the public."

"I see where he's coming from. I don't see you as a public speaker, but you should be able to find a job that pays well with the abilities you have. Some of the jobs that would be behind the scenes would be an accountant, data analyst, IT consultant, scientist, librarian, software developer, or technical writer." Mr. Freeman continued. "You will need to go back to school, but the test results indicate you would be a very good student."

As he left the counseling center, Mr. Freeman's summary flashed through his brain. The big five inventory made so much sense to Clifford. *Every ex-con should be evaluated and pointed in a better direction. Once out of prison, ex-cons are devoured by wolves, which forces them back into a life of crime. Maybe if I had gone into counseling sooner, I would have avoided prison. Where do I go from here? I'm broke, no money anywhere, and I need a job.*

20 The Attwood Farm

Vince and Sue had always dreamed about owning a farm. "It's a good place to raise a family," they would say in unison. "The kids would learn responsibility by doing chores, and they'd learn to love animals." Vince grew up on a farm, but Sue was raised in a suburb of a big city and had no idea how much work a farm required.

Shortly after Christmas, Vince and Sue had another addition to their family, baby Bertram. Vince got the boy he wanted. Bert became his nickname and he was a happy little fella. Vince and Sue were satisfied because they had a balanced family, two boys and two girls. The four children had boundless energy. From sunup to sundown, they played tag, climbed trees, crafted mud pies, and enjoyed their menagerie of animals on the farm.

As each year passed, the list of animals grew longer and the animals larger. They started with a sheltie named Sweet Pea, graduated to a full-sized collie, and then, a golden Labrador. Each dog became part of the family. The family circle widened to include several rabbits, two pygmy goats, a flock of chickens, a calf, a quarter horse, and an Arabian horse. As the children grew older, Vince hoped they would shoulder the responsibility of their pets and maybe participate in local 4-H activities.

Driving the children to school, doing laundry, making meals, and organizing doctor appointments for both the kids and the pets spread Sue's energies thin. The farm demanded a whirlwind of activity and because Vince was the main breadwinner, he had to drive two hours to get to and from Lansing for employment. The farm chores and working at the Department of Corrections exhausted him. Never deterred by rain, sleet, or snow, he was on the road by seven in the morning.

As his children got older, Vince planned to turn over the farm chores to them.

"Kids, come here!" Vince shouted. The oldest three children followed him like the pied piper down to the barn. "Here's a fifty-pound bag of chicken feed. Let me show you how to open it." The children watched as he turned the bag around. "This is the front because it has a picture of a chicken." The wide-eyed children nodded. "On the left side is a string. Do you see it?" The children nodded again. "Pull this string and the bag will open up all the way from one side to the other. It's easy. It's like magic. Sam, get the pails by the door."

"The white pails?"

"Yes. Take this cup and put two cups of feed in the pail."

"Okay, Daddy."

"John, bring this pail to the chicken coop and put the feed in the trays. Understand? If we're going to get eggs, this has to be done every morning before school and when you get home. Is that clear?" John nodded and the other two followed.

"John, you're able to read some, so I'll tack a sheet of paper with the step-by-step directions on the wall above the bag of chicken feed in case you forget. Okay?"

"Okay."

The three children handled the job pretty well for a couple of weeks, but soon Nintendo games and playing outside climbing trees called to them. The chores took second place. Vince gave them gentle reminders.

The next morning, John and Sam went to the barn to find an unopened bag of feed. John read the directions but started pulling the string at the wrong end, and the feed spilled all over the barn floor. The school bus came, and they ran out of the barn to catch the bus, leaving behind a big mess and the chickens without food.

When Vince got home from work, he opened the barn door to a disaster. "What in the hell happened?" he yelled. The children scampered to their bedrooms. After calming down some, he said, "Sue, send the children down here!"

"They're hiding from you," Sue said.

She gathered the children and carried Bertram in her arms, and the children dragged their feet to the barn.

"I think I know what happened," Vince said, trying to stay calm. "You opened the bag from the wrong side, the bag fell over, and spilled all over the floor. The chickens still need to be fed! Sam, grab the pails and fill the scoops. John, feed the chickens! Sam and Sarah, help me clean this up."

The family ate their supper in silence. Sue and Vince waited until the children were in bed to discuss the day's mishap.

"Vince, I don't think the children are old enough to do that chore. Maybe we can start by having them feed the cats and the dog."

"You're probably right, but dammit, I need help. I'll have to come up with something else."

Later that evening, in a moment of inspiration, Vince said, "I received information that Clifford is done with the transitional housing part of his rehab to reentry. He's looking for a job."

"Really? That went fast," Sue said.

"Probably faster for you than Clifford."

"I know you too well. You're hatching a plan."

"Yup!" Vince chuckled. "Maybe I can offer him a job doing the lawn and other chores around the farm."

Silence. "I don't know," Sue fretted. "I'm not sure I want an ex-con working around our yard."

"Clifford is different. You know he is."

"At the very least, call Jane and see how he did in transitional housing."

"Okay," Vince said.

"JANE, THIS IS VINCE. I'm checking with you to see how Clifford is doing in transitional housing."

"He's doing very well, but he'll be done in just a few days. He did the chores without complaining; he followed the terms of his parole; and he received a good report from his boss. The most important activity was AA, and he stayed focused on the steps; and from what he told me, he finished them."

"I'm considering hiring him as a farmhand at my place here in Powell. Do you think he could handle it?" Vince asked.

"I think so. I've got his file here, and I'm reading the report from Dr. Freeman, the career counselor." Jane read the summary of the testing. "Clifford has a high IQ, and he recommended Clifford go back to school for more education to improve his employability."

"Interesting." Long pause. "I think I could help him out. There're several colleges in Grand Rapids to choose from."

"That's true. All signs point to him being a good employee. Maybe you can ask him if he'd be interested. Good luck. If there's anything you need from me, just give me a call."

"Thanks," Vince said. "I'll give Clifford a call in a couple of days; I have to run this past Sue."

VINCE'S THOUGHTS JUMPED AHEAD. He assumed Clifford would say yes, so he had to convince Sue. *Our children are too young to do the work. I'd like to help Clifford and my family at the same time. It would be a win-win situation. Clifford has done well in transitional housing and I trust him with my farm and my family.*

Vince looked at his farm as he drove up the driveway. A two-story brick colonial home graced the top of a sweeping hill. Down the hill and to the right was a fenced-in pasture attached to a two-story barn. Mature oak trees surrounded the house and the barn, which was bordered by rows of sassafras trees and interspersed with sugar maples. The farm was at its best in the fall. Oak Hill Place was a suitable moniker for the farm located just east of Grand Rapids. The homestead had all the charm of country living with convenient access to a large city. Vince considered it to be the best of both worlds.

Adjacent to the farm was another ninety acres that Vince and Sue owned. Fifty acres of pine tree forest bordered the north end of the farm. Vince had brokered a deal with a real estate company to create a development at the north end. The other forty acres, which were between the homestead and the development, were barren scrub acres consisting mostly of a sandy loam. Plants that thrived there were hardy and drought resistant. Stinging nettles tangled their way along the hills and valleys of the land. Purple fuzzy bull thistles dominated the landscape and the seasonal yellow mustard plants invaded the empty crevices.

Many times, Vince walked that forty acres, scratching his head. *What can I do with this barren land, this infertile soil? There're ants all over here! Maybe I can sell ant farms to ant enthusiasts or for educational experiments. Or, maybe I could sell my sand to excavators who needed fill sand.* Excited by that prospect, he took John and a couple of shovels to the sand hill and they started digging. Eighteen inches below the hard, crusty surface, they discovered a fine, no. 2 fill sand often used by excavators.

"By golly. I think we've got something!" Vince exclaimed. John, eight years old, grinned and nodded.

Vince set up a sand-mining operation. He contacted the excavators in the area, notifying them of sand for sale at Oak Hill Place. The business grew because of good sand at low prices, and this spread by word of mouth. Vince received payment by using the honor system, a.k.a. a gentleman's agreement. Invoices were time-stamped, and the amount of sand itemized.

There was one lone trailer sitting on the one-acre parcel closest to the highway. A tenant had lived there for a few years, but left the area and abandoned it. Vince had a plan. *With some elbow grease and sweat equity, the trailer would be a nice place for Clifford to live. It has two small bedrooms, a bathroom, kitchen, and water from a nearby well. I'd have to get the electric turned on so the heater could run. But before I go any further, I have to run this by Sue.*

"Hi, babe. How're you today?"

"A bit rattled. I took John to the doctor. The neighbor's dog attacked Sweet Pea. John tried to separate them. That nasty critter nicked his hand with his teeth. The doctor cleaned the wound out and bandaged it. He said it should heal on its own."

"I'll take a look at it at suppertime," Vince continued. "I called Jane today."

"About Clifford?"

"Yes, and she gave him a glowing report. He was cooperative, got along with his roommate, worked, and finished the AA program."

"Wouldn't you agree it was a good placement for him?"

"For sure. Jane sent him to a career counselor for an assessment, and he's recommending further education."

"How would he get to his classes?" Sue asked, concerned she would have to drive him.

"He could live in the trailer by the highway. I would get an old truck for him because I need to get a farm vehicle anyway. He'd be able to use the truck to get to his classes."

"How's he going to pay for tuition and course fees?"

"Good question. That's what I wanted to talk to you about. What would you say if I agreed to give him minimum wage for hourly work like farm chores and lawn mowing, and pay more for major work projects?"

"I'd say he's getting a pretty good deal."

"That's true, but I would pay him out of the proceeds from the sand-mining operation. I like the idea of having someone there to keep an eye on the trucks going in and out."

"That makes sense. I've always wondered how honest those guys are. I can't see what they're doing from the house."

"I know, and I don't expect you to do that. You've got your hands full."

"Well, all you can do is ask Clifford and see what he says."

"So, it's okay with you?" Vince asked.

"Yes. Why not give it a try?"

That's what Vince liked about his wife. She was

open-minded but wise enough to be cautious when necessary. He was certain his four children would benefit from those qualities as well. He mapped out in his mind what he would say to Clifford. *I'll provide a place for you to live, a truck to drive, and a minimum wage for hourly employment. For special projects we would agree on a fair price.* He did a business calculation and was certain the earnings from the sand pit would provide Clifford's pay.

Vince called after four in the afternoon to make sure Clifford would be home from work.

"This is Vince Attwood," he said. "I visited you when you were in the hospital and in prison."

"I remember you."

"I understand you're almost done with transitional housing."

"I'll be done on Friday."

"I'd like to make you an offer. You can think about it overnight and get back to me." Vince spelled out his proposal, sharing the idea of him going back to college using the truck as transportation.

There was a long pause.

"If you don't mind me asking, what were you planning to do on Friday?" Vince asked.

"I was going to my parent's house in Mason until I could figure out what I wanted to do. I am interested in your offer, but I want to think it over."

"Great."

"I'll call you tomorrow about this time to let you know one way or the other?"

"I'll look forward to your call."

21   Last Confessions

"Grim." That word stuck in his head and became a thorn in his heart. His dad's phone call was anything but reassuring. Hearing those words, "grim prognosis," paralyzed him. He couldn't cry, speak, or even think, but he felt some relief when his father said, "Clifford, I'm coming to get you. She needs to see you."

The call came just one day before his discharge. He gathered his things and searched the house for Jane. She was in the kitchen working on the schedule. He stood silently in front of her with head bowed.

"What's wrong, Clifford?"

"My mother is very sick. She's in the hospital, and Dad is picking me up in an hour to go see her."

"I'm sorry," Jane said grasping his hands. There was a real moment between them before she switched roles. "We have some exit paperwork you must sign, and I need to call your parole officer to make sure it's okay for you to leave."

Clifford stood there listening with his banker's box on the floor next to him while Jane greeted the officer warmly and assured him that Clifford was ready for the next step. She explained that the circumstance of his mother's illness meant he would leave one day early. "Would that be okay with you?" Jane asked. "He'll need to take his tether off. I can do it here."

Silence, then Jane said, "Thank you! I'll do that."

"He gave permission," Jane said.

Clifford exhaled.

"Thank you, Jane," he said. "I have two books that need to be returned to the library. Would you return them?"

"You really are a bookworm!" Jane laughed as she reached for the books. "I'll be happy to. Make sure you keep learning and bettering yourself." She looked straight into his eyes. "Promise?"

"I promise."

"You're a nice person, and I hope you have the best life possible," Jane set the books on the table and hugged him. Her warmth renewed his deflated spirit.

SUE ATTWOOD ANSWERED THE home phone shortly after the family dinner.

"Hi, Sue, this is Jane Bartman. Is Vince there?"

"He is."

"I need to speak to him. When we're finished, I'd like to chat with you."

"I'd like that. Hold on. I'll get him."

"Hi, Jane. I'm surprised you called me at home."

"Something has come up for Clifford, and he wanted me to give you a call. He's accepting your job offer, but his dad picked him up and took him home to visit his mom. She's in the hospital and not doing well. He said he'd call you as soon as he can. Is it alright if I give him this number?"

"That's fine, but the poor guy has something else he has to deal with. It doesn't sound good."

"It's a family emergency for sure."

"Can I count on him to call me?"

"I don't know. His tether is off, but he still has to be accountable to the system through his parole officer. You'll be able to find him if he doesn't call you." Jane continued, "Is Sue there? I'd like to chat with her."

"Thanks for giving me the message. Here's Sue."

THE OLD BUICK DROVE up and parked by the curb in front of the rehab house. *Dad!* All that Clifford could see through the window from the front room was Dad's dark-rimmed glasses and his bald head above the steering wheel. Other than shrinking with age, Herman hadn't changed much. Clifford remembered that same image of his father behind the wheel, picking him up from school—punctual to a fault, but unwelcoming and distant.

Clifford waved to Jane as he climbed into the car. He shut the door and entered the world of silence—no greeting, no smiles, just driving.

"How's Mom?"

"Not good."

"How did she get sick?"

"Her heart."

"Did she have a heart attack?"

"Her weight, you know."

"No, I don't know. Is that what the doctor said?" Clifford asked.

"Yes. Severe blockages."

"Is she going to have surgery?"

"Don't know—need your help."

"Doesn't she want the surgery? What's the name of the procedure?"

"CABG."

"What does CABG stand for?" Clifford asked.

"Don't know."

Why is Dad so frickin' dense? If it was my wife, I'd be asking all kinds of questions and researching all the options. He's so damn passive. I need my mom; she's my only encourager, my cheerleader. Sharm's baby needs a caring great grandma. All I get out of Dad is: "Don't know this and don't know that."

"Have you seen Sharm?"

"Yeah. Sees Ma at the hospital. She's real big! So, I asked, 'You got twins in there?'" Herman laughed. "David does second shift at the GM plant in Lansing, so she comes to see Ma in the morning."

"It'll be good to see her again. How are David and Sharm getting along?" Clifford asked.

"Okay," Herman shrugged.

A comment like that coming from Mr. Insight isn't worth much. I'll have to find out for myself.

"Please drop me off at the library before we go to the hospital; I want to check on that medical term before I see Mom."

"Okay. I can do that. It's on the way."

The car stopped; Clifford jumped out while his dad

waited. He walked into the library and went directly to the reference desk.

"I'm hoping you can help me with a medical term," he said to the librarian. "I don't know what CABG means."

"My husband had that procedure," the librarian said. "It stands for coronary artery bypass grafting." Clifford's eyes lit up. "Is there anything else you need?" she asked.

"How did that surgery work out for your husband?"

"Good. He's alive. He watches his weight and does everything the doctor tells him to do. I can print out some information about the surgery and recovery for you."

"That would be helpful." Clifford looked at the new upgrades in the library as he waited for the copies. The children's section had been repainted and expanded. *I remember the old yellow walls. Mom took me here for story time. Afterwards, we would walk to the Michigan capitol building. The grounds were loaded with squirrels. I'd chase them, and she'd laugh at me. Good times.*

"Thanks for your help." Clifford took the copies and exited the library. *What are the odds of meeting someone who knew about the surgery? Maybe it's an omen.*

SPARROW HOSPITAL HELD A lot of memories for Clifford. His two children were born there. He took a short detour to the gift store to buy Mom some flowers. With a pot of gerbera daisies in hand, Clifford took the elevator to the second floor. The hospital smelled of disinfectant, but it was not as obnoxious as the prison smells. His mother had a private room with special nurses and was a few feet away from the ICU so she could be moved at a moment's notice.

Clifford stood quietly beside her bed, waiting for her to wake up. Her eyes opened and she beamed with recognition. She reached up, placing her hands on his face, and pulled him toward her. "Clifford, my boy. I've missed you so much," she whispered, and kissed him hard on his cheek. Tears welled in their eyes. Clifford pulled up a chair and held his mother's hand.

"So, what's goin' on with you, Ma?"

"I don't have any energy—no get-up-and-go. Herm took me in to see the doctor and they ran some tests. My arteries have blockages—big ones."

"Dad told me they're talking about open heart surgery," Clifford said.

"Yes, but that doesn't appeal to me. It's a tough surgery."

"They constantly make improvements in the operation and recovery. The outcomes and findings are really good."

"I've heard the recovery is long and I'd have to change my lifestyle. I'm kinda used to my way of living. I don't know if I can do change at my age." She pressed her lips together. "I don't want to talk about it anymore. What's happening with you?"

"A lot has happened—mostly good stuff," Clifford continued. "My parole officer approved taking my tether off early; I completed my transitional housing time; and I have a job and a place to live. Most important, I have *no* desire to smoke pot."

"You're turning your life around," she smiled. "I always knew you could do it."

"A career counselor tested me and found out I have a high IQ. He recommended I go back to school."

"You've always been smart. Taking you to museums and libraries was so much fun."

"I have a lot more I'd like to do with *you*, Ma," Clifford said. "You should do the surgery." She turned away and stared out the window. "At least think about it. I'll put the daisies on the table."

"Thanks for the flowers."

Clifford left with a heavy heart. *It's her life; she has to make the decision. I took a bumpy detour with my choices. Now that I'm finally back on track, Mom might not be around to share my freedom.*

Herman and Clifford climbed into his old Buick and drove to Mason. The stone-silent twenty-minute drive felt like forever.

"Where do you want me to stay?" Clifford asked as he lifted his banker's box out of the car.

"In your old room."

"Is it still a bedroom?"

Herman nodded.

An avalanche of memories almost buried him as he climbed the stairs to the second floor. He remembered the nasty accusations and threats followed by, "If you don't shape up, I'm writing you out of my will. You'll be a loser your whole life."

Then, I'd stomp up the stairs and slam the door. He put so many nasty words together when he yelled at me. It was the only time he talked in complete sentences.

Clifford took a deep breath and set the box on the floor. Spotting the books on his bookshelf, he ran his fingers down their spines. They were friends from long ago: Twain, Dickens, Tolstoy, and Steinbeck, among others, still stalwart and inviting. *Travels with Charlie* by Steinbeck piqued his interest, so he placed it on his bed for later.

I must check my cache. He shoved the dresser to the side, pulled a wood panel up from the floor, and there it was—his paraphernalia, along with a very dried-up bag of pot, probably fifteen or more years old. *Does pot get better or worse with age? Some say it gets better, like wine, but others say it gets stale. Maybe I should check out that theory. No-no-no! Dad could smell it and I'm done-done-done with that life.*

Along with the bag of pot, he found a percolator bong. He remembered how much better the lift was with his perc. It had a smoother hit because it cooled down and moisturized the smoke. He was determined to put this nightmare stuff in the trash and continue on his path to recovery.

"Supper!" Herman shouted.

Supper? Yuck! Would this be like so many others? There was either no talking, or one-word jabs. But he was sure it would be better than prison meals. *Dinner without Mom being the buffer could be a nightmare. I'm in my thirties now. I can handle whatever comes my way. When it's over, I can go upstairs and read Steinbeck.*

"Your favorite," Herman shouted up the stairs.

My favorite, he says. Macaroni and cheese? Colonel

Sanders chicken meal? Scalloped potatoes? How does he know what my favorite is?

"I'll be down in a sec," Clifford said. He gathered up his paraphernalia and stuffed it in a paper bag. He was going to dispose of it as soon as he could. "What's for dinner, Dad?"

"Spaghetti with garlic toast."

"Did you make it?"

"From scratch."

"Impressive." Clifford settled into his chair, the same one he had as a kid. He smiled at his dad and chowed down. "When did you learn to cook?"

"When I retired."

"Damn, it's good! How long has Mom been in the hospital?"

"Almost a week for tests and whatnot." Herm soured. "I miss her so much. Life isn't the same without her."

He's talking in complete sentences!

"I miss her too. She's a good woman," Clifford said.

"Yup." He lifted his shirt sleeve and wiped his tears.

"Don't worry, Dad. We've got a little time to convince her to do the surgery. What time is visitation tonight?"

"Seven to nine."

"You made dinner, so I'll do the dishes," Clifford said. "Why don't you watch the news and chill out."

"Okay."

I want Mom to do the surgery. If not for her, for me. I have to be convincing. She never had a whole lot of fight in her. Dad's a puzzle. He dominated her, but tonight he showed he loves her. Clifford stacked the dishes in the dishwasher and wiped off the table.

"Ready to go, Dad?"

"Yup."

"Do you want me to drive?"

"License?" Herman asked.

"Yes, I have one, and it hasn't expired."

"Okay." He handed Clifford the keys.

"Buckle your seat belt, Dad. When you ride with me, you gotta do it." Herm reluctantly pulled the strap and snapped it in place.

Clifford enjoyed being behind the wheel even if it was his dad's old Buick. He hadn't driven in almost two years. He clicked on the radio and cruised along the highway at seventy miles per hour and tried to reimagine his freedom. *Life is good. I've been liberated from the gates of hell.*

"You enjoying yourself, son?"

"Oh, yeah! I'm rediscovering life!"

He braked hard and drove into the parking garage, slipping into a parking spot near the hospital entrance. The two men, the same height and girth, walked together to the elevator to visit their favorite woman.

Celia, her hair neatly curled, was sitting up, gazing at the daisies on the windowsill.

"Hi, Ma," Clifford said. Her eyes lit up.

"How's my Cel?" Herman said. She smiled.

"Well, boys. I made a decision. I'm doing the surgery," she continued. "I'm so tired, it's like I'm already dead. At least the operation might give me a chance at a little more vim and vinegar."

"That's the Mom I know. I'm proud of you. It's the right decision."

"Ditto," Herman said. "Maribelle, Sharm, and Kevin need to know."

"I'll give them a call after you leave," Celia said.

"Do you know when they'll be doing it?" Clifford asked.

"Tomorrow."

"Wow, that *is* soon!" Clifford said.

"You know me. Once I decide on something, I run with it," Celia grinned. "They plan to do the surgery at nine in the morning."

"When you call the family, tell them to be here between seven and eight thirty—just in case they begin early," Clifford said.

"I'm the first surgery in the morning," Celia said.

"I'll be your cheerleader. You go for it, Mom! You're the best."

"Clifford, I'd like to talk to you alone for a while," she said looking at Herman.

"You want me to leave?" he questioned.

"Just for a few minutes."

Confused and hurt, Herman shuffled out of the room.

"Son, shut the door and pull up a chair."

He dragged a chair to her bedside, gazed at her smooth round face framed with tight curls, and gave her a broad smile. Her mood changed suddenly, like a switch in the weather. He froze, seeing her eyes change into dark pools of grief. His mind jumped into overdrive. *Is she mad at me? Is Mom dying right before my eyes? Have I or someone else offended her?* Clifford braced himself for whatever she would say … or ask.

"Are you okay, Mom?"

"I have something to tell you. It's been locked away for thirty-seven years. I'm afraid to seek out more information because I worry everything will fall apart. It keeps pressing, pressing on me. It never goes away, but my heart can't hold it any longer," she said, wringing her hands.

Celia sighed and continued. "I met your dad when I was seventeen, and we were crazy about each other. We were high school sweethearts. The summer after we fell in love, my dad hired Jason, a young man to help him in his hardware store. He was a cutie, fun-loving, and so smart. My dad couldn't say enough good things about him. On the weekends, when my mom and dad visited Grandma, I helped Jason in the hardware store. It was almost every weekend that summer. I guess it's possible to love two boys at the same time. I did … but I was so confused. One Saturday morning, both of us showed up early to open the store. He pulled me into the back room, and we made out—heavily…. We made love. I'm pretty sure that's when I got pregnant."

"Stop, Mom! Enough!" Clifford uttered with a painful expression. All he assumed to be true was a mirage. "But Dad and I have the same bodies—we look alike. He's my father—you've *got* to be mistaken."

"But … you have Jason's eyes. Without a doubt, you have Jason's beautiful eyes. They're beseeching eyes. The color is exactly the same, and your eyebrows are his. I have no doubt."

"Does Dad know?"

"We've never talked about it, but he might suspect. I

don't know. I often wonder if that's why he favored Maribelle."

"Why didn't you do a paternity test?"

"That's just it—I didn't want to know because knowing might shatter my life with Herman." Clifford stood up and paced.

"I have to go. I'll see you in the morning." Clifford's father, or maybe not his father, stood by the door when he exited the room. "I'll be in the car," Clifford said.

Herman entered Celia's room, gave her a kiss goodbye, and joined Clifford in the car. "I don't know about you, but I need a good stiff drink," Herm said. "I know just the place—Darb's Crystal Bar."

They found a table in the corner and ordered a couple of beers. Clifford could *not* relax. He sat with his back to the wall, ramrod straight in the chair, and then lunged forward with his elbows on the table. Caught in an awkward silence, Herm spoke first.

"Did Celia talk to you about Jason?"

Clifford, wide-eyed and surprised, said, "You know?"

"I've known our whole married life."

"Why didn't you talk about it?" Clifford said, still astonished by the revelation.

"I was grateful she decided to marry *me* when I asked. I loved her so much. I didn't want to lose her."

"Do you think he's my father?"

"I don't know. We were intimate too." Herm continued. "I didn't want to know—I just thought of Celia and the baby as a package deal."

"How did you know about Jason?"

"I visited her at the hardware store. I could tell by how nervous she was and how he looked at her. I was worried, so I decided to ask her to marry me on our next date."

For almost forty years they've had this surface tension, and nobody talked about it.

Herm and Clifford left the bar and drove home in silence. Up in his old room, Clifford's mind raced. *I have to get a paternity test. I'll check on that tomorrow.*

After washing up, he wrestled with the covers, pulled them over his head, and then flung them away. His dreams were vivid … Sometimes they were creepy, sometimes rhapsodic, but never calm or reassuring. The night was a long stretch of darkness. The first bleed of light through the window roused him. Tomorrow was yesterday and today was here. Enormous challenges were waiting. He had to be steady for his mother and find the way to his real father.

ONCE AGAIN, DAD SAT in the passenger seat without fastening his seat belt. Clifford waited, but his dad was clueless.

"Put your seat belt on, Dad," Clifford said, waiting for Herman to cooperate. "Dad, would you be willing to do a paternity test? I'm struggling with a need to know."

"I would."

They pulled into the same parking space they had the night before, walked into the hospital, and pushed the up arrow by the elevator. They were the first ones to see Mom.

"No food this morning," Mom pouted. "That's the only thing I look forward to in the hospital. It's nice not to have to cook."

"Have you seen the doctor?" Clifford asked.

"Not yet, but his nurse took my vitals." Celia continued, "Good to see you this morning. My insides are like Jell-O, and my nerves are killing me. I wonder when the rest will show up."

"It's eight. They should be here soon." Clifford said.

"Hi, Gram. Hi, Daddy!" Sharm kissed her and hugged her daddy.

"Good to see you, sweetie. Did you get the crib?"

"They delivered it about a week ago. It's a real pretty one. Thank you."

"I'll stop by for a visit before I leave Lansing," Clifford said.

He heard Herm talking with Maribelle and Kevin in the hallway.

"It's been a while," Clifford said, approaching Kevin. "Good to see you, son."

"You've done your time?" Kevin asked.

"Yes, it's behind me."

Kevin moved his hand forward for a handshake, but Clifford preempted with a bear hug. "I hope we can make up for lost time."

Kevin stepped back, shook off the hug, and stood very still. Gazing up at his dad, he smiled and whispered, "Me, too." Hope opened the door, just a little.

"Have you decided to give up a life of crime?" Maribelle chuckled. "How's my big bro?"

"I've changed a lot, but I can tell you're the same old Maribelle," Clifford smirked.

"So, what's next in your life?" Maribelle asked.

"I'll be a farmhand for a while, and then, back to school."

"Michigan State?"

"No, a college in Grand Rapids."

"They're getting ready to prep Ma for surgery," Herman announced.

The family gathered around her bed, and each in their own individual way wished her well. Clifford was last.

"You can see how much we love you. You have given us so much encouragement over the years. We'll pray you through this and be by your side when you open your eyes." He planted a tender kiss on her cheek. "Love you," he whispered.

The family watched in silence as the attendants rolled her bed down the hallway, disappearing into the surgery wing.

Clifford turned to Kevin. "Would you like to go out for coffee?"

Kevin nodded.

THE EXPERTS ESTIMATED THE surgery would take anywhere from three to six hours. Clifford and Kevin talked for an easy three hours. They discovered they had educational aspirations that were similar. Neither one wanted to be the center of attention, and both preferred working in the background. Clifford recommended that Kevin seek out the advice of a career counselor. He shared the results of his recent visit with Dr. Freeman and said he regretted that he hadn't done it earlier before he got into trouble. It was a good visit.

Sharm joined them, and Kevin and she reminisced about the good times in their childhoods. When they trespassed into the not-so-good ones, Clifford changed the direction of the conversation. This was about reconnecting, and not about regrets of the past. The three of them walked to the waiting room together.

A NURSE APPROACHED HERMAN. "Your wife is in recovery and is doing well." There was a collective sigh of relief. "You may visit her."

Herm went in first. The rest lined up in the hallway. He gave a motion to come in. They grouped around her bed. Groggy, but eyes open, she smiled when she saw her loved ones.

"You did good, Ma!" Clifford said, gently touching her hand.

"I'm so tired," she said, closing her eyes.

CLIFFORD VOWED TO VISIT his mother every day. It would be later that day because he found a place that would do a paternity test. He chose a lab near the hospital which used the RFLP DNA method, which had 100 percent accuracy. This lab cut the DNA and assessed the VNTR (variable number tandem repeats). The only downside would be that it would take two weeks for the results.

"Dad? You doing anything this afternoon?"

"No."

"I'm making an appointment for a paternity test at four this afternoon. We can do the test before we visit Mom."

"Okay, but don't tell her," Herm said.

"You have my word."

AFTER THE PATERNITY TEST, Herman and Clifford headed to Darb's Crystal Bar for a beer and a burger.

"Are there any other secrets I need to know?" Clifford asked.

"You need to know I had a gambling problem—a big one."

"Really? The penny-pinching Herman gambled?" He sat back in amazement.

"I told Celia I was going to Detroit on business. I drove to the airport and bought a plane ticket to Las Vegas. I watched the blackjack tables for a while before I jumped in. It was Bill Benter's heyday. He was my hero and the best card counter I'd ever seen," Herman continued. "The first night I played the tables, my betting level was fifty dollars, and in two hours I made five thousand dollars. I was hooked from then on."

"I remember you as someone so tightfisted, you'd put a milkshake on layaway," Clifford laughed.

"Oh, come on! I'm not that bad!" Herman said, but he smiled. "After two years of losing, losing, losing, Celia caught on and threatened to leave me. So, I tried to stop, but I switched to betting on horses, dogs, athletic games, you name it. The lure of easy money sucked me in. But she caught me again and I finally went to Gambler's Anonymous. That's when everything started looking up."

"It's probably similar to AA for my pot addiction. I just completed the program."

"I'm pretty sure they use the same steps for gambling," Herm said.

"As long as we're confessing, I'm sharing a secret from long ago. Last night I opened up the floorboards in my old bedroom and found my stash of marijuana and my bong from fifteen years ago."

"I'm surprised the mice didn't find it—that would have given them some happy squeaks," Herman chuckled.

"Dad, time to head to the hospital. Mom should have had her dinner by now."

THEY TOOK THE ELEVATOR to the second floor. The door opened to a flurry of nurses and doctors with white coats bolting into Celia's room. Herm and Clifford were shoved aside so they could hustle a large machine into her room.

"What's going on?" Clifford asked a nurse.

"It's a code red."

Clifford charged into his mother's room like a battering ram, pushing medical personnel aside. He took one glimpse at her pale, motionless face and sobbed. "What happened? Less than twelve hours ago, she was tired, but smiling."

"Sir, you have to leave. We're trying to resuscitate her."

Clifford was so shocked by her visage, his awareness of the surroundings was blurred. He heard only the muttering of distant voices. He struggled to move closer to his mother, to no avail. His body was moving in slow motion. He snapped to when one of the medics pulled him out of the room.

"You *must* stay out," he commanded.

"How can everything go so wrong so quickly?" Clifford cried.

"They're doing the best they can," Herm said, with head bowed.

"Are you praying, Dad?"

"Yes, with an urgency like it's the end of the world."

"It just might be," Clifford muttered.

A metal cart with the flashing machines was pushed out of the room, and only a few remaining medical technicians lingered behind. A physician walked out, looking for someone or something.

"Is Herman Ratz here?" he asked.

"Over here," Herman raised his hand.

"I'm Dr. Brahms. I'm sorry to have to tell you this, but your wife didn't make it. She had a massive stroke, which caused a brain bleed. We tried to resuscitate her, but it wasn't effective. If she had survived, she would have been bedridden for the rest of her life, or at best, facing an extremely long, painful rehabilitation." He made occasional eye contact with Herman, but mostly his explanation was cold and clinical. "Please call your funeral home and arrange for transport of the body. I'm sorry for your loss."

Clifford and Herman embraced and wept inconsolably. Clifford composed himself and offered to call the funeral home.

"Do you want Gorsline-Runciman Funeral Home in Mason, or one in Lansing?" Clifford asked.

"Gorsline-Runciman. I'll stay with Cel."

"Okay."

Clifford called for the transport van from the funeral home. It would arrive in forty-five minutes. Clifford pushed the button to the second floor and walked toward his mother's room. He stopped, horrified—she wasn't there. Two women were busily changing the sheets on her bed. "Where is my mother?" he yelled.

The head nurse appeared in the doorway. "She's in a small room next to the back entrance," she said. "I'll take you there."

Clifford didn't know if he was angry, worried, or defeated. He hadn't felt this awful in a long time. As they walked through the hallways, he smelled the mild disinfectant and heard voices in the background. Chatting with his own mom would never happen again.

"Was Celia your mother?" the nurse asked.

"Yes."

"She was a pleasant woman. All the nurses liked her. She was proud of you and the rest of her family."

"Thank you for sharing that." His eyes moistened, and tears escaped.

Clifford found Herman hunched over her body. "I will miss you, sweet Celia. I will miss you *so* much."

Clifford gently placed his hand on his dad's back to comfort him. Herman's face was wet and blotched from sobbing. Clifford gave him a Kleenex from his pocket, and then held his mother's hand while he solemnly studied her face. The good times of his childhood flowed through his mind like a gentle spring rain. *You nourished me, made me laugh, helped me grow and taught me about the world. I will cherish you, those special times, and endearing memories forever.*

THE FUNERAL TOOK PLACE at the United Brethren Church in Mason. It was a simple ceremony. Clifford wrote a memorial to his mother, positioned the microphone next to her coffin, and read his speech to the congregation.

"My mother was a kind and loving woman. She was a great mother—fun loving and affectionate, and my best cheerleader. I always thought of her as the queen of clichés. She could rattle them off faster that you could blink an eye. She collected them: 'When you wallow with pigs, expect to get dirty'; 'Never corner anyone meaner than you'; 'I have vim and vinegar'; 'Don't put all of your eggs in one basket'; 'The apple doesn't fall far from the tree'; 'Like a kid in a candy store'; 'We're not laughing at you, we're laughing with you'; and 'Time heals all wounds.'

"She was a very wise, caring woman. I will miss her every day of my life and I must wait to see if time does heal all wounds." Clifford looked at her casket. "I love you, Mom."

22 Baby News

"**M**r. Attwood, this is Clifford Ratz. I lost my mother last week," he said over the phone.

"Sorry to hear that."

"I have one more visit in Lansing, and then I'll be ready to work on your farm."

"There is a crew cleaning the trailer as we speak, so we're getting ready for you to move in. When will you head this way?"

"Tomorrow. I should be there about ten in the morning."

"The exit number is fifty-two. Turn right and go two miles," Vince explained. "If you get lost, call me."

HE HAD PROMISED SHARM a visit before he left Lansing. He drove through an unsavory neighborhood and found the address. Her apartment looked like a landlord's afterthought, all cobbled up. Clifford had seen so many rental units like this one, a cheap way for the owner to get more income.

Clifford was carrying a Colonel Sanders bucket in his

left arm as he knocked with his right hand. He smelled pot. "Who's there?"

"Your father."

"Alright. I'm coming." A pregnant Sharm waddled to the door. She was carrying a big tummy on a small frame and was in a miserable mood.

"Good to see you, Sharm. I brought supper."

"Smells good. All I have in the fridge is stale pizza." The thought of food lifted her mood.

The apartment was as he expected, a pigsty. The kitchen floor was sticky, and wrappers and fast-food bags were tossed everywhere. Clifford swallowed his comments to keep the peace. He wiped the table with a rag and set the bucket in the middle to share. He made two place settings on the table with napkins and plastic silverware. Getting ready to tackle the food, Sharm pushed her sleeves up, exposing a nasty looking inflammation.

"What happened to your arm?"

"I got a tattoo. Want to see?" She pushed her sleeve higher and revealed a face of a person.

"Who's that?"

"Grandma," Sharm said, surprised he didn't recognize it. "I *never* want to forget her face. She was more of a mother to me than Wanda was."

"Creepy." Clifford crinkled his face in disgust. "It's huge! Couldn't you just carry her picture around?"

"Not the same. Her face is always handy and forever with me. I love it," Sharm retorted. "When you die, I'll have you engraved on my other arm. You're my two favorite people."

Not amused, Clifford grimaced. "No, thank you!"

"That's *my* choice."

"How much did it cost?"

"About three-hundred fifty dollars."

"What! That's enough for two months' rent."

"Good grief. You sound like David. He's always complaining about money."

"Let's change the subject," Clifford continued. "Tell me about the baby. Is April fourth still the due date?"

"Yup. I feel like I'm as big as a horse. At this point, I don't care if I deliver a hippopotamus; I just want it over. I can't sleep in the bed because once I'm on my back I *can't* turn over. I sleep on the sofa so I can move myself around to my side. One thing for sure, I'm happy I'm out of the nausea stage. Men just don't understand how awful that is. You're always on the verge of hurling. It's like you're chained to the toilet. You can't leave the house, not ever!"

"That does sound miserable."

"You got it!" Sharm continued. "After a while you can't even see your feet. One morning, I bent over to flush the toilet and I tipped forward and hit my head hard on the wall. My belly was so front heavy, I almost fell over."

"How are you and David getting along?"

"Are you sure you want to know? ... Horribly!" Sharm snarked. "He's on second shift, now, but they're talking about moving him to third. That would be dreadful. His sleeping is off now, and I can't even imagine what it would be like if his days and nights were completely upside down. He yells at me whenever I make noise. I feel like I'm in prison."

"Did they say when there would be a shift change?"

"No, that's what I hate about this company. You never know when or if they'll spring it on you."

"The pay is pretty good, though," Clifford said.

"I suppose so, but David constantly complains about money. 'We don't have any money for extras, only for food and rent,'" he says. "He scolds me like a child. 'Why did you buy this?' 'We *don't* need that—you're stupid!' I'm really sick of his attitude."

"I'll be living in a renovated trailer outside of Grand Rapids. You can come to visit me any time."

"Will you have a car?" Sharm asked.

"Supposedly. He's getting a work truck for me."

"Wow! Cool! Do you think you can come and pick me up?"

"Maybe. Dad's giving me a lift over there tomorrow, so I'll be able to see what he has for me."

"I want to show you the crib you bought. It's very nice. David put it together."

Sharm showed him the way to the bedroom, and just inside the door was the crib. He ran his fingers along the headboard and remembered the crib he'd put together for Kevin and Sharm. He recalled the good memories and great expectations. The cycle of life never stopped. It went on and on and on …

Clifford said his goodbyes and walked down the rickety stairs. He shook his head as he turned around to take one last look at their apartment. It was even more cobbled up than he'd thought. Somehow the landlord carved a bathroom, kitchen, bedroom, and living room out of the remaining two-hundred fifty square feet. The front door was slanted at the bottom, so someone added a piece of floorboard to make it shut tight. The renovation project in the utility room left the room in disarray with the washer and dryer unhooked, the walls unpainted, and the sink disconnected. At least, there was a tiny bathroom that was functional.

I guess it's all they can afford.

TODAY WAS MOVING DAY. Clifford carried his banker boxes downstairs. He'd purchased enough clothes and toiletries to make a smooth transition from his dad's home to the trailer. He stowed the boxes in the old Buick and slammed the trunk.

"Ready, Dad?"

Herman picked up his pace, climbed into the passenger side, and settled into the one-hour trip.

"Seat belt!" Clifford rolled his eyes and sighed.

"You act like you're my father," Herm grinned.

"I am," Clifford smiled. "Just a younger version."

Herm chuckled. "I hope this works out for you. Even if the paternity test says you're not my son, you'll always be my son at heart."

"Aw, thanks, Dad."

"Did you give the lab my phone number?" Herman asked.

"Yes, they should call sometime this next week." Clifford continued, "The first thing I'm doin' is getting a phone in the trailer, and I'll give you my new number. I want to know who my biological father is."

They watched the exit numbers go down from ninety

to fifty-two, indicating they had to make a right turn. Two more miles and they would be looking for the Attwood farm. Resplendent vistas of rolling hills and forested homesteads surrounded by corn and wheat fields accounted for much of the countryside. It was similar to the farmland around Mason. Clifford drove past the farm and down the hill, where he spotted a trailer by the side of the road.

"That's it! I think that's it," Clifford exclaimed as he drove in.

It was an old trailer, off-white on the top section, with dark green skirting along the bottom. Concrete blocks formed the stairs to the only door. Random blotches of rust mottled the off-white exterior, but sandpaper and a can of paint could take care of that. Alongside the trailer was a gravel two-track. Clifford followed the trail into an active sand-mining operation. *This is all new to me. My dad dealt in life insurance, so I don't have experiences with farming and sand mining. Mr. Attwood is giving me a break. I'll do my best.* He circled around the pit, drove back around onto the two-track, and parked by the trailer. A red Chevy truck rumbled down the road and pulled in.

"Howdy," Vince yelled.

"Mr. Attwood, I'd like you to meet my dad, Herman Ratz." They shook hands.

Vince had on an old cowboy hat with sweat rings around the band, obviously a work hat for the farm. Clifford surmised from his jeans, plaid shirt, and boots that he was in his down-home mode. The suit jacket and tie he wore when they first met was expected attire for office only.

"Let me give you a tour," Vince said. "This here's the trailer. Have you gone inside?"

"Not yet. We just got here."

"Come on in."

It was small, but adequate. Vince turned the faucet on at the kitchen sink to demonstrate the water pressure.

"You've got your own well," Vince said as he pointed to a cistern to the left of the trailer.

"Sue made those blue-and-white checked curtains for the windows over the sink."

"I like 'em," Clifford said.

They walked down a hallway which had just enough room for Vince's shoulders. On the right were two storage closets with pocket doors and next to them was a small bedroom which barely fit a full-size mattress and a dresser. Across the hall on the left was a long skinny bathroom with a tub, shower, commode, and sink; rust stains marred the appliances.

"I just put in a water softener, so that should help with the rust," Vince mentioned.

In the back of the trailer was the master bedroom, which housed a queen-sized bed, a dresser, and a small closet. It was all done in blue and white, with yellow accents—bright and cheery. Sue's touches were everywhere. Clifford got a closer look at the kitchen as they headed out the door. There was a new microwave, a tiny oven with a range top, and an adequate refrigerator. This was more than he expected. He could enjoy the quiet of the countryside, which was decidedly better than the grating bedlam in prison. Making his own meals and sleeping in a bedroom without bars and disruption was nirvana.

"What do you think?" Vince asked.

"This is more than I hoped for."

"Good! But, of course there's work to be done on the farm."

"I know," Clifford smiled.

"Well, son, it's time I go back to Lansing," Herm said. "Be sure to give me your phone number." He took the two boxes out of the trunk. "Where do you want me to put these?"

"I'll take 'em," Clifford said, and set the boxes on the concrete steps. "I'm calling the phone company today to get my phone."

Clifford waved to his dad as he drove out. Vince headed toward the red truck, and Clifford's stomach churned with a fear of failure. *I've never been a farmer. Vince will have to be patient with me. I'll take notes, review the material, and do what I need to make it work.*

"I heard how the trial turned out yesterday. Blak got life for first degree murder. He's the one that plotted and executed Delores's murder. The others went along for the ride, so their sentences are less. They're a rotten bunch of hombres. I'm glad they're behind bars and out of the prison system."

Clifford nodded. "Their careers are over! Justice was served."

"Getting back to the farm chores, I've written a contract, so you'll know exactly what I expect of you. The jobs need to be done every day, but if you get into a routine, you should have plenty of time for schoolwork."

"My daughter, Sharm, wants to come and visit me. Would that be okay?" Clifford asked.

"That should be fine if she doesn't get in the way of doing farm chores. What's more important, I don't want any illegal activities on my farm."

Clifford nodded and heeded the warning.

Driving up the road to the farm, Clifford was impressed. "This place is organized and neat. I like it," he commented. "I've never worked on a farm before, so I'll be taking notes as we walk the property."

"Good, that's what I like about you—you're conscientious."

Clifford and Vince walked through the barn with the animals. There were chickens, horses, and pygmy goats. All the animals, except the chickens, seemed tame. Vince called the horses by name and they ambled up to him, giving him a peck on the cheek. The goats were another story. They came when called, but the rascals head-butted each other. The two dogs, a sheltie and a lab, circled them as they walked the grounds. A pair of cats with tails high in the air sashayed around the fence line. Clifford jotted down their names, the kind of food they ate, and how often they were fed.

"The goats forage in the wooded areas, but I throw them some hay once a day and make sure they have water in their trays," Vince said.

"They're smaller than other goats I've seen," Clifford said.

"The pygmy goat is a smaller breed for sure. They're cute, but Sue gets irritated with them because they eat all the red flowers around the farm. The kids call them Rocky and Bullwinkle. Don't worry about the cats and dogs. The children feed them inside," Vince said, walking toward the house. "I'd like you to meet Sue."

Clifford followed him in. The place was lovely but not ostentatious. He heard the children playing in the backyard and stopped short when he saw Vince's wife. Her cheeks were ruddy; her hair a strawberry blonde. Her plain face sported a radiant smile. She lacked the svelte, sophisticated look of a lawyer's wife, and looked more like a farmer's wife. She was friendly and unassuming, a good combination. *She's okay. I like her.*

"I leave for Lansing about seven in the morning and I'm home somewhere between five and six in the evening," Vince said. "When I'm gone, if you have any questions, you can ask Sue. She knows everything about the farm. I have some jobs to show you before I hand over the keys. Follow me."

With notebook and pen in hand, Clifford accompanied Vince to the part of the barn with farm equipment. "This is a hobby farm, so we don't have huge tractors, cultivators, or other large farm equipment, but we have a riding lawn mower. Have you ever used one?"

"Yes, my dad had one and I mowed the lawn every two weeks," Clifford said.

"Good. Was it a John Deere?"

"Yes, indeed. He swore by them."

"So, you know how to sharpen the blades and do the routine maintenance?"

"Yup."

"The sand-mining operation isn't in full swing yet. I have to wait for the frost laws to be lifted. We'll go over what I expect when the excavators start hauling."

"Frost laws?" Clifford asked.

"During the spring thaw, the roads get soft, so when a heavy truck goes over the roads, it makes them crumble," Vince said. "Usually, those restrictions are lifted around the middle of April. Do you have any questions?"

"Not at this time."

"Alright. Let's get the contract signed."

The contract was written in legalese, but Clifford grasped most of it. Essentially, the farm work needed to be done daily, the lawn mowed weekly, and the sand-mining operation monitored as needed. If Clifford wanted time off, he would have to talk to Vince. The pay was fifty dollars a day, which would be paid every two weeks. He could increase his earnings by doing other projects. The amount paid for individual jobs would be negotiated. He could use the truck but would be responsible for buying his own gas. He could not have anyone else live in the trailer without prior permission. Most importantly, he needed to fulfill the requirements of his parole, and any illegal activities would be reported to the police. Clifford considered the terms reasonable, and he certainly didn't want to violate parole.

"My daughter would like to visit me. Could I take the truck to Lansing to pick her up?" Clifford asked.

"You have to pay for the gas, but the truck is yours to get to class, to check in with your parole officer, do chores around the farm, and visit family and friends.

I'll pay for the insurance and for maintenance within reason. If you do kitty-hinders in the winter and blow the tires—it's on you."

Clifford laughed. "I haven't done anything like that for fifteen years!"

They signed the contract and shook hands. It looked like a good deal for both, a win-win, as Vince would say. He gave him the keys to the truck.

"Could I use your phone?" Clifford asked. "I want to get one in the trailer ASAP."

"Go ahead, ask Sue. I'll do the chores today, but you'll start tomorrow."

"If it's okay, I'll do the evening chores with you."

"Sounds like a good idea. I'm usually in the barn by five on Saturdays."

THE PHONE COMPANY SCHEDULED the installation for Monday morning. He said goodbye to Sue and hustled off to his new dwelling. *I'll work hard, save money for college, and create a better future for me and my family.*

Clifford opened the refrigerator and the kitchen cabinets. All bare like Mrs. Hubbard's cupboards. The closets were empty too. Fortunately, he had almost a thousand dollars saved from his job at the bakery, so he could get the food and supplies he needed to set up housekeeping. He found the closest grocery store in Powell and stocked up with food, milk, a broom and dustpan, toilet paper, Rust-out for the sinks and, a little luxury, a cheap patio chair. He looked forward to sitting outside in the evenings listening to the birds and watching the sunsets.

For lunch he had tomato soup, grilled cheese, and a glass of milk, which reminded him of lunches with his mom. His favorite comfort foods were just right for settling into his new home. He sat on the bench by the table and savored every bite. He had two windows; one looked out on the road, and the other, the natural wonders: oaks, sassafras trees, and early spring blooms. It was every bit country. After lunch, he unpacked his banker boxes and put his clothes in the closet. *I have officially moved in. This is home.*

Promptly at five in the afternoon, he climbed into his truck and drove the quarter mile south to Vince's farm to watch him do chores. Clifford had a stake in doing them right.

"Howdy," Vince shouted as he walked out the front door. "We'll do the horses first. Matt! ... Tonka!" he yelled. The horses galloped to their feeding trough. They knew when it was time to eat. Vince climbed the stairs to the hayloft, threw the bale outside into the trough, and filled the buckets with fresh water. "In winter we plug in this deicer to thaw the water, but we don't need to worry about that now. Spring is here." Vince smiled his appreciation. "You need to feed them twice a day."

"Next, the chickens." He reached into the feed bag and scooped out enough feed to fill the chicken feeders. He put fresh water in the tip-over pail, which dripped into a large bowl. "The chickens don't eat at night, but they need food all day long, so make sure you give them enough. The water needs to be changed every day to keep them healthy." Vince continued, "Let me explain how to open the bag of chicken feed. I showed this to my kids, but they spilled the feed all over the barn floor. That made me realize they were too young for the job." Vince pointed to the pull cord and emphasized the left to right direction. Clifford jotted this down in his notes.

CLIFFORD FINISHED SUPPER, TOOK his aqua-and-white webbed patio chair out of the closet, and set it behind the trailer, away from the road. An aura of magic descended as he watched the sun set and listened to the birds. He heard a robin with its sweet throaty song and the mesmerizing croak of the baby toads. The soothing hoot of the horned owl ushered in the twilight. No city lights disrupted the black wall of night. The brilliant stars were like low-hanging fruit; he could almost pick them right out of the sky. Clifford was tired. It had been an eventful day. He lay on his new bed enveloped in the fresh sheets and slept soundly.

THERE WAS NO WAY he could tell time—he'd have to get an alarm clock. The persistent rays of the sun nudged him awake. He threw on his work clothes, grabbed a yogurt and orange juice, and climbed into the truck. Coming up the driveway, he saw Vince looking out the window of his house. *Is he checking on me?*

"Matt … Tonka," Clifford called. The horses stood stock-still. *This is going to take some time. I'm an interloper.* Once the hay flew out of the hayloft, however, they galloped to their feeding trough. The little goats, Rocky and Bullwinkle, were next.

"Little goats, time for food." They clambered toward him as he threw half a bale in their direction. He emptied the dirty water in their containers and filled it with some fresh. The chickens were a messy job. Chicken poop was everywhere. The fumes were so bad he felt like they ate the nose off his face. Clifford hosed out their feeding troughs and water dishes and replenished both. Caring for the livestock took less than an hour. He waved at Vince, got in his truck, and returned home. Parked by his trailer was an old beat-up Toyota with the motor still running. Sharm was in David's car. *How did she find me?* He walked toward the car carefully. He peeked in the window and saw Sharm snoozing with her head tipped back on the driver's seat.

"Sharm! Is everything okay?" he said, trying to open the locked door.

"Hi, Daddy," she said pushing the door open. Clifford caught a faint scent of pot. He chose to ignore it.

"How did you find me?"

"Grandpa gave me directions. I wanted to give you a call first, but you don't have a phone."

"Come on in. I'll show you around." Sharm struggled to pull herself out of the car. "Let me help you," Clifford said as he reached for her hand. "I don't think it was a good idea for you to drive here all by yourself."

"I had to get out of the house. David's doing over-time, and I get so lonely I can't stand it." Sharm continued, "When he does come home, he's tired and in a bad mood. We get into screaming matches immediate-ly. I had to get out of there." Clifford helped her up the concrete stairs and into the trailer. "This is pretty nice, Daddy," she said, appraising the trailer.

"I think so. I bought supplies yesterday, so I could fix you some lunch." Clifford noticed the time on the microwave. It was past eleven and he realized he was late doing chores. *I have to get an alarm clock, so I wake up early enough to do chores on time.*

"That sounds good. I'm really hungry."

"How about grilled cheese and tomato soup," Clifford suggested.

"That reminds me of old times. Sounds good."

Sharm slumped on the bench by the kitchen table. "Is the small bedroom you showed me where I would sleep if I come to visit you?"

"Yeah, it's not much, but I put clean sheets on it and the blanket is new."

"It looks comfortable to me. I'm not sure I want to go back to Lansing," Sharm said between her sips of hot soup. "David doesn't know I took the car. He drove it to work today."

"What! Why did you do that, and how did you get it out of the company parking lot?"

"I had a spare key, and I told the parking attendant I had a medical emergency, which I sorta did. My mind hasn't been working right."

"Won't David worry about you?"

"No, but he'll be pissed I took the car. I'm an inconvenience to him. He's *always* mad at me."

"You've got yourself in a pickle," Clifford said, shaking his head.

"Daddy, could I stay with you?" Sharm pleaded.

"What about the car? You've got to take it back, so David has transportation."

"I'm so miserable," Sharm whimpered.

"Do you have any doctor appointments scheduled?"

"I do—on Tuesday."

"We'll have to get you back for the appointment because you're due in a couple of weeks." Clifford was exasperated. "This is getting so complicated. Next time, you need to think it through before you do something like this."

"I know, Daddy. I know. My mind isn't working right," Sharm sobbed. Clifford sat next to her on the bench and comforted her with an embrace. She wailed uncontrollably as he rocked her back and forth.

"It's hard right now, but you'll get through this, sweetie." Clifford sighed.

Sharm caught her breath, looked at him, and said, "I love you, Daddy."

"I must call David—he needs to know you're okay and that you have his car. There's a phone booth at the gas station in town," Clifford said. "Do you want to come with me?"

"Okay."

They found the red phone booth just a couple of miles from the farm. The conversation with David didn't take long and he sighed with relief knowing where his pregnant wife was. Although he wasn't overjoyed, he accepted Clifford's promise that he would get her and the car home sometime on Monday.

"This little town has a large grocery store open twenty-four hours. It has everything you need. I have to get an alarm clock so I feed the critters on time," Clifford said. On the way home from the grocery store, he picked up a Little Caesars pizza for supper. After some warm food and conversation, Sharm was ready to sleep. She relaxed and settled into the small bedroom, but left her door slightly ajar.

The next morning, the irritating jangle of Clifford's new clock woke him. It was a little after six when he got dressed. He left the trailer with Sharm snoring away in the guest bedroom and drove his truck to the farm. Vince was backing out of the garage when Clifford arrived.

"I got a new bag of chicken feed," Vince said, as he rolled down his window. "Good to see you up bright and early."

"I bought an alarm clock last night. It worked." Clifford smiled and waved.

"The adjustment to country life takes a little while," Vince said.

Matt and Tonka trotted toward Clifford and nuzzled him. He rubbed their noses before he climbed the stairs to the hayloft and threw down a bale of hay.

Clifford took out his notes and reread the directions for opening the bag of chicken feed. "Yup, it's left to right like I remembered," he mumbled. He picked at the string, but it wouldn't release, so he found a screwdriver and with one firm stroke, released the string and the rest unraveled. It was easy. The pygmy goats head-butted his knees. They were tired of being last on his list. *They're cute little buggers.* He tossed some hay their way. After he freshened up all the water containers, he drove back to his trailer to check on Sharm. She was still snoring.

He fixed a country-style breakfast with scrambled eggs, bacon, and wheat toast with strawberry jam. Sharm caught wind of the bacon, stretched her arms wide, and joined him for breakfast.

"This is great. I wish I had somebody makin' me breakfast every morning."

"We've got to get you home sometime today. I don't want you driving alone, so I'll follow you to Lansing. I have to be back by five because that's feeding time on the farm."

"I don't have to be home until eleven tomorrow morning for my doctor's appointment," Sharm said, hoping she could stay longer.

"I need to talk to David," Clifford said. "He should go with you."

"I'm not sure he wants to go. He's staying as far away from me as he can."

"That needs to change."

A loud knock startled them. "Phone company here," a technician said. "I'm here to install a phone. For your information, this place is wired already. I just need to give you a phone number and check on the jack to make sure it works."

"Come on in."

"Here's your number. I have push-button phones in the truck. If you want one, I'll put it on your bill."

"I want a red one. You got that color?"

"I do." He retrieved it from his truck.

The technician slipped one end of the cord into the jack and the other into the phone. Clifford smiled when he heard the dial tone. "Yay! I'm connected."

"Write the number down for me, Daddy."

"Here it is. Make sure you give me a call when that baby is born."

"I will, for sure," Sharm smiled.

"We've got to leave for Lansing. You have some mighty important business to tend to."

Clifford followed Sharm all the way to Lansing. He worried about her swerving and erratic speed, but she got there. She pulled off at a gas station to fill up. Clifford was right behind her.

"I need money for gas, Daddy."

He waited until the tank was full and went inside to pay. There was no way he would give her cash. He didn't trust her.

"Is David working today?"

"No, he did overtime on third shift last night. Right now, he should be home sleeping."

"I need to talk to him."

"Good luck with that," Sharm retorted.

Clifford helped Sharm climb the shaky fire escape stairs. David was asleep on the couch. Frightened, he sat up quickly when he heard the door open. "Who's there?"

"Sorry to wake you up," Clifford said. "I have something to ask of you. Sharm needs you to bring her to the doctor's appointment tomorrow." David sighed. "Will you do that?" Clifford continued. "It seems like the baby is coming soon and I can't be here for her because I have to work at the farm."

"What time is the appointment?" David asked.

"Eleven," Sharm said.

"I'll have to ask for the morning off. I better call them now," he said, shuffling to the phone.

"Tell them it's a family emergency. They'll understand," Clifford said. "Sharm, do you have your hospital bag packed?"

"No, but I can do it now."

"Good. It's important you're prepared and ready for the baby," Clifford said. David and Sharm stared at him wide-eyed, surprised by his serious tone. "Give me a call if anything comes up. You have my number, right?"

"I do. Thank you for your concern. I love you, Daddy," Sharm said, giving him a hug.

Mission accomplished, Clifford drove back to the farm.

How could David and Sharm be so naïve? Granted, this is their first, but I'm sure they've seen this stuff on television. He remembered when he was that age and dealing with the same thing. *They have no idea what's about to hit 'em. But I'm here for the little person that's about to be born.* Clifford hoped they would rise to the occasion and find the maturity they needed to be good parents and keep their household going. He drove up just in time for evening chores. The animals were hanging out by the fence, waiting for supper.

As Clifford drove back to his trailer, twilight sparked some end-of-the-day thoughts. *I wonder how Simon's doing. I can still see him smiling at me, with his hands gripping the bars. I can call him tomorrow.*

After supper, he took his patio chair around back to catch a couple of hours of calm. Listening for the night sounds was pure pleasure. It soothed the jagged edges of his life and helped him sleep better.

THE NEXT MORNING, HE woke up to rain, a much-needed spring rain. The horses stood still and stoic, enduring the downpour. The chickens stayed in their coop, but the goats acted the way they always did—butting heads and kicking up mud. Clifford wasn't sure if Vince had different procedures when it rained, so he decided just to follow the same routines. He would ask him the next time he saw him. Rain dripped down his face and his boots were soaked with mud, but thankfully, his Carhartt jacket kept him dry enough to get the job done.

He worried he might miss Sharm's or David's call when he was away at the farm doing chores. *Don't know if I can afford an answering machine.* He drove to a Radio Shack in Grand Rapids and found they ranged in price from one-hundred fifty dollars to two-hundred fifty. He looked at his checkbook and saw a balance of about five-hundred fifty dollars, rounded up. He wrote the check.

I need to call Simon. He called the prison and asked for him. It was a hassle getting through the mechanical prompts, and he didn't have enough credit for a credit card. The operator agreed to send him a bill for the phone call. He waited almost thirty minutes before Simon finally lifted the receiver. He realized what an imposition he had been on his family while he was in prison. *Thank heavens, those days are over.*

"Clifford, it's you!" Simon said. "I've been waiting for your call. How the hell are you?"

"All things considered, I'm doing pretty well." Clifford continued, "I lost my mom from a stroke last month, but we're adding a new baby to the family soon." The two men chatted about the goings-on in the prison, and Simon shared a bit of good news.

"The priest from St. Albans asked me to sing solos in the chapel," Simon said. "You remember him?"

"I sure do."

"I'm helping him with the service. He's takin' a likin' to me."

"That's good news. Did you hear what happened to those bastard guards?"

"Yup! They f**ked up their lives! That's better than screwing with us!"

Clifford managed to get out "I'll give you a call next month" before they lost the connection.

SETTING UP THE ANSWERING machine was more than Clifford could handle. He was mystified by all the jacks and cables the salesperson gave him. The technology had changed so much since he was in prison. He decided to use the trial and error method to make a connection, when the phone rang.

"Clifford, this is David," he said, hyperventilating. "Sharm is being wheeled into labor and delivery. She needs an emergency C-section."

"What happened?"

"During the doctor's visit this morning, they listened to the baby's heart rate with a fetal monitor and immediately sent us to Sparrow Hospital Emergency Center."

"Is her doctor there?" Clifford asked.

"I don't know. I'm worried. I hope and pray that everything goes okay."

"Me too," Clifford said. "I can't drive to Lansing now, but keep me informed. Do you have my phone number?"

"Yes. I'll give you a call if anything changes."

"When I finish my evening chores, I'll hightail it over there."

Clifford spent the rest of the morning and most of the afternoon making the answering machine work. Once the green light came on and the message said "on," he was convinced it was working. He took a jaunt to the sand-mining operation to calm down. Walking up the two-track road, he spotted a truck filled with brush parked in the mine. He approached the vehicle.

"Howdy," Clifford shouted. "What ya doin'?" An older gentleman turned his head.

"I'm cleaning up the brush on the land. They're planning to open this area for mining."

"I'm Clifford Ratz. I live in the trailer behind this berm."

"I'm Bob Sykes. Vince gives me a call when he has a job that needs to be done."

"Do you have to worry about the frost laws?"

"No," Bob laughed. "That's only for the heavy gravel trucks—mine's just a pickup. Next week a crew will be here to harvest the trees on top of this hill. They'll fell the trees, wait 'til the frost restrictions are off, and then a logging truck will come in here and haul 'em away."

"Thanks for letting me know," Clifford said. "I have to get to the farm to feed the critters."

When Clifford came home, a red light on his answering machine was blinking. He rewound the tape and played it back.

"This is David. We have a big baby boy. He weighs eight pounds two ounces and is nineteen-and-a-half inches long. Sharm is recovering from surgery—both mother and baby are doing well."

"I'm a *Grandpa*," Clifford mused. He sat on the kitchen bench, enjoying the moment. "My hope for a better future is here! I have to call Dad."

He dialed his number, but the answering machine gave the standard response. "Leave your name, number, and a message, and I'll get back to you."

Clifford left a cryptic message. "You're a great grandpa, now. I'll call you later with more news."

He hustled through the farm chores, ate cold pizza for supper, and drove off to Lansing. *One minute I'm muddling along with my life, not knowing where I'm going, and the next moment, life is as clear as a bell.* A trip that normally took fifty minutes took him just forty-three to get to Sparrow Hospital. There was little traffic and he expertly accelerated around every curve in the road. His heart was running on high gear.

At the information desk, Clifford asked for the location of the maternity ward, and specifically, for Sharm Atkinson's room. He purchased an arrangement of daisies at the gift shop and pushed the elevator button to the third floor.

David and Sharm were glowing. David was seated next to her, holding her hand. They had just witnessed a miracle as old as time, the wonder of birth.

"Our baby's amazing," Sharm exclaimed. "I love him so much."

"How are *you* feeling?" Clifford asked.

"I'm not feeling any pain, but time will tell—the pain meds haven't worn off yet."

"I would like to see the little guy. Where's the nursery?"

"Down the hall to your left," David said. "I'll take you there."

The two men peered through the glass at Baby Boy Atkinson, who looked like a purple pickle.

"Does he have a name?" Clifford inquired.

"Not yet. We're working on it," David smiled.

"The two of you have done a good job—he looks like a healthy baby boy."

"Thanks," David said sheepishly.

They walked back to Sharm's room. "When will you go home?" Clifford asked.

"They told me three days, if I do well," Sharm said. "C-sections take a little longer to heal."

"I'll call you every day," Clifford said. "Give me a shout if you need anything." He gave Sharm a kiss on the cheek and shook David's hand. "See you soon."

Clifford was relieved that Sharm and the baby were healthy. It made the ride back to Powell a relaxing trip.

A new baby in the family gives meaning to my life. Baby Boy Atkinson is amazing.

A red light blinked on his answering machine.

"This is Dad. I got a phone call from the lab. Give me a call back when you can." He called Herm.

"Sit down," Herman said. "They told me over the phone—we'll get the details in the mail shortly. Who do *you* think your father is? You've got one guess."

"Come on, Dad," Clifford snapped. "Just tell me. I don't like guessing games."

"The test results say I'm your father."

"Well, well, that's terrific," Clifford said. "Everything is as it should be."

"You've always been brainier than me, so I thought maybe you got his brains."

"Did you get my message about Sharm and David?

"Yes, and I'm planning to visit them tonight. It seems like everything is turning the corner," Herman said. "I've got to eat some supper and get to the hospital. Talk to you soon."

CLIFFORD DID HIS FARM chores, mowed the lawn on Friday, and called Sharm every day. He even shared his glorious family event with Sue and Vince. As expected, they were supportive. Sharm healed quickly from the C-section and after three days, they left the hospital. Before they were sent home, the nurses did their best to prepare them for parenthood. The nurses gave them lessons on feeding, bathing, playing with infants, and the importance of bonding with their son. Sharm and David were as ready as any could be for the joys and challenges of parenting.

A few days later, on a Sunday morning, Clifford received unexpected visitors. An old blue Toyota drove up the two-track and parked. Clifford was sitting on his patio chair behind the trailer, soaking up the sunshine. David and Sharm walked around to the back, carrying a swaddled bundle. David gently placed the baby in Clifford's arms.

"We'd like you to hold your grandson, Cliff Allen Atkinson."

Clifford was awestruck. One grateful tear rolled down his cheek.

23   Baby Blues

The phone lines between Powell and Lansing were busy. Clifford and Sharm talked every day, sometimes more than once. Sharm had a baby boy to love, and she was elated. Breastfeeding came easily for her. Clifford was pleased with Sharm's more than sufficient mothering instincts. Nurturing seemed to be a perfect fit for her. David, on the other hand, was miserable. He had bills to pay, a bawling baby to tolerate, and sleep to catch up on. Baby Cliff's squawks and coos grated on his nerves.

"David's irritable," Sharm revealed. "He's angry when the floor squeaks. I tiptoe, but it still bothers him. He says, 'Gosh, woman, can't you just be quiet.' When the baby cries, he paces the living room and says, 'Shut the kid up!'" Sharm continued, "Daddy, what am I supposed to do? He's just a baby. He can't help it."

"That's what babies do," Clifford said. "Where does David sleep?"

"In our bedroom."

"So, the baby sleeps in the living room? Try switching it around. See if that helps," Clifford said, trying to offer solutions. "You can turn a fan on in the living room to block out the bedroom noise."

"I'll give it a try. Thanks, Daddy."

Sharm took his advice, switched bedrooms, and turned on the fan. It helped for two weeks, and then everything fell apart again. Baby Cliff became colicky, David became ornery, and Sharm was frazzled.

"Daddy, I'm so tired. I need a break. Will you come get the baby and me and take us to your place?"

"I'll come and get you after my evening chores around seven. Make sure you bring everything you need for the baby," Clifford said. He was eager to see the little fella again.

Clifford climbed the shaky stairs to the apartment to help Sharm and the baby with their things. She had never been organized, but when he opened the door, Clifford discovered a disaster. Diapers, baby clothes, empty bottles, onesies, blankets, and burp cloths were scattered everywhere on the floor. The combination of the pot smell and dirty diapers almost gagged him.

"What in the hell is going on here?" Clifford asked. Sharm dissolved into tears.

"I'm so tired, I don't know which way to turn," she whimpered.

"Well, let's get started by sorting out what needs to be tossed and what should be kept," Clifford continued. "Where's the garbage can?"

"David took it down to the curb yesterday—it's probably still there."

"I'll get it. While I'm downstairs, put all the dirty diapers over here and put the clean ones in his diaper bag."

"Okay, Daddy." Sharm didn't hesitate to follow his directions. She knew he meant business.

After they hustled about cleaning the apartment, it looked and smelled much better. Clifford didn't want to bring up the pot smell. He remembered from his pot-smoking years when he was chastised, he just got sneakier. Clifford wanted the relationship he had with Sharm to be open and transparent with nothing hidden. He decided not to say anything, but it continued to niggle him.

Baby Cliff was fastened in his car seat between the two of them—no back seats in the truck. It was a bumpy ride, but Cliff cooed and smiled all the way to the trailer. Sharm had a gentle mother's touch and was attentive to him. Clifford sighed with relief, knowing he must have done something right when raising her. He had never seen her so happy despite the challenges she had with day-to-day living. *Would she ever find her way through it?*

"We're here. Home sweet home," Clifford said. "You take the baby and I'll get the rest."

Sharm and Cliff settled into the little bedroom off the narrow hallway. Muted streams of twilight filled the room. It was cozy and warm. After Cliff's evening feeding, he fell asleep and stayed that way until three in the morning, when he woke up with a blast of noise. Clifford bolted out of bed at the first shrill scream.

"Man, that little bugger has a powerful set of lungs," Clifford grumbled.

"Dad? You up?" Sharm yelled from her bed.

"How could I *not* be—he's window-shattering loud!"

"His bottle's in the fridge," Sharm said.

Clifford took the little guy out of his playpen and gently bounced him up and down. The warmth of Clifford's body and the soothing repetition of shhh … shhh … shhh quieted him. It was pitch dark in the trailer, so he clicked on the stove light. Holding him with one hand, careful so the baby's neck wouldn't flop, Clifford managed to get a pan of water to the stove. He set the cold bottle of milk in the pan and waited for the water to heat. He then shook the bottle and sprinkled a little on the top of his hand to make sure the nipple was working and that the milk was warm enough. *I remember Mom doing this when she fed Maribelle. It's amazing how memories come back when you need them.* He turned off the light, settled on the couch, and fed the baby. The two of them fell into a deep sleep. Clifford was awakened by daylight. Where did the time go? The alarm went off, signaling it was time to do chores.

"Sharm! Get up!" Clifford yelled. "I have to hurry. Vince wants to talk to me this morning." There was only silence in her bedroom. She was sound asleep. Clifford opened the door and placed the baby next to her. That finally roused her.

He dressed quickly, grabbed a banana off the counter, and started up the truck. Vince was waiting by the barn.

"Mornin'. You need to get some hay from the Sykes farm today," Vince ordered. "We're running low. His farm is two miles north of Powell. Take a right just after the Propane Gas Company."

"I've been by that place. When should I do that?"

"This morning. He's expecting you."

"Do I need money to pay for it?"

"No, he'll send me the bill."

With the chores done, Clifford went by the trailer to check on Sharm before he drove north to get the hay. He checked each room; Sharm wasn't there. He looked around the back and went inside to check the bathroom. He couldn't find Sharm or baby Cliff. Panicking, he ran outside. "Sharm!?" Clifford yelled. His heart pounded hard. *Did she run away? Was she kidnapped? Did David pick her up? Why didn't she leave a note?* "Sharm? Where are you?" he yelled at the top of his lungs. He looked in the woods and walked up the hill toward the sand-mining operation. Sharm sauntered down the two-track, carrying Cliff on her hip.

"Where were you?" Clifford said, clearly upset.

"I took a walk to see the nature around here," Sharm smiled. "Daddy, you worry too much."

"I worry because I care," Clifford said. "I'm picking up hay and hauling it back to the farm but should be back by lunchtime."

"Want me to make lunch?" Sharm asked.

"That would be nice."

Clifford enjoyed his solitude, bouncing along in the truck, doing chores here and there. He hadn't grown up on a farm, but it was a good fit for him right now. He was eager to start classes at the local junior college. Dr. Freeman's advice made so much sense: go back to school and work behind the scenes. Clifford accepted that he was an introvert. His voice was still raspy, but people could understand him, and he had no problems carrying on conversations. When he scanned the list of classes offered, a business degree triggered his interest. Understanding business would be practical and useful in many occupations.

Clifford decided he would register for classes as soon as he could, but right now, he wanted to spend time with Cliff. The baby was four months old and he smiled at Clifford whenever their eyes locked. Grandpa's eyes twinkled. When Clifford left to do chores, he looked forward to returning to the trailer to play with Cliff. He bounced him on his knees, repeated his coos, fed him, and took naps with him. Sharm watched their relationship grow and nodded with approval. Sharing the baby-raising chores with her father made life easier for her. Clifford bought a baby carrier to strap around his middle. He guided Cliff's little feet through the holes and fastened him in. They took walks around the trailer, up to the sand-mining operation and into the woods. Listening to and identifying the bird sounds was a delightful pastime. Clifford would whistle and sometimes the birds whistled back. The baby's eyes were on high alert, listening, and cooing. His feet and hands waved with excitement.

ONE MORNING, CLIFFORD DROVE to the farm to do chores and a toddler tumbled out of the front door and waddled down to the barn.

"Howdy, little one," Clifford greeted. "Does your mommy know you're down here?"

"Bertram?!" Sue shouted. "Where are you?"

"He's here in the barn," Clifford shouted back.

"Thank heavens," she huffed, walking into the barn. "I let him walk outside, but he's roaming. I'll have to rethink that."

"Little ones love exploring," Clifford said. "If he wants to help me feed the animals, I can come and get him in the morning."

"Nice of you to offer. He watches you through the window and is curious about what you're doing," Sue said. "How's everything going at the trailer?"

"I like it there. My daughter and grandson are visiting me," Clifford said. "I talked to Vince about it and he gave me the go ahead."

"How old is your grandson?"

"Four, going on five, months."

"He's a little too young to be Bertram's playmate, but in time, that might be good for both of them."

"I bought a baby carrier—one that I strap on. Would it be okay if I bring the baby along to do evening chores?"

"That's fine with me."

When the time came for evening chores, Clifford placed Cliff in the carrier and off they went. The little pink feet dangling out of the carrier surprised the horses. Curiosity got the better of them and they nuzzled Cliff's feet. He giggled. He stared at the horses, peered at the goats, and studied the chickens pecking the ground. The baby's alert eyes were like a sponge soaking up all their antics.

The next morning, Sue came by with Bertram. "Hi, Bertram," Clifford said, bending down to shake his hand. "Come with me. We'll feed the animals." He was a cute little chunk of a kid with rosy cheeks and a shock of golden hair. Clifford looked up at Sue. "Do you mind if I call him Bert?"

"Bert's fine. I told him he would do chores with you this morning. He's excited."

Bert held Clifford's hand and babbled all the way to the barn. He liked the horses the best and squealed when he touched their noses. He laughed when the pygmy goats jumped up and down. Clifford walked toward the chicken coop, and then suddenly, a rooster stormed around the corner, heading straight for the little guy. There was almost a mid-air collision before Clifford rescued Bert from the charging fowl. Bert was so scared he couldn't stop crying. Clifford carried him to the house.

"Sorry, Sue. We encountered a hell-bent rooster."

"I understand," Sue said as she embraced her frightened son. "We'll try it again another time. Thanks, Clifford."

He finished the chores and headed home. The old blue Toyota was parked beside the trailer. Clifford sat in his truck and listened to the conversation.

"Please, Sharm, come home. I miss the baby so much," David pleaded. "I won't complain. I'll be nicer to you and the baby."

"Daddy and I and Cliff are getting along great," Sharm responded. "I don't want to go back to Lansing."

"You can have the car anytime you like," David sweetened the offer. "You can come here for visits as often as you want."

Clifford stepped out of the truck and opened the door to the trailer. He smelled marijuana and flew into a rage.

How dare they smoke pot in my trailer. "Why are you here?" he yelled. "Did you smoke a joint in my trailer?"

"We *both* smoked," David said, cowering.

"Don't you ever do that again!" Clifford demanded. "If anyone found out, I'd be back in jail for a parole violation! Take the baby and get out of here. All three of you."

Sharm, wide-eyed and quivering, gathered her things and carried the baby out of the trailer. Tears streamed down her face. David grabbed the diaper bag and the sack of toys, slamming the door. Without so much as a word of apology, they drove off, out of sight. Clifford was left with the broken pieces. He realized he might never see Cliff again, and he would miss him terribly. For a moment he thought about calling them back, reversing what he had done. *Maybe if I apologize, the happy times would return. But, if I do, it won't be fair to me. David and Sharm are babies raising a baby. I'm tired of them running over me and I'm left with picking up the pieces. They gotta grow up!*

Clifford shrugged, went into the trailer, and shut Sharm's bedroom door. He had to stock his empty refrigerator.

24   Out of the Shadows

A Saturday morning on the Attwood farm was relaxed. Even the animals sensed it. Clifford arrived to find the goats jumping and head-butting in the grassy area near the house. The children were climbing trees, throwing frisbees, and chasing the goats. It was time to play.

Clifford parked his truck next to the barn just as Vince sauntered out of the house. He barely escaped the frisbee flying through the air. Vince joined Clifford by the fence next to the horse shed. The horses trotted toward them expecting a treat, or at least some head rubs. They obliged. Vince wore his work-worn hat and cowboy boots. With elbows on the top fence rail and a foot wedged on the bottom rail, he chewed the stalk end of a timothy weed. Clifford followed suit.

"I've been thinking," Vince posited. "Officer Blak really f**ked us over. That son of a bitch strong-armed me, assaulted me, tied me to a chair, and threatened me *and* my family." Vince's voice escalated. "I'd like to screw with him like he did with us."

Clifford nodded, rubbed his forehead, and forced his tears back. "That sleazebag thought he could get away with framing me for Delores's murder. I couldn't take it.

She was like a second mother. We proved him wrong—the bastard's behind bars, sittin' in his own misery—but I almost died slitting my throat."

"I remember that all too well. It was a close call," Vince continued. "A few years ago, Congress gave the victims more rights. So now, they can confront their perpetrator if the situation calls for it. I'm itchin' to give him a piece of my mind. I have a lot to say to him. Thought you might want to do that too."

Clifford gave him a blank stare. He'd never thought of the possibility. "Oh, I dunno," he said softly, shaking his head.

"Give it some thought. We can talk about it later," Vince said.

They parted company. Clifford fed the animals and Vince corralled the kids for lunch.

I'VE NEVER HEARD OF victims' rights before. For sure, they have rights, but would it help me to confront him? Looking into Blak's eyes scares the hell out of me. He's a freakin' maniac who enjoys inflicting pain. He would have gutted me like a hog if he could have gotten away with it. And what did I do about it? Not a damned thing. I was a f**king coward. Well ... not anymore!

Clifford grabbed his patio chair and set it on level ground behind the trailer. His thoughts ran through his prison experiences and his unresolved anger toward Blak. *Justice has been served but I'm still screwed up. I need to dump my anger where it belongs ... at Blak's feet. I can do it. I will do it.*

The next morning was Sunday; Vince was hanging out by the fence, the same place they met the day before. Clifford joined him.

"Howdy," Clifford said. "Thought it over. I'm in."

The look in Vince's eyes was like a friendly hand-shake. "Good. I'll set up a time and make it happen."

No more words were needed between them. Clifford did the chores and Vince spent time with his family. Clifford stewed over what he would say to Blak. For him, it was painful to dredge up his prison memories and the hell Blak put him through. He sat in his patio chair and wrote, scribbled out words, wrote more, and scribbled it out ad infinitum. The project took several days of remembering and searching for the words that rang true. He wanted to deliver a short speech, but one that would gut Blak—the same way he'd gutted him.

For Vince, it was easier. He had wrangled with words throughout his careers, and he would finally let his heart speak the truth. He got a phone call from the warden at Jackson State Prison.

"This is Warden Canfield from Jackson Prison. I've set up a time for next week, two o'clock on Thursday. FYI, Blak is in a separate cell away from other inmates. He verbally harassed the other inmates to the point of mayhem."

"I'll be there," Vince said. "I'll have another victim with me, Clifford Ratz. Blak set him up for the murder of Delores Kin."

"The cook?"

"Yeah. Damn shame. She was a nice lady."

ON THURSDAY, VINCE PICKED up Clifford at the trailer and they drove to Jackson State Prison, about two hours away. Clifford was visibly shaking. He viewed it as running the gauntlet for his own mental health. He'd never been a public speaker, and he was less afraid of dying than he was of public speaking, but Vince's confidence helped him relax.

"You need to be first," Vince said. "I want to have the last word."

Clifford nodded reluctantly. *If I go first, I'll be done first.*

Vince parked the car in a visitor parking slot close to the front door. Warden Canfield gave them a warm welcome as they entered the prison.

"Blak's in his cell. He's been segregated from the other inmates. I'll have a guard stationed nearby as a precaution. Do you have any questions?"

"No. Just ready to get started," Vince said.

Warden Canfield took them to a room nearby, opened the steel door, and left. A guard stood by the back wall. Clifford and Vince approached the cell. At first glance, no one was in there. Only a slight shadow shifted between the toilet and the bunk in the dark recesses. Clifford's hands twitched as he took the notes out of his pocket and approached the bars. "Inmate Blak … I …"

Blak hurled out of the shadows, grabbed Clifford by his shirt collar, and yanked his head forward against the bars. He clamped his teeth around Clifford's nose. With his free hand, Clifford grabbed Blak's groin and twisted it until Blak shrieked in agony. The guard lunged forward and clubbed Blak's arms until he released Clifford. Cursing, the guard dragged Clifford to the other side of the hallway. Clifford's heart pounded hard against his chest as he slumped down, shaken to the core.

Vince knelt down to assess Clifford's injuries. He lifted him up and placed Clifford's arm around his shoulder and walked him to the infirmary.

"We'll be *back*!" Vince shouted.

"Maaaybe," Blak snorted. His evil laugh could be heard in the hall.

One look at Clifford and the intake nurse grabbed towels to clean up his face and treat his nosebleed before calling the doctor. "Your face is banged up pretty bad. What happened?" she asked.

"Blak slammed me into the bars of his cell."

"He's got quite a reputation around here. Many fear him. Nobody likes him."

"Put me at the top of that 'nobody likes him' list!"

"Somebody has to put him in his place!"

"Maybe that someone is me," Clifford mumbled under his breath.

"What did you say?" the nurse asked.

"Nothing. Never mind."

The doctor came in and carefully inspected Clifford's injuries. "You'll be okay. There's a bite mark on your nose, but your skin is mostly intact. A regular application of antibiotic cream should take care of that. Your cheek is bruised, and your right eye is beginning to swell. You'll probably have a shiner. If it's not better in a week, have your doctor look at it. Blak is the inmate from hell."

Clifford nodded and reconnected with Vince in the

waiting room. "I'm so damn mad. I want to go back and confront him."

"Sounds good to me," Vince replied.

The guard opened the door for them. "I handcuffed him, so he can't grab you," the guard said. "I'll be standing by the back wall."

"Thanks!" Vince said.

Vince hung back and Clifford stepped forward, his bandaged face close enough to confront him, but far enough away to be safe. Blak, sensing a change, stood in the shadows, silent. Clifford glared at him, his body straight and commanding, his face creased with anger. He crumbled up his notes, threw them on the floor, and with an icy stare said, "You are a sorry piece of shit! You had life by the tail—a good salary, a pension, and a secure future. You threw it all into the crapper. You were driven to get more by hating more and that destroyed you. Lust and greed wormed their way into your heart, chewed up any human decency that was left, and spit the spoils on the ground. For a short while your power almost destroyed me. *But you didn't succeed.* I'm a free man, but you'll rot in prison for a long time … a very long time. You'll die grieving your ruined life." Clifford's words were as clear as a bell, straight from the heart. He served them up cold, piercingly cold.

Vince was next. Blak stayed in the shadows of his cell. "I've had two careers with criminals, one as a cop and another as a judge. You are the biggest coward I've encountered. Only a gutless coward ties up his victim, hurls threats at him, and runs away when the police come. Cowards torture their prey when they're helpless. Strong men fight fair, eyeball to eyeball. You slither away like a snake when people see your evil heart." Blak surfaced out of the shadows, gave Vince a cutting stare and balled spit in his mouth, getting ready to fire. Vince jumped back out of range, having seen that trick before. "Blak, you're the one who's tied up now. I like seeing you behind bars destroying yourself."

Clifford and Vince walked down the hallway and exited Jackson Prison. Their steps were lighter somehow. It was a sunny day—auspicious. They felt the warmth and freedom of the outside. Clifford exhaled and smiled. He felt cleansed. It was the right thing to do.

SIX MONTHS PASSED AND Clifford didn't hear anything from either Sharm or David. He wondered how the baby was doing. Every day, he did the farm chores, mowed the lawn, and did special jobs for Vince. The sand-mining operation was going gangbusters. Once the frost laws were off, the trucks came in to haul sand for building projects in the area. A local excavating company used Vince's sand for a bridge, and the state bought it for a road project. Clifford expected Vince to give him some sand-mining jobs, but he used somebody else.

"I'm just checking in with you," Clifford asked. "Is there anything you need me to do for the sand business?"

"No, the business is doing just fine. I trust the haulers and the companies they work for. They're honest men." Vince continued, "They invoice the amount taken and send me a check. 'If it ain't broke, don't fix it' is my motto. If anything comes up, I'll let you know."

When the fall season came around, Clifford did more jobs around the farm. He raked oak leaves into six-foot high piles and burned them. He swore there were more oak leaves on the Attwood farm than all the trees up north. It was an endless job. One crisp fall day, Bert came out of the house in a full toddler run and jumped into a huge pile of leaves Clifford had raked. He threw his arms in the air. Next, he made a couple of crazy dives into the pile, scattering leaves everywhere. He grew tired of the leaves, so he ran pell-mell around the yard. Clifford laughed and chased him behind the barn. "I'm going to get you." Bert squealed with delight and continued running in circles.

25   Family Tear

Clifford's phone rang. Bleary-eyed, he looked at the clock—three in the morning. Still groggy, he struggled to get his body up and legs moving. He managed to get to the phone before the call went to the answering machine.

"Daddy?" Sharm was hysterical. "David beat me up."

"Are you okay?"

She gulped through the sobs. "I think my arm is broken and my face is bloody."

"Call the police right now," Clifford demanded. "How's the baby?"

"He's asleep in his bed."

"I'll get over there as soon as I can. Make sure the police stay with you until I arrive."

"Okay," she whimpered.

Clifford threw on some clothes and drove like a madman to Lansing. "Oh, no. I'm low on gas. I don't have enough to get there." He filled up at the closest station and made a fast forty-two-minute drive to Sharm's apartment. The police and the ambulance were still there. He parked just as the EMTs carried Sharm down the stairs on a stretcher.

At the bottom of the stairs, Clifford stroked her hair.

"I love you, Sharmbee," Clifford whispered. "I'll make sure the baby is cared for."

"Thank you, Daddy," Sharm said as her voice trailed off. The paramedics lifted her into the ambulance and drove off with the lights flashing.

"She was beat up pretty bad," the police officer said. "There's a baby in the bedroom. If there's nobody here to take care of the baby, we call Protective Services."

"I'm his grandpa. I'll take care of him."

"Okay. Do you know anything about this David Atkinson?" the officer asked.

"He's decent. As far as I know, he's never been violent before."

"How long have they been married?"

"Almost two years," Clifford said. They both heard the baby crying. Clifford climbed the stairs to check on him.

"Well, that's enough for right now," the officer called after him, getting in his car to leave.

Clifford was apprehensive when he opened the door. He hadn't seen Cliff for six months and questioned if the little guy would recognize him. He approached his crib cautiously.

Cliff cried so hard, it would break anyone's heart. "Mommy! Mommy," he yelped between the tears.

"I'm your grandpa, Cliff. Your mommy has an owie and she went to get help from a doctor. Shhh … shhh … shhh. I love you. I'll take care of you. You can come home with me." The baby stopped crying. Clifford wondered if he remembered the "shhh" he'd used to calm him six months earlier. Cliff was standing up in his crib, clutching the top railing. Clifford reached his hands toward the baby, signaling he wanted to pick him up. When he didn't object, he lifted him up and out of the bed. Tears and snot ran down Cliff's face. Clifford didn't care—he held him tight.

He looked at the little boy, surprised by how much he had changed. He admired his curly blonde hair, his chubby arms and legs, and azure blue eyes. *He's a nice-looking little boy.* Cliff reached for a book and gave it to Clifford to read—*The Little Engine That Could,* by Watty Piper. Clifford read it with expression and the baby was exuberant when the little engine made it up the mountain—he clapped with excitement. He slipped off Clifford's lap and crawled around the living room. The room was babyproofed and much to his surprise, the apartment was clean and organized. *Sharm seems to be getting her act together. I wonder how she is doing at the hospital.* The first call to the ER was unproductive. She was sedated and couldn't talk to him. The next call was to Vince.

"Vince, this is Clifford. My daughter is in the hospital. I need the day off tomorrow."

"Is she going to be okay?"

"I don't know. I'm going to the hospital to check on her."

"Of course, you can have the day off. Sue and Bert can do the chores."

"Thank you. I plan to be back tomorrow," Clifford said.

He needed to find provisions for the baby, and he

wanted to visit Sharm before he left Lansing. The baby crawled from the kitchen to the bedroom and back again while Clifford scrambled to find diapers, baby food, bottles, wipes, and clothes for the little guy. He had a few things at the trailer, and he could go shopping if he needed more supplies. If only he had brought the strap-on carrier, he wouldn't have to keep checking on him. *Where is the car seat? Does David have it in his car? Babies nowadays have so many more things to keep track of.* Finally, he found the car seat in the kitchen closet behind the broom. He packed up the car. *I'm getting too old for this gig. Raising babies is for the young. It's hard for me to organize the pieces to make everything work.* He fastened the seat belt around the car seat, gave the baby a bottle of juice, and drove to the hospital. He rode the elevator to Sharm's floor, Cliff in tow.

"Hi Daddy! Hi, sweet little boy," Sharm said as she stretched her right arm to tousle Cliff's hair. Her left arm, in a cast, lay useless beside her. Clifford cringed when he saw her puffy face and black eye.

"Mommy," Cliff cried, reaching toward her to give her a kiss.

"Have you talked to the doctor?" Clifford asked.

"Yes, he stopped by early this morning, as did the hospital social worker," Sharm continued. "They want me to go to a women's shelter."

"In Lansing?"

"Yes, it's near the hospital, but I need help caring for Cliff. Can I go home with you?"

"Have you been discharged?"

"Not yet, but I will be some time this morning."

"You can come home with me, but you *cannot* smoke weed!"

"I understand, Daddy." Sharm said glancing away.

A discharge nurse entered the room with papers in hand.

"Is this your family?"

"Yes. This is my daddy, and my little boy," Sharm smiled.

"Nice to meet you," she said, shuffling through the papers. "Sharm needs to stay safe, so we're recommending she go to a women's shelter until this is all ironed out."

"I want to go home with Daddy—he'll take care of me and Cliff."

The nurse looked up from the papers and at Sharm. Then, at Clifford. Clifford nodded. "Does your husband know where he lives?" she asked.

"Yes, but it's fifty miles away and in a different county. I'll either be home or close by," Clifford said.

"I feel safe with my daddy."

"Okay, but make sure you get counseling. It is so important, considering what you've been through."

"Yes, I will." Sharm promised.

"I'll make sure she does," Clifford said.

"Good," the nurse continued. "You need to find a doctor and have him check your arm in a week to make sure it's healing right. Use an ice pack as needed for the swelling on your face. I'll send one home with you. Here is a prescription for pain medication. Follow the directions on the label. Drink fluids and get plenty of rest.

Any questions?" Sharm shook her head no. "I'll have an assistant bring her to the north exit in a wheelchair and you can meet her there with your car," she said, looking at Clifford.

As Clifford left to get the truck, Cliff bellowed, "Mommy?! Mommy!!"

"Your Mommy will meet us downstairs," Clifford said. "She'll ride in a moving chair." Cliff kept crying, squirming to get down.

"Shhh … shhh … shhh … Mommy will come home with us."

Clifford buckled the sniffling baby in his car seat and drove the truck to the north exit. The assistant helped Sharm in the car and fastened her seat belt.

"Daddy? I need to pick up a few things at the house."

"Okay, we'll head over there."

Not wanting to upset the baby, Clifford climbed the stairs to the apartment to fetch the clothes and things she needed. His legs were getting weary from climbing the rickety stairs. He hauled the crib down the stairs and placed it in the bed of his truck. He tipped it on its side and tied it securely with bungee cords. He made one last trip up the stairs, rummaged through dresser drawers and closets, and gathered enough stuff to fill a garbage bag. He dropped the garbage bag at Sharm's feet, and she checked the contents. After a quick inventory, she straightened in her seat.

"All I really need is you and the baby. Let's go," she said.

Clifford backed away from the stairs and circled around the block to get to the freeway. One street down, they saw the old blue Toyota parked under an oak tree. David was slumped down behind the steering wheel. Sharm looked at Clifford, rolled down her window, and gave David the finger as they left town.

"Was that helpful?" Clifford scolded, irritated by her antics.

"No, but it felt good," Sharm sneered.

"I'm going to have to get you into therapy ASAP," Clifford mumbled under his breath.

After waking up in the middle of the night and coping with the police, sirens, and crying, Cliff was exhausted. He slept all the way to Powell.

I wonder what will happen with Sharm and David. Seems like there's way too much hostility between them. Clifford recalled his marriage to Wanda and remembered that once a child was involved, relationships could get pretty messy. He wanted to give her a load of advice, but it wasn't the right time. He'd talk to her later after she was healed. First and foremost, he wanted to help Sharm and Cliff settle in, provide good food, and make sure Sharm was healthy enough to take care of the baby. All of this would complicate his life.

CLIFFORD WOKE UP EARLY the next morning, still tired from the night before. Sharm was sound asleep. He fed the baby, changed his diaper, buckled him in his car seat, and drove to the farm. He plopped Cliff in the baby carrier as he began the chores, surprised he didn't protest. After all, it was over six months since the last time they were together. The carrier didn't bother him either. *Did he remember the fun he had the last time we did chores? It's hard to believe he could remember, but he's a smart little bugger.* Once he saw the horses, Clifford was sure he remembered; he had no fear, just excitement. He giggled when he saw the goats perform and stared at the chickens pecking the ground.

By the time they got back to the trailer, Sharm was up and moving. The lesions on her face were healing. There was less puffiness and she had more pink skin showing. Long hours of resting were curative for her. She greeted Clifford and Cliff with a smile and a table set with sandwiches and oranges.

"That's a nice surprise. Thanks for making lunch. You did it single-handedly!" Clifford praised. The threesome gathered around the table, enjoying a family meal together. Clifford noticed her furrowed brow and her mood change.

"What're you thinkin' about, Sharmbee?" Clifford asked gently.

"My future. How can I raise a son all by myself? I don't know how I can get the income I need to keep food on the table and pay the bills." Sharm continued, "I love my little boy and I want him to have what he needs. I feel so lost without David. I don't know if I can do it alone."

"You need to get yourself healed, and then we'll worry about that. Have you made an appointment with a counselor?"

"Not yet. I don't know which one to choose. I looked in the local newspaper and checked the Yellow Pages, but nothing jumped out at me."

"I'll ask Sue tomorrow if she knows of anyone who's

good. We need to get you in sessions as soon as possible."

"Down. Down!" Cliff insisted. He wriggled out of his high chair as Sharm guided him to the floor. He crawled to the end of the hallway to get his blankie.

"That means he's tired and ready for a nap. Chores must have worn him out. Ready for a nap, Cliff?" Sharm asked. He rubbed the blankie on his nose, holding it close. Grandpa carried him to the bedroom for Sharm. Sharm had only one working arm. She kissed him and shut the door behind her. He didn't protest. "He's starting to feel at home here. Thanks for all you've done, Daddy."

"You keep healin' up and things will get better," Clifford said.

HIS WORDS DID NOT reassure Sharm. She was not convinced her future would get better. She took Sue's suggestion and made an appointment with the counselor she recommended. She tried therapy but, in all honesty, her heart wasn't in it. During the counseling session, she slumped down in her chair and stared at the floor. The counselor did her best to engage her, but in the end, she was not successful. She had no reason to believe therapy would work this time. Her cynicism won out. After four appointments, Sharm abandoned therapy.

The last time Sharm had been in counseling was when she was just nine years old. Her parents were angry and fighting about everything, but mostly over the kids. She tried to please her therapist by sharing her concerns openly, hoping that her parents would stop fighting.

All she ever wanted was for her mommy and daddy to stay together and be happy, but her world turned upside down. One of the sessions was scheduled for the whole family. The therapist commented on how the family came in and who they sat by. He saw the family dynamic even before he started talking. Sharm would never forget what the therapist said:

"I see in front of me a family that has taken sides. Wanda and her son, Kevin, are sitting together on one side of the room, and Clifford and his daughter, Sharm, are sitting on the other. This family is divided." Sharm's heart and head went numb—the truth stung. She didn't remember anything else that was said. Therapy didn't work, and her parents became more vitriolic and sometimes vicious with each other until they finally divorced. That was the end of the family as she knew it.

Sharm thought of herself as Daddy's girl. She was his special gift—perfect, a cut above the rest. Kevin belonged to Mom. He was her special gift. Their family had separated into opposing camps and the children were possessions to be coddled and fought over. She vowed that when she had a family, she would *never* do that to her children.

Her thoughts turned to David and the few good times they had together. She convinced herself she couldn't live without him and was certain she couldn't make it financially on her own. Most of all, she didn't want Cliff to be raised in a divided family. Sharm didn't want to repeat the mistakes of her mother and father.

FOR THE NEXT SEVERAL months, Sharm and Clifford followed their morning routine. Sharm slept in, and Cliff and Clifford headed off to the Attwood farm to do chores. This changed, however, when Cliff learned to walk. Life took on a new and more uncertain turn. Clifford had to corral the toddler to make sure he didn't get into trouble on the farm, and the baby carrier was the easiest way to do that. He wanted to keep Cliff safe in spite of his emerging independent streak.

"Down, down!" he protested over and over again. Grandpa was reluctant at first but grew weary of Cliff's incessant demands.

"Alright, I'll put you down, but stay near Grandpa. Do you hear?" Cliff toddled off behind the barn and wanted Grandpa to chase him. It took Clifford twice as long to do the chores. He kept disappearing and Clifford had to track him down.

One day, he was not to be found. Clifford shouted, checked behind every building and around every pile of hay. Where was he? Panic set in when he didn't know where else to look.

"Cliff! Cliff!" he yelled. No answer. Clifford knocked on Sue's door, hoping she might have seen him. She was just as surprised as he was and joined him to search for the little toddler.

"Maybe you should call the police," Sue said.

"I will. I have one more place to check. A couple of days ago, I walked through the woods with him rather than drive the truck." Clifford continued, "Maybe he took that path back to the trailer. I'll give you a call one way or the other."

Clifford raced through the woods but did not find him. On a run, he called out, "Cliff, Cliff! Bumpa is looking for you. Where are you?" He approached his trailer and saw the door ajar and tire tracks in the sand leading to the main road, an ominous sign. Clifford opened the screen door and cautiously entered the trailer … Nobody there. He knelt down and checked under the beds and in the closets. With an exasperated sigh, he walked back through the kitchen and saw a note on the table.

Dear Daddy,

David came to pick us up. We're going to try to work it out. David found Cliff walking along the edge of the woods and carried him the rest of the way back to the trailer. Cliff was glad to see his daddy. David said he bought me a car, so I can come and see you anytime. I'll give you a call when we get to the apartment.

Love,

Sharm

Clifford balled the note in his hand, covered his face, and sighed. *What makes Sharm think she can save her marriage? I put her fires out the best I can, and she runs back into the flames. Those flames might devour her this time.* Clifford let Sue know the baby was safe and then prepared a lunch of comfort food—tomato soup and grilled cheese. The phone rang.

"I'm okay, Daddy," Sharm said. "David set up an appointment with a marriage counselor for this evening, and we'll see if he thinks we can save this marriage."

"I hope you can," Clifford said. "I'm here if you need me. Give Cliff a hug for me."

"I will, Daddy. I love you."

The routine of evening chores brought some measure of relief from the emotional turmoil of the day. His thoughts kept circling back to David and Sharm. He didn't believe in miracles, and saving their marriage would be nothing short of a miracle. He was tired. Tired of living through the emotional whipsaw, and the drain on his time and energy. Weary of shouldering the responsibility for a young family. He hoped David, Sharm, and Cliff would find happiness, but it was his turn to take care of himself. College classes would start in just a few months, and he was eager to get started. He hauled out his patio chair and carried it around to the back. He listened to the rustling sounds of the deer and squirrels in the woods. The smell of pine was in the air. Twilight descended with its purple and pink hues; it was a beauty of a night—serene and still. He heard two hoot owls communicating back and forth and the evening robins chirping at sundown. Peace at last.

26   Courage to Change...

God, grant me the serenity to accept the things
I cannot change,
The courage to change the things I can,
And the wisdom to know the difference.
—Serenity prayer

Clifford hopped in his truck and drove to the center of Grand Rapids. He planned to sign up for classes. While walking through the halls of the junior college, he took an inventory of himself. He was almost forty years old and just getting started. His hair was thinning, his girth expanding, but his mind was inspired and ready to gain knowledge. AA had taught him what he could change and what he couldn't. He learned not to sweat the small stuff. After squinting to read tiny print on the pages of course offerings, Clifford realized he needed glasses. Everything blurred after the first few lines. He scheduled an appointment with an optometrist, took an exam, and waited for the results.

"Mr. Ratz, you have presbyopia."

"What's that?" Clifford asked.

"Basically, old eyes."

"Old eyes! I'm not even forty!"

"Around age forty, eyes become less flexible and your vision changes. Do your eyes get blurry when you read?"

"Yes, and sometimes I get a headache."

"You definitely need glasses. Do you have insurance?"

"No, I'll pay out of pocket." *Isn't that a kick in the head! I'm going to classes with teenagers, and I have old eyes. This is going to be quite the experience. Mom used to say in her own clichéd way, "Nothing ventured, nothing gained."*

Clifford decided on a business curriculum, but he had required classes to take to graduate from junior college. Math, English, physical science, and social science were core classes he had to get out of the way first. He went to the "pit" to register. The pit was a place overrun with teenyboppers, with only a few in their twenties and thirties. He found himself in the middle of a pack herded up and down the stairs. It was like running an obstacle course. He finally got to the gymnasium. Once there, the herd broke into a run, scrambling to sign up for the classes they needed. Clifford sized up the system of tables and conserved his energy by finding the shortest lines. He enrolled in all the classes he needed except for physical science. That would have to wait until next term.

At the registration exit area, he found a kiosk advertising student organizations. Delta Sigma Pi, an organization for business majors, caught his interest. He tucked a pamphlet outlining its history and how to apply into his shirt pocket. At the very bottom of the brochure was the name and number of the contact person for the local chapter. *Would they accept me into their group? Am I too old? Would they find my life experiences an asset or a liability? I'll think about it for a while and test the waters. I'm not going to rule anything out—not yet.*

His first class was Monday morning at nine. He was done with chores and on the road by quarter after eight. He had his routine worked out in his mind. Simple, right? The traffic was horrific; people slid in and out of lanes, honking at the line of cars, and blocking the one lane that led to downtown. "Heh," Clifford snorted. "I can't believe this—it's already nine o'clock. I'm going to be late for class." Finding a place to park was another challenge; every spot was taken. He followed the road to the left and found a parking ramp. *I'm late, but I'm here! I'm not giving up.* He found the room, peeked in, and opened the door and marched in. The young faces turned, looked at him, and gave him the stink eye. He searched for a seat.

"Sir, the continuing education classes are down at the end of the hall," the professor said.

"I'm here for Math 101," Clifford replied.

"You're late. Take a seat." He walked toward Clifford, waving the syllabus for the class.

"I will. And, thank you."

"We're on page four."

Clifford took his seat and leafed through the pages. The professor's name, Dr. Douglas Garbow, was print-ed on the cover sheet. The objectives for the course were mapped out in the syllabus. After perusing it, he felt confident he would excel. Learning the subject was easy compared to the hardscrabble world in prison.

The assignments were listed by subject, date of lecture, and when the assignments were due. He was eager to get started. The class was three hours long, held once a week, and he had a research paper due at the end of the semester.

The next day, he went to his Introduction to Business class at ten in the morning. He gave himself more time to get through traffic, but to his surprise, the traffic between nine and ten in the morning was easier to navigate. He arrived on time, and noticed a female professor sitting at the front desk. Also, there seemed to be an older group of students in this class. Three rows ahead of him sat two attractive females he thought were close to his age. Life had a way of coming around right. Clifford remembered what Maggie Sweetwater said to him: "You're a nice guy, Clifford—someday you'll find someone to love, and that someone will love you back." *Maggie, what a gal! She fought for me to the bitter end and saved my ass. There is no one like her . . . Oops! Get focused. We're starting.*

Dr. Lena Van Til announced her name with a Dutch accent. She suited up exquisitely. Her blonde hair was pulled back with a silver clasp, which created a long flat ponytail. She had a ruddy square face with a widow's peak above her thick light eyebrows. Her most remarkable feature was muscular calves. She was either a cyclist or an avid walker. Despite the Dutch accent, she was fluent in the English language. Her expertise was international business. Clifford considered it a privilege to be one of her students. He looked forward to her classes that were held two days a week. He had to drive into

Grand Rapids only three days a week because his other classes met in the afternoon after his business class. Next semester he would try to organize his classes better to save on time and gas.

According to Dr. Van Til's syllabus, a research paper was due at the end of the quarter. Clifford decided to check out the library, a.k.a. Library and Learning Commons, for research and reference materials.

"Where's the business section?" Clifford asked the student librarian.

"Two aisles to the right of the check-out desk."

He followed her guidance and was surprised to find a shortage of books on business. There were a few outdated journals, but essentially, they weren't sufficient to conduct an in-depth research project.

"Is there another business section in the library?" he asked.

"That's all we have, but if you need more, the Grand Rapids Public Library is just down the street."

Clifford took her suggestion and walked to the larger library, a massive three-story building. He scanned the floor plan in the lobby and marveled at how comprehensive it was. The librarian at the resource desk gave him more information. She described the lending library opportunity, which expanded the pool of resources for patrons to every library in Kent County. The library system impressed Clifford.

So far, his life experiences consisted of a short stint in college, factory work, selling drugs, and time spent in prison; but now, his world was opening up in a grand way. He signed up for a library card, his ticket to thousands of books and other resources. Card in hand, he scouted out the business section and was pleased with the variety of sources. He could read forever and still not exhaust all of the publications. His appetite for more knowledge was fueled, and he felt like an alcoholic in a distillery. At least for the moment, learning became his new addiction.

A RED LIGHT BLINKED on Clifford's answering machine.

"Hi, Daddy, I'm just checking in to see if you're okay. Cliff misses you. Call when you get home."

Clifford decided to call her back after doing the farm chores and eating supper. Farm chores were at the top of his list. When he went into the chicken coop, he was horrified to see that all the hens were dismembered and mangled. Some nasty critter had sneaked into the hen house and killed all the chickens. He collected the few remaining eggs and brought them to Sue at the farmhouse.

"Is Vince here?" Clifford asked as he handed her the eggs.

"No, he's doing hearings on the east side of the state, so I don't expect him home for another hour."

"Well, when he gets home, have him give me a call. A predator—probably a fox or a weasel—got in the chicken coop and killed them."

"Oh, no! How did they get in?"

"I don't know. That's what I want to talk to him about."

He was baffled by the blitz on the chickens. The outside pen was securely wrapped with chicken wire, but maybe a weasel could have slipped through. Somehow, he couldn't shake the feeling he was responsible for the loss.

CLIFFORD'S COLLEGE CLASSES TOOK center stage at this time in his life. He enjoyed the business class with Dr. Van Til and was often called on in class. He excelled in class discussions and spent countless hours researching the first five-page paper. His grade reflected his efforts. She gave him an A and wrote an encouraging comment: "Mr. Ratz, this is an excellent paper. It is well-researched and well-written. Your insights and organization will advance your future career." Clifford saved that paper and whenever he belittled himself, he reread her comments. Never before did he consider working in an international business, but it was now on his radar.

Sharm called once a week or more. Clifford looked forward to talking with Cliff. He enjoyed hearing him speak and learning new words. Cliff's vocabulary was expanding.

"Bumpa? Ball?" Cliff asked enthusiastically.

"I'll play ball with you when you and Mommy come to visit," Clifford said.

"Bye, bye, Bumpa."

Sharm took over the phone. "Dad, what're you doin' tomorrow?"

"I have class, but I'm free on Wednesdays and Fridays after I do chores."

"I'll drive over on Wednesday. What time is best?"

"Any time after ten in the morning."

"That's doable. See you on Wednesday," Sharm said.

He sighed and his shoulders drooped. *Dammit! Just when things were going right in his life.* Sharm always brought turmoil with her. She reminded him of Joe Btfsplk, the world's worst jinx from the *Li'l Abner* cartoon. The rain clouds hung over his head, following him wherever he went. Problems followed Sharm too.

Clifford reminded himself that college was the one positive thing he had going for him. He arrived early for his Tuesday classes. One of the women sat next to him.

"What's your name?" she asked.

"Clifford Ratz."

"You're one of the old guys—maybe I should say, older—kinda like me," she smiled.

Clifford smiled and nodded. "What's your name?" he asked.

"Sara Peters."

"What brings you to this class?"

"I work for one of the downtown banks and I'm hoping for career advancement. My employer was willing to pay for this class. I couldn't pass it up," she said.

When Dr. Van Til entered, all conversations stopped. She was well-disciplined and expected the same from her students.

SHARM AND CLIFF CAME for their Wednesday visit and, as expected, she was full of angst.

"I'm so frustrated, Daddy. David and I have a love/hate relationship. That's what the counselor said." Clifford just listened. No words came to him. "Everything is going along well and then one of us blows up and the nasty arguments start, and they don't stop!" Sharm continued, "When David comes home, the bickering escalates. I'm so sick of it!"

Clifford nodded with understanding. "Did the counselor say the marriage could be saved?"

"He said it would take lots of work and we might be in counseling a year or more."

"That's a long time!" Clifford said.

"If we break up after counseling anyway, it wouldn't be worth it."

"It's a tough decision. I'll support you as much as I can." Clifford sighed.

"If we break up, could Cliff and I stay here until I get on my feet?"

"I'll have to ask Vince, but if it's up to me, you can."

"Thank you. I love you, Daddy."

Grandpa and Cliff played ball in the afternoon before his nap. When Cliff threw the ball every which way, he knew the little guy was to the point of exhaustion.

"Time for a nap," Clifford announced. Cliff started yelling and running in circles. "No, Bumpa. No."

Bumpa captured him in his arms and carried him kicking and screaming into the trailer. With lights out and the bedroom door closed, Cliff finally stopped wailing and nodded off to sleep. He was still asleep when Clifford left to do the farm chores, so he did them by himself. When Clifford returned, Sharm was walking with Cliff out of the woods and down the trail toward the trailer.

"What're you doin' up there in the woods?" Clifford asked.

"We went for a walk to get some fresh air," Sharm said. "Lovely up there."

"Yes, it is. Looks like Cliff enjoyed it too."

It was a good visit with Sharm and Cliff, but Clifford was happy to see her red Toyota turn around and head back to Lansing. He needed to study for his classes, and he relished seeing Sara Peters in class again.

"HI, SARA," CLIFFORD SAID, smiling.

"Did you finish the assignment?" Sara asked.

"Yes, I did, but I had to think about it long and hard."

"Me too," Sara continued. "I've *never* thought about how computers would change business twenty-five years from now."

"Those twenty-five years are what we'll experience when we graduate from here," Clifford said.

"I know. The question is a good one. It's going to be our future," Sara said.

Clifford enjoyed their conversations. He liked the cadence in her voice—it had a lilt to it. Her hair was light brown and straight, barely touching her shoulders. Her black thick-rimmed glasses offset a plain, but symmetrical face. A nicely tailored blouse accentuated a small waist and long, slim legs. Without a doubt, her appearance would be an asset in the banking industry. She looked the part. Best of all, he liked her welcoming smile and their easy conversations.

I wonder if she's married or has a boyfriend. Maybe

we could go to a concert together. No ring on her finger, but that doesn't tell the whole story. I wonder if she'd date an ex-con. I'll give it some time.

CLIFFORD CAME HOME FROM class and once again, Sharm and Cliff were walking down the two-track. Sharm's hands were dirty, and Cliff was filthy from head to toe.

"What's going on in the woods? Do you have a secret life up there?" Clifford asked jokingly.

"Cliff and I have a humongous sandbox up there and we're having a blast."

"Without a doubt, Cliff needs a bath!" Clifford said, as he filled the bathtub with warm water. He grabbed Cliff's bag of bath toys out of the closet and found his favorite towel and a bar of soap. "Bath is all ready for you." Cliff squealed with delight and ran down the hall toward the tub. Sharm could barely hold him long enough to get his clothes off.

"I got you, you little fish!" Sharm bantered as Cliff squirmed away from her. It didn't matter whether it was dirt or water, everything was his playground.

While Sharm bathed her son, Clifford drove to Powell to pick up pizza and pop for supper. On the way back, he saw Vince turn into the driveway.

"Good evening," Clifford said as he slid out of the truck.

"Howdy," Vince replied. "Just wanted to stop by to let you know I'm going to need your help. Tomorrow a new excavator is coming to haul sand, and he doesn't have the best reputation." Vince continued, "He's starting the haul at sunup and should finish before noon. Do you have class tomorrow?"

"Yes, I do, but I don't have to leave here until nine thirty in the morning."

"That should work. You can keep an eye on how many loads the driver takes from the sand pit between six in the morning and nine thirty. I want to see how honest this guy is."

"I'll give you a report at the end of the day when you get home from work."

"Sounds good," Vince said. "By the way, how's your daughter and grandson?"

"Not so good. Her marriage is falling apart, so she came for a visit. I've been meaning to talk to you about that. Would it be okay if she stays here until she gets back on her feet?"

"I don't have a problem with that as long as you do the jobs on the farm and make sure nothing illegal occurs on my property."

"For sure. Thank you, Vince," Clifford smiled.

Dinnertime was disorderly. Cliff didn't like the pepperoni on the pizza and started to whine. He picked up pizza bits and threw them on the floor.

"Somebody's ready for early bedtime," Clifford said.

He had homework due for his classes, so Sharm was charged with putting Cliff to bed and cleaning up the kitchen.

"I'm going to Lansing early tomorrow," Sharm said. "I have an appointment with my attorney. I've made a decision."

CLIFFORD WAS UP EARLY too. Just after the crack of dawn, he heard the truck engine roar up the two-track. Sharm gathered her items, dressed Cliff, and went outside. Clifford fastened him in his car seat and noticed a shovel in the back seat. "What's that for?"

"I've been planting flower bulbs at the apartment," Sharm answered.

"Bye, bye, Bumpa!" Cliff waved.

Clifford counted three hauls between six and nine thirty in the morning. With that information, Vince could verify the morning count from the excavator. On the way to class, he passed the same truck on its way to get another haul. That would make it four.

Once in class, he lit up when he saw Sara.

"Hi, Cliff," Sara smiled. "I like Cliff better than Clifford."

"So does my daughter. She named her son after me, but left off the 'ord.'"

"Do you mind if I call you Cliff?"

"Whatever makes you happy," he smiled. "Are you up for a dinner and a concert sometime?"

"It depends," she flirted.

"On what?"

"If you want something serious … or not."

"I don't understand."

"My boyfriend's at Fort Bragg."

"In the army?"

"Yes. But … we have an understanding. We can go out and have a good time but can't get serious."

"I'm okay with that," Clifford said after a pause. "What kind of music do you like?"

"I'm a big fan of Neil Diamond."

"Really? Huh, I'll keep that in mind."

Dr. Van Til walked in with her arms loaded with books, ready to start class.

CLIFFORD OPENED THE TRAILER door to a red light on the answering machine. "Daddy, this is Sharm. I filed the divorce papers—David will be served tomorrow. I don't know how he'll react. He might get really angry. Cliff and I will be staying at your place. I hope that's okay."

Clifford sighed. He had a premonition this would happen. *They'll be arriving soon. Gotta stock the shelves with groceries, and the laundry is backed up.* Fortunately, he'd be there all day for the next few days to keep them safe. *I wish I had a gun, but I'd be breaking the terms of parole and that would be stupid. I can call the cops if needed.* He had an axe under his bed in case David threatened the family.

Sharm and Cliff pulled up alongside the trailer with a car packed so full it was like a moving attic. Sharm stepped out, frazzled and filthy from cramming all her things into her small car. Cliff was fast asleep. "I don't know where you're going to put all this stuff," Clifford said. "My trailer is small."

"I'll bring in the bare essentials and the rest I'll leave in my car. I'll try to find a cheap storage unit."

"Good plan!" Clifford continued. "I have to get groceries, but we need to do it together. I don't want to leave you home alone." The whole family piled into his truck to get provisions.

JUST A SHORT TIME LATER, the divorce was final. David and Sharm didn't have many material possessions, so they didn't quibble over nonexistent assets. Basically, they took what they had brought into the marriage, which was next to nothing. Sharm received a small alimony based on forty percent of David's income. The judge at the hearing gave Sharm a cold stare and said, "Get a job, girl. You've got a long life ahead of you and a son to support." David covered his mouth and coughed to hide a smile. He knew Sharm would get pissy about the judge's statement. Sharm got primary custody of the child, and David would have to pay child support until Cliff was eighteen. He would have supervised visitation at first. Sharm's bargaining chip was the police report of spousal abuse.

Neither one hurled threats at the other. It was clear they were tired of fighting and trying to salvage a dead relationship. David left the courtroom and moved on with his life. He was an adequate father, and modestly supported Cliff both emotionally and financially. Sharm and David met once a week during David's visitation and smoked a joint together, the only activity they had in common. David changed jobs, made a little more money, and started dating. Sharm, on the other hand, lived with her father through the winter and fretted about supporting herself without Cliff's father around.

Clifford provided for his daughter and grandson as much as he could. His better judgment told him he had to charge her rent. She was surprised when he had her sign a rental agreement. She never considered living with a parent to be a business deal. It was Clifford's idea because he wanted to create an incentive for Sharm, hoping she would become independent. In time, he wanted his daughter to be strong and self-sufficient. He encouraged Sharm to take classes at Grand Rapids Community College that would lead to a professional degree.

She balked at the idea initially, but grew weary of his insistence and agreed to take one class in commercial art. Her fatal flaw was she didn't accept criticism, and that was what the class was all about. The students created an art piece based on the teacher's assignment. Then, the teacher, and sometimes the other students, critiqued it. Initially, they tried to soften the blows of criticism, but soon the critiques became almost brutal. The first time that happened, Sharm interpreted it as public humiliation. She tried not to take it personally, but when her teacher said her work was like a child's, she ran out of class and never came back.

Cliff was two years old, and he hit all the developmental milestones either on time or a little ahead of the curve. He had an extensive vocabulary and memorized the books Clifford read to him. He would recite the stories, mimicking Clifford's expressions and laughing at the same passages. Clifford and Cliff were a delightful team, and the little guy was the one bright spot in their lives. Sharm's mothering skills diminished as her self-preoccupation increased.

"When I'm out, you've got to feed Cliff and play with him," Clifford said, glaring at her. He was tired of her moodiness.

"I don't know what's going on with my brain," Sharm mumbled. "It's running slow, like molasses in winter."

"Make an appointment with the counselor!" Clifford snapped. Sharm tightened her lip and sulked all the way to her bedroom.

Clifford's life was a triumph. He enjoyed his classes, his grandson, and the friendship he had with Sara. He bought two tickets to the Neil Diamond concert at the Joe Louis Arena in Detroit and surprised her with them. At first, Sara was speechless, but then squealed with joy. He earned the top grades in his classes and was busily completing assignments for his winter semester. Vince and Sue continued to be happy with his work around the farm. Vince started another brood of chickens in the late fall, and one of Clifford's jobs was to bury two fencing strips under and around the top of the pen. Vince was certain there was no way a weasel or a fox could slink through.

AFTER CLASS, CLIFFORD OPENED the door to a message on his answering machine.

"Hey, Clifford. This is your dad. Would like to come visit you guys sometime this week. I miss Cliff," Herman said. "Give me a call back."

It had been a long time since he had seen his dad, and Clifford's life had made such a turnaround, he felt like bragging about it to someone.

"Hi, Dad. We'd love to see you. How about coming for supper after class on Thursday? You can play with Cliff before he goes to bed."

"That time works for me. See you on Thursday."

Clifford told Sharm that Grandpa was coming for dinner, and her face was all smiles. "Good! Cliff and I miss him," Sharm said.

Herman drove up in his old Buick and parked next to the trailer. He had a bundle of gifts for Cliff. Sharm and Cliff ran out to meet him.

"Hi, Grandpa!" Sharm said, giving him a warm over-sized hug. Cliff clapped and jumped.

"Papa is here!" Cliff announced.

"You look good, son," Herman said, gazing at him.

"Thanks. It has been going pretty good here. I like my college classes."

"I'm proud of you, son—and Sharm, it's good to see you. I brought some presents for Cliff," Herman said, handing him a shopping bag.

Cliff excitedly grabbed the bag and searched for the best toy. He pulled out the pegboard and hammer and started pounding away. He had found his favorite.

"What's been happening in your life, Sharm?" Herman asked.

"A lot, not all good," Sharm frowned.

"I heard that you and David got a divorce." Sharm nodded and sat next to him on the sofa. "I was sorry to hear that, but sometimes making a change like that can turn out for the better," Herman said, putting his arm around her.

"Grandpa, I miss Grandma so much," Sharm said. She pulled up her sleeve and showed him her tattoo. Herman's eyes opened wide.

"Wow! That really looks like her."

"If I want to remember something about her, I just look at my arm. Gram was a great lady."

"Yes, indeed. I miss her," Herman sighed.

"Supper's ready," Clifford announced.

The dinner fare was Celia's favorite: casserole, biscuits, green beans, and apple pie. The meal was satisfying on many levels.

"Dad, I want to show you something before you leave," Clifford said. He went to his bedroom and retrieved the paper from his business class with Dr. Van Til's comments. Clifford read them out loud, beaming with pride.

"You have a good future ahead of you. I'm glad you're my son," Herman said.

Clifford hugged his father before he got in the car. "Thanks for all you've done to help me."

"Anytime, son."

THE LAST TIME HE talked with Vince, he had mentioned he wanted Clifford to play a more active role in the sand-mining operation. Vince said the new hauler turned out to be crooked as a rattlesnake. None of his records agreed with Vince's, and the trucker hauled far more sand than he reported. Vince positioned a trail camera in a tree, which recorded the trucking activity.

"We'll have proof of who's honest and who's dishonest," Vince said. "I've strapped it in about eye level on the oak tree just north of the operation. I want you to be in charge of the camera. It was expensive and I don't want it falling out of the tree."

"I'll check it out after class today. How often do you want me to view the footage?" Clifford asked.

"About every two weeks … maybe more during the summer, when the hauling increases."

"I can do that."

As spring arrived, Sharm's ill temper seemed to dissipate. She took long walks with Cliff past the sand-mining operation and up through the woods. Both of them came back filthy. Clifford just smiled at them when they returned. They were two kids playing in a giant sandbox. He was grateful Sharm's ugly mood had lifted. Sharm drove into Lansing twice a week for David and Cliff's visitation. They smoked joints together, claiming it dispelled any animosity they felt toward each other. Sharm still hadn't found a job and was dependent on the small alimony she received from David and on her father's good graces. Nothing motivated her; even the judge's admonition had not moved her to seek employment. She had other plans.

27   The Pit

One spring day after her usual trip to Lansing, Sharm pulled in the driveway and popped the trunk. She lifted Cliff out of his car seat and hauled his bag of toys into the trailer. Clifford stopped by on his way to class and noticed large planting trays in her trunk. Sharm flew out of the house.

"What are you up to, Sharm?" Clifford asked.

"I thought it would be lovely to plant something around the trailer. It was supposed to be a surprise. I stopped at Horrocks in Lansing and bought some flowers," Sharm said as she pulled out a tray of petunias and quickly shut the trunk with her right elbow. After setting the tray on the steps, she went inside to check on Cliff.

Clifford packed a brown bag lunch, waved goodbye, and headed to class. *If that makes Sharm happy—who am I to say she can't plant flowers? Having a happy mama helps Cliff too. I still worry about her resisting further education. She'll have child support, but her alimony will be done at the end of this year. One of my mother's clichés is so apt: "You can lead a horse to water, but you can't make them drink." I'll have to trust she'll find her way.*

SHARM WAITED UNTIL CLIFFORD was gone. She put Cliff down for a nap, put on some old clothes, and hauled the planting trays up beyond the sand pit to an open spot north of the woods. She placed the trays on the dirt she'd loosened a couple of days earlier. She returned to the trailer, filled a bucket of water, and hauled it up to the plot.

"David did a good job with these seedlings," Sharm mumbled. "They're a vibrant green—good and healthy." She'd been planting marijuana for almost two hours when she remembered Cliff was napping in the trailer. With the empty planting trays and the empty bucket in hand, she hurried through the woods, past the pit to the two-track road beside the trailer. Cliff had been awake for a while. Alone, he didn't know where his mommy was. Tears streaked his cheeks as he ran to hug her.

"Mommy's working to give us a good income," she said. Cliff didn't understand the words but was relieved to be safe in his mommy's arms. Sharm cleaned up and organized the food for dinner.

"It's going to be a taco night," Sharm said. Cliff clapped. "Let's plant flowers by the trailer." The project was a team effort. Cliff tried to scoop out the dirt, and Sharm plopped a plant into the hole and patted the ground. Cliff fed the plants with water from the outside faucet. He did his best to target the flowers, but he got himself wet and even sprayed his mom. Sharm laughed it off, and they teased each other with a water fight. When all was done, they created petunia patches to the left and right of the steps, making the front door the centerpiece.

"Bumpa is going to be home soon. You need to help

me make the tacos." Cliff climbed up on the stool and filled a bowl with shredded cheese while Sharm cut up the tomatoes and the onions. She browned the hamburger and added the taco seasoning, stirring until the aroma was tantalizing. Clifford opened the trailer door and made a pleasant comment about the petunias and the delicious smell coming from the kitchen.

"This is the best welcome home gift," he said. "Cliff, did you help your mama?"

"Dirt and cheese … Mama and me," he chattered.

They enjoyed the meal together. Cliff took a bath, tried to brush his teeth, and Bumpa read him a story. After he was tucked in, the lights went out and Clifford shut his bedroom door.

"Sharm, we need to talk."

"What about, Daddy?"

"First of all, thank you for the flowers and the delicious meal." Clifford continued, "I'm worried about you. Your alimony ends soon, and you haven't even looked for work."

"Daddy, I'm on it. You have to trust me."

"Have you been filling out applications?"

"I have a plan based on my contacts in Lansing."

"Is David a contact?"

"Yes, he's one of them," Sharm answered.

"What kind of job is it? Can you make money at it?"

"Yes, lots of money. You'll find out soon enough."

"Is it a sales job?"

"Sort of. Daddy, you just have to trust me," Sharm snapped. "I *don't* want to talk about it anymore." She stormed off, slamming her bedroom door behind her.

SHARM PACKED UP CLIFF'S things and headed for Lansing early the next morning. It was a visitation day for father and son. David had several more trays of marijuana seedlings ready for her to plant.

"This is the last of the crop," he said. "Did you plant the other ones?"

"Yes, I did. They look good all lined up in a row," Sharm continued. "The toughest part was hauling the water up there. Water is heavy. I watered them in the trays first before I carried them up, and then after I planted them. Mother Nature always does a much better job of watering, so I prayed for rain."

"These seedlings are mighty fine—bright green and the stems are strong. We should have a really good crop when it's harvest time," David said. He turned his attention to Cliff. "Wanna play ball?"

Cliff grabbed a ball and ran to the backyard to play with his dad while Sharm put the trays in the trunk. When the playing was done, Cliff had lunch and took a nap. David and Sharm chilled out with a couple of joints. The stirrings of their toddler waking up brought them back to reality. Sharm gave Cliff some food, placed him in his car seat, and made the one-hour trip back to Powell. On the way, her imaginings were excited by the prospect of making lots of money over the summer, getting her own apartment, and selling the best pot in Lansing.

THE SAND PIT'S BUSINESS activity was in full swing. Truckers were in and out, hauling several times a day.

The front-end loaders gouged out the hillsides and dumped the sand in the bed of the trucks. The beeping signals filled the air when the front-end loader backed up. When the gouge dented the hill, it caved in, making a million grains of sand cascade down like a waterfall to the ground. The tree roots and topsoil with a myriad of plants mired the pure sand the excavators wanted. It was time for a cleanup.

"Bob, Vince here. I need you to do a job for me. The brush needs to be removed from the south hill of the pit. Are you available any day this week?"

"I have some time at the end of the week."

"That's good enough. The haulers will have to work another part of the pit until then."

Bob drove his trusty pickup into the pit and started hauling brush. About an hour later, he saw a young woman carrying trays up the two-track. She walked around the pit and headed north. She disappeared like vapor in the air.

"What in the heck is she doing?" he mumbled. He scratched his head but kept working—he wanted to get the job done. Bob worked a good share of the afternoon chopping tree roots, hauling brush, and pulling tree branches out of collapsed sand. After a while, the young woman came out of the woods, walked around the pit, headed toward the two-track, and entered the trailer.

"I'm following her tracks up through the woods," he whispered. "I wonder what she's up to." The tracks in the sand were easy to follow, but the footprints in the woods were another story. He walked due north until he saw an open field. Planted rows of some kind of vegetation came into view. *What on earth is that? I've never seen anything like that before. It's not corn. It's not beans. It's not alfalfa.* He plucked the top leaves off, put them in his shirt pocket, and left for home.

Bob set the leaves on his dining room table and cleaned up for supper. His teenage son came home from school.

"Who put this on the table?"

"I did," Bob said.

"Dad, it's marijuana! You smokin' weed?"

Bob rolled his eyes. "I found it growing in a field. Where did you see marijuana? Are you sure?"

"I'm sure. We've seen pictures of it in health class."

"I better let the boss know about this," Bob said under his breath.

"What?"

"Nothing," Bob said, clipping the conversation short and putting the leaves in a baggie.

AFTER SUPPER HE MADE the call to Vince. "Bob Sykes here. I spotted some marijuana growing out in your field north of the woods. A young lady from the trailer was carrying planting trays to that field."

"What!? Are you serious?" Vince exclaimed. "Are you absolutely sure?"

"Dead serious. I've never seen the stuff before, but my son saw pictures of it in health class," Bob said. "He is certain it's marijuana."

"Thanks for letting me know. I'll get right on it." Bewildered and upset, he headed out the back door and walked through the bramble past the sand pit. *I'm pretty sure he said the field north of the woods, which is the field near Old Baldie.* He kept trucking until he spotted even rows of new plants. It was marijuana! Vince exploded and under his breath he threatened the people responsible. "Who would have the gall to plant pot on *my* property. Bob said he saw a woman from the trailer carrying planting trays. That's got to be Clifford's daughter. I made it perfectly clear that any illegal activity would break the contract between Clifford and myself. I won't tolerate it!" Vince snarked under his breath.

Vince deliberated a few moments, and then called the local police.

"I want you to check out a marijuana field on the Attwood property." He gave them a detailed description of the location, and Bob Sykes's phone number.

INCHING ALONG LIKE A snake on its belly, a car with headlights off pulled alongside the road with just the faintest crunch of tire on gravel and parked. Two men opened their doors and closed them carefully so as not to alert the inhabitants inside of the lone trailer sitting next to the towpath. It was a pitchy night—the dense darkness encircled both men like a shroud. It had rained hard just before nightfall and the damp chilly air sculpted a vaporous mist, blurring the lines between grass and trees. The overcast sky blotted out any star or moonlight. Darkness crawled into every dimension, suffocating any hint of light.

The men walked side by side, hunched and intense.

A distant sound of crackling twigs and the rustling of underbrush disrupted the hush surrounding the fir trees. Grabbing their flashlights, the sharp beams pierced the darkness. Glowing eyes stared back at them—frozen in fear. With a sudden dash, deer leaped, bounding through the woods into the distant open fields. The deer's hooves kicked up the pine needles, triggering a sharp sweet smell.

They continued walking, looking over their shoulders to check to see if the persons in the trailer had started investigating—the lights were still out. In front of them, just a trace of the towpath was visible, and a flashlight beam lit the way. A "No Trespassing" sign in neon letters appeared out of the mist, but they disregarded it and pressed on, inching their way toward the shadowy woods. The men trudged through underbrush wet from the evening's rain and ferns high from summer growth. Their shoes, pants, and legs were damp, and their weary bodies cold.

Beyond the woods, a field of even rows emerged as they quickened their pace in excitement. Their flashlights beamed up and down, twirling around the field, certifying their discovery. They snatched off a leaf, noted its spiky points, smelled the earthy, unmistakable scent, and tucked samples in baggies, stuffing them in their pockets.

"I think we can nail the little bitch."

28   Trail Cam

Early in the afternoon, Clifford came home from the Attwood farm. The chickens were growing nicely, and all the other animals were healthy. He liked days like this, and he felt satisfied that all was well. Sharm and Cliff would be coming home for supper, and he would heat the leftovers in the fridge. In the meantime, it had been two weeks since Vince installed the camera in the pit. He walked up the two-track and removed the cartridge from the trail camera. Clifford considered it an ingenious invention. When the infrared beam detected an object, the sensor triggered the camera shutter to open and a photo was taken. From the pictures, Vince would know how many loads were retrieved by the different haulers. Clifford slipped a new cartridge into the camera and took the film to a store in Powell to be developed. He would pick up the developed film and review the footage after supper when the house was quiet.

Sharm and Cliff drove into the driveway, hungry from their travels. Unfortunately, farm chores would have to wait until after supper.

"What's for supper?" Sharm asked.

"Last night's tuna noodle casserole."

"Really?" Sharm scowled.

"Oh, come on—you'll survive," Clifford said, teasing a smile out of her.

"I'm going to bed right after supper," Sharm exhaled her exhaustion.

They finished off the casserole. Sharm went to bed, and Clifford tucked the toddler in for the night with a hug and a kiss. He drove to the farm to do chores.

AFTER THE DINNER DISHES were washed and put away, Clifford picked up the pictures from the store and took them out of the envelope. He was curious to see how well the camera worked. The pictures were black and white, but the images were clear and distinct. There were several truck pictures and a couple of deer photos. The next picture floored him—Sharm with a tray of marijuana plants. Clifford's eyes bugged open, and a huge ache hit his stomach—like a rock. He wanted to puke. *What is she up to? Am I living with a traitor?*

"Sharm!" Clifford screamed. "Get out here!"

"What is it, Daddy? Is Cliff okay?" she asked, stumbling out of the bedroom.

"I am holding a picture of *you* with a tray of marijuana plants." His scream sucked the air out of the room. Sharm dropped into the chair.

"I was going to tell you, Daddy, but I couldn't find the right time."

"Tell me what!?"

"That I was getting into the marijuana business. I'm growing the best crop in west Michigan. It's a little plot behind the woods—nobody goes there. It's hidden from view. I'm sure nobody knows."

"Are you that stupid? It's *not* your property. It's illegal. If anyone finds out, I'm heading to jail or back to prison for sure. I'll die before I go back to prison," Clifford yelled. "They need to be removed! I mean *all* the plants, and … burn them so nobody knows. Is that clear?"

"Yes, Daddy. But you need to know that I *never* smoked pot in your trailer or on this property. I kept that promise."

"What you did was *far* worse. It was sneaky and illegal. If anybody finds out, you'll get *no mercy* from me or anybody else. Is that clear?"

"Yes, Daddy. I'll take care of it in the morning." Sharm slinked back to her bedroom and shut the door. "Dad's crazy. Nobody's going to find out. He's a f**king neurotic!" she mumbled under her breath.

Clifford could not—would not sleep until all the marijuana was burned and any evidence destroyed.

29 "I Have a Warrant ..."

With the sun barely up over the horizon and the crow of a rooster from the Attwood farm disrupting the morning stillness, two police cars drove up alongside the trailer and parked. Clifford heard the vehicles settle to a stop and the squawk of a police radio as the car doors opened. He peeked through the slit of his blinds to confirm his suspicions. His heart started beating so fast it throbbed in his ears and threatened to choke him. Beads of sweat seeped out of his forehead as he sucked in air. He was in a trap with no way out. *I could climb out the window, run up the embankment, and disappear into the woods.* Moving through the hall, he saw Sharm's bedroom door ajar. He looked in. Mother and baby were sleeping soundly.

"I love you so much," Clifford whispered. "More than you'll ever know. Good or bad, you're still my little Sharmbee."

Clifford pulled on pants and returned to the window.

The officers stepped out of their cars and patted the holsters on their belts, checking their weapons, and walked toward the trailer. They pounded on the door, waking the baby.

"Deputy Livingston here. Open up. I have a warrant."

Clifford moved his legs toward the door, but his thoughts flew out the window past the sand pit and up through the woods. With each labored step he sank deeper into hopelessness. Suicidal feelings surged within, just like when he was blamed for Delores's murder. His legs inched forward towards the door. It opened. *Did I open it?*

"I have a warrant for the arrest of Sharm Atkinson," the deputy said, holding up a document. "We believe she lives at this address and has been growing marijuana north of the woods on this property."

Clifford read the warrant, tore it up, and threw it on the floor. Then, he pushed past the officer and stumbled against the table. He jumped the stairs and ran, surprising the backup around the police cars. Ducking around Sharm's car, he ran toward the two-track, heading for the woods. One officer reached out for Clifford's arm, but tore the sleeve from his T-shirt. Clifford stumbled and another officer slammed him to the ground but failed to pin him down. He wrestled his way further up the hill.

"Hey, hey, take it easy. We're not here for you." But Clifford was beyond reason. He lunged forward and ran like a flash of lightning up the two-track towards the woods.

"Stop! Put your hands up! Stop!" Deputy Livingston shouted. Clifford slowed and turned to take one last look at Sharm and Cliff. Sharm was as pale as a ghost, wide-eyed, and scared. Cliff was wailing. There was no consoling him.

Clifford yelled out, "You've got it all wrong. They're

my marijuana plants." He charged up the hill and ran like a madman toward the shadow of trees. Officer Palmer scrambled up the hill behind him, tackling him. He pulled out his gun. In one last leap for freedom, Clifford threw himself forward, reaching for the gun. A loud explosion burst through the morning air, blasting through Clifford's chest and kicking up the sand behind him. He grunted and dropped backwards. Officer Palmer stood up with weapon in hand, sweating and huffing.

Sharm, clinging to her wailing baby, shrieked, "Daddy, Daddy, no!"

Vince heard the gunshot from the farm and jumped into his vehicle. "No, no, no, no!" he muttered like a litany as he sped in the direction of the gunshot. The deputy ran up the hill to check on Clifford. Officer Palmer felt for a pulse. They slipped their guns in their holsters, and the deputy called for an ambulance. Vince raced up the driveway, skidded to a stop, and burst out of his car. Once he knew it was Clifford, tears filled his eyes. "Clifford, I'm so sorry." He knelt down beside Clifford. He covered his hand with his and said, "Clifford, my friend. Sorry it has come to this."

The blare of the sirens grew louder and louder as the ambulance closed in on the scene. They swerved into the driveway and braked. Clifford lay motionless on the ground. His eyes had opened wide with fright, shocked by the force of the bullet. Vince stayed by his side.

"Does he have a pulse?" the paramedic asked.

"A weak one," the officer said.

One of the paramedics wrestled a stretcher to the

scene. They carried Clifford into the ambulance. Looking at Sharm, they asked, "Which hospital?" Sobbing uncontrollably, Sharm didn't respond. In desperation, she held her terrorized baby close to her. They turned to Vince and asked, "Which hospital?"

"Butterworth?" Vince repeated. "I'll follow you, but first, I have to take Sharm and the baby to my house— my wife can watch them while I'm gone."

The ambulance left with lights and siren off. The policemen got in their cars and drove away. The deputy went back to the office to file a report, and Officer Palmer followed the ambulance to the hospital.

By the time they got to the emergency entrance, Clifford was DOA. Officer Palmer was there, and Vince showed up a little later. Palmer had paperwork, and the hospital had their records to complete. It was all about covering themselves. They didn't want anybody or anything to come back to bite them. From the time Vince was an investigator, he knew the standard operating procedures for hospitals and the police departments.

"Who is Clifford Ratz's next of kin?" the officer asked.

"His daughter, Sharm Atkinson, and his father, Herman Ratz," Vince answered. "Those are the only two I've met. Sharm was at the trailer and witnessed the shooting. She's in shock as we speak, so you should notify Herman Ratz. He lives in Lansing."

"I'll call his father. Maybe we can get this wrapped up by noon."

"Wrapped up?" Vince asked. "Are you sure he planted the marijuana?"

"He confessed to it."

"He did? When?"

"As he was running away, he said it was his crop of marijuana."

"Oh?" Vince stopped the conversation. He had to reevaluate his thoughts about Sharm.

I guess Sharm could have been doing Clifford's bidding by planting the marijuana. The evidence he had incriminated Sharm, but maybe she was only an accomplice. *Sharm could have been acting alone without Clifford's knowledge, or maybe she was just following her daddy's orders. The only one who knows is Sharm. She's in such a state right now, she's not sure of her own name.* He was surprised they were wrapping this up without an investigation, especially with a fatality. They wanted this case closed—to be done with it and move on. They were accepting Clifford as guilty. *I'm not so sure. On the other hand, we'll never be able to get all the facts—Clifford is dead. For now, I'll be patient and see what happens to Sharm and the baby.*

The officer called Herman while Vince sat in the waiting room.

"That was a helluva difficult call to make," the officer said. "His father will call Gorsline-Runciman Funeral Home. He was clear he didn't want an autopsy. The gunshot wounds was the cause of death. I didn't order an autopsy either—we know what happened. He ran when we told him to stop. He reached for my gun and I shot and killed him."

"Is there anything else you need from me?" Vince asked, his body sick from Palmer's report.

"No, and thanks for your help."

Maybe this might not have happened if I would have handled it differently. What rotten luck—Delores Kin, and now this. Clifford was doing so well. It's such a tragedy he's dead. Vince swiped at his tearing eyes. It was so unfair; Clifford had so much promise. *I'll miss him—he was a good friend. Clifford knew that discovery of that patch would land him back behind bars. If Sharm secretly planted the marijuana crop without her dad knowing, this was a betrayal of the worst kind. She needs to pay the price for what she did.*

As far as the farm went, this couldn't have happened at a worse time. The sand-mining operation was in full swing. He had to destroy and burn the marijuana plants north of the woods—pronto! Sue had her hands full with their children. The farm animals needed tending and there was nobody to help. He'd call the office on Monday to request time off.

Vince drove up his driveway and a feeling of peace washed over him. It was as if Clifford was there comforting him. Suddenly, out of nowhere, a mandate, seemingly a heavenly mandate, caught him off guard. It was someone or something instructing him to help Sharm and not to punish her.

"Are you telling me she's the guilty one?" Vince asked the presence.

"Yes," the spirit said. "The quality of mercy is not strained. It droppeth as the gentle rain from heaven upon the place beneath. It is twice blessed—it blesseth him that gives and him that takes."

He shook his head, trying to bring himself back to reality. *That's me talking to myself. I'm in English class in high school reading Shakespeare. But Sharm needs mercy, not punishment.*

Vince stepped out of his car and walked in the front door. His family and Cliff were sharing a hot dog lunch together. Sharm was sitting on the floor in the corner of the room, comatose. Vince looked at her dispassionately. He was not ready to give her mercy. It was only noon. So much had happened since early morning, he felt he was in a time warp … 6:00 a.m. to eternity.

Vince's four children enjoyed Cliff and considered him to be the newest member of the family. They played and laughed together. Vince joined them at the table and Sue handed him a hot dog.

"You're a great gal," Vince said to his wife.

VINCE CALLED HERMAN TO make sure the funeral home transported Clifford's body to Mason.

"You need to know you had a wonderful son. He was a good employee and I considered him a friend," Vince said. There was no response at the other end, only deep guttural sobs.

"Thank you," Herman sputtered.

"I have Sharm and Cliff at my house in Powell. Sharm is not in any condition to care for … Cliff." Vince stumbled over the baby's name. Clearing his throat, he continued, "We need to make a plan for them."

"I'll call Wanda, Sharm's mother. We'll come up with something and get in touch with you," Herman said as he hung up.

After Bert and Cliff had their afternoon nap, the whole

group went outside to play while Vince did chores. He found the animals different somehow—it was like they knew Clifford was dead. The chickens acted like they always did, scratching, clucking, and pecking, but the horses looked him over and moved slower. The goats didn't jump as high. The children ran around the farm, picking flowers and playing tag. Cliff fit right in and became Bert's buddy.

Vince answered a phone call from Herman. "I'm hoping you can do us a favor and keep Sharm and Cliff overnight. It took me a while to track Wanda down," Herman said. "She's out of town and can't be here until tomorrow morning. We'll take two cars to Powell. That way we can move Clifford and Sharm's things out of the trailer and bring Cliff and Sharm back to Lansing."

"What time do you plan on being here?"

"Late morning is my best guess," Herman said.

"That should work just fine."

Dinnertime came and Sue coaxed Sharm to the supper table. She was famished, but never acknowledged anyone around her, including Cliff. She fixated on the food. After supper, Sue guided her to the guest bedroom and showed her where the bathroom was. She placed fresh towels on the bed. Sharm was like a stone. She didn't make eye contact with Sue or speak. When all the children had gone to bed, Vince and Sue watched the news. Suddenly, Sharm came out of her bedroom, bolted out the front door, and disappeared into the night. A thick blanket of clouds hid the sliver of a moon. Vince switched on the security light and looked outside, but couldn't see her. He slipped his shoes on and the chase began. Vince had no idea which direction she had gone or where she was. The horses neighed a warning. This meant she must have run by them into the woods. He grabbed a flashlight from the barn and continued the trek through the bramble and the dark shadows underneath the oak trees.

He saw a fresh Kleenex on the ground. Perhaps it slipped out of her pocket. The trailer was coming into view, a logical destination because it was familiar. He continued past the dark empty trailer. Up the hill on the two-track he spotted a shadowy figure hunched over the very spot where Clifford was killed. He cast the flashlight beam in that direction and what he saw was horrible. Blood dripped from one of her wrists. Her face was as white as a sheet. Vince's adrenaline kicked in. He raced toward her, ripped off his shirt, and removed his sleeve. He created a tourniquet and fastened it on her arm. He was relieved when he watched the bleeding slow down.

Meanwhile, Sue had put John in charge of watching the children and took the car down the main road, looking for Sharm and Vince. She drove up next to the trailer and her headlights revealed the grisly scene. Two figures huddled together on the two-track. Sharm was crying, and the sleeve Vince had wrapped around her wrist trying to control the blood flow from her wrist was crimson. He comforted her as much as he could.

"Thank God you're here. Call the ambulance ASAP," Vince yelled. "Sharm tried to kill herself."

"Is she okay?"

"The bleeding has slowed down, but she needs medical help."

Sue hurried back to the house and had an ambulance dispatched. When the paramedics arrived, Vince shared the events of the day, and they hustled her to Butterworth ER. He knew she needed more intervention than treatment for her self-inflicted wound. She was in shock and once she was stabilized, she needed to go to Pinehurst Psychiatric Hospital. He would go to Butterworth and advocate for her. Once again, the ambulance came to the same place where Clifford was shot earlier that day. They helped Sharm walk to the ambulance, placed her on a gurney, and treated her wound. They left for the hospital.

Vince walked with weary steps through the shadowy woods back to his home. Once again, he felt Clifford's spirit reassure him he was doing the right thing. Choosing the path of mercy and compassion over punishment and revenge was Clifford's message from the other side. Vince's footsteps lightened; he had a purpose, an affirming lodestar. He would be lenient with Sharm and support her in every way he could. He would exercise compassion.

LATE MORNING THE NEXT day, Herman and Wanda showed up in two cars. Vince shared the events of the night before and strongly emphasized the importance of sending Sharm to Pinehurst for treatment after she stabilized and Butterworth discharged her. Vince said he and Sue would visit often and encouraged them to do the same.

"Cliff is welcome here anytime," Sue said. "Bert and

Cliff are good friends. They play well together. Would you like to come in for coffee?"

Herman and Wanda declined the offer, saying they needed to start getting Clifford and Sharm's belongings out of the trailer. They hoped Sue would be willing to watch Cliff while they worked. Sue nodded with a smile.

As they packed Sharm and Clifford's personal belongings, Herman found a packet of photos on Clifford's bed. He opened it expecting to see pictures of baby Cliff. Instead, he saw snapshots of trucks and deer and …. "Is that Sharm? What is she carrying?" he whispered under his breath. Herman's hands started shaking and the blood drained out of his face. He looked at them hard and slipped the Sharm pictures in his back pocket and put the rest back.

When everything was packed, Herman and Wanda went to see Sharm at Butterworth. Both of them suggested a placement at Pinehurst, so when she stabilized, the ambulance drove Sharm to the psychiatric hospital.

THE PERSONNEL AT THE check-in desk allowed Herman to visit, but her doctor indicated Sharm was not ready to see Wanda. They encouraged Wanda to check back often. They informed them that family therapy was part of the treatment and reunification was one of the goals in therapy. The staff was confident Sharm would welcome her mother at some point.

Herman hugged and held Sharm as much as she allowed. The words she uttered over and over again between tears were, "I'm so sorry. I'm so sorry …" There was no real dialogue during the visitation. Herman said goodbye with a promise to visit again soon. He was surprised when she didn't ask about Cliff. *Maybe the pain is too great to see outside of herself. She's locked inside and nobody else matters.* In time, he hoped that would change.

Wanda and Herman picked up Cliff and returned to Lansing. They had so much to manage. Cliff needed a secure home. They needed to contact David; the funeral details had to be finalized. Clifford's things needed sorting, but that could wait. He had no last will and testament, nor any property to speak of. His life was cut short just as it had started to rise.

"He had plenty of promise—a gentle soul," Wanda said. "It was the beginning of a new life for him. We competed with each other over how many books we could read—he always beat me."

"For sure, he was smarter than me," Herman said.

"I worry about Sharm. I don't know if she can live without him," Wanda continued. "I'd be surprised if we ever see eye to eye."

"Other than the family breaking up, why is Sharm so angry with you?" Herman asked.

"She was her daddy's favorite and I've always been the enemy."

"Maybe that can change."

"I hope so. We need each other," Wanda said.

"Our job is to take care of Cliff the best we can."

"I agree. That might be what finally reunites us."

Herman knocked on Vince and Sue's door, ready to pick up Cliff for the ride home.

"Hi, Bumpa. Where's Mommy?" Cliff said, running into his arms.

"She's still at the hospital. We'll pick her up later." Herman continued, "Vince, I can't thank you enough for all you've done. I found something on Clifford's bed that belongs to you." Herman handed him the packet of photos.

"Thanks for giving them to me. They're probably pictures from my trail camera."

With Cliff in his arms, Herman said goodbye and headed to his car.

Cliff was exhausted from playing so hard with the Attwood children. He slept all the way to Lansing. Wanda and Herman arrived at his house about the same time. Grandpa Herman carried him into his house while Wanda set up his portable bed. He laid him gently on the mattress, and Cliff was out for the night.

"I'll watch Cliff tomorrow while you sort out Clifford's belongings," Wanda offered.

"Thank you. Will you contact David and let him know what's happened?" Herman continued. "I don't want Cliff staying with David. There was and may still be a lot of smoking in that house, and the little guy doesn't need to be exposed to that."

"I couldn't agree more," Wanda said. "I'll contact him tomorrow. If he wants to see Cliff, he can come over to my house."

"Good idea."

When Wanda left, Herman collapsed on his couch, exhausted from the events of the day. He couldn't handle going through Clifford's boxes. The pain of his loss was still too fresh. Maybe tomorrow. He woke up from a knock on his front door. He stumbled around the boxes and opened the door to find Wanda ready to pick up Cliff, who was fast asleep.

"You're early," Herman said.

"Not really. It's after nine."

Herman scratched his head. "Where did the time go?"

Wanda heard Cliff cry from the bedroom; she gathered him up and took him to her house, leaving Herman with a gaggle of packed boxes. He plopped on a chair, trying to decide which one to open first. He opened the one marked "bedroom." Inside was a set of sheets, an alarm clock, and a quilt that Celia had made. He unfolded it to see the design, which was an organized arrangement of concentric circles. The colors were a beautiful combination of blue, green, and red. His eyes saw Celia in the quilt, and his nose smelled Clifford. The memories of the two of them washed over him like a tsunami. It was more than enough for one day.

CLIFFORD'S FUNERAL WAS A somber affair. It was held at the Church of the Brethren in Mason. Sharm's doctors advised that she not attend the funeral. When Herman asked why, they said she would relive the trauma, and she was not ready for that. They emphasized the importance of continuing treatment. Herman and Cliff came to the funeral together, but Cliff had no idea what was happening. When Herman lifted him up to see Bumpa in the casket, he grabbed his hand.

"Bumpa's cold. Is Bumpa asleep?" Cliff stuttered.

"Bumpa is dead," Herman said forthrightly. Cliff gave him a quizzical look.

Vince's entire family was there—they filled up a pew. When Cliff saw his buddy, Bert, he scooted next to him and left Herman by the door greeting people. Cliff and Bert goofed around so much that Sue moved to sit between them. That quieted them some. Most of Clifford's family was there too: Wanda, Herman, Kevin, and his sister, Maribelle. All the close relatives were there except Sharm. Sara Peters sent a beautiful vase of sunflowers, and Simon sent a sympathy card to Sharm by way of Herman. Vince shared a brief eulogy.

"I've only known Clifford for a short while, but what impressed me about him was his drive to get better and his care for others. He laid his life on the line and made the ultimate sacrifice. He worked hard and was a conscientious employee. I trusted him with everything I have, including my own life. He was a true friend. He loved his family." Vince paused to look at the family members seated in the pews and continued, "Clifford loved every one of you! He was a good role model and actively pursued a better future by being conscientious every day. His life's story is a shining example of how a person can persevere through tough times, overcome their mistakes, and *never* lose heart." Vince teared up and before he sat down, he touched the casket and said, "Goodbye, my friend," his voice gruff with emotion.

Tears flowed in the audience. After a moment of silence, the men from the funeral home lifted the casket and carried it down the aisle and out the church door.

After sliding it into the hearse, they shut the doors and started the long procession to the cemetery. Clifford's family and friends followed.

The group gathered around the open grave and as the casket was lowered, they said the Lord's Prayer in unison. Herman held Cliff's hand and whispered something in his ear. He handed Cliff a white rose, lifted him up, and approached the edge of the grave vault. Cliff dropped the rose on top of the casket. This was followed by a moment of silence. The group slowly wandered back to their cars and left.

30   Cry of Contrition

Sharm sat in her therapist's office, clueless that her father's funeral was over. Her thoughts were stuck on suicide; like a scratched record, her circular thoughts kept coming back to the same place. Suicide was her only way out. Every cell in her body yearned for a mindless space that would free her from her guilt and mental torture. The full realization that she had caused her father's untimely death was gut-wrenching. Contrition would come at a cost. She would have to face herself and accept all the ugliness and stupidity she'd buried deep down. All the pretty dresses, makeup, or nail polish couldn't hide the muck inside. A defensive stronghold mired in self-deception waited to be released. She had no justification. Accepting her role in her father's demise was far more painful than taking her life by her own hand.

Sharm's eyes were hollowed-out sockets, empty and weary. Her bouncy bobbed hair was now shoulder length with frizzy tangles at the ends. Her body was emaciated from a lack of food; she had no desire to eat.

"I killed my father," Sharm repeated over and over again.

"No, you didn't," Ida, her therapist, answered emphatically. "The police killed your father."

"Why did they kill him?"

"He ran away when the police told him to stop," Ida said.

Sharm frowned and pursed her lips, straining to understand.

"He didn't listen?" Sharm asked.

"That's right."

"Why did he run away?"

"I don't know. We'll never know because he's dead now."

Sharm curled into a fetal position and sobbed. The therapist was an empathetic presence but wanted Sharm's suicidal thoughts to stop. If that meant reinforcing half-truths, so be it. Hospital stays were time-limited, and Sharm's time was running out. *Maybe more medication, or a different one, is the answer.*

"You need to see the psychiatrist sometime today," Ida said. "He needs to check on your medications."

Sharm smiled. "I like Dr. Farrington. He's a lot like my dad and my grandpa."

Ida picked up the phone. "Dr. Farrington? This is Ida, Sharm Atkinson's therapist. I don't think her present medication is helping her obsessive thoughts. Her suicidal ideation isn't stopping. She can't get them out of her head."

"I'll try something else," Dr. Farrington promised. "Let me know if you think it's working."

HERMAN DECIDED TO BRING the quilt Celia had made for Clifford to Sharm as a comforting reminder of her father. She took it with care, nuzzling her face in its folds. She caught the scent and smiled.

Herman made the one-hour drive to Grand Rapids to visit Sharm twice a week. He had called Sharm's therapist to get permission to bring Cliff to visit her. Ida was adamantly opposed, indicating it would be best to wait until Sharm was further along in therapy. Vince and Sue visited Sharm in the hospital as well. Most of the visits involved talking about the weather and the food at the hospital. One of Vince's visits was very different, however. When Sue couldn't find a babysitter, he came alone.

"Howdy, Sharm. How's it going?" Vince asked.

"Okay." She looked furtively at Vince. "Please tell me what happened to Daddy," she pleaded.

"Do you want the straight scoop?"

"Yes," she said softly.

"Are you certain you want me to tell you?"

"Yes."

"Okay." Vince cleared his throat and sat straighter. "Someone planted marijuana on my property. That's against the law. My worker told me he saw a young woman carrying plants to the plot north of the woods and watched her return and go into the trailer. He checked out the plot after she left and discovered marijuana plants. He called me and told me what he saw, and I called the police. Two officers checked out his claim that evening. They found the plot and took samples back to the lab. The officers verified it was marijuana, so they got an arrest warrant for the woman in the trailer. They knocked on the trailer door and told your father they had the warrant. According to the officers, he took his time reading it. Then, without a word, he tore it up and dropped it on the ground. He bolted, running toward the woods. They ordered him to stop several times, but he kept running. As he ran, he yelled back at them, 'They are my marijuana plants.' Clifford admitted guilt but did not go calmly. He wrestled with the officer and in the squabble the policeman fired the shot that killed him."

Sharm let out a prolonged high-pitched wail and ran out of the room. Vince was flummoxed. He stood up, not sure what to do next. After he regained his composure, he walked to the registration desk and briefly described what happened during his visit with Sharm.

"I'll contact her therapist," she said.

Vince had a jumble of thoughts as he drove back to the farm. *I always thought the truth sets you free, but Sharm reacted like a terrified animal. Maybe she can't handle the truth—at least not yet … maybe never.*

WHEN SHARM ENTERED THE hospital, she was encouraged to meet Ariel, the art therapist. At her first session, she stared vacantly at the white surface with a brush in her hand. Her mind was empty, void of imagination. The canvas remained blank for two sessions. Finally, Ariel placed a mirror on the shelf next to her and suggested she draw a self-portrait. Sharm carefully lined up the blacks and the grays, and the skin tones: reds, blues, and yellows. She stroked the ends of the brushes and looked at herself in the mirror for a long time. She moved in closer to the mirror, squinting and widening her eyes. From her first strokes, two eyes emerged, raccoon-like gray eyes underscored by black half circles. Next, she painted shoulder-length squiggles of black hair with separated strands. The painting looked like Edvard Munch's *The Scream*. She changed brushes and reached for the flesh tones, whites and yellows. After combining all the colors, she made one sweeping brushstroke, shaping her bony shoulders with thin arms dangling at her side. She freshened her paint, added pink, and deftly painted her breasts and the rest of her torso. She looked up and saw Ariel smiling. Sharm smiled back.

The next art therapy session was very different. Sharm entered the art room in a huff, stood by her easel, and angrily selected her paints. She selected the red, the black, and the gray tubes, opened them, and squirted them on her palette. Her brush attacked the canvas first with black swathes of paint, then red and gray blades. It looked like a smoldering brush fire. She hastily cleaned up and left in the same angry mood. Ariel noted the change and contacted Ida.

"This is Ariel. Sharm just left art therapy in an angry mood."

"That's good! She's been turning her anger inward. Finally, it's coming out. That's progress. Depression is hard to work with. I can work with anger."

The next session with Ida was pivotal. Sharm stomped in the room, plopped on the chair, and glared at her therapist.

"How are you feeling?" Ida asked.

"Mad." Sharm crossed her arms and sat with her legs apart, feet firmly planted on the floor.

"That's encouraging," Ida said. "Who are you mad at?"

She pursed her lips and furrowed her eyebrows. "Many people: the police, David, and how rotten life is…" Her nose twitched in a sniffle. "Mostly, at myself," Sharm said softly.

"Tell me more about that."

"My dad was good to me. I made a mess of everything. I took advantage of his kindness." Sharm clasped her hands together, put her elbows on her knees, and hung her head. "He helped me when David and I were struggling. He took care of Cliff and gave me food and a place to live."

"You had a good father," Ida responded.

"Yes, I did … I was a bad daughter."

"You don't feel you measured up as a daughter?" Ida asked.

"I failed big time. I was sneaky. I put my father and my family in danger," Sharm said sheepishly, tears welling in her eyes.

"How did you put your family in danger?"

"The police came for me. My name was on the warrant."

"You caused the police to come to your home."

"They came to arrest me. My father took the fall. He told them he was guilty."

"Your father died to protect you."

"Yes."

"He gave you an amazing gift," Ida responded, nodding her head.

"I will never be able to repay him. I'm worthless."

"So, this is about you forgiving yourself."

"Yes." Tears ran down her face. Ida's silence opened the way for Sharm to release a cry so huge that it cleansed.

"What did your father want for you?" Ida asked.

Without hesitation, Sharm said, "He wanted me to finish school and be happy."

"Is that something you want?"

"Yes, with all my heart," Sharm said between sobs.

Ida gave her time to take deep breaths and calm herself. "How can you make that happen for you?"

"Little Cliff makes me so happy. I want to be the best mother I can be for my son."

"You find happiness in caring for your son."

Sharm nodded and folded her hands on her lap.

"Caring for yourself and building your self-esteem will help you be a good mother for your son. How can you do that?"

"My father wanted me to finish school and find a career that I enjoyed. I can start by getting my GED. When I'm finished, I can go to college and find a job that's right for me."

Ida nodded. "Therapy is about accepting responsibility for your mistakes, for your wrongdoings and learning from them. It is also about understanding and being kind to yourself. You're on the right track!" Ida gave her a reassuring smile and Sharm smiled back. "When you come to your next appointment, we'll develop goals to help you create the life you want. You have worked hard, and it shows."

Sharm nodded.

AS SHARM HEALED, HER paintings had greater detail. She immersed herself in bright colors and her subjects were less sullen and more animated. The colors she chose in her dark period were black, red, gray, and white. Her next set of paintings was murky and uninviting, but at the end of treatment, the light broke through the shadows. Oranges, yellows, pinks, greens, and blues joyously played on her canvas. She was becoming stronger and happier every day.

"I WANT TO LET you know about the turnaround I've seen in Sharm," Ida reported. "She hasn't talked about suicide in over a week and she's participating in a group. Her mood seems to be improving. I've actually seen her smile a couple of times."

"That's good news," Dr. Farrington said. "We'll keep her on the same meds but let me know if anything changes."

Ida was pleased with her progress in group participation. Another patient who often sat next to Sharm was recovering from major depression. During group therapy, Dahlia knitted. She knitted sweaters, scarves, baby clothes, and stocking caps. Oddly enough, Sharm played a role in her recovery.

"Dahlia, I want to learn how to knit. Will you show me how?" Sharm asked.

"Yes," Dahlia said. Sharm's interest gave her a purpose.

Before the next session, Dahlia put extra yarn and needles in her tote for Sharm and carried them to the group. The two stayed after the session so Dahlia could teach Sharm the basic stitches. Sharm was a natural. She caught on so fast it was as if she was born with knitting needles in her hand. Her work was exacting, and she created splendid designs that were uniquely hers. Her knitting became the topic of conversation.

"Sharm, you have talent and an eye for color," her friend Beth said. "You should go to school to study art."

"You think so?"

"Hasn't anybody told you that before?" she asked.

"No."

"You have so much potential," Beth continued. "The world needs you."

"Oh, stop!" Sharm blushed and hung her head in embarrassment. She lapped up the praise and let it settle inside. *Maybe I can try to study art again; I do enjoy the creative side of me—it helps me focus. When I knit, I lose track of time and I feel peaceful.*

31   Knitting Together

"Herman, this is Ida, Sharm's therapist at Pinehurst."

"I've met you before. I hope you have good news."

"I do. Sharm is ready to see her family. The next time you come to Grand Rapids, bring Wanda and Cliff."

"Do you want me to call you before I come?"

"No. Sharm says she's ready to see all of you."

Herman hung up the phone, pleased Sharm was making progress. He didn't want to tell anyone, but Cliff made him so tired. Just carrying, lifting, and chasing after him was getting to be a chore. But he loved the little guy, and he was determined to keep Cliff's care within the family. Herman had heard so many shocking stories about children in the foster care system. Without a doubt, Wanda was helpful. They split the week in half. Wanda took the first part of the week and Herman took the second part. The middle day, Wednesday, they split in half. It worked out well for both of them. Herman was pleasantly surprised that Wanda and he were getting along. Cliff was the catalyst for the harmony.

"Wanda, I have some good news." Herman said excitedly. "Sharm wants to see you, Cliff, and me sometime soon. It seems that there's been progress in therapy."

"I guess Tuesday works for me," Wanda said with some apprehension.

"I don't have a job right now, so anytime is good."

"I'll have Cliff at my house, so I'll pick you up," Wanda said.

"What time?"

"One thirty in the afternoon. Cliff will take a nap in the car."

Herman usually dropped by Darb's Crystal Café for a couple of cold ones, but this Tuesday he would skip it for an even better treat. Ever since Clifford died, Herman hoped Sharm would regain her health so she could take care of her son. He knew Sharm loved Cliff.

Wanda showed up at exactly one thirty. She drove an old red Hornet built by American Motors. It was considered a compact muscle car. Herman sat in the front seat, enjoying the ride.

"Wow, this car rides smooth—like floating on a cloud," Herman exclaimed.

"It's a gas guzzler, but it is fun to drive. You know I'm a James Bond fan." Wanda continued, "This brings me back to the Hornet stunt in *The Man with the Golden Gun*."

Herman chuckled. He recalled when Wanda and Clifford got married. They were both nineteen, still kids, and a little bit crazy with oodles of dreams. Herman looked in the back seat to check on Cliff, finding him fast asleep. "You must have tired him out," Herman smiled.

"He's pedaling a tricycle now," Wanda said. "His feet

just barely touch the pedals, so I'm pushing him. He's having a blast," Wanda said.

They walked through the door of Sharm's residential treatment center, registered at the desk, and sat staring at the mint green walls. Soon, Ida walked toward them in the waiting room and greeted them. "Good to see you. Sharm is waiting for you. Follow me." Wanda and Herman each held one of Cliff's hands, and the threesome walked through the hall. "I'll let you have time to visit privately before I join you."

"Where's Mommy?" Cliff asked.

"The lady is taking us to her," Wanda said.

The door opened. Sharm sat in a rocking chair with a ball of red yarn in her hand. She was knitting with her needles clicking in a rhythm, creating a sweater. In front of her on the floor were partially unraveled skeins of brightly colored yarns. She raised her head as they entered, and her face lit up. Her eyes zeroed in on Cliff. The little boy hung on to Wanda, not so sure about Mommy.

"Yes, Cliff. It's me, your mommy."

He glanced at her and looked down, tightening his grip around Wanda's legs. Slowly he relaxed his grip and walked toward his mother.

"I love you, Cliff," Sharm said. "You're my little boy." Tears dripped down her nose and her arms opened wide. Cliff ran to her, accepting her love.

"Mommy!" Cliff echoed. Sharm lifted him on her lap and hugged him. He nestled his head on her shoulder.

Wanda and Herman witnessed the beauty of primal peace between a mother and son. Sharm reached for

Herman's hand and he responded in kind. Her sleeve slipped off her arm, exposing the tattoo of her grandmother's face.

"Thank you, Grandpa, for all you've done to help me and Cliff," Sharm said. "I love Grandma too … always will."

Wanda tentatively moved closer to her daughter.

"Hi, Mom," Sharm said as she gave Wanda's hand a playful squeeze. "I need you more than ever."

Wanda knelt down and gave both Sharm and Cliff a giant hug. "I love the both of you," Wanda whispered.

Sharm reached into the tote by her side and pulled out a fire-engine red sweater. "This is for Cliff, my handsome little man." She held it up to him. "Ahhh, yes! Red is your color." Next she pulled out a long green-and-white scarf. "Grandpa, this is for you, my favorite Michigan State fan. It will keep you warm in winter. Mom, I knitted you a red wool scarf to match your car." Sharm draped the scarf around her mother.

Ida walked into the room and sat down. "Sharm is doing well and we plan to discharge her next week, on Monday. We want to observe her over the weekend for any reaction to the medication we just added. So far, everything looks good. The final meeting before discharge is a family meeting with everyone who is part of her daily life. That is scheduled for Sunday afternoon. I usually don't work on the weekends, but I will be here for that meeting! Sharm and I talked about who should attend, and we've made a list. Herman, I hope you can contact them and they'll agree to be here," she said as she handed Herman the list.

"I'll do my best," Herman said. "What time on Sunday?"

"Two in the afternoon," Ida said.

"Okay." Herman's shoulders sagged under the weight of family responsibility, which was getting heavier by the minute. He'd been watching over Cliff, acting as a supportive father figure to Sharm, and now, as facilitator for the rest of the family. *I miss Celia so much. If only she was here to help me. She was much better at this than I am.*

Wanda kneeled to whisper something in Cliff's ear. He turned around and looked directly at his mother and waved. "Bye, bye, Mommy." Holding hands as they walked down the hall, Herman, Wanda, and Cliff represented three generations of the Ratz family. Life had crippled them, but they were determined to be strong enough to take care of Sharm. The three amigos found their places in the Hornet and Wanda drove them back to Lansing.

"I'm dyin' to know who's on the list," Wanda said. Herman ceremoniously pulled it out of his breast pocket and read off the names: "Me, *you*, Cliff, David, Maribelle, and Kevin."

"Phew, I'm on the list," Wanda said. "Sharm hasn't wanted me in her life for a long time. At least I'm considered an important part of her family. I wonder why Vince and Sue aren't on it."

"Maybe they're too far away, and they were really Clifford's friends. I think they continued to see Sharm because Vince suggested therapy. It's just Sharm's family,

I guess. I'll give them a call and let them know she's being discharged. They've been so helpful."

"They're nice people, that's for sure," Wanda said.

ON SUNDAY AFTERNOON, THE family meeting was just around the corner. All had agreed to come except Maribelle, who was out of town. David drove his own vehicle, so Kevin, Wanda, and Cliff rode with Herman. Herman focused on the road and tuned out the conversations, but Cliff and Kevin had a great time chatting it up. Kevin taught Cliff how to do shadow puppets with his hands, showing the images on the backs of the car seats in front of them, and they played a game identifying the farm animals grazing in the fields along the freeway.

One by one, the family arrived at the hospital. Ida greeted them, asked their names, and introduced herself. She guided the family and Sharm into a small conference room off the visiting area. Ida summarized Sharm's treatment at Pinehurst. "Sharm entered the hospital in an unresponsive state after witnessing a horrible tragedy. She has made considerable progress and her prognosis is good. To protect her privacy, I've cleared what I can share with you with her. Sharm is on two medications, one that helps with depression, and another that manages her anxiety. She will need these medications for six months to a year. Weekly CBT, which stands for cognitive behavioral therapy, is strongly recommended." Ida continued, "It's critical she find a therapist in Lansing. If you need help finding one, let me know. Support from her family is critical. She needs *all* of you."

"I want you to know my family means a lot to me," Sharm began. "You took care of Cliff and stuck with me during this terrible time. I've been the wild child in the family." Kevin and Wanda made eye contact and smiled at each other. "Well, the wild caught up with me and really kicked me in the butt. I can honestly say I've learned my lessons. I'm now ready to be a mother to my son and find work to support the two of us."

David nodded and smirked.

"Does anyone have any questions?" Ida asked.

"I do," Kevin said, straightening in his chair. "Will Sharm become suicidal again?"

Ida frowned. "That's a delicate question … but reasonable. If she continues the medication and therapy sessions, it's not likely. Her suicide attempt was a reaction to the loss of her father. Her diagnosis is PTSD, which means post-traumatic stress disorder. This disorder happens to normal people who have experienced extraordinary trauma. Does that answer your question?"

"I'm not one to believe someone is *cured* after they've been in the hospital only three weeks," Kevin said.

"For sure, she needs the help of her family to continue to improve," Ida said. "What the hospital stay does is give Sharm time to reflect on what happened, to meet other patients with similar difficulties, find the right medications, and develop goals that will give her a plan to follow. It's just the start of her life's journey."

"So, you're saying she's just starting to put the pieces together," Kevin said.

Sharm was livid. "I'm not like you! I'll *never* be like

you! You're Mom's favorite and you were a pansy in school, blindly following all the rules."

Ida stepped in.

"This is the place to air family conflicts," Ida said. "That's why we're having this family meeting. Kevin, will your differences keep you from helping Sharm?"

Ida paused, waiting for Kevin's answer. Wanda and Herman fidgeted in their seats. David lowered his eyes to stare at the table in front of him.

"She's my sister, and my nephew's mother. She's part of the family."

"Good answer," Ida said. "But do you really mean it?"

Kevin paused, seeming to think it over.

"I do. Cliff's a neat kid. I want what's best for him, and I want to be part of his life."

Sharm looked at Kevin intensely and said, "He does mean it! For sure, Cliff and I want you to be part of your life."

Kevin sighed, relieved he was off the hot seat.

"What's this 'you're Mom's favorite' about?" Ida asked.

Wanda raised her chin, looking straight at Ida. "Their father and I didn't get along well. It seems so immature now, but we picked favorites. I chose Kevin, and Sharm was close to Clifford. We never worked it out. After the divorce, we each took care of our favorite one." Wanda shook her head. "That was wrong!"

"How are you going to change that?" Ida asked.

"Even before Clifford died, I've been hoping Sharm and I could get counseling to get our relationship on the right track."

"This is a good time to do that." Ida turned to Sharm.

"Tomorrow before you leave, we'll add that to your list of goals."

Sharm nodded and said, "I want to improve my relationship with Mom."

"Any more questions or comments?" Ida asked again. After a short pause, she addressed the family. "First, we have to determine where Sharm and Cliff are going to live. Sharm will need a place to stay, and she'll need help taking care of Cliff."

Both Wanda and Herman enthusiastically offered Sharm a place to live. Sharm was pleased with both offers, but anxiety set in when she was pressured to choose.

"That puts me on the hot seat," Sharm said. "I don't know what's best for me."

Ida hoped the family would solve the problem, but after a long pause, she said, "I'm going to make a suggestion. Remember, it's only a suggestion. You've been close to Herman for most of your life, and while you and your mother want your relationship to continue developing, it will take time to establish a comfortable one. When you leave the hospital, you need comfort and familiarity."

Wanda, Sharm, and Herman agreed that living with Grandpa Herman was the best option for now. Herman agreed to take her to therapy and help monitor her medication. David, Wanda, and especially Kevin volunteered to help with Cliff's care.

"When Sharm lives with me, I hope she'll help take care of Cliff. I'm getting too old to chase him around." Herman winked at the little guy.

Cliff giggled. Sharm gave him a hug.

"Grandpa, are you coming to pick me up on Monday?" Sharm asked.

"I will. Is noon a good time?"

"Yes," Ida said, as she ushered them into the waiting room. Before they left, she pulled Wanda and Herman aside. "Cliff saw the tragedy, too," she said. "You might see him react later to the incident. He seems like a typical two-year-old now, but if you see a change in his personality or if nightmares start, you need to take him to a child psychologist."

Wanda and Herman listened intently, fully aware of their responsibility for Cliff's well-being.

HERMAN CALLED VINCE AND shared Sharm's discharge date, which prompted Vince to find a time to visit her before she left the hospital. Sunday night, Vince showed up alone. Sue stayed home with the children. It might be the last time he would see her, so he wanted her to know how much Clifford had loved her.

"I hear you're being discharged tomorrow," Vince said.

"The family meeting went well. I'll be living with Grandpa."

"Herman is a good man. Your father was a good man too. He spared you and little Cliff a miserable life."

Sharm stared at the floor, deep into her thoughts. She caught her breath and slowly raised her head. A single tear ran down her face. She was beginning to understand the magnitude of her father's sacrifice. She ached with love and a gratitude she had never known. Vince knew the truth. He knew she was guilty on *all* counts, but he was compassionate and merciful. She met his eyes and gave him a soft smile. "Thank you for your kindness," Sharm said. As if carrying a full measure of love, Vince stood slowly, reached for her slumping body, and hugged her as if she was his own daughter.

"Please be well. Live well. You have received an amazing gift," Vince said, gazing at her one last time. He turned to walk away. Sharm teared up and waved goodbye.

She went back to her room to organize her belongings. The last item she packed was the quilt her grandma made for Clifford. She stopped packing for a moment, sat on her bed, wrapped the quilt around her, smelled the sweet smell of her father, and bowed her head.

"Thank you, Daddy," she whispered.

Acknowledgments

The writing of this psychological suspense novel generated many trips. The first trip was to the Upper Peninsula of Michigan, to the Peter White Library in Marquette. There I found a wealth of information about the Tiroler Hof Hotel, the Marquette State Prison, and articles about the assault on Governor G. Mennen Williams. The librarians were gracious, helpful, and even emailed me needed information during the pandemic when the library was closed. The next trip was to Marquette State Prison, where I was given a tour of the administration area, which included the offices under the large rotunda. I also walked through the flower gardens in front of the prison that were tended by the inmates. During that tour I was introduced to the book *One Hundred Years At Hard Labor* by Ike Wood, and was given a centennial edition. This was an invaluable resource for me. It detailed prison escapes, the early history of the prison, and highlighted fascinating stories about life behind bars.

The Citizens Police Academy in Grand Rapids, Michigan, was another stop on the journey. Under the watchful eye of Sandi Jones, I toured the insides of a correctional facility, learned about the use of force, and experimented with firearms and tasers. Chief Judge Jeffrey J. O'Hara, who successfully runs a drug rehab court in Grand Rapids, gave an informative presentation about what happens inside the courtroom. The relationships and the struggles among the police, the prosecuting attorney, and the court system was a frequent topic of conversation. It is this experience that has given *Prison Shadows* its authenticity.

My dear writer friend, Katharine Robey of Empire, Michigan, helped me determine which cover best conveyed the book plan. I am deeply grateful for her insight and her ability to see humanity in faces.

Every Friday at 2:30 p.m., I met my writer's group in Vero Beach, Florida, via Skype. Their comments were both affirming and critical, which is immensely helpful to a writer of novels. Larry Davis did a good job with my "trash and trim" directive. It added a necessary veracity to the story and characters. Also, praise goes to my beta readers, Jon Den Houter and Judith Konitzer, for sharpening both my vision and voice. Chad Kremer has crafted an exceptional book trailer for *Prison Shadows*. Special thanks go to Doug Weaver for his brutal honesty, and to Tanya Muzumdar and Heather Shaw for their brilliant contributions. Although this novel has had much support, it has been a long journey. Fashioning the characters created a disturbance in me, as I hope it does in my readers. This is a psychological suspense story, so enjoy it, but beware!

About the Author

Kathryn Den Houter has been actively writing since retiring from her work as a psychologist in 2014. Her last novel, *Cobalt Chronicles*, has received three awards: a Readers' Favorite Award, a Kops-Fetherling International Book Award, and it was a finalist for the Eric Hoffer Book Award.

Prior to her career as a psychologist, she served as a college professor, a K-12 teacher, and as a directress at a Montessori school. She holds a doctorate in psychology from Michigan State University.

Her most beloved career, however, was raising four children with her late husband, Leonard Den Houter, on a hobby farm near Lowell, Michigan. She now has seven grandchildren.

She lives in Caledonia, Michigan, in the summer and in Indian River County in Florida during the winter with her husband, Jim Jackway.

Kathryn enjoys hearing from her readers, so feel free to email her at: kathryndenhouter@gmail.com or kvdhwriter@gmail.com

Also by

KATHRYN DEN HOUTER

Cobalt Chronicles

Abigail's Exchange

Resilience: A Workbook

*Powering Through Adversity
to Find Happiness*

Van: A Memoir of My Father

Made in the USA
Columbia, SC
14 May 2022

60324949R00209